Midnight
OMEN

Midnight
OMEN

MARTI
MELVILLE

For my Grandchildren

Isabel, Boone, Abigail, Mikaela, Alice, Alexis, Aubrey, Ryan…

…and the rest who wait to join us in this lifetime.

By Marti Melville

The DÉJÀ VU SERIES

Book One: Midnight Omen

Book Two: Silver Moon

Book Three: Onyx Rising

Book Four: Cutthroat's Omen: A Crimson Dawn

Published by
Doce Blant Publishing, Dana Point, CA 92629
www.doceblantpublishing.com

Cover by Fiona Jayde Media
Interior design by The Deliberate Page

ISBN-10: 0-9971023-4-9
ISBN-13: 978-0-9971023-4-5

Library of Congress Control Number: 2016906558
Printed in the United States of America
www.doceblantpublishing.com
First published in the United States of America 2010

Thank you to the many people who continued to believe in this series. In particular, Wendy Hickman, Sue Beckman, Karen Zabriski, Lissa Buchi, Lois Cozens.

To my children (Rich, Jeff, Brett, Rachel, Brooke), their spouses (Kindall, Kaycee, Tom, Eric), and my husband, Mark, thanks for putting up with the distraction, daydreaming, and constant talk of Caribbean pirates.

Kevin du Toit, thank you for your honesty and editing skills with the screenplays, which made for a richer plot.

Additional gratitude must be given to the very talented Fiona Jayde for her brilliance with finally capturing the Caribbean "feel" of the story on the cover. After many "eyes" had looked at the text, Karen Kohler nailed the edits and forced a deeper look at the way the story had been written. Thank you for your skill with the interior's design, Tamara Cribley.

Lastly, thank you to the fans of *The Déjà vu Chronicles* for your devotion and love of the characters. It is for you that this 3rd edition was comprised.

"Luna, every woman's friend,
To me thy goodness condescend
Let me this night in vision see
Emblems of my destiny."

(Ancient British divination practiced at the
Harvest Moon)

"And so the warnin' be given to all who sail the seas of El Caribe—Beware the Midnight Omen."

(Kathryn - Chirurgeon of the *Revenge* 1721)

Prologue

DARKNESS CRAWLS LIKE TENTACLES THAT reach out as death's fingers from my body. Inky shadows extend beyond these appendages, snuffing out all light from the night sky. Only the moon refuses to hide. My lips curl at her defiance, and I cast a pall in retaliation. Mist rises from below and the brilliant orb is encased. Now all shall see it.

I scan the water below, but cannot see him. My thoughts command the elements as I move forward, gliding effortlessly, as is my right, high above the inky sea. Even the creatures flee, and this is good. I cannot be trusted with innocence – a truth I do not attempt to hide.

Humankind is weak. It is my prey when death overtakes its ravaged human body.

Fools, to think you can run from me. Your instinct only weakens you.

Ahead, I hear voices – men's voices. They celebrate, or mourn. Perhaps they know I seek them out. Perhaps he is with them.

The waves reach up toward the blackened heavens, and their currents stir beneath me as I pass overhead. I cannot help myself, and I scoff at the folly of Mother Nature – pure, sacred, and vulnerable to my whims.

My hand moves only slightly and a single wave from the water becomes lethal. *Maelstrom*, I believe mankind calls it. Let them have it, then – a maelstrom sent from Morrigan. It will be a gift to the weak, who will certainly choose to offer their lives as a sacrifice for their comrades. Foolish, malleable mankind – so easily manipulated to give me all that I seek. And as they die, these brave, silly men, I will be waiting to collect their souls.

He is not there.

If that be the case, then they must all die to pay the price. *He* was meant to be on that vessel, and he is not.

I feel my anger seethe and the waters below mirror my fury. Indeed, the dead belong to me – in silence, in the dark, in death. My eyes glance upward once again as the voices sound from below, urgently fighting to save their beautiful ship and pathetic lives. Tossed to and fro upon the angry seas that I control – as I also do the night sky – I watch the futile effort of drowning men fighting my wrath. Now I see life ebb slowly from those who sacrificed themselves first, and I choose to laugh at the futility of human life. My voice carries over the wind – hissing, screaming death's greeting.

I am here. I come to collect the souls of the dead and carry them with me to hell.

The moon remains defiant, a light among the darkness. My pall encircles her, a warning of my presence.

Those who are wise will heed the warning of the Midnight Omen.

PART ONE

Fate

One

SPLINTERS PITCHED FROM THE SEA-ROTTED beam as the dirk imbedded itself deeply with the hilt swaying upon impact.

"Close, but not quite, you dirty maggots...now drop 'em! I won't be sayin' it again!"

Seth Brooks still felt the sting of the last fist he'd taken to his right cheek. He was grateful the blade had missed him – a dirk to the face would slow him down, especially coming from a blaggard like Cuddy. A filthy cuff from that pirate would be humiliating... and painful. His fists were the size of boiled hams.

Seth cocked his pistols, aimed them at different cut-throats, and stood ready to fire at the least provocation.

"We'll see you dead before we be givin' up our gold, pup!"

Spittle flew through the air as the salty sailor spat though black teeth, most of which were missing from his mouth. A single gold ring dangled from one ear.

"I won't be askin' again, sir," Seth said coolly, and shifted his weight to position himself between the pirates and the gaping pub door. Just then, a brute, with a torso covered in tattoos and raised scars, charged at Seth. He easily sidestepped the thug's bulk and cracked the butt of his pistol over his bald scalp. The man stiffened and fell, whacking his head on the pitch floor. One of the other pirates called out to his "mate" lying motionless on the wood planking. There was no response.

"Who's next? I could do this all night, dogs!" Seth called out. He aimed the barrel of his pistol at a rusted chain that supported an elaborate chandelier dangling overhead. He pulled the trigger and fired. The first of the three chains snapped and the iron candelabrum teetered, spilling flaming tallow sticks and hot wax over the heads of the gathered men. A few slapped at the ooze and embers raining down upon their exposed skin, and, as they did so, their cutlasses clattered to the floor.

"Now, the rest of you…drop 'em!" Seth barked. This time, hands rose above their heads as dirks, pistols, and long-blades were surrendered. The heap fell at Seth's feet.

"Excellent! See now, we can all get along and be friendly." Seth kicked the weapons to one side and out of the reach of the cutthroats. "Ladies? If you please."

A pair of voluptuous doxies sauntered to the pirates and lined them up against one wall.

"You know you're my favorite, now, don't you?" Seth whispered and pecked the painted cheek of the blonde as she sashayed past him. "Indeed," he added as an afterthought.

Her nimble fingers made way along the pirates' appendages, stealing into hidden pockets and apertures meant to conceal weapons. Sultry smiles lifted the edges of the painted ladies' ruby-stained lips each time a firearm or blade was discovered. A pirate treasure hunt, to be certain! A growing mound of pistols and dirks took shape, filling the farthest corner, as the women collected the weapons. Seth glanced at it and shifted his weight. With his arms still extended and pistols aimed at the cutthroats, he barked the same order.

"Now…*drop* 'em."

Their weapons had been relinquished. The pirates stood with hands in the air, eyeing each other with dumbfounded expressions. Seth waved the barrel of his pistol at the pirates' knees.

"To your heels…drop 'em! I won't ask again," Seth shifted his weight again, steadying his aim.

"Our bloody britches?" The voice was elevated and indignant.

"Aye," Seth replied, unable to hold back the grin that crossed his lips.

One by one, the ruffians dropped their trousers to the floor and returned their grimy hands overhead. Seth circled the captives and flinched at the sudden display of bare bums. He made his way behind the lineup. In truth, he could barely look at the shiny backsides without laughing.

"My, my, gentlemen," he chuckled. "There certainly seems to be no lack of glare off your unsullied, bright rumps."

Ahead of them, the painted ladies giggled between themselves, pointing now and then. On one end, a scruffy pirate with a rounded belly and yellow eyes glanced at his neighbor's bare bum. His eyes drifted to the faded ink scrolled across one pale cheek. The tattoo spelled out a name with a roughly drawn heart next to it.

"B-R-U-C-E? Who's Bruce?" he asked through yellowed teeth.

The tattooed pirate shrugged as color flooded his face. Shuffling stirred the entire line of men at the opposite end.

"What?" The response came from the last of the lined up men.

A burly pirate standing to one side beamed a toothless smile at Bruce, who waved back. Apparently, Bruce was well known among the pirates. Seth cleared his throat and the ladies giggled again.

"Now that's a piece of fancy, if ye ask me," the bawdy lady said as she reached the end of the line.

"No one asked you, Cecily. Just gather their bounty and bring it to me," Seth said.

"Indeed, I will." Cecily grinned and eyed Moody lustily.

"The gold bounty, my dearest." Seth's voice took on an edge. He couldn't lose control of the situation – not now that he had the men where he wanted them. The ladies were proving to be more troublesome than the thick-fisted pirates. At least their weapons were visible and made of steel. The same could not be said about the bawdy women in the room. "Please, darlin'," Seth added.

Cecily immediately began gathering an assortment of leather pouches sagging with coins fastened to the pirates' dropped trousers. Just for fun, her wandering touch would slide up a hairy leg and tickle the nether-regions most hidden from sunlight. More than a few pirates squirmed as Cecily frisked them.

Once she'd collected a fine haul, she glanced to one side, and, thinking no one was looking, dropped a handful of coins down her corset. Cecily shook her ample bosom to make certain the coin had settled in a place where it would not fall. Finally, after gathering what seemed a treasure trove of gold doubloons and silver reales, she deposited the rest into two waiting leather satchels tied snugly around Seth's waist.

"Watch your hands, love," Seth warned and flashed Cecily a steely smile. She answered with a simper and glanced over at Martha, who had finished tying up the second satchel. The weight pulled them against his hip, and they jingled noisily with each movement Seth made. Without taking his eyes off the bare backsides of the captives, he flipped a few more coins down both ladies' bustiers and kissed them each on the cheek.

"That is for your efforts, my sweet Cecily, and for you, dear Martha," he said. Then pulling the draw-strings tight, using the fingers of one hand while clenching a pistol in the other, he backed toward the doorway. "As for the rest of you…my highest regards and deepest gratitude for your generosity toward me cause. My advice be simple, men: do not think on fol-lowin' me, as your precarious state will certainly garner the notice of the parish constable. I'm certain ye don't want your true identity as cutthroats…er…exposed."

Seth glanced at the bare bums and widened the gap between himself and the line of pirates, leaving the women as guards for a short moment. Then, keeping his pistol carefully aimed, he gathered any remaining coins, and skillfully stuffed it all into his own pockets. When he finished, he carefully positioned himself in the archway of the door and faced the bare-bummed buccaneers one last time.

"Once again, gentleman…thank you for your generosity, donating to my cause, as it were." He half-bowed, keeping his eyes and barrel locked on them. "And now, if you will excuse me…"

In a sudden switch, Seth ducked out the doorway and bolted down the main road, losing his footing only once on the slippery cobblestones. Doubloons spilled from his bulging pockets, causing him to pause only briefly before thinking better of it. The telltale marker left behind would likely be a deterrent, as much as a trail. Seth decided to take his chances on the former and hope the pirates would stop to gather the gold lying along the cobblestones – though he couldn't be certain. These were scallywags, after all.

Just ahead, the fish carts that lined the path to the docks came into view. He was almost there. Seth crossed the roadway and caught sight of a beggar squatting against a dilapidated building. Tossing a coin, he shouted over his shoulder, "For you, mate. If anyone asks, I went the other way."

The beggar nodded and bit into the coin just to be sure it was real gold, before he tucked it down his pants. "Aye, lad. I never saw ye!" he shouted back, whistling through the holes in his gums that should have been filled with teeth.

Seth made for the path, certain he was home free, when suddenly, two lanky salts sauntered up the dirt path toward him. The gold earrings they wore gave them away, along with the curved blades tucked against a hip.

More pirates! Perhaps the same crew.

Seth careened in the opposite direction and darted down an abandoned alleyway. Behind him, he could hear shouting – the voices of his victims, no doubt. A blast sounded to his left, and he knew it would only be minutes before they discovered where he'd gone. *Damn those cobblestones*, he thought and shoved the coins deeper into his pockets.

Sure enough, the voices grew louder, and Seth realized they had entered the alley.

It seems these blokes have been here before. The thought unsettled him, and he picked up the pace. If he couldn't outsmart them, he could certainly outrun them. He turned the corner and disappeared down another alleyway, followed by bloodthirsty cutthroats hot on his heels.

PART TWO

Futurity

Two

"CHARGING TO 200."

The blonde standing closest to the body lifted her chin only slightly, announcing the next step. "I'm clear. You're clear. We're all clear."

The assemblage took one step backward and watched silently. They waited impassively, ready for electricity to be delivered. The ritual was set with protocols that everyone in the room had memorized. A few eyes drifted to the white box situated at the head of the bed, then dropped back to the blonde as she pressed the red button. The body arced, its back hyper-flexed by electrical current before dropping hard onto the surface. All heads turned to the monitor.

"No change. Still in V-fib," a nurse said as she glanced at the clock and yawned.

"Can anyone feel a pulse?" A tenor voice sounded from near the body's feet.

"No pulse." The response came from somewhere to the right. The voice sounded high-pitched and grating inside the tiled room.

The energy inside the room remained as flat as the dead man's pulse. The result of boredom, most likely. The Code Team had done this too many times. Their careers were filled hourly with the dying.

A large man with a round face and white beard bent over the body's head, snowy hair dropping below one eyebrow. He puffed against it, but the silvery locks refused to stay in place. He wore a badge fastened askew to his white coat. A name and the title, *Respiratory Therapy*, was scratched in bold black letters over the surface. No one bothered to look at it. His appearance suggested an air of rushed professionalism from a man who'd done this for too many years.

The respiratory therapist attached a blue, oblong bag to the tube protruding through the body's pale lips. Slowly, methodically, he began to squeeze. The rhythm of his movements delivered an artificial breath with each compression of the bag. The corpse's chest rose just before the therapist relaxed his grip. He delivered another breath and shifted, as his stomach growled, and glanced at the clock without noting the time. Eyes locked on the ER physician, a tech waited to pound on the chest as soon as the signal came.

"Resume CPR." The physician's lips barely moved as he spoke. He wore a pressed white jacket draped over starched indigo scrubs. He was equally unruffled by the room's activity. No one noticed the physician's brows knit together as he glanced at the clock, then back to the gurney. Shifting his weight, he folded his arms across his chest and nodded. The tech immediately began to push against the body's chest while the Ambubag bellowed oxygen into the lifeless lungs. Eyes watched as the torso rose and fell in time with the tech's movement. Their actions – a choreographed dance designed to sustain life within a barren carcass – appeared to be a mechanical performance of medical professionals.

"Go ahead with one more Epi," the physician ordered.

A nurse, with hair the color of sugared chestnuts, moved closer to the body. She wiped clear plastic tubing with alcohol then jabbed it with a needle. Below a neat row of craggy bangs, her deep brown eyes glanced up at the clock. She pushed clear liquid into the IV from a syringe without blinking.

"One amp of Epi at 1716."

The oxygen and liquids forced into the body circulated while the young tech urged the silent heart to beat. The team was indeed a consummate virtuoso, each part played in calm unison.

"Okay, stop CPR," the physician announced.

On cue, the tech stopped bouncing and stood upright. His youthful fingertips massaged his throbbing left wrist as he waited for evidence that the heart would beat on its own. A second nurse casually tucked another ampoule neatly into one pocket of her scrubs, then placed two fingers on the creased skin at the body's right groin. No palpating artery responded. She tossed a glance at the doctor standing to her right and shook her head.

His jaw stiffened, arms still crossed over his starched white jacket.

"So, what do you want to do?" the nurse asked, and removed her fingers from the dead man's groin. The physician ignored her. All eyes were glued to the green lines snaking their way across the screen that hung from the wall. Nothing had changed.

"Still in V-fib," someone called out from the opposite side of the room as if it needed to be said.

"Let's shock him again," the physician announced, reluctantly. Lunch was already an hour late and his accountant was waiting for a return phone call. "*Ille mortuis,*" he said under his breath.

"Charging."

They all stepped back as the warning to "clear" sounded out again. The nurse pushed the red button for the second time. Again, the body arced and then fell back onto the hard surface with a dull thud. Eyes flew to the monitor, and the tech stepped on the stool, anticipating another chorus of resuscitation. The doctor remained motionless while the green line crossing the monitor screen ran flat.

"Asystole," he stated the obvious. "Resume CPR."

Instantly, it all began again – pounding, pushing, and bellowing in rhythm – a synchronistic assault upon the old man's body. But despite the warm hands the cold, mottled corpse began to stiffen. Their composite efforts had failed. After a few more minutes, the doctor lowered his hands to hide them within the pockets of his lab coat and glanced up at the clock on the wall in front of him.

"Stop CPR." There was no pulsing from the still heart inside the chest. Eyes shifted to the doctor, anticipating his next words.

"Whaddya wanna do, doc?" Someone asked the question on everyone's mind.

"If no one has any objections to the contrary, let's call it."

Heads nodded. The tech stepped down from the stool, peeled off his gloves, and flung them into a garbage can on the other side of the room. "Two points!" he called out, and flipped his right hand to mimic a basketball dunk. No one paid attention.

The respiratory therapist lifted one corner of his mouth, a reflexive smile, and systematically detached the bellows, then set it aside. No one spoke. The nurses began to scribble on sheets of paper or tap on a computer, and the doctor cleared his throat.

"Time of death: 1721." The voice was clear, female, and nervous.

The physician turned to see who had pronounced the death from behind him. Standing in the doorway, watching the Code Blue, a nurse shifted her weight and smiled. Her brilliant blue eyes, framed by a pair of black-rimmed glasses, blinked then opened wide. She glanced from the clock to the corpse. The physician shot a sour look at her. She shrank back and pushed the black frames back up her nose.

"I'm…so sorry…excited. I'm the new RN…I…"

"What's your name, 'new RN'?" he snapped as he walked toward the door.

"Katherine. I'm really sorry…" she said, and dropped a pen that rolled underneath the gurney. "Oops," she whispered and stepped closer to see where the thing had finally landed. No one paid any attention to her as Katherine made her way to where the dead man lay. She leaned away from the body in an attempt to avoid the dead mass lying there. But curiosity got the best of her. After all, this was the closest she'd ever been to a real corpse. Katherine glanced up to take a peek at death's handiwork just as the tech lifted the sheet, shrouding the body's face.

"They say that the ghosts of these dead guys are seen in here at night," he said.

Katherine shot him a look, and then dropped her eyes back to the dead man. Something had caught her attention. No one showed any real interest in the new nurse. Silent glances passed between co-workers. Some even shook their heads or shrugged a shoulder in dismissal at her curiosity over a dead guy.

Muffled noises filled the space within the walls of Room 13, the Code Blue Room, as the team cleared out their equipment. It was true. Many had claimed to see ghosts in Room 13 long after the bodies had been removed to the morgue downstairs. But the spirits were absent now.

Katherine glanced up at the monitor just as a nurse snapped the power button to *off*. The screen greyed out and Katherine felt a bit of remorse that it was over. She could use some experience, and Codes were the best to learn from.

Just then, the screen blinked and the windows outside lit up as violent lightning crackled in the darkened sky. She glanced back to the monitor just as the ghostly image of the dead man flashed over the darkened screen. Katherine jumped but was unable to tear her eyes from it.

"Did…did anyone…see…?" she stammered. But nobody seemed to notice. She locked eyes on the screen again, waiting for any sign that the face was real. The clock had stopped, but the tick…tick…tick of the second hand continued to snap in place.

Suddenly, the corpse flexed one hand and seized Katherine's arm. Its cold fingertips dug slowly into her warm flesh and stole the air from her lungs. Overhead, a large surgical light swayed, flicking shadows into every corner of the room. Echoed whispers danced within the light, inhuman, foreign, and menacing.

Kathryn.

She screamed as larger hands seized her from behind, pulling her backward into the shadows. "I've got you, newbie," the tech said.

The ER physician began to pace. "What the hell was *that*?" he barked at no one in particular. "Somebody get security and call maintenance. These lights are messed up in here!"

A linebacker-sized tech jogged out of the room as Maya, stepped forward. Her ampules clattered inside her pockets. "Are you okay, Katherine?"

Katherine glanced back at the body. Its arm dangled loose over the gurney's edge. Her eyes locked on patterns tattooed over its skin, a symbol of some sort. Katherine's skin crawled. She peeled her eyes away from it.

"Yes, thank you." She forced a smile then faced the tech, who had covered the corpse. "That was definitely creepy."

"Reflexes, most likely. I hear it happens all the time downstairs, long after they're tagged and bagged." He shrugged and his smile looked more like a grimace as he waited for her response. Katherine only nodded.

"That can be disturbing, don't you agree, Katherine?"

She spun around to see Alex, whose sultry voice hinted at a deeper meaning. "I…yes, I guess so," Katherine stammered. She blinked and locked eyes with her boss. "Hello, Alex."

"Get the body downstairs where it belongs," Alex stated and looked at the ER physician, who simply nodded and pressed his lips together before making his way outside.

"I…I need to get back to my patients," Katherine said, and followed him out through the door. Halfway down the hallway, she picked up the pace. Katherine ran until she was at last safely situated inside a vacant patient room with the door closed. In desperation, she clutched at the closest garbage can. As she did so, she caught sight of a dead man's grip imprinted on her arm. Her stomach heaved at the sight of the death's fingerprints on her skin.

Suddenly, without warning, she relinquished her breakfast.

Three

KATHERINE WAS CONSIDERED A "HEAD-TURNER" on most occasions – not really what you'd consider movie star material, but definitely someone to notice. Her eyes, as blue as the Pacific Ocean, were frequently framed by dark-rimmed glasses that gave her that sensual, nerdy look. Her dark hair fell in tousled waves down her back. It was easy to see that beauty came naturally to her.

With a penchant for discovery, Katherine spent most of her free time with her nose in a book. There would always be other ways to seek the adventure she hungered for, but books were her favorite.

Katherine's mind was sharp. In school, she was unusually quick to understand intricate ideology – particularly medical theories. For those reasons, she'd graduated from high school almost two years ahead of her classmates and had decided to study nursing. It was another frontier to be discovered, as she navigated her way through the inner workings of the human body. Needless-to-say, she graduated with honors, and was well on her way to becoming a good nurse.

Alex stepped into the hallway and glanced at the empty space where Katherine had been. Her thoughts rarely drifted from the young woman. Katherine was indeed gifted – qualities Alexandra Crane recognized.

She glanced at her reflection in a window nearby. Alex had once possessed the same youthful beauty as Katherine – stunning, yet elegantly sophisticated. Alex gracefully mixed an enchanting air of aesthetics and authoritarianism. The same held true for Katherine. If you watched her, even for just a moment, you'd notice she had a gift – something she didn't really think much about, but when needed, knew how to use to her advantage.

Alex walked to her office.

"Good afternoon, Alex," Eric said from the other side of the hallway. "I guess that didn't go as planned." He glanced to Room 13 and gave her a half smile.

"No – not the outcome we'd hoped for," she replied.

"Too bad Katherine freaked out."

Alex shot him a look. "I wouldn't call it freaking out, Eric. She's new to trauma and just needs some experience with it. I remember when you were the same."

"Yeah." Eric dropped his eyes and hurried away.

To say that Alex was protective of Katherine would be a gross understatement of truth. It was her job from the beginning. Katherine's grandmother had introduced Alex to a very young Katherine one autumn day when the wind whipped as crisply as the leaves it carried. The meeting took place in her grandmother's garden, on Katherine's eighth birthday.

Mariel and Alexandra had been friends for centuries, and their loyalty to one another ran sacrosanct. Frequently, the two women would chat over tea and discuss Katherine's future – nothing out of the ordinary, except for the hour – long conversations conducted at night.

Today, however, Alex sat in her little office situated within the ER. It was cramped but functional. Photos of friends and good memories over the past years hung on the wall above a cluttered desk. She straightened a scattering of sticky notes and glanced up at a photo taken only a few years ago. Katherine's hair was darker then, pulled back into a ponytail that dangled nearly to her waist. An athlete wearing skins smeared with the USA's red, white and blue, stood sandwiched between the darker-haired Katherine and another nurse, Raquel. The parkas they wore displayed the red and white snowflake designating the medical team for the most recent Olympics.

Alex had been there – watching the games, watching Katherine.

Standing inches from the ice was mesmerizing – something she would never forget…and never repeat. The decision to leave her home and travel away for the games had happened on a whim, but listening to those impulses had proven invaluable. Alex was glad the arrangements had been made in secret and that Katherine had never found out. There would be no purpose in that. And, besides, it was Mariel's idea anyway.

"Let her discover life, Alexandra. The girl needs to learn what she is capable of under stressful conditions… particularly near foreigners." Mariel's advice had been given with no option to question it. So, Alex agreed to make a phone call. Soon afterward, the Olympic Committee notified Katherine that her services as a nurse were required.

That was a long time ago, when life seemed simpler.

"I wonder if peace is in the cards for either of us," Alex said aloud. Her gut twisted on itself, screaming a warning to her conscience. Something *felt* bad. The impulse to get away from the ER festered, but Alex had too much to do to end her day just yet. Things had already started out bad, with a Code Blue that couldn't be salvaged. Rarely did the Code patients make it, so the idea of another non-survivor wasn't the issue.

A message of warning. Perhaps that was it. *But what was the message? And who was it for?*

Alex shook her head to clear it. She was the "boss" for the dayshift in the forty-eight-bed Emergency Department of St. Luke's General Medical Center, servicing the seaside community of Salt Bay Beach. 'Losing it' was not permitted, at least not in Alex's world. She pressed her lips together tightly. The noises of the Emergency Department just outside her office door rose slightly, indicating the need to 'get in the game' and back to work.

Certainly the body in Room 13 would have been moved to the morgue by now so we can get back to normal. The thought wasn't convincing. She opened the office door and prepared herself for whatever lay in wait.

"*You* people are crazy! I'm in*vin*cible," a shrill male voice blasted from somewhere along the adjacent hallway. She looked to her right, hoping to spot the hysterical patient, and caught sight of a familiar face. The man scrambled around the enclosed room, wearing a cape and ski mask. She knew him, and knew his *modus operandi* would require a shot of Haldol to settle his mania.

Ronnie had been in the ER before, and was delusional, as always. This time he'd been brought in by the local police department. Ronnie's attire suggested his aberration was based upon the latest superhero. It made sense. Artel Comics had just released a new TV series filled with superheroes battling zombies.

At least he doesn't think he's part of the living dead. Her eyes drifted toward Room 13, and the thought unsettled her.

Alex watched for a moment as Ronnie tried to escape. Three ER techs surrounded him. Ronnie allowed them to encircle as he "stunned" them with laser vision.

"Okay, okay, buddy…this way. We need your super power to help us in here…"

A little scuffle followed as Jimmy, built like the Hulk and with moves like a professional wrestler, escorted the patient toward Room 22. That was the room reserved for the "crazies" that showed up almost daily. It was serene and soft, though the walls and ceiling were plastered with the latest technology, complete with surveillance cameras and reversed locking doors.

Alex sighed and crossed the hallway as she made her way toward the central nurses' station. A placard on the wall displayed beneath a faded photo reminded her that she worked in a *community based and well-respected establishment* – something she tried to remember over the protests from the superhero.

She pressed her back against the tiled wall and waited as the superhero was escorted to his designated room. The strict distance she maintained in her personal and professional relationships kept her in proper focus at work. Alex was innately private and cautious. She felt safe when she was in solitude.

She made a quick round of the department, then returned to her office to face a computer filled with unanswered emails. It seemed endless, and the volume had increased substantially in just the few short minutes since she had broken away from the chaos outside. Her stomach groaned, and she decided perhaps it might help to eat something. A half-eaten bag of seasoned kale chips and a tall diet cherry soda sat on the desk next to her, the visible remains of her scant lunch. She pushed it aside and opted for the protesting stomach instead.

"For heaven's sake!" she grumbled, and looked at the monitor in dismay. Twenty-four new emails had appeared. This was definitely one of those days. "I can't do this, not today." She closed her eyes and rubbed her temples.

Slowly, her mind wandered.

Memories of her first days of school in fifth grade at Sherman Penn Elementary surfaced. Sitting was never easy for a little girl when the sun was out, beckoning her to come and play. She would frequently stare outside and allow her mind to amble elsewhere. It was too warm to be at school in early September. A hint of summer's remnants would shine through the classroom windows, and the faint breath of fresh air from outside often sighed through the bottom half of a wedged-open window to taunt her. She would peer through the dirty glass at hopscotch paint and tetherball poles. At least for a time, she would be transfixed in a daydream until a disruptive "ahem" from the front of the classroom would snap her attention back to where Mrs. Crane stared at her with arms crossed.

Alex smiled at the memory.

That same sun shone outside the ER on most days and beckoned her to the ocean. She squirmed as she found her focus drifting to sandy beaches just outside of the already busy ER. She blinked her eyes open, and leaned in to the monitor, as if that would somehow bring her mind back to work.

"Impossible," Alex said. "How can I focus?"

On the other side of her office door, voices talking at once combined with the clamor of alarms going off in patients' rooms. She had heard this same commotion for so many years that she had become impervious to it. That is, until one of the alarms blared its warning tone. It was that one offending noise that jolted her into a secondary state of hyper-vigilance. Instinctively, she would join her co-workers and move through the protocols. This afternoon, however, was a steady mellow for the ER, except for the superhero in Room 22 and the dead guy in 13.

"There's a shift in the air currents. The energy has changed," she had said to Mariel only last week over tea.

"I feel it, too, but that doesn't change our course. It's still your job to watch over her, Alex." Mariel had given her *that* look. "Katherine isn't ready yet. There's much she must learn before she goes back."

"Yes, but if time and circumstance calls to her – even before she's prepared for it – what can be done? I really don't think there's time, Mariel." Alex's tea had grown cold, and so had her wits.

"Then you must work harder and keep watch for the man. He will be coming for her. The responsibility falls to you, as watch keeper." That had been the end of the discussion, but Alex hadn't been able to put it aside. Over and over again the signs had shown themselves, and Alex could not ignore the inevitable. She wished that Mariel would stop her stubbornness, just this once.

Alex rubbed her temples again and tried to focus on the computer screen in front of her. Shifting in her chair, a familiar burning sensation shot down her neck and into her left pinky. She tilted her head to the side and rubbed her fingers with her unaffected hand. As usual, it did nothing and the irritation continued – a constant reminder that Katherine still had not answered Dr. Farrell's question.

"They call it sympathy pains," Mariel had stated that same afternoon at tea. "You will be privy to the same suffering as she…in order to protect her properly."

As much as Alex had argued to the contrary, there was no escaping the physical and psychic symptoms that she experienced. Katherine's unresolved issues were instantly transferred to Alex, who experienced them as if they were her own. It would remain a constant thorn in her side … until Katherine finally dealt with whatever the concern was. Health problems were always vexing. Alex suffered enough from her own aches and pains, but add a young woman's youthful traumas into the mix, and Alex could spend a full day in agony.

The manifestations weren't nearly as difficult to deal with – unless, of course, there was some dark secret lying in wait for the young girl. Wendy was really much better at seeing the future, so when these visions presented themselves to Alex, she could only sit back and view them as if in a movie theater…and wait. Katherine's sister had been questioned about nearly every vision, but Wendy's psychic prowess still did not relieve Alex of the images that floated uninvited into her psyche now and then. It was an irritant, really.

Alex's neck ache had flared up only last week, along with the burning sensation. And when Alex had asked Wendy whether she'd had any premonitions related to necks or arm pains, Wendy had only shrugged and said, "asphyxia."

"That is not a term you should be familiar with, Wendy. It's purely medical and usually references strangulation. Why in the world would you come up with that term?" Alex had asked her.

"It just popped into my mind, but honestly, Aunt Alex…I haven't a clue why." Wendy had responded rather flippantly, and then added as an afterthought, "Ask Katherine."

And so Alex did.

Katherine had avoided the topic altogether. She simply had no clue how she had come by such an injury and had remained silent when sent to an orthopedist for an exam. He'd probed with difficult questions that she simply had no answers to. When the orthopedist had called her later that afternoon with the results, she'd had enough.

"What the hell did you do to your neck? It's bone on cord. Did you fall on your head or something?" The orthopedist's tone had taken a "don't mess with me" slant.

"Well, not that I can remember." Katherine's sarcasm had carried through the receiver. "I would have known if I'd done something like that, wouldn't I?"

The call had ended with more unanswered questions and the not-so-gentle suggestion for a change in lifestyle. "Yeah, right" she had snapped before she'd hung up the phone.

Deep down, Alex knew Katherine was right. How could she fix her neck, or her lifestyle, when she didn't know what was wrong either? And, anyway, it was always painful to make empty promises to others – something Katherine's nature wouldn't allow. The doctor made her pledge that she'd adjust her workload and find time for recreation. Katherine knew it would be a lie, but she made the promise anyway. Soon after, the phone calls stopped coming.

But the burning pain in Alex's neck hadn't stopped. In fact, it had gotten worse. She decided to make her own lifestyle change in the hopes that it would help, if even on a subconscious level. But no matter what change she made, the ever-present burn on the left side of her neck remained as if it needed answers, too. She retreated in silent defeat with no immediate resolution. The only answer today was to rub her left hand, dismiss the irritation that festered, and move on to the next email.

Her brain simply would not cooperate with her eyes. She gave up the battle and let go, leaning back in her chair as her stomach growled again. Her mind wandered mercifully away from the conflict taking place on the inside.

Just five minutes, she thought, and closed her eyes again.

Soon, Alex found herself drifting to another place, another time – daydreaming again to be sure, but this dream was familiar. Here was a darker, ancient place filled with the familiar aromas of saltwater and damp wood. Her senses drank it up for what seemed like only minutes when the scene suddenly shifted. The dried grasses of a forgotten meadow swayed against a dry, hot wind. Blinding sunlight assaulted the view. She blinked against it and images appeared – hazy shadows in the bright light of noonday. Slowly, the images took definition. Try as she might, she could not look away. Without moving, she found herself standing to one side of a makeshift platform, and was forced to crane her neck just to see what was going on there.

She recognized the body suspended in mid-air from a large crossbeam. Its eyes were closed and the head tilted ghoulishly to the left. Death embraced the body. It hung limp, dangling freely from a thick rope tied overhead. She could not tear her eyes off its face. It seemed too familiar. The face rolled, vacant and lifeless. Horror passed through her soul and Alex watched as the irises dilated to black, then suddenly reappeared as blue. She couldn't look away. The crowd gathering below couldn't either.

No one moved. All eyes stared upon a woman's lifeless body … upon Kathryn's body hanging there.

Four

SOMETHING SCREAMED.

Alex jumped and blinked a few times before she awoke fully. Somewhere in the distance, an alarm wailed from one of the patients' rooms. She realized she had dozed off.

A hanging?

She had been to that place before and had seen a woman's body dangling from a gallows pole. Most of the time she dismissed the whole thing as a meaningless nightmare. But this time it had been Katherine.

Why her?

Alex shuddered. She had much to discuss with Mariel at their next tea. For now, it was over. The screaming alarm reminded her to come back to reality, and back to work.

She stood up from her computer, feeling the familiar ache in her neck, and stretched.

Come on! Cut me some slack today…just for a few minutes. Just long enough to allow her to shift focus to the blaring noise going off in the next hallway.

"Here we go." She voiced her thoughts knowing no one else could hear.

The ER continued to grow restless. It was busier than most Tuesdays, and Alex's superstitious mind wondered if some other employee had spoken aloud the dreaded Q-word. No one dared say it. The tiniest slip-up, the slightest breathed utterance of that dreaded word "quiet" would guarantee an onslaught of patients.

Alex poked her head out of her office and saw the scuffle of nurses rushing to their various charges. "Someone said it," she whispered. Shaking her head, Alex stepped out of the safety of her office.

As she walked into the hallway, she glanced to her right. The alarm wailed. She looked at the large red letters printed meticulously on plate glass sliding doors. EMERGENCY stood boldly, stamped in the color of fresh arterial blood. Occasionally, those letters separated as the glass yawned its welcome to paramedics and EMT's. Only the rescue and fire trucks were allowed to park there to offload the endless cargo of patients strapped to rolling gurneys. On busy days, the circular drive would be full of red and white rigs, but now it was empty.

Alex pressed her lips together as she glanced through the glass panes at the vacant bay. "This is not a good sign," she breathed. "Why is the ambulance bay empty? Where's security?"

To make certain the emergency vehicles only policy was followed, a security guard had been deposited on a small chair next to the doors to make sure that no one got in (and no one got out) without proper identification. Usually he was asleep with his head on his chest, which is how Alex found him sitting there now.

I wonder if sleeping on the job is one of those fragile rules made to be broken, she thought. Her infamous smirk escaped as she gave the guard a gentle tap on the shoulder.

"Come on, Pete, we need you awake and alert right now." The guard's eyes flickered, then closed, followed by a muffled snort in protest.

She turned away from the useless guard and tried to locate the alarm. Most nurses could tell within moments where an alarm originated and Katherine was no different. She had already started in the general direction of the awful wailing. Alex walked to one side with her lips pressed together, tightly accentuating the circles that darkened her bright, goldenrod eyes.

"Good morning … again, Alex," Katherine said without stopping.

"Kat. Do you need…?"

"I've got this," Katherine said and disappeared around a corner.

"Yes, you do, my girl," Alex said and smiled inwardly, as she watched Katherine jog away.

Amber filtered in through patterned fingerprints scattered along the glass and spilled dusk's light across the front counter. Sunset gently washed the hallway amidst the chaos, suggesting the end of the workday was close.

A few hospital employees walked along the sidewalk opposite the ambulance bay, headed for their cars in that steady gait reserved for tired employees who'd just ended their shift. For the staff of the ER, however, the busiest time of the day was just about to begin. Katherine could tell that others sensed it, as well.

One person stood out.

Katherine paused to look at the setting sun. Without warning, the light consumed her. Her body trembled and her mind shifted. Images of the ocean, pale turquoise saturated with a kaleidoscope of colored fish filled the shadows of her senses. Her tongue traced the edges of her lips and found there the salty flavor reserved for seafarers onboard wooden vessels far out at sea. A gentle sunset dancing over water crests and low rolling swells swam before her eyes. Katherine was caught up in a vision, hallucinating.

Images of water, deep sunsets, and the bow of a ship emerged. Slowly, then gradually increasing in speed, one image at a time flashed into her mind's eye – a slide show that paused only momentarily as each scene became a catalogued memory of something familiar.

Ocean...sunrise...water...turquoise...sunrise... waves...sunrise...crossed blades...crystal green...

Over and over the images flashed, faster and faster, until, finally, they were nothing but a blurred polychromatic film of color. Everything suddenly halted and a strange symbol grew brighter before her eyes, burning itself into her brain. Wavy lines beneath a single inverted half circle. The outside end looked like the tip of a femur bone. Centered behind it was the image of a skull with a gaping jaw. Its teeth clenched tightly across an arched blade.

A skull and cutlass.

And underneath it was etched three small marks: *Q.A.R.*

The symbol held Katherine in a trance. Raw fear crept through her body as her mind fixed on the image emblazoned there. This was something she knew, something familiar, yet she could not recall it. But she sensed its evil. An entity had attached itself to the image.

Something was terribly wrong, and Katherine couldn't break free of it. She was transfixed by the terror that held her captive to the image.

Raspy laughter whispered faintly, as if the vision itself was mocking her. She began to panic, unable to break free from the horror of it, and a man's voice bellowed.

"Kaycee, call for respiratory in Room 23." Dr. Woodson's head poked through a curtain as he spoke.

Katherine jumped, the trance broken by the chaos erupting in the next room. She blinked several times and shivered as she turned her back to the glass doors and the fading sunset outside. She rushed around the corner toward the nurses' station, pushing her glasses up the bridge of her nose as she scurried. Three of the most experienced nurses dashed into Room 23 ahead.

I probably won't be in on this one, either. The thought soured Katherine's face. Ahead, the curtain flew outward as an athletic blonde nurse with a visibly toned body and a cut attitude pushed her way out of the clustered room.

"This should have been called as a trauma," she said to Alex from across the hallway. The disgust in her voice was palpable. Katherine stood to one side as Alex's stern look was met with silence. "This guy's bad. He needs to go to the OR quick or we're going to lose him."

The blonde rushed past Katherine and down the hall toward the department's stash of drugs. Two more EMT's made their way into the room. One carried dressing material, and the other pulled a suture cart.

I really need to be in on this one, Katherine thought and pushed a little farther into the room, hoping to be lost in the crowd for a moment. The worst thing would be to get an assignment elsewhere, to be told to go away, or help in Fast Track and miss out on the trauma altogether.

Katherine felt eyes boring into the back of her head, and she knew she'd been discovered. She glanced up and saw Alex staring at her. Alex nudged her head toward the patient, so Katherine took the cue and moved to one side of the gurney.

Alex stepped forward and quickly surveyed the room's activity in one brief glance. Katherine followed suit, keenly noting the activity of the other nurses. She picked up a pair of gloves and tried to look official and busy like the rest of them. The screaming monitor continued its outcry, which added to the anxiety mounting in the claustrophobic space. Alex reached up, tapped the "silence alarm" button, and the keening instantly stopped.

"This guy fell from scaffolding. His back's involved, to be sure, but I'm worried about that leg." A thin, bearded doctor in a white coat spoke without taking his eyes off his patient.

Alex nodded and Katherine stepped around the end of the gurney, intent on getting a better look at the injured man. The distraction of a fresh trauma would certainly snap her back to her inquisitive, rational self. Stepping forward, her legs trembled. She tried to focus her attention on the gurney but suddenly felt herself reel.

Get a hold of yourself, Katherine! The thought propelled her closer to the victim lying strapped to a long blue board, blood seeping everywhere from underneath paper sheets. The tech's gloved hand lifted the drape, and she stumbled – unprepared for the grisly image lying there.

Five

A MANGLED HUNK OF BLOOD, gristle, and tissue that once resembled a human leg was heaped on the gurney, staining a stark-white sheet. The resident leaned over the nearly amputated appendage and pushed wire-rimmed glasses back into place with his left forearm. Holding the scalpel in his right hand, he poised himself to cut loose the debris and dead tissue. Unexpectedly, the coppery-sweet aroma of raw meat assaulted Katherine's nostrils. Her focus blurred and voices grew distant. One of the younger techs standing alongside caught hold of her shoulders just as her knees gave way.

"Somebody get a wheelchair," he announced. With the skill of an athlete, he directed her toward a chair.

Voices reverberated and faded into hollow echoes as Katherine shuddered again. Her vision narrowed to only a pinpoint focused somewhere distant where whitecaps belted against the groan of a ship's timbers.

"Repulsion…horror, I cannot do it, Capt'n…" Katherine's voice was faint. She reeled, and gentle hands lifted her into a wheelchair. Someone asked who she was speaking to, and another called out her name, the pronunciation incorrect and choppy. She couldn't answer.

"Kat…open your eyes and look at me…Kat," a male's voice spoke. Katherine's response would not escape her clenched teeth. "Take her into Room 29 and I'll be in there in a minute."

She heard the voices say her name over and over again, followed by comments about someone passing out. Conversations materialized around her, sounding as if they were taking place inside a hollow tunnel somewhere. A hand patted her on the shoulder and she felt air rush past her face. She was moving, and moving fast – escorted into the curtained room down the hall.

Apparently the crew is concerned. Is this about me? Why? What's going on? Why can't anyone voice me name properly?

Her mind drifted, swimming in saltwater and a faint sent of sandalwood. She breathed in the scent deeply. Her body lifted with each inhalation and fell into the rhythm of ocean swells. It felt like home and where she wanted to be. The gentle rolling of sea currents and swells rocked her as if she were in a giant cradle, bringing her peace. Katherine allowed herself to go a little deeper into the moment, holding on to every sensation of the delicious daydream.

"Has anyone told Alex yet?" the voice echoed behind her.

"No." It was a whisper that carried fear with it.

Alex had seen more than her share of battered, mangled body parts, and had handled each incident with skill and professionalism. Katherine's reaction was a common one for new nurses. Most had never seen anything beyond what TV or films decided to project on a screen. The initial, first-hand, graphic display of freshly torn flesh was always unsettling. But there was something different about Katherine's reaction.

Apparently, someone had told Alex, because, moments later, she walked into the room.

"Has she said anything?" Alex sounded concerned.

"She's talking gibberish about a crew and a captain or something," the tech answered as he pushed the empty wheelchair a little too rapidly out of the tiny room.

"Very weird, if you ask me," Rachel said, stepping up to prime an IV.

"A captain?" Alex repeated. She leaned in closer, examining Katherine's dilated pupils and glassy eyes. Something related to her daydream was dragging Katherine into a nightmare. Alex's gut feeling had been right – an entity more powerful than she had imagined was pulling at her. Ready or not, Katherine had been chosen. Mariel was wrong…this time.

Mariel, damn! You really need to text, Alex thought as she fingered her phone. She would call Mariel as soon as she could get away. For now, her role was to watch over Katherine – a duty she had been given the day of her birth.

"Get her onto the gurney and I'll go find Dr. Rich," Alex said and made her way out of the room, leaving Katherine in the hands of her coworkers.

"I've never seen her react like this," a voice over Katherine's shoulder whispered. It sounded familiar, and Katherine thought perhaps Jimmy was near.

"Yeah, there's definitely something wrong," said someone else. She couldn't place just whom it was speaking, but concern laced the tone.

"Maybe she's worked too many back-to-back shifts. No sleep will get to you eventually," Jimmy said.

"I know, I know." Rachel's voice shifted behind and to her left.

"Whatever. It happens all the time. These new nurses get all excited, and then pass out at the first sight of blood." Another voice.

Strong hands reached underneath her arms. "One, two, three…" Katherine landed hard on top of a cushioned gurney and lolled backward onto a pillow thrust beneath her head just in time. Bars clicked on either side of her and she heard the voices move toward her feet. Something still pulled at her – something not human.

Kathryn…come home.

No one else heard the whisper. No one else felt it reach inside her soul to grasp and pull it from her body. Was this death's grip?

"Where's the doctor?"

Another shuffle followed near her heels. Then a light washed over her face. Katherine winced and felt the pull let loose. There was someone else in the room.

"Katherine. Katherine, can you hear me?"

She nodded but stayed silent, waiting for her clouded mind to clear. Her head dropped slightly and something warm was draped over her body.

"Let's go ahead and get an IV in her."

Katherine shook her head "no" as her fear of needles suddenly brought some clarity in her foggy brain.

"Keep that blanket on, sweetie. You'll feel better. It's just out of the warmer and one of the perks of this place." Katherine recognized the voice and opened her eyes. Maya finished tucking the blanket under her feet, and then faced her patient. Her mocha skin matched the dark brown eyes framed by a perfect round face with dimples on either side of a wide, soft smile. Chin-length hair highlighted to look as if the sun had kissed each lock fell meticulously around her face as Maya leaned forward. She patted Katherine's hand.

A ghostly sigh evaporated, along with its presence. The entity had vanished.

"What happened?" Katherine asked.

Maya shrugged and turned to fuss over something on a cart against the wall. "I'm not sure. Rachel said you passed out. Do you remember anything?"

"I don't know. It was so weird. I ..." Katherine stopped short, knowing she couldn't explain her own reactions to herself, let alone to Maya. "Help me up, will you? I'm okay now. I think I just got a little light-headed." She pushed up on one elbow and the room began to spin.

"Oh, no…stay still. You're not going down again if I can help it." Maya sounded like she meant it, so Katherine obeyed. Her mind retraced the past few minutes, and she remembered the hunk of meat with a foot attached in Room 23. Her gut heaved and she fought back the urge to be sick. Something about that leg had affected her.

Surely, that wasn't it, was it? I saw that kind of stuff in school. The thought never made it to her lips, and she swallowed hard against it. No, there was something else about the injured man's leg that had set her reeling.

"I'm going to give you a little IV fluid, and I think you'll feel better," Maya announced as if she were awarding the Purple Heart.

Katherine shook her head again. "No, Maya. Really, I just need to get something in my stomach and rest a minute. I don't want this to be a big deal when it's just…just too much work and no breaks. I don't want to lose my job over it, either."

Maya stared at her, one hand holding the IV bag while the other held a needle suspended in mid-air. "Whatever, Katherine."

This was a battle Katherine knew she wouldn't win, and so she surrendered and laid back. Offering an arm, she waited for Maya's assault.

"Hello." A head popped in through the curtain. "How's the patient behaving?" Dr. Rich's face was transparent as his eyebrows pressed together across a bony forehead.

"She's not, as usual," Maya said with her head down, eyes trained on the needle she had just pierced through Katherine's skin.

"Ouch!" Katherine grimaced and glanced at Maya, who ignored her. Dr. Rich offered a counterfeit smile. She knew his concern was really for her wellbeing, but anxiety flashed behind his hazel eyes – a telltale sign. The sight of blood and bone had thrown Katherine into a stupor, and everyone knew it. Either she was too soft to be an ER nurse or something else was going on.

Katherine's gut told her the truth.

"Well, let's see how you feel after a little rest and some fluid, okay?" Dr. Rich smiled at both nurses and ducked out.

"I think we're going to get really busy tonight," Ryan grumbled as he walked past. His ponytail swayed as he glanced through a crack in the curtain. "Oh, hey, Katherine. Hope you feel better."

As quickly as he'd been there, he was gone – scooting down the hallway and into another room. Katherine listened to the exchanges taking place outside. They were all talking about her 'event'. She needed to get back to work – to look more like a nurse and less like a patient.

Her temples throbbed but her thoughts were clear now. It was time to pull her attention away from the shattered leg in the room down the hall. She glanced down at her arm where Maya was pressing transparent tape around the IV catheter.

I guess this will help…it can't hurt.

"What's going on…out there?" she asked, trying to sound nonchalant as Maya flipped the dial and cool fluid dripped into her veins.

"Honestly? It's starting to get a little crazy now." Maya stood and pulled the curtain closed.

"They all think I'm soft, don't they?"

"No." Maya cocked her head and looked at Katherine with skilled nurse's eyes. "I know this is difficult for you, being on this side of the gurney, but do me a favor and at least let the IV do its job. You'll feel better, and you can rest for a minute in the meantime. I can tell you need some of that. The dark circles give it away, you know."

"Is it that bad?"

"Yup." Maya nodded. "The rest of the ER can wait. You can't."

Katherine lifted her free arm to cover her face and block out life for a moment. "Thanks, Maya, really."

The waiting room had filled to capacity and buzzed with the stirrings of sick bodies. All in all, there were about fifteen people waiting to be triaged. Though no one seemed critical, the nurse knew everyone waiting was convinced they were destined to meet their Maker that very night. A few "regulars" snoring off their daytime drunkenness were slumped backwards in the farthest seats, as if they were part of the décor used to fill the room's empty corners. The rest of the waiting room waited.

"Still no room," Kindall said and offered the best smile she could muster. Triage had been insanely busy from the moment she stepped into her shift there. "I promise, we haven't forgotten you."

That promise never helped. The interior of the Emergency Department was already filled to capacity, and every gurney was mounded with a body. *You're taking up valuable space that someone else needs, Kat.* Katherine's guilt mounted as she lay there waiting for the IV to finish. She groaned and closed her mind against it.

"How you doin', kiddo?" Alex's voice jolted her back. Clearly, Alex was hiding something. "Your spirit seems to be in turmoil today – uncharacteristic of a strong trauma nurse."

"Alex, I'm just tired, really. There are too many patients for me to be lying here. I really want to get back to work…really," Katherine insisted.

Alex eyed her for a moment. Something had happened in the Code Room. There was a connection between Katherine and the corpse. It was obvious, Katherine was keeping some piece of vital information to herself. Alex shifted her gaze to the window and caught a glimpse of the eerie moon. *I really need to talk to your grandmother.*

"Go home, Katherine. Get out of this place. Go elsewhere and…"

Katherine thought about the patients. Perhaps she could still help, especially with those patients that were less critical. *At least the ones still alive need me.* The thought was not reassuring. Alex was right – she should leave.

"Two more medic runs due any minute, one with minor complaint of neck pain, status post rear-ended MVA. ETA five minutes," the nurse operating the pre-hospital radio announced to no one in particular.

"Thanks, Alyssa," Alex said, looking out through the open curtain in Katherine's room. The alarm sounded and Alex watched as Alyssa ducked back in to take another call.

Katherine doesn't belong here. The thought hit hard, and Alex looked back at Katherine, who shook her head.

I've got to go. Katherine reached over and clamped off the fluid dripping into her arm, then opened a packet of gauze dressing and covered the needle site. Within seconds, the IV was pulled and her arm bandaged. Alex watched in silence.

"You're right, Alex." Katherine stood just as Maya entered through the curtain.

Alex said nothing but her face revealed everything. Katherine couldn't fool her. She never could, even as a young girl. It was as if Alex knew her very soul.

Maya grunted and shook her head. "I guess I'm not surprised," she said flatly. "Are you feeling better?"

Katherine nodded.

"Liar." Maya glanced at Alex and rolled her eyes. "I guess I can't convince you to stay here for just a minute while I get Dr. Rich?" Maya's expression suggested she already knew the answer.

"Nope." Katherine grabbed her belongings and made for the hallway, then stopped to rest one hand on Maya's shoulder. "Thank you, Maya. You really are a good nurse, and a better friend."

Maya mumbled something as Katherine slipped out of the room and into the hallway. Alex watched in silence as she skirted down the hallway in the opposite direction.

"They're bringing in a 'chest pain' next." Alyssa stuck her head out of the radio room again. "Hope you're better, Katherine," she added just before disappearing inside to field another call.

"Thanks, I'm fine," Katherine said and rounded the corner, as Alex made her way to the tiny radio room.

Alyssa bent over the large radio and scribbled notes on a sheet of paper. The radio squawked, a hollow-sounding voice that gave the report for the next incoming patient. Alex waited a moment before asking her only question.

"What's their ETA?"

"Three minutes. The patient's pain has decreased to 4 out of 10," Alyssa replied. The voice on the radio crackled before interrupting with a set of failing vital signs.

Silently, Alex calculated the priority of the incoming patient, and knew this one would need a bed upon arrival. The EKG tech had been summoned, and a nurse already assigned. Labs would be drawn by the phlebotomist and sent off for stat results. Everything ran like a well-oiled machine when the real emergencies showed up.

On the opposite side of the ER, Katherine grabbed her belongings and quickly summed up her options: *Either walk out through the glass doors now or be faced with a new assignment and the probability of another "event." I should probably go.*

"I agree…and sooner is better than later," Alex whispered.

"What?" Alyssa looked up from her notes.

"Nothing." Alex had been caught reading Katherine's thoughts before. "Good work, Alyssa," she added and stepped into the doorway to wait. Her eyes followed Katherine as she headed toward the exit. Alex felt protective, as always – knowing her young charge would be stepping into a realm where she could be joined. Katherine simply did not know what lay ahead. Perhaps it would be safer for her to remain in the ER tonight.

"Fate!" Alex said aloud, and her thoughts betrayed her as she watched the glass doors whoosh closed behind Katherine. *I hope she faces it well.*

Six

ALEX TOOK A DEEP BREATH and forced a smile at no one. "I can do this…I can do anything for three more hours," she lied to herself.

Her eyes wouldn't focus, and her head pounded in rhythm with her pulse. A wave of nausea raised its nasty self in the back of her throat. Katherine was gone and she was left to manage an ER that demanded too much. *Lord help me!* She needed to get away from everyone for just a moment.

Alex spun on her heels and walked down the hall into an empty room. Her heart raced. She began to feel sick as her stomach twisted in an unrelenting wrestling match with her intestines. Fighting the urge to be sick, she quickly washed her hands in the sink next to the medicine cabinet and splashed some of the cool water over her flushed cheeks. This was not about the ER … this was about Katherine.

The room spun and the floor began to rise up. She leaned sideways to catch hold of the empty gurney next to her and held on. *Calm down, Alex!* Her body refused to listen and she retched. Quickly pressing her left hand against her abdomen, she held it there, as if its job was to subdue whatever was clawing to get free through her skin. *Breathe.* Her lungs obeyed. One forced breath followed another until she was finally calm. Alex stood upright and lifted her hand from the gurney she had been leaning on.

The white sheet moved.

Her body froze. A new feeling crept over her – a spreading sensation as she watched the sheet directly underneath her hand rise off the gurney. Katherine had vacated refuge – she could feel it – and her presence was gone. And now *this* had happened to Alex? Could there be a connection? Her face blanched and the room darkened.

Immediately, she dialed Mariel's number on her cell phone. The incessant ringing told her that Mariel wasn't near her phone.

"Dammit, Mariel! Pick up!"

A soothing voice on the other end urged the caller to leave a message, followed by a standard beep.

"Mariel – I've got to speak to you. This is very urgent." She paused for just a moment before adding, "It's happening."

Alex clicked off her phone as tiny blue sparks leapt from her hand to the sheet and back again. She turned her palm upward and broke the spell. The sheet dropped lifelessly to the gurney.

Hissed laughter whispered in the room and the lights flickered to black.

PART THREE

Impunity

Seven

April, 1721 ~ Youghal, Wales

"THE BLAGGARD'S SCALED THE WALL." The shouts sounded breathy in spite of the short distance he'd run from the pub to the open street market. "And it looks like he's gettin' away."

"Can't lose him, mate. He's taken all me gold," another pirate piped up from behind.

The scuffle of footsteps thumped against the cobblestone, sending a flurry of chickens and children into abandoned corners along the street. Within moments, Seth had leapt over another barrier and scaled the side of a ratty edifice to its roof. Dust scattered through holes in the thatch, raining particles that glimmered frosty amber to the floorboards below. A bag of coins clanked hard against his thigh – a reminder of their value as he darted across the building's main beam.

"Thar he be!"

Seth didn't stop to find out where the voice had come from. Instead, he jumped from the shaft onto another protrusion in the structure's framework. It gave way and he plummeted through moldy thatch and landed on what was once the crossbeam of an abandoned fishery.

"Ooph!" The wind had been knocked out of him, and the sound of it gave away his position. He heard the cutthroats changing direction and heading straight for him. He pushed upright and tried to run. Tiny bones and slime covered the rotting wood, and Seth found his balance vexed as he skated across grease that coated the surface.

"In here." The voice shouted just outside a tattered door that gave way an instant later and toppled into pieces as three pirates shoved in.

"There!"

The scrawny one they'd called Bruce shouted with a grimy finger pointed directly at the youth.

They'll never make it across this slime. Seth grinned and tucked into a somersault to drop onto an outcropping. The pirates immediately followed suit, running headlong onto the same ledge that suddenly disappeared into an empty vat of tiny bones and dried fish guts. Seth was right. The pirates lost their footing on the slick surface and fell in a mass heap of tangled limbs and brawny bodies.

"*Adieu*, gents," Seth called out, tapping his brow as he tiptoed around the rim of the tank and out through an open conduit. The sun kissed the horizon as he threaded his way around a makeshift byre set up for wayward visitors. Donkeys brayed in protest at his intrusion and scattered the threshing with hooves that kicked at shadows fading as fast as the daylight. "Hush," he urged the beasts, but they refused to be quieted. Within moments, the pirates had located him.

"Thar's the little bugger!"

Closing in on one side, the irate pirates scuttled toward the double doors and waited for Seth to emerge.

"You smell like fish, Cuddy," a thick pirate said and stepped to one side, fingers pinching his nostrils together.

"You smell worse, like ye haven't had a bath in a month!" Cuthbert said and cuffed the pirate over both sides of his head.

"I haven't!" The pirate rubbed his ears just as Seth emerged from an open window on the farthest side.

"It's all yours if you can catch me, mates," Seth taunted, then lobbed a gold coin into the dirt and sprinted in the opposite direction. He stumbled, losing his balance only once before regaining it. With little time to waste, he lunged for a wall of stone rising out of nowhere.

As if on cue, the pirates tore after him, tripping over one another in their pursuit. Seth bounded along a low palisade. The moss growing between each stone made for tricky passage, but he gingerly hopped from one to another until the barrier gave way to an open field. He glanced down at his plunder and realized some of the precious coin had fallen loose from the bag. Glancing back, he saw gold glinting in the fading sunlight, and for a moment considered returning the way he'd come to gather it up.

"Bloody pirates!" He berated himself and bolted through knee-high grass. "That's what ye get, Seth, for being cocky." Tucking the offending bag with its remaining coins into his shirt, he made for the cliffs. Within moments, the pirates were on his trail, curses flying as fast as their feet. *The boys can run – I'll give 'em that.* The thought propelled Seth into a quicker pace.

"You've got nowhere to run, boy," a deep bass shouted from behind.

"There'll be little left o' ye after we're done skinnin' yer hide," another hollered.

Seth glanced back and saw that the motley crew had gained some ground. He shifted to his left and picked up speed in hopes of widening the gap between himself and the pirates. It worked. He smiled to himself as he dashed across the open field, certain he had lost the marauders.

Just then, something whizzed past his ear. He heard the shot a moment later and realized the pirates were shooting at him. Another whoosh passed the other side, followed by the sound of a pistol discharging.

"You're shootin' at me?"

He changed directions and ran straight for the threshold of the precipice. Amber sunlight blazed from the edge where the cliff suddenly disappeared. Seth realized there was nowhere else to go and dug deep for resolve. Another discharge sounded from behind and the dirt at his feet erupted as the bullet dug into it. *This is not the time or place I'm going to die.* The thought drove him forward, and he took one last step, launching himself into the unknown.

"The ruffian bloody jumped off the edge o' the cliff!"

"Aye, and he's taken our gold with 'im!"

A chorus of pirate obscenities echoed from the abyss as the tirade of cutthroats stopped abruptly at a craggy overhang.

"Shoot 'im. I want me doubloons back," Cuthbert shouted, and fired his weapon into the expanse. The others joined him, and, seconds later, iron bullets rained down from the cliffs.

Seth flailed with arms and legs spiraling in all directions as he plummeted toward the open sea. The iron shot continued to follow him non-stop, when, suddenly, a blast from below sent blinding fire upward. The cannon ball that followed was far to one side, crashing into the outcropping just below where the pirates stood. Another barrage of curses bellowed from where they stood.

Bobbing at anchor, a magnificent merchantman sat directly below, its cannon still smoking as Seth arched, then tucked his knees and rolled into a dive straight for the mainsail. With skill akin to a Japanese pearl diver, Seth catapulted his body into the sail and landed full force against the tarpaulin. Head over heels, his body bounced down the sailcloth until he landed with a thud, sprawled out over the burnished deck of the great ship. It was a miracle he'd survived the fall. Gold and silver spilled out, blanketing the deck where Seth lay.

"Ooph!" Seth heaved, the wind knocked out of him once again. He rolled to one side and gasped for air. A pair of boots planted themselves just inches from his nose.

"Well, well, well," a deep voice said above him. "And what have the Gods rained down upon me ship this day, I wonder?"

PART FOUR

Crossway

Eight

BY THE TIME ALEX REACHED her office, her lungs were sucking air through bronchial tubes the size of coffee straws. The event with the sheet had unsettled her, to say the least, and the significance of it meant Katherine would not return. Alex lowered herself into the chair behind her desk and closed her eyes. *Reality has shifted.* She lifted her head, opened her eyes, and stared down at her own hands with wonder.

Mariel said she's not ready...not yet. I've failed her!

The thought repeated itself over and over again in Alex's tired brain. She studied her hands. Her palms were pink and sturdy. No longer did blue sparks dance from them.

Static electricity, someone else would have called it that. Well, maybe. Mariel will know.

She reached for her cell phone and dialed Mariel's number again. After nearly six rings, Mariel finally answered.

"Alexandra, I've been waiting for you to call." The silky voice sounded breathy.

"You really need to learn how to text, I'm telling you."

There was a sigh on the other end of the phone. "Yes, yes…you've said that before. But you've really too much to tell me for a text anyway. Better to speak about it directly."

"I suppose you are right." Alex paused and wondered how to explain Katherine's behavior.

"Just spit it out, Alexandra," Mariel interrupted her thoughts.

Uncanny how she always does that. "I believe the time has come. It started…today…she's receptive, but unaware."

"Did she recognize anything?"

Alex cleared her throat and glanced at the door to her office. It was closed tight. "I don't think she recognized any*body* in particular, but she definitely witnessed the symbols."

"Ah, then it presents itself slowly." Alex heard Mariel sigh.

"Slowly? Are you kidding, Mariel? It hit her like a Mac truck. She passed out and…"

"Symbols you say?" Mariel interrupted.

Alex sighed. "Yes." She glanced at a photo of a nine-year old Katherine poised with her face to the ocean as the sun set in brilliant colors of rose and lavender. Katherine was but a shadow against the brilliant light – another symbol in Alex's mind. "I've failed this time, Mariel."

There was no response.

Tears surfaced along the outer edges of Alex's eyelids and she blinked them away. *She's the prey to an unseen predator and I can do nothing.* She pushed against the thought, but it wouldn't leave. *Something wants her ... something not of this world. Why now... before she's ready?*

"The timing seems odd, doesn't it, Mariel?" Alex glanced out of her office window, looking for the sunset. The sky had grown dark.

"Perhaps not. It's a space-time relativity that Albert put into a math equation or something. I never understand his prattle. In all of my years, I've never met a man with such a lack of attention! If I hadn't told him to 'write it all down'…"

"Einstein? As in Albert Einstein?" Alex cut her off this time.

"Why, of course, Alexandra. What other Albert with theorems would there be?"

"You knew Albert Einstein? You never told me." Alex was incredulous.

"We were in school together. Dated a few times, but it never went anywhere, obviously. The man was a dreamer and couldn't focus on anything! Least of all me. And you know how that interrupts a budding romance."

"Mariel, how does this relate to Katherine?" Alex, exasperated, still reeled from the impact of Mariel's romance with Einstein.

"Yes…yes, I drifted off topic. I apologize. And don't be so shocked, Alexandra – there are many things you do not know about me. Still, we can talk of those later." Mariel cleared her throat. "Now, can you think of anything related to time…a date perhaps?"

"Let me think a moment." Alex glanced at the moon, her thoughts lost in the day's events. "Nothing comes to mind. She reacted strangely to some of the patients here, but, then, most new nurses don't handle their first trauma well."

"Trauma? Exactly what was it?"

"Some guy lost his leg. Katherine took one look at the leg and fainted. That's not unusual, really."

"Perhaps…perhaps not. If anything about that… that dismembered leg is reflected in time. An event, let's say…" Mariel sighed as her thoughts drifted again. "Remember, it presents itself slowly in subtle messages – mostly as signs and symbols. What else?"

"I don't know. We had a death – actually, he was dead long before we ever got him, but…"

"That may be it," Mariel interrupted. "Tell me more. Was there anything unusual about the body? Anything you can remember? A birthmark, scars, unusual wounds, injury markings of any kind?"

"No, at least not that I'm aware of. I never inspected the body for anything specific. But Katherine reacted as if something pulled her toward it. She screamed when she glanced at its face. No, wait! The corpse grasped at her arm."

Silence.

"What did you say?" Mariel's voice was hushed.

"It would be the usual death reflexes, most likely. At least, that's the way it was explained. Happens all the time down in the morgue." Alex flinched as she heard herself repeat the tech's commentary. "Do you think the body actually grabbed her purposefully?"

Silence again.

"Indeed," Mariel finally answered. "There are no accidents, no coincidences, as you well understand, Alexandra. There must be something about that body that resonated with Katherine. She would know."

"I should have paid more attention to…"

"What was the time of death?" Mariel's voice piqued.

"1721." Alex gasped. "You don't think…?"

Mariel inhaled deeply and let the breath out slowly. "A time-space shift – the symbols are plain when viewed through eyes that do not see boundaries."

"He was dead when we got him. The actual time of death…"

"Time only has meaning when it's reflected through some medium – something like a clock or a date."

Alex shuddered. It had been right in front of her and she'd missed it. "Hidden in plain sight. I should have seen it, Mariel. Deep down, I knew it. I said so even then. '1721, as it should be'."

Alex wrung her hands as she envisioned the corpse lying in Room 13. Katherine had reacted, and now strange happenings had found their way to Alex.

"Are you experiencing events, as well?"

The question unsettled Alex further. Initially, there had been no accounting for the hallucinations or the electrical current jumping from her hand. It just had happened.

"Yes."

"Ah, then the symbols lie in the death. If death is not acknowledged, it will continue to present itself elsewhere again and again until given validation." Mariel paused. "What else has occurred…not just to Katherine, but to you, as well?"

For a moment, Alex was unable to answer. "I…I lifted a sheet with the energy of my hand. It looked like tiny blue sparks. That's not my *Gift*, Mariel. You know that."

"No…your *Gift* lies with insight and protection. I do not recall you ever manifesting the *p er mellt*."

"No. The power of the skies belongs to the Mellt Sosye, which I am not!" Alex could not contain the fear creeping into her voice. "If strange events have disturbed me, then certainly they profoundly affect Katherine. You sense it, Mariel. I do too, although I've been in denial, I admit it. Katherine is surrounded by an aura that attests to the truth of it. I just refused to see it."

"That you would manifest such power could mean many things. Likely, you are manifesting for Katherine." Mariel paused. "This is dire, Alexandra. You know Katherine has been born with the *Gift*."

"Yes," Alex said. "I remember the library."

"As you should. Katherine is very gifted with spells, though she doesn't know it yet."

"She was very little when it first showed itself, wasn't she Mariel? That time in the library."

"Aye." Mariel sighed. "She's calling on her Gift even now, in this century."

"Yes…yes indeed." Alex paused to remember the little girl in Mariel's library years ago.

It was not the first time Katherine had made magic. Alex had been witness to the very first time it happened. Tea time at Mariel's had always been suited for deep discussions of past events, present moments, and planning, as it were, mostly for Katherine's future. Alex remembered clearly Katherine's *ability to make* things happen.

In the earliest days, there had been times when objects near a young Katherine moved without ever being touched. Once, when she was just a little girl of six, a favorite book of fairy tales flew through the air and landed on the table in front of her. She was playing in the library at Mariel's house when it had happened.

Katherine had thought it a marvelous trick at the time and returned the book to its original place on the other side of an antique game table under a bay window. As she focused on the little book, it would shift ever so slightly. Bending down so that her nose had just touched the edge of the table, she stared a bit more intently at the book.

"Move again," Katherine had commanded in her pint-sized voice.

Mariel had sensed her granddaughter's intention and glanced to the library at young Katherine. "This one's powerful," she had said and given Alex a knowing look as they sipped their tea. Both women had waited with eyes glued to the carved oak library door while the little girl cast her spell from inside.

As if the book understood, it twitched a little harder this time. Once more, Katherine had made her demand for movement.

"Come to me."

The book slid from one end of the table to the opposite side of the room where she sat. With a faint whoosh, it landed just inches from her face, almost hitting her nose before it stopped. Alex and Mariel exchanged looks as they watched the little girl discover her new abilities. It became a game that afternoon. Katherine amused herself with commands and the book responded, flying back and forth from table to table. This lasted well into the late evening. Outside, a mourning dove had cooed as the sun dropped below the palm trees that lined the grounds.

"It is no accident." Mariel had stated the obvious and Alex had nodded in agreement.

Then, without warning, the bird had ended its song and the magic disappeared just as Katherine's mother had popped her head inside the library door.

"It's lovely to see how you enjoy the library, my dear. But we have to leave now. Come and say your goodbyes to mum and Auntie Alex."

Mariel had immediately concluded tea with Alex, waiting in the garden room – a timeless, magical place.

"She's been in the library again," Sara had apologized and squeezed Katherine's hand. "I'm afraid she's made quite a mess of your books in there, Mother."

"Little Kath*ryn*..." which was how Mariel pronounced her name, with a slight roll of the *r*, "...is special. She has the *Gift* passed down from our line."

Mariel had explained the magical *endowment* to Katherine's mother, Sara, years before Katherine's birth. Sara had not inherited the *Gift* like Mariel had inherited from her own mum. "A broken link," Mariel had called Sara. It had always been difficult for Sara to be different from the other women in her family line, so she chose to ignore their magic...especially Katherine's *Gift*.

"Not broken, Mother ... just different." Sara's response always resulted in a snort from Mariel.

"Call it what you like, my dear. The child possesses the Gift and you simply do not."

It was a well-known fact that the McCauley women were unusual. Katherine was no different, and showed early promise as a talented healer, as had the generations of McCauley women before her – all except for her mother, Sara. Alas, Sara was destined to remain a typical human female deprived of any magical abilities, except to give birth to a talented, beautiful daughter.

Tugging on her daughter's hand, Sara had walked the little girl out of the garden room and away from her grandmother. Mariel had peered through the corners of her bright silver eyes. It was no secret that her granddaughter had been up to something in private with magic, kept hushed in the booked-lined walls of the elaborate library.

That's my good little girl.

A slight shift in her grandmother's face had given away her thoughts. Katherine had felt Mariel's eyes upon her and pulled free from Sara's grasp. Little legs carried her back to Mariel's arms.

"I don't want to leave you, Mum."

"Aye, and I don't want you leaving, either. But you have much to do at home, now don't you? School awaits, and your mother needs your spirit with her."

Katherine had pulled back and gazed into her grandmother's silver eyes. "Yes, mum."

"I know what you've been up to in the library, little miss, and I'm proud of you for it. Now take those abilities home with you and practice them when no one else is looking, especially your mother. Be certain to harm no one. That is the first rule. Then help your mother by loving her most. That is the second."

Mariel's eyes had danced as she spoke, and Katherine caressed her grandmother's cheeks with her little girl's hands.

"I promise I will," she had whispered.

Mariel had smiled. Behind her, a mourning dove settled upon a branch and watched them.

"I love you, dear girl," Mariel had whispered back. "Now scoot before your mother grows impatient with us both."

Katherine scurried back and had reluctantly clutched Sara's outstretched hand.

"She's an old soul, that little one is," Alex had said softly.

The bird had cooed again and two sets of shrewd eyes observed the prodigy and her mother as they passed through the front entrance and out of the great house. Nothing more had ever been said about that day in the library until many years later, well after Sara had passed from this lifetime.

That was long ago.

Leaning back slightly in her office chair, Alex pondered Katherine's *abilities*. A sigh escaped her lips and carried the last of her stress with it. *Well, she can live with being unusual. Wendy certainly does.* The thought gave no reassurance. *No one would ever suspect Katherine and Wendy of being sisters. How could they? The two are completely different! Unusual indeed.*

Unusual was Alex's norm, something to account for the hospital sheet lifting beneath her palm and blue sparks accompanying it. But that type of manifestation did not belong to Alex, and she could not recall the blue sparks attaching themselves to Katherine, either.

Time seemed to narrow to this day, and Katherine seemed too young for what lay ahead.

"Alexandra," a voice cut into her thoughts. "Are you still there dear?"

"Oh, Mariel, I am so sorry. Daydreaming, I suppose. I will keep a weathered eye out for anything else that seems significant and let you know. In the meantime, Katherine is leaving the hospital now. Perhaps you should follow up with her?" Alex sighed, and Mariel could hear the fatigue in her voice.

"All right, then, I'll do as you suggest. Thank you, my dear friend. We'll speak again soon."

With that, the phone clicked to silence.

"Goodbye, Mariel," she said to the dial tone.

Nine

"THERE'S A PHONE CALL FOR you from radiology on line two, if you can take it," Kaycee said as she popped her head in through the office doorway.

"Will you see if Maya can field this one? I'm tied up for a bit," Alex lied.

Maya's was always the right nurse to have around when things needed sorting out. Yet she could be easily distracted under the right circumstances. In truth, Maya was occasionally too spontaneous for her own good. Those traits made her the perfect fit to Alex's cool-headedness. Their friendship was easy, and casual enough for both women to be comfortable. Alex was grateful for that.

"Will do." Kaycee disappeared and the sound of gently placed footsteps echoed behind her. They belonged to someone else, and the patter instantly lifted Alex's spirits.

Almost immediately, the outline of a curvy, womanly figure stepped through the narrow office door. Almond-shaped, mocha eyes peered in. She smelled of cinnamon and her face radiated peace.

"Cindy!" Alex smiled. "I'm so glad you're here."

Cindy moved with a breezy benevolence that commanded the chaos in her path in much the same way Moses had parted the Red Sea. A sideways glance revealed a hazy golden glow surrounding her entire form that blended into the color of watermelon. But nobody noticed the aura – no one except a true intuitive … and Alex, who couldn't take her eyes off of it. This magnificent aura entered the office first, radiating through the doorway just moments before Cindy entered. She smiled.

"Are you okay?"

Her voice reminded Alex of a lullaby sung on a hot summer night. "Kaycee mentioned you were tied up with something. That's not you." Cindy placed one hand on Alex's shoulder.

Her touch sent a wave of tranquility rolling throughout Alex's body. Cindy was someone with whom she could share the deepest part of her soul. Fortunately, this included the horrifying details of Katherine's hallucinations, and Alex's feelings of failure when it came to protecting her.

"It happened again, Cin." Alex barely spoke the words. "It's happening with much more intensity, and I'm not sure what to do."

"Is she handling it well?" Cindy asked without emotion.

"Hard to tell. She's responding, but I'm not convinced she's accepted everything coming to her."

Cindy sat down. The focused look of a nurse facing a terminally ill patient crossed Cindy's face as she studied Alex.

"Okay, I'm listening."

Alex recounted the images and Katherine's subsequent reaction to the injured man's leg. Occasionally, Cindy would nod and mutter, "uh-huh" as she listened.

"Mariel said to watch for symbols," Alex continued, and began a narration of the day's events. When she had finished, she crossed her arms, then sat back and quietly searched Cindy's face for answers. Cindy's eyes were soft and deep and secretive. Her friend had taken in every word. Silence passed between them for what seemed an eternity. Then, suddenly, Cindy reached over to the desk, and, in one smooth motion, took up a small blank sheet of paper lying on top of a note pad. She pulled out a pen from one of her pockets and wrote something on the paper, then slid it across the desktop to Alex.

"What's this?" Alex asked.

"She needs to call him, the sooner the better. Then stay away from this place until it settles. You should try to figure out what's going on as quickly as possible. It appears Katherine won't be able to wait very much longer."

Alex glanced at the name written in very graceful handwriting.

Gary L. Strickland (Shaman)

The phone number written next to it had a local area code. She looked back at Cindy and was met with a warm smile, her eyes masquerading the thoughts behind them.

"Just make certain Katherine calls the number, Alex." Cindy nodded at the paper in Alex's hand.

"A shaman? I appreciate this, Cin, really, I do, but I think this is way beyond a shaman's capabilities." Alex tried to hand back the slip of paper. Cindy refused.

"You know she needs to do this. He's good and he'll help. Tell her. In fact, go talk with her in person. I've got it covered out there for the rest of the day." She bobbed her head in the direction of the main ER. "If anyone asks, I tell them you've gone home early." Although it wasn't really early, as far as the clock was concerned.

Evening had come and the change in staff for the night shift had already started. Alex didn't protest, relishing the peace that followed the golden-rose aura as it took leave of her office behind her friend. She looked once more at the sheet of paper with the name written on it before tucking it into the back pocket of her leather billfold. As she gathered her things, she thought of how much she would like to take Cindy's energy home with her.

Maybe she's right. A shaman couldn't hurt.

Alex hastily scribbled a note to the night charge nurse, something about going home early, adding as an afterthought:

Call me if you have any questions...A.

Flipping off the lights, she walked out of her office. No one observed Alex as she made her way toward the glass ambulance doors. Perhaps the staff was just too busy to notice her – perhaps they were relieved to see her abandon the chaos. It was definitely time to get out of there. Her heartbeat picked up a little as she thought about going home.

"Hey, Alex," a cheery voice called from her right. "Glad I caught you."

"Hi, Kindall, I was just leaving."

The smile dropped slightly from the triage nurse's lips. "Um, well, I guess it's a good thing you didn't, because they just walked Brooks back to Room 15."

"What?"

"Sorry. Something about his arm. He's fine, I'm sure." Kindall threw out a hasty smile and darted back the way she'd come.

Alex groaned, made an about-face, and headed to the opposite end of the ER – away from the waiting glass doors and her escape. Ahead, the curtain had been drawn, encasing the occupant of Room 15 – all but the loosely tied tennis shoes belonging to a teenage boy. Alex clasped the curtain and flung it open.

"Mom!"

"What happened this time, Brooks?" Irritation spilled into each syllable as Alex gave her son the once-over.

"Mom! It totally wasn't my fault."

"It never is," she said, then placed her belongings on the only chair and sat down on the edge of the bed facing him. Hazel eyes danced, electric with the energy that matched young Brooks' spirit. Golden curls that refused to be combed added to his surfer image. Most kids his age would spend hours in the sun and never imitate that look. Brooks' carefree attitude came naturally, and his appearance vouched for it.

"For real this time, Mom. They put up over forty to anyone who could base jump the lighthouse. I totally had it nailed until ..."

"Dollars? Seriously, Brooks? You'd risk your life for forty dollars?"

He dropped his gaze to the floor and Alex knew she'd bruised his ego. "You don't get it, Brooks. We're all we've got – just each other. I can't keep paying for these guys to put you back together every single time you decide to be stupid."

That was a little too harsh. Alex winced at the words and bit her lip to stop herself from saying more. He turned his back on her and blinked back tears.

"Why do you always have to make such a big deal about stuff? Why can't you just have a little confidence in me for once?" His voice cracked as he spoke.

Alex rested a hand on his knee, but he pulled away from her. She studied him for a moment and decided a little space might be good for them both.

"Honey, I'm sorry. I've had one helluva day. I just want you to think a little bit about some of the situations you're willing to put yourself into. Life is so fragile – look around here, if you doubt that."

He glanced up at her, and resentment flashed behind his eyes. "Why do you always have to be so cryptic?"

"Don't go there, Brooks," Alex whispered. "Too many unseen events…so much you aren't even aware of…it's all real."

He cocked his head, unsure of what she meant. Mostly, he was disappointed that his mother hadn't been impressed with his use of a really cool word he'd just picked up.

Cryptic. He has no idea. Alex knew better than to try and explain. She stood and picked up her things. "I'm going back to my office to put these away. I'll be back in a moment, and we'll get you all fixed up before much longer," she said, glancing at his arm suspended in a sling.

"I'm fine. I don't need you here."

She'd been too hard on him and felt bad about it. She cupped his chin in her palm and lifted his eyes to meet hers. "I love you, Brooks. No matter what it sounds like, I just want to protect you. That's my job." He nodded in silence and refused to look her in the eyes.

"Hey, there, young man," the animated voice of an energetic physician pierced their exchange. A broad smile spread across his unshaven face and lit up the room as he entered. It was obvious that the young doctor had been working well past his scheduled shift. Alex was relieved he'd stayed. Alex smiled warmly, grateful to have someone break the tension in the room.

"Hi, Eric. I'm glad you're still here," she said. He directed his smile at her and moved to Brooks.

"So what's this make? The second time already this month?" he said.

"Third," Alex cut in, and Brooks shot her a look.

"Well, then…" He attempted to make light of the situation by keeping his focus on Alex. "Let's get going on the X-rays and a few other tests. I'll get him something for the pain. We'll try to make this happen quickly, but you know how it can be around here. He's likely to be with us for a bit…"

"I'm right here…hello?" Brooks snapped. "I can hear everything you're saying."

"Of course you are." Eric smiled even broader. "See you in a minute."

Brooks grunted as Eric darted out through the curtain and left him alone with his mother again. Alex looked at her son and decided to follow the doctor's example.

"I'll be right back," she said, and slipped out through the curtain. Brooks was left to himself, frustrated and hurting. He glanced at his arm in the sling.

"This is so lame."

Ten

HEAVY FOG SHROUDED A FULL moon, while apparitions haunted the quiet evening ocean. There was no peace in nightfall as Katherine nudged her glasses up her nose before threading her way to the little blue sports car. Goosebumps made their way to the surface of her skin and crawled over her shoulders, clawing along her spine. She shivered and fumbled with the keys inside her bag. Katherine glanced at her phone. The weather app flashed, announcing a balmy 82 degrees, along with a surf alert for tomorrow morning. *I shouldn't be shivering.* She really wasn't feeling cold.

Suddenly, she felt the prickly stare of eyes upon the back of her neck. Instinctively, her focus darted from one side to the other and then trailed behind her. Nothing. But she could *feel* a presence there. Fear shaded her vision and she blinked several times, hoping to see something, anything. She was met with shadows cast by the eerie moon overhead.

"Who's there?"

Her voice sounded hollow. She cleared her throat and called out again, but the only sound was a gust of wind through leaves. Katherine scanned the parking lot again. Nothing but darkness and the rustle of trees in the ocean breezes. *My mind must be playing tricks on me again. What is wrong with me?* Given the circumstances of the day, she dismissed it as fleeting paranoia.

Until she saw the figure.

Inky appendages moved through patches of moonlight, illuminated in bits of floating silver. Katherine blinked. The oppressive black of night made it difficult to separate shadows from objects. She blinked again and caught a glimpse of the form as it moved through her peripheral vision.

"Who's there? Brett? Maya? No more jokes, okay?"

The shadow moved again and her skin crawled.

"I'm calling for security," she shouted, but did not move.

Out of the corner of her eye she saw it again. Black hate stared from glistening sockets. It had no body, just a dark form with an arm limply dragging something behind. Katherine's teeth chattered with the ice that flowed through her veins. This was the same evil that had gripped her forearm in a dead man's grasp. Perhaps the old man had revived somehow and followed her out to the parking lot.

Ridiculous!

Her thoughts jumped with the movement of the figure. She reached for her phone, but her hand came up empty. Too afraid to peel her eyes from the shad-owy image, Katherine refused to blink. Her fingers fumbled again, unable to identify anything hidden in her bag as she searched frantically for her keys, phone…anything.

The form shifted into the moonlight just slightly to reveal one side of a ghostly torso with its arm now luminescent and pale. Her eyes caught sight of a dark mark visible on the surface, bold against the pallor of its flesh. She squinted, but couldn't make out the details.

Reveal yourself! Her thoughts commanded it and the form came into focus. Katherine stumbled backward. Her eyes snapped open wide, terrified. Emblazoned in black ink on the lurid, leathery skin, curvy lines overlaid the same set of letters she had seen earlier: *Q.A.R.*

"No! It couldn't be…you're dead," she half whis-pered, and fumbled again inside her purse. Frantic fingers finally found the velvet rabbit's foot chained to her keys. She snatched them and scraped the key against the door lock of her blue Mustang. A white line remained where the paint had peeled away. "No!"

"*Witch…*" Wheezy laughter closed in around her.

"Stay away from me!" she screeched at the shadow, not daring to look behind her. The raspy laughter grew louder, and the sound of footfalls advanced. Black eyes affixed to the back of her neck burned white hot. She jammed the key into the lock again, but missed.

Another long white line was scratched unevenly along the side of the door, intersecting the first, forming a cross.

"*I know ye, lass,*" hissed a raspy voice somewhere from behind her, closer now. *"John Rose Archer never forgets."*

She could feel frigid breath upon her neck as it wheezed again. The entity was only inches from her now. "I don't know a John Rose Archer. You h-have the wrong p-person." Jabbing blindly again at the lock, she felt the key hit its mark with a soft click.

"Aye, but ye do! Ye be the one I come for. A pox, indeed. It's revenge…"

"No!"

In jerky movements she turned the key, opened the driver's side door, and slipped across the leather seat behind the steering wheel. Somehow, the door slammed shut and instantly locked. Katherine set the alarm and readied for what might happen next. Eyes wide, she scanned the darkness through the window. The full moon pierced the black night, and her eyes drifted to the moon's omen.

"Cursed Midnight Omen! I know what you are," she whispered, and then dropped her eyes to the window where the glass was transparent. Fog from the breath of something on the other side blurred any view to the outside. Without warning, her car rocked – side-to-side it struggled to stay upright. Then just as suddenly, stopped.

"*Ye be known, witch,*" the voice hissed, and a soggy chuckle spewed, then faded, as the voice grew distant. Echoes of the sea crashing against the sand in full tide melted into the frothy laughter. Soon only the ocean sounded outside of her locked car.

She peered out of the window as the pane began to clear. Nothing was there – nothing but moonlight dancing against an inky night sky. She traced the ground and saw the glimmer of damp pavement blanketing the parking lot. Empty. She was alone once again. Straightening herself, she took in a better view of the passenger window. The imprint of a hand against the steamy glass began to fade. Her breath caught and she shuddered back against her seat. Her view had been through this handprint – the view that had allowed her to see the ghost.

"Got...to...get...home...Katherine," she said in great breathy gasps as shaking hands turned the ignition and started the coarse purr of her Mustang's engine. Lungs screamed for oxygen and she felt a sharp, unexpected jolt of pain searing across the front of her throat. Panic! She forced a hard swallow, then inhaled deeply through a narrowing trachea.

What does it want with me? Who the hell is that?

Tears burned against her flushed cheeks, and she wiped her face with the back of one hand as the other dropped to the stick shift. As she pulled out of the hospital parking lot, she took one last look at the place where the shadow had been. The light flickered and she caught sight of a man standing where her car had been. He lowered the hilt of a curved sword and tucked it into a sash tied about his waist. Atop his head a scarf tightly shrouded his scalp. Below it, from one ear, dangled a gold earring.

Katherine pressed hard on the gas pedal and rubber screeched in protest against the wet pavement. The sports car took the road intersecting the main highway without slowing. Within minutes, the tires made their final turn, hugging the narrow road winding up the coastline and away from St. Luke's Emergency Department.

Nearly thirty minutes later, Katherine pulled onto the final stretch of road leading to her small home at the end of a beachfront cul-de-sac. Steering by reflex into the small, two-car garage, she stopped the car and turned off the engine, then sat for a moment, unable to remember how she got there.

Eleven

NEARLY THIRTY MINUTES HAD PASSED before Brooks was deposited into his room. The X-rays took much longer this time. A new guy was in training, and Brooks, apparently, was his guinea pig. After several attempts, the trainee finally positioned Brooks arm against the hard surface of the X-ray table, reciting the well-practiced dialogue he'd been taught to say: "Okay, now hold still." As if Brooks could do anything else.

"Dude, that really hurts." Brooks flinched and the trainee smiled in response.

"This will be over soon."

Something clicked in the background and the trainee jogged out from behind a glass wall to reposition Brooks' arm.

"Be careful not to injure the affected limb."

The instruction came from an unseen person through a loudspeaker overhead.

"Ouch. Dude! Be careful what you're doing ... like your boss said. That freakin' hurts!"

"This will be over soon." The trainee smiled and jogged back behind the glass wall.

After two more rounds of repositioning and clicking pictures, they eventually finished, and the trainee wheeled him back to Room 15, where Brooks was left alone on the hard gurney. That was how Kaycee found him when she bounced in and presented him with two white tablets resting in a tiny cup.

"This will help with the pain," she said, and handed him some water to chase it down.

"Thanks. Those guys in radiology are rough," he said, handing the cup back before laying down on the gurney.

"That…" she nodded toward the empty cup in her hand, "…will help, promise. Someone will come by in a minute to check on you." Kaycee smiled and slipped out through the curtain. Brooks waited until she was gone before tipping back onto the pillow.

"I hope it's not my mom."

"Nope, just me," Eric said, and stepped inside the curtained room. "I'm guessing a fracture, not too bad, but we're probably going to have to do something more than just let you lay here. I'm guessing you're planning a way to escape this place without your mom finding out."

Brooks tossed him a look and snorted.

"That's what I thought. Okay, well, do me a favor and don't leave just yet. I'll get in trouble if you take off." Eric glanced down at some papers in his hands. "I don't want us both in trouble with Alex. That would suck!" He grinned again and lifted his eyes to look at the teen, who was desperately trying not to like him.

"Yeah, okay." Brooks let the corner of his mouth turn up.

"Cool." Eric held out a fist to his patient. Brooks just stared at him. "Oh, oops! I guess you can't do that, can you?" Eric chuckled. "Knuckle-bumping is out for a while." He laughed out loud this time, and then collecting himself, tucked the papers under his arm and backed through the curtain. "Okay, someone will be back in a minute, so just hang out here like you promised."

"Right." Brooks eyed the curtain. "Like I'm going to do anything else."

He was beginning to feel the effects of the pills anyway. Laying back on the gurney, he stared at the ceiling and decided not to count the dots in the tiles – some of which looked like they weren't meant to be there. He lay there for what seemed only a few seconds, when, suddenly, the lights flickered. Brooks bolted upright. The overhead panel, illuminated with two long rods, randomly blinked off and on. Outside, a high-pitched wheeze filtered through the curtain.

"Seth." The voice grated with an old man's rattle as it spoke. *"Seth, I know you're here."*

Brooks glanced at the curtain. It moved as gnarled fingers pulled the fabric slowly to one side. Aged eyes, bleary with years of staring at sun-kissed seas, wandered to the teen's face. The old man stepped into

Room 15 and grinned. Yellowed teeth peeked through thin lips, accenting the amber of his eyes. He pulled up a chair and sat, leaning forward so his nose was only inches from Brooks'.

"What are you doing?" Brooks shouted. "Get out of here, creep…before I call for someone."

The old man only laughed, and Brooks could smell his breath. "I know you, Seth."

"My name is Brooks, not Seth. Now get out of here, freak!"

"I've seen you on the ship. You're *his* cabin boy, the one who knows the sea. I know, I've seen you there," the old man wheezed.

Brooks wriggled farther onto the gurney, his back against the wall. "Someone get in here!" he shouted, but no one answered. "You better get out of here, creep. Go harass someone else. You got the wrong guy."

"Look, Seth…remember?" The old man held out his forearm. Brooks gasped and couldn't pull his eyes from the faded mark on his weathered skin. The shape was familiar – a curved line with archaic letters beneath. The teen leaned in for a closer look at the tattoo.

Scrolled in black the word Revenge had been penned just below an anchor. Brooks gasped and his eyes darted to his own forearm. A birthmark — at least, that's what he had been told – stood out pale and gnarled against his own flesh. Its outline was the exact same shape as the tattoo inked into the old man's arm.

"There, see? Now you know it's true, Seth."

Brooks shook his head. "No, you've got the wrong guy, I'm telling you."

"Remember, Seth. Think back to when you was onboard, leapin' from the yardarm, workin' the lines." The old man laughed again, and Brooks screamed for help. "*Remember…remember…*"

"My name is Brooks!" he cried, and peered out through the opposite end of the curtain. "I need help in here. Someone help!"

Kaycee glanced up from the desk and saw the Brooks' face peeking through the far end of the curtained room. She jumped up, and in one quick motion, pulled open the curtain, and stepped inside.

"Brooks, what is it? What's wrong?"

He turned his head and motioned toward the chair next to his bed. "The old man. Get him out of here!"

"I don't understand…" Kaycee stepped forward, shaking her head.

"There." Brooks pointed again and turned to look where the old man sat.

The chair was empty.

"Lay back and relax, Brooks. I think maybe the medicine is making you a little anxious." Kaycee lifted a blanket over Brooks' legs. He lay back, shaking his head.

"There was someone here. I'm telling you the truth," he said and rolled to his side. Just then, Alex stepped into the room.

"What's going on?" she asked and moved to where her son lay trembling.

"I think he's having an anxiety reaction to the meds," Kaycee said. "I'll get the doctor."

She slipped out of the room and Alex moved closer to her son. He stared at the wall, as he whispered "no" over and over again. Alex glanced around the room and noticed the chair had been placed precariously close to the gurney. She touched the seat and was surprised by its warmth, as if someone had recently sat there.

"Who was in here?" Alex asked Brooks. He rolled dolls-eyes to stare beyond his mother's face. "Brooks! Was somebody in here with you?" No answer. Alex snorted and stood in a huff. "No one is allowed inside the room except for the hospital staff. It's ER policy. Brooks is a minor, and visitors are not allowed without parental approval. Unacceptable," she said under her breath.

Marching out of his room, she scoured the hallways for Kaycee. Maya stood at another station – within view of Brooks' room, at least. Alex made her way to where Maya stood typing.

"Hi, Alex," she said without looking away from the monitor.

"Did you see anyone go into Brooks' room recently? Anyone that isn't family or staff?" Alex's toe began to tap against the linoleum floor.

"No. Who…?" Maya glanced at Alex.

"Nobody at all?"

"No." Maya's brows furrowed. "Why?"

"Nothing." Alex turned from her and marched back to Room 15. Maya watched her for a moment, shrugged her shoulders, and went back to typing.

Brooks hadn't improved. Upon entering his room, she saw that while he had stopped repeating the word "no," his blank stare remained fixed on something in the distance. She glanced at the chair and a chill ran down her spine. Something was wrong.

She pushed it slightly and surveyed the metal base. Nothing. Leaning over, she saw a tiny piece of cloth caught underneath one of the chair's feet. Carefully sliding it out from beneath, she held it up. It smelt of salt water and rotted wood.

The fabric is not from this time.

The thought sent chills down her back. *Someone has been in here.* Someone had frightened Brooks – her son, who knew no fear.

"Brooks, who was it?" Alex whispered, praying he could hear her. He held out his forearm, the one with the birthmark staining his young flesh.

"The old man."

"What old man?"

"The one from the sea," Brooks breathed.

Alex's eyes shot up to the clock on the wall overhead. It had stopped at exactly 5:21 p.m.

"1721," she said. "It *has* begun…"

Twelve

Something's happening – something Alex tried to warn me about. Mariel or Wendy will know.

Katherine's heart pounded in her chest, drowning out the voice in her head. However, her nerves refused to stop their work of shaking her hands and knees. Unwilling to leave the safety of her car just yet, she glanced in the rearview mirror. An empty driveway lined with lavender and jasmine met her gaze. *It's over,* she reassured herself, and while she didn't completely believe it, she decided to listen to the rational side of her wits. Perhaps the hauntings had been left behind in the ER.

Katherine reached for the visor and hit the button on the remote that opened the garage door. *Okay, you're home, Katherine.* She couldn't stop trembling. *He's gone. It's gone…that ghost is…*

In response, her stomach groaned its displeasure at having been ignored most of the day. She glanced around the garage once more, checking the shadows in particular. Nothing.

"Pretty weak, Katherine," she joked. With more than the usual effort, she exited the sports car and ran through the adjoining door and into her kitchen.

Some say that the kitchen is the heart of a home. For Katherine, this was true – even more so tonight, and it was peaceful and inviting as she stood in the doorway. She breathed a sigh of relief. *Home.* The aged mahogany table had been a treasure she'd found in a forgotten antique store in the backwoods of South Carolina. It smelled of the sea. She quickly replaced the solitary candle in the sterling silver candlestick with a black one and lit it. Then, pulling a bundle tucked deep inside her great-grandmother's sideboard, she ignited some sage and began wandering. Absently dropping her backpack and keys on the countertop, she began the work of cleansing her living space.

"Glanhau y sanctifica illum sagrado."

She chanted the words over again – something akin to Gaelic and Latin that Mariel had forced her to memorize when she was still quite young. As she made her way into the shadowed corners of her house, and the dark spaces of her thoughts, she felt her spirit ease. The entity hadn't followed her home. Chanting in no more than a whisper, she made her way from room to room, swirling the pungent smoke in elongated ovals above her head. Finally satisfied that the house had been smudged properly, she laid the bundle next to the candle in a polished abalone shell and allowed the smoke to curl at leisure.

Katherine flicked on the stove, and put a kettle on. Within moments, she was seated near her favorite plate-glass window, a steaming cup of lavender and mint tea in hand. *At least it's safe here*, she thought, nibbling on one edge of a sourdough biscuit. Her eyes scanned the room once more.

Again nothing.

A soft clicking across the tile floor caught her attention. She set the biscuit down and waited.

"There you are," Katherine cooed. Black eyes piercing through tufts of caramel fur stared affectionately at her. She reached down and stroked the soft coat of her Sheba Inu. The Japanese-bred dog closely resembled a small fox, though graced with the attitude of a lynx. Sheba positioned herself and crossed her front paws.

"How was your day, girl?" she asked.

Sheba dropped her nose to her paws as Katherine lifted the teacup to her lips. The moon glistened against the windowpane, casting odd light throughout the room. *You cannot reach me here.* Katherine glanced at the smoldering sage and flickering candlelight, but wasn't completely convinced all was well. She hadn't completed the rituals. There was solace inside her home, lavender lined her driveway, and sage encircled the perimeter of her yard. Still, there was one last thing to do.

She stood, and, just to be safe, struck a match and lit the lantern nestled in the windowsill. Mariel had taught her this as well – a simple talisman made with fire to bring protection to the house. *I guess if it's always worked for Mariel, it can work for me, too.*

She returned to her place with tea in hand and Sheba at her feet.

Outside, the moon radiated its surreal gleam. Something spectral about it made her draw her knees to her chest. It was an ominous moon, and, likely, she would hear from her cousin or grandmother soon.

Beware the Midnight Omen and her wicked sister, the Silver Moon.

The words popped into her head without invitation. Mariel had said them. Katherine's eyes locked on the pallor that encircled the moon and silently prayed it wasn't the Midnight Omen, although her gut told her otherwise.

Mariel would have plenty to say about it in the morning. For now, Katherine would rest and sip on tea. It seemed this was the only quiet moment of the day, and as Katherine relished it, her body screamed for sleep. Moments later, she'd snuffed out the flame and sage, and the smoke curled into nothing.

"Come on, then. I've had one hell of a day. I'm exhausted." Katherine stood, and Sheba took the clue to follow. They made their way to the upstairs bedroom, and, within moments, Katherine had thrown off her scrubs, showered, and donned a simple T-shirt and silk pajama pants. The bed seemed unusually welcoming, pulling Katherine's body into its folds. There was no fighting the slumber that would eventually overtake her, so she just waited for its arrival. Curling up on the floor next to the bed, Sheba softly snored. Katherine limbs grew heavy. Cradled in down pillows and comforter, sleep found her swiftly and her mind, finally, was still.

Silence filled the house as peace hovered in the darkness...for the moment.

Thirteen

IT WAS 4:30 A.M. WHEN shards of apricot and amber sunlight sliced through the steel grey sky. Katherine awoke for no apparent reason. Her eyes darted to the window. Dawn hadn't officially arrived, although the incessant coo from a mourning dove insisted otherwise. Her body ached – evidence of a restless night.

"Sheba," Katherine whispered, and dropped her hand over the edge of the bed. The little dog lifted her nose into Katherine's palm, and then rolled back into a ball next to the bed. "Well, I'm glad somebody sleeps."

The mourning dove cooed again. Katherine studied the creature as it dropped to perch on the windowsill. She shifted the down pillows to one side and the bird hopped in through the open window.

"Well, aren't you daring," she said. It seemed odd that Sheba hadn't been alerted to its presence.

Jasmine-laced breezes rushed against the trees, sending a crystal tinkling of chimes singing in the morning air. The hazy glow of moonlight faded beyond the window that faced the sea to the west. Sunlight would soon eclipse the last of night's obscurity. But for now, Katherine reveled in the dusky daybreak that washed over her like warm honey. She was completely at peace, allowing the gentle breeze to swirl around her, and whisper softly in her ear. With each breath she took, serenity expanded within her body. The whispering crescendo blended into syllables and formed a wispy voice that sighed in her ear.

From time long before memory recalls, the Gift be yours by birth.

Katherine dared not move. She waited for it to speak again.

The Gift is most precious and must ne'er be neglected.

Her pulse pounded in her ears as her gaze locked onto the omen moon pale in the dark morning sky. "Who is this?" she breathed, and the voice answered, soothing, gentle and female.

Use it well, and bless with its power.

Her spine tingled and the dove cocked its head, and cooed again. She trailed her eyes across the dim moonlight that filled the corners of her room. "Who are you?"

God be the source, and your hands be His tool. Ne'er to do ill and blessed ye be.

Katherine lay still watching the dove. There was nothing there. She was not afraid, yet she dared not move. She waited for the whispering to return again, but the voice had faded back into a gentle breeze. The message had been delivered.

She stared at the sunrise as it approached, lost in her thoughts, when suddenly she caught a glimpse of a woman's face – elderly yet timeless, with silvery tresses that matched her pale eyes. The face smiled just moments before melting into the dawn's light. Katherine caught her breath and outside the mourning dove cooed.

Sheba's steady breathing suddenly stopped. Katherine looked to dog and saw coal-black eyes tuned in to the windowsill. A low growl rolled from her throat. Katherine reached one hand to Sheba's head, and, instantly, the solid black eyes peered at her. Pointed ears matched the color of Sheba's curly tail that arched over her back.

"I guess it's over. You saw it too, huh?" Katherine said.

Sheba relaxed underneath her fingertips as they traced through the thick fur coating her head. "It's a gift, me girl," Katherine whispered, repeating the words she'd heard. "I have the *Gift*. Mariel will be overjoyed when I tell her about this one. I guess Alex is right … I need professional help."

She sighed and found the paper with a name and number written on it. Alex had texted the information to her the night before. Apparently, it was Cindy's suggestion she talk with a shaman. And while Kathryn trusted Cindy's judgment implicitly, the thought of talking to a "shrink" was more than she could digest. Perhaps a shaman would be different. She'd scribbled the info onto a sticky-note and tucked the scrap away, then promptly forgot about it. Now, it lay crumpled upon the nightstand.

It seems there's a reason I couldn't throw it away. I guess this is it.

Katherine smoothed the edges and dropped her feet to the floor. Her eyes scanned her loopy handwriting. "Dr. Strickland…I guess we have a date."

Sheba trotted down the stairs and into the kitchen. Katherine soon followed, swinging the paper in one hand. "I don't want to do this."

As she pivoted into the kitchen, she caught sight of Sheba waiting by the silver food bowl on the floor. The canine needed no reminder that the kibble laid hidden away in the breakfast nook.

"Okay, Your Highness, now what do you want to eat?" she said, pouring the dog food into the bowl on the floor. She glanced at the abalone shell and candlestick that lay undisturbed on the table. Her eyes then drifted to the amber skylight, and she breathed a sigh of relief that darkness was banished for another day. Turning her attention to the refrigerator door, she opened it to discover its contents looked neglected and rather bare.

"I've worked way too many days this week," she said and pulled out a carton of eggs and some juice. Plucking out two, she broke one egg raw over the dog food in the bowl and dropped the other into a frying pan. Sheba turned her attention away from Katherine and back to her bowl. For a moment, the little piece of paper still clutched in one hand was forgotten. Still, the promise she had made to call him festered – there was no use trying to ignore it. She decided to make the call.

The Gift is most precious and must ne'er be neglected.

The voice from early this morning replayed over and over again, still fresh in her mind.

…your hands be His tool.

"His tool to do what?" she said and scooped the eggs onto a plate. As she thought about it, she felt a new sense of urgency. Far too many occurrences over the last twenty-four hours had thrown Katherine off guard – events she could not dismiss.

Ne'er to do ill…

Someone was calling to her. She was supposed to do something, she supposed. From another place, another time, perhaps.

"An impossible task," she muttered as she walked her breakfast to the table. "Yeah right, 'Ne'er do ill'? Everyone does ill at some point…"

Without warning, as if given wings, the paper flew out of her fingers and into the air. She reached out for it, but it swooped forward just ahead of her. Puzzled, Katherine watched as the paper floated to the ground. She bent over to grab it, and it swooped oddly, as if some invisible string had pulled it away from her. Again and again she grasped at it, only to have the paper take flight just out of reach. As it moved toward another part of the room, Katherine dove after the moving object again.

What the...? Who is doing this?

For several minutes she chased it, lunging and weaving after some invisible force that played keep-away with her. Exasperated, she looked around the room to make certain no one was toying with her, but the room was empty.

"I'm done with this," she stated and dropped her fists to her waist. The paper drifted slowly, fluttering down in a feather-like zigzag until it came to rest upon the small table in front of her. Lying next to her cell phone, it waited only a moment before it suddenly burst into flame.

Within seconds, the tiny paper was reduced to ash. "No! No...no...no!" Katherine blew against the particles of ash. The residue scattered, leaving behind an indiscrete black mark where the flame had been. *"Not the antique...not the antique!"*

She licked her thumb and ran it over the scorched wood in hopes of erasing the damage. As she rubbed, dark symbols were exposed, etched deeply into the grain. Numbers – a series of ten separated by two dashes – glared up from the end table. *A phone number!* Katherine recognized it – the one written on the tiny piece of paper.

"Not subtle," she whispered, and considered calling Mariel first.

There was no denying it – something wanted her to talk to a shaman, now! She tapped on the phone icon and glanced at the numbers burned into the wood.

"Unbelievable!" she said, hoping there would be no one to answer at this early hour.

"Gary Strickland's office. How may I help you?"

The weight of that question hung in the air as she tried to find an answer. Her lips parted, but her voice failed. The silence was unbearable, and Katherine decided to hang up. Suddenly, a voice from the receiver spoke.

"Katherine? Katherine, is that you calling?"

She yanked the phone from her ear and stared, horrified, at the cell phone in her hand. *How does this person know...?*

"Katherine?"

Fourteen

THE VOICE THROUGH THE RECEIVER sounded too skill-fully practiced for normal conversation. For a moment, Katherine couldn't speak.

"How did…? Who is this?" Katherine finally found her voice.

"Katherine McCauley? Is that correct? How may I help you? Professionally pleasant, the voice waited for Katherine's answer.

"How did you know? I only just…" Katherine stammered.

The voice on the other end of the line cut her off. "Your friend Cindy notified us about five minutes ago – a sort of head's up that you might be calling. She mentioned you would like a session with Gary?" Her voice rose at the end of her statement, a rehearsed inflection, to be certain. "Excuse me. I mean, Dr. Strickland."

Katherine sighed. "Yes, that is correct. She referred me to him yesterday."

"Wonderful! He is available to see you next week, unless you are able to come in later today around 4:30?"

"Today would be best for me."

"Please state your full name with the correct spelling, dear." It was a request delivered with pristine courtesy.

"Katherine McCauley."

"No middle name?"

"No."

Katherine was sure she could hear a muffled gasp of exasperation through the receiver. "Okay, fine. Now your date of birth, please."

Katherine provided her date of birth, as well as two separate phone numbers where she could easily be reached. The voice on the other end cleared her throat.

"Please allow plenty of time before your session in order to fill out the necessary paperwork. We take cash the day of your appointment … that would be today. Also, Dr. Strickland prefers that you eat organic and drink lots of water the day of your appointment. Since you will be meeting with him this afternoon, I guess you need to do the best you can, under the circumstances."

How does she know what I eat, anyway? Katherine's cheeks grew hot for the second time in less than five minutes. "Okay."

"Focus on what you eat for the next several hours. Oh, and no sugar whatsoever. Thank you and we'll see you between 4:00 and 4:30."

The conversation ended as crisply as it had begun. She stared at the receiver again, her mouth slack and voiceless. *The audacity! What a twit!* She hung up the phone. "Pick your battles, Katherine." She berated herself aloud and shook it off.

Glancing at the clock on the wall, she noted there would be a little more than six hours before the appointment and no time to fuss about a faceless trill that sounded more cyborg than human. Right now she needed to plan out the rest of her day. Katherine rushed up the stairs and into the bathroom, then set to work properly grooming for a session with a shaman, whatever that would require. After drying her hair and dabbing on lip-gloss, she picked up the phone again and dialed one other number.

"Wen, it's me. I need to ask you a huge favor."

St. Cimarron was only twenty-five miles up the coast from where Katherine lived. Wendy's house was located in the middle of winding roads filled with magnolia trees and oleander. Sweet orange blossom and eucalyptus taunted tourists with an invitation to stay as they passed through the quaint seaside town.

A contrast in dark and light – with her wavy dark hair and olive complexion, Katherine looked foreign compared to Wendy, whose curly blonde hair just touched the tops of her shoulders. A China doll's skin and watermelon lips accented her blue eyes. Wendy was bright and wonderful and family.

"Hi, honey! What's going on?" The pause was only milliseconds. "Of course, I'll do anything, you know that. What do you…?" Wendy's manicured nails clicked against the phone as she waved the other hand in the air. "Your voice. It's in your voice. Honestly, Kat, I can tell there's something…"

Katherine cut her off mid-sentence, a tactic she frequently deployed just to get a word in edgewise. "Wen, if you'd just come up for air, you'd remember exactly what we were talking about." It was meant in jest, but there was some truth to it – and part of Wendy's charm. Always a puzzle, Wendy could deliver one continuous thought after another without pause and never ran out of things to say – another difference between them.

"I have a last minute appointment." Katherine hesitated, not wanting to disclose too much information. She was in a hurry and had no time to explain everything that had happened, at least not right now. "I…I have a doctor appointment."

"You have no such thing!" Wendy snapped.

"Really…it's just a checkup, but I have to be there early, and I don't know how long it will take. Can I bring Sheba up to stay with you while I'm with the…um, doctor?" She couldn't bring herself to say "shaman." And anyway, it was an excuse to spend a few minutes with her sister. Wendy was psychic and someone she needed some time with. Sheba was always a great excuse.

"Of course you can bring her here…and be serious, you cannot fool me. Call this appointment whatever you'd like. We both know it's not that. Lucky for you,

I'm too busy to dig the truth out of you right now. I have to meet with a client in a couple of hours, but the front door is open, and the key is in its usual place, in case I miss you."

"Thank you," Katherine breathed, grateful that Wendy hadn't pushed her for more.

"Just come in and make yourself at home – you know where everything is. Of course, if you need anything…"

"I'm leaving shortly. I should be there in about forty-five minutes, traffic permitting."

"Oh, of course, honey. See you then."

There was a click and Katherine knew her sister was off doing something else, no doubt chatting blissfully to herself the entire time. Her eyes dropped to the plate of scrambled eggs waiting on the table, and Katherine's stomach rolled. Eggs were *organic*, weren't they? She would have to eat something if the day were to go as planned. Her gaze drifted out through the double-paned windows that lined the breakfast nook.

Stressed pine window frames accented the bright blue of the Pacific Ocean. Her heart jumped every time her eyes met the rolling water. She found comfort in its presence. Off to one side, hummingbirds darted back and forth from trees to blossoms. They had made a game of flitting in and out of the bright orange Butterfly Weed that grew on the side of the hill behind her house. It had become a morning ritual with the birds – just like the cooing of the mourning doves.

This is almost paradise. She smiled and offered a silent prayer of thanks. Then, something else caught her eye.

Below the window, tucked inside a row of shelves, a cooler-sized chest lined with cedar lay nearly forgotten. In fact, Katherine hadn't noticed it for quite some time. The chest was over three hundred years old and incredibly weathered. Leather strips encircled salt-pocked oak crumbling in places at the touch. The interior had all but rotted away, with tongue-and-groove edged corners holding the sides together. Katherine treasured the chest – a gift from her parents when she was just fourteen. Within it, her most precious things were kept safely buried.

Katherine forced a forkful of egg into her mouth, and then made her way over to where the chest rested. She brushed the dust from its surface before gently lifting it. The arched closure groaned against worn hinges as she urged the lid to open. Inside, lay a treasure trove collected for centuries by family members she had never met. These precious objects had been slowly gifted to Katherine over the years – her treasures. Some appeared broken and unusable, but they remained priceless in her eyes, and she could not bear to part with any of them. Katherine stared into the trunk, fascinated. *Riches indeed*, she thought. *Buried here within my very own treasure chest.*

She lifted out an ancient astrolabe – the entire disc carved out of solid gold. Etched over the surface were elaborate markings, and long hatch marks snaked in varying lengths, decorating the surface. It housed a cutout rete. Katherine had called it a "compass" when she'd first laid eyes on it. However, her great-grandfather had quickly corrected her, labeling the object a "star seer" instead. It sounded mystical and mysterious when he'd said those words, and while she did not know what the astrolabe was used for, the object fascinated her.

Lace doilies tatted by her great-grandmother were draped over an old photo that framed unrecognizable faces. She stared at it and thought she noticed the shadow of a man and woman staring back. She didn't recognize their faces, but something familiar shadowed their features. Strangely, each time she looked at the photo, the images captured seemed different than she remembered – there were always new faces, or so it seemed. Mariel had given it to her long ago and charged her to keep it close, delivering it with a warning: *"In no way ever let it out of your possession. Promise me, girl."* Katherine had agreed, though she could never seem to find the right location for its display in her house. Because of that, she had decided years ago to tuck it away in the chest for safekeeping. She smiled and set it aside gently.

Katherine lifted an ancient piece of linen and draped it over the lid to search for one item in particular. This one was unique, given to her when she was a little girl, and not too long after the day she made magic in the library. Underneath a pink puckered quilt, she caught the tarnished glint of sailor's brass.

"There you are," she said as she lifted an oddly shaped object wrapped in ancient, rust-stained muslin that was blackened and burned in places. The object was heavier than she remembered, which surprised her a little. She placed the piece on the center of the kitchen table, then sat back to study it for a moment. The cloth was worn, stained, and very old. Its threads appeared to have survived a fire at one time, and the edges were burnt with scorched patches over most of the surface.

What a story you would tell, if only you could speak of your past. The thought was not a new one. She untied the ribbon holding the worn linen in place and let it fall open to reveal a centuries-old, bronzed hourglass. Katherine stared in awe at its beauty. Simply adorned in scrollwork that ran the length of both handles, the hourglass was breathtaking. She wondered why she had never bothered to display the marvelous object. Perhaps it was safer tucked away in the treasure chest where she, alone, could resurrect it and enjoy its brilliance at her whim.

"My, you are a beauty," she said as she ran a finger along the scrolled brass.

Gently, she lifted it by the handles and turned the hourglass upside down. Creamy sand spilled from the top in a smooth stream, producing a miniature pyramid into the bottom chalice. The top and bottom of the glass base were overlaid with heavily embellished symbols that were blackened with years of tarnish.

These were Celtic knots for luck, she had been told. Mystery surrounded this hourglass, something she couldn't quite put her finger on. But at the same time, there was a sense of familiarity about it – something that surfaced from deep within her heart. It was as if she'd seen this very hourglass before.

"Impossible!" Katherine said aloud. "It belonged to Mariel's great-grandmother nearly two hundred years ago, and that is only as far as Mariel will talk about. Someone must have owned it before then!"

In fact, the hourglass *felt* ancient. It was a timeless piece that belonged to its own century – much like the strange images seen in the ER the day before, she realized. Katherine shuddered at the thought. Something in her past connected her to the hourglass, and that somehow tied her to the ghost.

"How can that be, Katherine?" she reprimanded herself. "You're such a beautiful thing and that … that dead guy was so repulsive." Chills ran down her spine.

She flipped it over and watched the sand drip. A definite energy emanated from the timekeeper. It even seemed to radiate its own aura. Katherine studied it for a moment. *This gives off the exact opposite vibe from that damned symbol tattooed on that dead man's arm in the ER. They can't be linked.* She tilted the hourglass slightly to expose the underside. On one edge of the dulled bronzed brass the letters *JPB* had been inscribed. Something else had been scratched there, but it had faded and worn off. Whatever it had been, Katherine was certain these must be someone's initials. Just whose, she did not know, but she had been told that it had once belonged to privateers. She ran her thumb over the initials and a surge of deep sadness washed over her.

"That's the very reason you've been tucked away," she said aloud.

In spite of the overwhelming sadness that gripped her heart every time she looked at the hourglass, she couldn't return it to the chest. Instead, she carefully placed it on top of the fireplace mantle, and then stepped back to admire it again. The sand fell gracefully – truly an entity at work.

"If I didn't know better, I'd say you were a living thing," Katherine said, cocking her head to get a different view. She shrugged then turned back to the chest. Gently fingering the astrolabe, she studied it for a moment.

It is not your time – not yet.

She slipped it between the folds of cloth that had shrouded the hourglass, whispered a blessing of peace, and tucked the bundle back into the chest. Then closing the lid and latch, she gently urged the chest back into its place below the shelf. Glancing once more at the timepiece on top of the mantle, she felt a familiar longing for the sea, for another time, another place. Katherine sighed, turned her back on the hourglass, and set about preparing to leave for St. Cimarron. She desperately needed to be with someone who loved her – with family, with Wendy.

Katherine gathered her belongings then called for Sheba. When the little dog caught sight of the leash in her hand, she trotted to the door and waited. Katherine snapped the leash to Sheba's hot-pink collar, took a deep breath, and stepped through the front door and into the hands of a shaman.

"But not before we chat with a psychic," she said as she shut the door behind her.

Fifteen

SALT-CREEK'S COASTLINE ROSE AND FELL in uneven curls, allowing for an occasional glimpse of the Pacific Ocean from the main highway. Katherine's Mustang hugged the curves that followed the shore-line. Typically, she rarely slowed for the picturesque seascapes of ocean and sunlight. Today, however, Katherine allowed herself the luxury of snatching brief glimpses of azure water as it danced in and out of view. Sheba had situated herself, paws crossed, atop a pillow on the passenger's seat with her head raised, alert to whatever passed before the windshield. Minutes flew by as the convertible made its way up the coast. The drive seemed shorter than she'd remembered, and Katherine soon found herself pulling onto the street that marked the entrance to Wendy's cul-de-sac. She inhaled the unique scents of lilac and eucalyptus as she passed by.

Ahead, the short driveway was lined with terra cotta pots filled to overflowing with pink and lavender blossoms. Her sister's black BMW was still parked in the garage. The door was open and the car looked ready to be backed down the driveway in a hurry.

She never closes that garage, Katherine thought and shook her head.

Wendy always bustled about, with thoughts far from the immediate surroundings, unless coffee was involved. Open doors and unlocked houses were never her concern. With the doors and windows left wide open for intruders, Wendy would suddenly remember the abandoned house and simply command the house to lock itself – and the house would obey. Wendy's *Gift* served her well and kept her safe at the same time. *Thank heavens for that!*

"Wen…Wendy…are you in here?" Katherine called out as she walked in through the unlocked front door. Sheba trotted ahead, making herself at home in the kitchen, Katherine made her way into the attached solarium. There she found her sister darting around the sunlit room, waving her perfectly manicured nails in the air.

"Hi, honey. This damn dog knows my weakness." Wendy's chirpy voice rang out as she tossed a morsel of something to Sheba. She then greeted Katherine with a quick air kiss to her cheek. Everyone was welcomed, kissed, and fed within a few moments of arrival – Wendy-style.

"Love that skirt! Make yourself at home. I've just got to finish this one thing and…" The thought left Wendy's head almost as soon as it had entered.

It was never clear, exactly, what Wendy was busy with at any given moment, but it was obvious to Katherine that she was in a hurry. Katherine paused, unable to hold back a grin as she watched her sister flitting from counter to counter in the cluttered sunroom. *She's that hummingbird outside my window in human form,* Katherine thought, and the grin shifted to a chuckle.

Off to one side, a solitary coffee cup sat unnoticed on a table, steam rising from the rim. A cloud of whipped cream magically appeared, expanding to the top of the otherwise forsaken cup. Katherine tossed her sister a sanctimonious glance. It was the unwelcomed busted smirk that caught Wendy's attention. She followed Katherine's eyes to the coffee cup.

"Oh, jeez, I can never find that when I'm in a hurry," she said, dismissing Katherine with the wave of her hand. "You know how I am about whip cream in my coffee. It's really a blessing the cup fills itself like that."

Wendy picked up the coffee cup and tossed her a *don't judge me* smile from across the room. Rarely would the sisters discuss the *Gift* they shared, obviously due to its taboo nature. In truth, the alchemy possessed between them had remained an unspoken family secret. Wendy's was different from Katherine's, which was not an uncommon trait among family members who shared a talent for making magic. She used it haphazardly, in Katherine's opinion, but when focused,

Wendy's psychic insight could be invaluable, and at times, life-altering. In truth, Katherine admired Wendy.

"I'll leave the leash here on the table," Katherine said as she dropped it onto the table.

"Of course … fine. Sheba's settled in anyway, over there, next to the fireplace." Wendy was pre-occupied with kitchen gadgets, occasionally sipping from the cup in her hand as she waved the other in the air. It was the signal she agreed with everything. After a quick pat on Sheba's head, Katherine kissed Wendy goodbye on the cheek.

"Wait!"

Wendy stared hard at her younger sister. Her eyes glossed whenever she used her *Gift* to scrutinize someone. She lowered her cup. Katherine moved to the door.

"I'm really in a hurry."

"Just you wait," Wendy said through ruby lips that were no longer smiling. "What's going on, Kat? Something's wrong with you…I can *feel* it."

Katherine paused. Deep down, she was relieved her sister had finally noticed something extrasensory about her. But at the same time, she felt anxious. If Wendy really knew what Katherine was up to, there would be no way to keep it secret. Katherine would be forced to disclose the dark parts of the past two days – events she had hoped to keep to herself.

"Nothing…really." Katherine glanced at the front door.

Don't even think about it, Kat. We have to talk first. It was as if Wendy could read her mind. Actually, Wendy *could* read her mind, and, apparently, speak to it as well. She was doing it now.

"Sit down, Kat, and get comfortable. I want to talk to you for a minute."

I'm in for it now. How do I explain this mess I'm in?

"Just start from the beginning," Wendy replied, again answering Katherine's unvoiced thoughts. Wendy's keen preternatural discernment kicked into full gear and stopped Katherine cold. She sat down, a surrender of sorts, as her shoulders shrugged and her gaze dropped slightly. To avoid Wendy's psychic awareness would be impossible.

"I think someone is following me…or something like that. Only it feels like more than just a crazy stalker. I think it wants to destroy me, Wen," Katherine confessed, and looked up at her sister. She could not hide the fear behind her eyes.

"Well, does he?"

"I…how do you know it's a *he*?"

Wendy smirked and cocked her head in a *you didn't really ask that, did you?* kind of way.

"I…yes, I believe so. It *feels* like a predator going in for the kill…and I'm the prey," Katherine said. She searched her sister's face for answers.

Wendy said nothing but stared at her sister, nearly looking through her. She then stood and began to circle Katherine.

You're reading my aura.

"Yes. Now be still," she ordered, and Katherine complied. After the third loop, Wendy closed her eyes and her lips moved in silence for what seemed like an eternity. An interruption would not be tolerated, so Katherine remained silent, waiting for her sister to speak. Finally, Wendy opened both eyes and locked her gaze on Katherine. When she spoke, her voice was deep and throaty – the voice of a spiritual entity.

"My sister, you are in grave danger. There is an energy surrounding you that is not of this world...not of this time. It seems to beckon you. I believe you must return to wherever...whenever this energy comes from. Your task is to find the one who seeks to destroy you, and the meaning behind a mark that is worn upon his forearm."

"You've seen it?" Katherine could not help herself. Chills ran down her spine.

"Yes, I've seen it, but I do not know the meaning of it." Wendy's voice grew dark. "The symbols have meaning, and you alone possess the ability to unlock the mystery of it all." Suddenly, she paused, and then blinked repeatedly. Stunned, Katherine waited as Wendy's eyes cleared.

"Wait...I..."

"Well, that's all I have for you, so you'd best be on your way." Her blonde curls bounced in dismissal as she retrieved her steaming cup. It was the signal there would be nothing else. Katherine could do little else but accept that the answers she was seeking lay with the man she was about to meet.

"A shaman isn't such a bad idea, Kat. Keep your mind open," Wendy said between sips.

Katherine shot her a look and watched as the coffee cup refilled itself with whip cream again. "I'm not sure how long this will take, but I'll call you when I'm done. Thank you…I owe you one."

Again, Wendy's hand fanned the air. "Don't worry about a thing. Sheba will be fine. Be safe and have fun!"

Have fun? Was she kidding? What fun could I possibly have with a shaman? She climbed into the front seat and turned on the engine of her sports car.

Don't answer that, Wen.

Sixteen

It was already 4:15 p.m. and the city traffic had grown heavy by the time Katherine arrived at the shaman's office. The building was rather unassuming, with his name printed in black lettering on the pane of a white door: *Dr. Gary Strickland.* He was a doctor after all, which brought Katherine some relief when she read the title.

"Dr. Gary Strickland, indeed. I hope that means medical," she whispered as she turned the knob and entered. The interior was simple and inviting. Oriental throws and jade shrubbery filled the expanse of an otherwise colorless room. A fountain stood alone in one corner, cascading water over a rock wall. Katherine glanced behind a counter and discovered a crown of red curls bobbing over a whining printer. They popped up instantly and large brown eyes welcomed her.

"You must be Katherine McCauley?" The voice was familiar, the same one Katherine had heard over the phone earlier. It lifted precisely at the end of the sentence to change the statement into a question – a rather condescending inflection, Katherine thought. She forced a smile.

"Yes, I'm here to see Dr. Strickl…"

"Oh, yes, he's expecting you." The red curls bounced in all directions as the woman cut her off. "Please, sit down. Someone will be out for you soon." She pointed with candy-apple polished fingernails to an oversized sofa on the opposite side of the room.

Beads of sweat spotted Katherine's forehead, and she rubbed clammy palms together as she made her way to the sofa. Soft light fed the room with rays that, on any other day, would have felt warm and comforting. Today was different, somehow. Katherine's heart pounded in her chest.

What is wrong with me? What in the world am I so bloody nervous about?

She tried to force her interest on a large, framed glossy of an open lotus blossom on the solitary wall facing her. Her mind raced and her clammy hands tingled.

"You must be Katherine. I'm Gary Strickland. It's a pleasure to meet you."

He stood well over six feet tall, with arms that hung limply to his sides, giving him that lanky nerdy look. The man padded to where Katherine was seated and extended a wide hand. *You could have been a pro basketball player*, Katherine thought and noticed the corner of his mouth lifted slightly. *Did he hear that?* She wiped her right hand on her jeans and met the doctor's palm with a firm handshake.

"Katherine McCauley. Thank you for seeing me on such short notice," she said.

"Did you fill out the paperwork Candie gave you?"

Immediately, the red curls popped up from behind the counter and the face flushed to match the color of her hair.

"Oops, I completely forgot, Gary. Wait just a minute and I'll get them." She ducked back behind the counter, the sound of crumpled paper accompanying her voice. There was an odd familiarity with which the bouncing receptionist addressed her boss. Katherine inadvertently bit the inside of her lip, fighting back the urge to smile. The name fit her perfectly.

"No, Candie, hold off. We can do that later," Dr. Strickland replied with a voice as smooth as silk. "This way." He motioned for Katherine to follow.

A narrow set of stairs led up to an oversized door that had an elaborate symbol carved into the burled pine exterior. Katherine recognized it – her grandmother called the symbol "Brahma," and there had been little else said about its meaning, except that monks chanted it as "Om" when they meditated. Something Mariel had said about the symbol seemed strangely wonderful: "Every tone is contained within that one syllable. It's very sacred and should be spoken with the utmost respect."

Katherine touched the carved wood momentarily before she entered the dimly lit studio. Instantly, her senses were assaulted with rich scents from India and China. Inside, the air was heavy with the earthy smells of sandalwood and musk. A large massage table covered in crisp cotton with a single plump pillow was set in the middle. *An altar to shamanism*, she supposed.

Katherine watched Gary Strickland walk in measured steps as he lit variously sized candles in each corner of the studio. He appeared gangly, and she thought he would be awkward in a place this serene, but his movements were as fluid as the smoke rising from the long sticks of incense he held purposefully between his tapered fingers. These were placed in shadowy corners, creating a canopy of colored smoke that crawled across the ceiling. It was obvious to Katherine that he was at home with the ethereal. Japanese wooden flutes suddenly began to play softly from an unseen speaker, and Katherine felt herself relax slightly as she watched the shaman perform his ritual.

I guess this is harmless – expensive, but harmless, she thought.

He motioned for her to take a seat on top of the table and waited with hands clasped in front, the way morticians pose a corpse. *Don't be so macabre, Katherine*, she berated herself. She awkwardly positioned herself in the center of the table and waited for the Shaman's next move.

"Just lie down and relax," he said with a reassuring smile. The man's soft brown eyes reflected a constant state of peace behind them.

Yeah, right. Her heartbeat accelerated. The Shaman seemed to sense her discomfort and cocked his head, lowered the lights, then turned his attention back to Katherine and began a series of questions meant to put her at ease.

"Tell me why you're here," he said. "Just take your time with the details. You don't have to worry about holding back information. Everything said here remains private." His smooth voice was a little too slick.

Katherine squeezed her eyelids together and tried to block out the idea of telling her secrets to a total stranger. It took a moment, but finally, she was able to open up. Beginning with the ER, she told him about the dead man and her hallucinations. She paused occasionally, opening her eyes to look at him, waiting for any sign of disinterest, or worse. But he only looked at her more intently as her story reached its crescendo – a graphic description of the eerie figure that had haunted her in the parking lot. "A ghost that came up from the beach, I guess. Anyway, it seemed to want me, to destroy me there in the parking lot," she said, and immediately felt stupid for saying it. Katherine quickly concluded her tale, hoping Dr. Strickland would be gentle in his opinion.

After a brief moment of silence, the shaman smiled and nodded his head as if he understood. Perhaps he found the whole story akin to a poorly delivered joke, something to pity her for…but he never laughed. In fact, he never even really smiled with his whole face, just bared his teeth now and then, and nodded. Katherine stared at him in bewilderment.

"Have you ever heard the term, 'past life regression', Katherine?" he asked.

"Well, only a bit here and there. My grandmother spoke of it once, but the actual act of mentally going back in time…" She shook her head. "No, not really."

His lips curled into the grimace again, a practiced look of tolerance, most likely. As he spoke, his voice shifted to a softer, gentler tone – *his shaman voice*, she guessed.

"I believe you are experiencing glimpses of a previous life, maybe several lives. These sound like only brief moments, a little like watching trailers from a movie."

"But how does that explain the dead guy in the ER…or the leg…or…"

"I can take you back and we can explore a little of what is coming through for you, if you are willing." His voice was almost a whisper.

Katherine could barely breathe. *He speaks the truth. I know it…I feel it with the same intensity I felt when the entity was near my car.*

He waited as if for her thoughts to finish. She stared at him – his black shiny hair, high cheekbones, and angular face were a stark contradiction to the soothing voice she heard coming from it. Katherine nodded. The concept of another life, another time, other places – this was truth, and perhaps the first tangible explanation she'd heard.

"Close your eyes. I am going to use my hands to guide your energy. You will hear me whisper sounds to encourage you to regress. Try to relax and experience whatever happens. Don't judge or control it – just be still and observe."

"Okay." It was all she could muster.

"Now clear your mind. Soften all of the muscles in your body. Let go." She heard him exhale. "Good." The smooth voice became almost hypnotic. "Listen to the chimes and feel the rhythm of your breath. Ride the breath."

Instantly, the delicate chime of a cymbal vibrated around her. She breathed in deeply the earthy scented air in the room. The cymbal chimed again and her mind accepted the whispered syllables spoken by the shaman. The air above rustled with the movement of hands, although she did not feel anything touch her. Still, her skin warmed with awareness, and she discerned the familiar sensation of her limbs turning into liquid as she began to feel her soul lift from her body. Another chime rang, and Katherine floated on a soft breeze, peaceful and happy. *Teeng*, the chime sang, and she moved deeper into stillness. A gentle floating consciousness propelled her senses through astral dimensions. Tranquility transformed her spirit, as she became the dense air she breathed. In and out, with each exhale, Katherine floated through space. Time ceased to exist and only the moment mattered.

Unexpectedly, she felt something cool embrace her thighs and run down to her ankles. She recognized the sensation – a feeling of being grounded, support from soft Mother Earth. Katherine's vision dropped down to the deep black soil and lush green of a garden. The air had changed somehow – sweeter, fresher, and moist. Time was no longer as she knew it.

Just beyond, the ocean pounded against jagged rocks below.

PART FIVE

Destiny

Seventeen

"DROP 'EM."

A hardened pitch betrayed the seasoned seafarer's voice. His tone sounded a big sarcastic, but given the circumstances, Seth didn't blame him. The pirate pulled back on the hammer and the pistol in his hand clicked a menacing warning.

"Don't make me ask again, mate."

Behind him, a cluster of scallywags burst into an uproar, slapping one another on the backs as insults flowed as freely as the rum passed behind them. A rather seedy mate stepped forward and grinned, exposing yellowed teeth and holes where others were missing. Spittle drizzled from the gaps and stuck to the bristle covering his chin.

"Ye don' want to be crossin' the likes of us, pup," he said, and dropped one hand to a pistol that rested against his hip. As if on cue, two more broke free and stepped forward with weapons aimed directly at the youth.

Seth lowered his hands to pull a pouch from his trouser pocket. He dropped it and slid it along the deck. Coins scattered over the burnished wood, but no one moved to gather them up. The floorboards shuddered as two more pirates jumped from the yardarm in tandem.

"Hold!" An imposing mate cocked a third pistol tied to a ribbon about his neck, and the two men froze. "Now, this be the last I'll ask. Drop 'em," he said, and one corner of his mouth lifted.

"Funny…I was tellin' a motley crew to do the same thing just before I had the misfortune of landin' on this little boat." The sarcasm in Seth's voice did nothing to help his situation. "They looked a lot like your collection of miscreants here." Seth flashed a toothy grin at a beefy bloke fingering the filigree along one side of his flintlock.

"You'd best consider your position, boy." The wiry man had a single gold ring hanging from one ear. He picked at his teeth with an oversized dagger; its blade was stained black and the surface scratched, although the serrated edge had been polished and kept razor sharp. Truth be told, it was a rather nasty dirk.

Seth produced another bag and let it fall. On cue, a beastly chap covered with tattoos and scars lifted the pouch with the tip of a polished cutlass. "What's your name, boy?" he asked, dangling the loot from his weapon.

Seth dared not move a muscle. Unexpectedly, his voice betrayed him as his eyes traced the brute's outline.

"Seth."

"Well, Mister Seth," he said while eyeing the pouch, "it seems you're in no position to bandy with pirates, now does it?"

Seth gulped.

"Who's the captain? I'll speak only with the captain under the rights of appeal in the Black Book."

"Parlay? The lad seeks to parlay wit' the capt'n?"

The pirates shared astonished looks, and a few more drew their cutlasses.

"This ship gives no quarters, boy," the beastly man spat.

"Aye, but you're not at battle, and I'm unarmed, so there's no point in calling for no quarters, now, is there?" Seth replied. He eyed the gathered crew that had increased in size and had begun to encircle him. There was only one way out of this, and that was to buy time.

"He's a quick-witted lad, he be," a stout pirate said, and the surly mate spat again.

"Ye can speak with the capt'n when I'm finished with ye, boy," the brute said and brandished the cutlass overhead.

Just then, a cavalcade of bullets rained down onto the deck, just missing the pirates that surrounded Seth. Above them, voices shouted from the cliffs, calling out indistinguishable insults and all kinds of foul curses. Seth glanced upward and saw the familiar group of faces he'd plundered from the pub.

"Put a stop to those muttonheads' show, Mister Archer." The command boomed from the helm

"Aye, aye, Capt'n," the beastly man responded and moved to the guns.

Seth raised his eyes and was met with the cool gaze of the captain. He towered over most of the crew, with chestnut hair tied back with a single green ribbon – the same color as his eyes. His bronzed skin remained youthful, in spite of the years obviously spent at sea. His presence alone held Seth's respect.

"I hear ye seek the capt'n, lad," he said and stepped forward. His steely gaze never wavered. Seth could feel his soul being scrutinized and dared not test his luck any further.

"Aye, sir."

Another volley of gunfire railed the deck from the cliffs above, which was immediately answered by cannon fire.

"Do they not know they fire on their own ship?" The captain snapped. "I haven't the time or interest for such folly. Take this pup portside and keep him safe, Mister Slade. I wish to speak with him further."

"Aye, Capt'n," came the response, and Seth felt the tug of strong hands against his shirt collar.

"Put an end to this, Mister Archer, else I seek a new crew by nightfall!" the captain shouted.

Within moments, Seth had been deposited portside and his hands were secured with hemp that was tied to the capstan. The volley continued until finally, the one they called Archer called the order to brandish the colours. A black flag painted with the figure of a man holding a spear and an hourglass whipped open in the wind. Two ends had been attached to a line affixed to the mainmast, ready for rising to its top. Seth noticed the pierced heart suspended at the end of the figure's spear, and a chill ran down his spine. These were more than mere sailors – these men were best not trifled with.

"Hoist the colours," the captain called, and the flag began its ascent up the lengthy mast. As soon as the black flag had reached its pinnacle, the shower of bullets stopped.

"Cease fire!" Archer called out, and the ship fell silent. Spiraling skyward, the remnants of smoke from the cannon became the only evidence that there had been gunfire exchanged. Of course, tiny iron balls littered the deck, with an occasional pockmark left where one had stuck fast. These were quickly collected by a few men and added to a barrel near where the powder monkeys manned the guns.

"Blaggards! Send a boat after them, and quickly, Mister Slade. I fear we've awakened the settlement. There'll be hell to pay should we be forced to engage in true battle, says I." The captain turned on his heel and studied the cliffs.

A small crew of men scrambled to unleash the longboat lashed to one side of the ship. Within moments, they'd set it into the water and manned it with five men carrying oars and brandishing firearms.

"Deploy another skiff and take the injured merchant with you. I've no need for another body left in an empty sick bay, not with the absence of a surgeon onboard."

"Aye, aye." The response sounded simultaneously as two men disappeared for a moment then returned, dragging what appeared to be an unconscious sailor, half-wrapped in a burlap bag. Seth couldn't tell whether the fellow was alive or dead.

"Is he departed?" He asked the stout mariner standing guard.

"Nay, lad. Ol'e McCully'd be shark bait by now, if he be dead. The capt'n be a generous bloke, if ye ask me. Most would send him off to Davy Jones' Locker in such state, but then yer aboard a fine vessel o' sailors that follow our own set o' laws, ye be."

"Ah," Seth muttered, somewhat relieved to see a shred of mercy was possible – even if it was reserved exclusively for those onboard. "Perhaps my fate will be as fortuitous."

"Highly unlikely," the man stated, and bit into a biscuit pulled from his pocket. Seth watched as the man's yellow teeth bit through a maggot that was still wriggling from its nest within the hardtack. The sailor did not seem to notice and popped the rest in his mouth without pause. "We kill the likes o' you. Let ye dance the hempen jig from the mast."

Seth glanced up at the mast and caught sight of a noose tied just below the Jolly Roger and the crimson heart dangling from the spear as the flag waved in the wind.

"Pirates," he whispered, and awaited his fate.

Eighteen

April, 1721 ~ Youghal Coast, Wales

HER GRANDMOTHER'S CELTIC LILT RANG through rows of foxglove and primrose. She spoke Gaelic in long, melodious sentences as she passed in and out of the cottage door with bundles of freshly cut flowers cradled in her arms.

"Kathryn," her grandmother called out, rolling the "r" as she said her name. "Don't ye forget to mind the edible roots for supper, now."

Kathryn. So that's how you pronounce it – not the stark Kath-er-ine, as I've always assumed. Her name sounded most serene when spoken in this strangely familiar place. She buried her hands in the soft earth and wrapped her fingers around a dense root. Gently tugging with both hands, it succumbed, exploding free from the dirt. She held it up, examined the carrot in the soft light, and admired the contrast of the black soil on deep terra cotta. Ahead, nestled in straight rows, fragrant mint, chamomile, and anise fragranced the air. She set the carrot in a basket lying next to her and reached into the ground in search of another.

"And take up some leaves for tea, Kat," called her grandmother from an arched doorway. Mariel fervently placed pieces of broken bread and salted meat on a stone, left outside for the sidhe – mischievous sprites and gentle faeries that would visit in the deep nights, or so she believed.

Mariel hummed, occasionally interjecting Gaelic lyrics reserved for telling tales of days gone by. Katherine glanced lovingly at the elderly woman and pressed her hands into the soft earth. Her name – Mariel – the same as her grandmother. Katherine's heart swelled, and she fought back tears that threatened to spill onto her cheeks.

Nearby, something rustled the sun-kissed bush that spilled lavender blooms near the rail fence lining the garden. She turned toward the sound and caught sight of curls the color of flax. They belonged to a young woman about her same age. She was bent over a wooden bowl and was pressing small red berries into a shiny pulp. She lifted her face to Katherine and smiled, mischief dancing behind eyes that flashed just before returning to the berries. Katherine watched as she lifted a finger, smeared with ruby paste, and touched it to her lips, staining them scarlet.

"Winne, what are ye doin', lass?" Mariel called out, hands on her hips and a soft smile on her own pink lips.

"Nothing, Mum."

"Don't be wastin' those berries, missy. We need them for jellies, we do," Mariel said, shook her head, and then turned her attention back to the cottage.

Winne. The girl was called Winne. Katherine watched with delight the bubbly blonde across the garden. She was her cousin – the same bubbly blonde that would return to be with her again in another lifetime as Wendy, her sister. *Indeed, it is true. I will never be alone in this lifetime or the ones to follow.* The thought brought a broad grin to Kathryn's face. She chuckled softly.

This was real.

A twentieth-century Katherine had somehow transformed into the youthful Celtic Kathryn. While in the shaman's office – she could barely remember what the place looked like – something had sent her back in time to a place that had existed centuries earlier. *The shaman was real too, wasn't he?* Katherine could barely remember. She glanced down at her hands and buried them in the moist black earth again. This was real; she could feel it, smell it. She lifted the carrot to her lips and took a bite. Yes, she could even taste it. Katherine didn't exist anymore. She was becoming a memory.

"Kathryn!"

Again her name, *Kathryn*, had been called from the cottage door. That was her name, this was reality, and the rest was a dream.

"Stop lollygaggin', bonnie Kat. It's gettin' late," Mariel said, and Kathryn dug her fingers back into the earth to search for another root. This was a peaceful time, and Kathryn would stay…for now.

She smiled and felt at home for the first time.

"Kat!"

She snapped out of her daydream and began the job of pulling the rest of the tubers from the soft earth as Winne giggled and bobbed her golden curls in and out of the tall stalks of rosemary. The girls worked their tasks in the pristine garden and listened to the ballad their grandmother sang. Mariel's voice rang with fluid pitch, and as she moved, the silver hair that draped nearly to her waist danced and swayed.

Long be the days and full be the moon that shines o're Rhiannon, beautiful Rhiannon

For her spells be cast and tho' be wrought to heal infirmed and godforsaken souls

They tied her to the stake and set her afire, Rhiannon, beautiful Rhiannon

Still she could not be felled

Her life was her own

And laughter rose high above with the smoke of the glowing pyre

At the stake of Rhiannon, the beautiful Rhiannon.

Sadness resonated within the tones of her voice as she sang the ballad of the golden-haired healer tied to a stake – the "white witch," as she was called, who looked toward the heavens and laughed as the flames leaped higher and higher, until they consumed her.

"And then, a white-winged dove rose out of the flames, up to the skies from the smoke as Rhiannon's fair face fell, and the flames roared aloft, grasping at that beautiful grey dove with white wings. But they could not catch her. All eyes watched as the dove took flight to the heavens," Mariel said and folded her hands into her lap.

She smiled with tear-stained cheeks at her two granddaughters, who stared back with unblinking eyes. "Remember this when ye are graced with the song of the dove, my daughters."

Kathryn's heart nearly burst in her chest at thoughts of a grey dove and smoke rising in sync into a starlit night. Winne had gone back to her berries, but Kathryn could not contain her emotions as she held the image in her mind.

"But what happened then? Did Rhiannon burn away to nothing?"

"It's said that her body disappeared into that of the dove's and lifted high above the flames so they could not touch her. When they came to gather the ashes, there was no trace of Rhiannon."

"Does that happen with all good witches?" Kathryn's incessant questions brought a smile to Mariel's face. As if she understood, Mariel gently placed a hand under Kathryn's chin.

"You are a precious one, you are, Kathryn. Do not forget it."

She kissed her granddaughter's cheek, rose slowly, and then returned to the cottage, wiping her hands briskly on the front of her white apron. Kathryn watched the woman in awe. Such beauty and grace she had never seen in anyone except…the memory had faded to almost a shadow…her own beloved grandmother from another time and place. Without thinking, she lifted the back of her hand and wiped her cheek.

Just then – *splat!* Kathryn jumped, startled by something that had stuck to her cheek. She touched it to find sticky slurry that came off red and shiny on her fingertips. *Thwack!* Something hit the back of her head. She looked at Winne and saw a tiny red berry flying through the air that nearly hit her shoulder. It flew past her and splattered on the white fur of a Siamese cat lying on the straw mat in front of the cottage door.

The cat lifted its head, arched its back, and then circled the mat. Mysteriously, its fur changed colors from pale ivory to a dark, striped caramel. Gracefully, it lay down again and pointed its tail defiantly towards the two girls in the garden. This cat was *Gifted* as well. No one knew where the cat had come from, but one day it appeared, walking proudly along the cobblestones between the lavender until it made its way through the front door to the fireplace hearth. It settled in with an air of ownership, and Mariel never questioned the feline's rightful place in her home. Likely, the cat's soul belonged to a person of dignity, who had once inhabited the cottage. That it had returned to claim a place near the hearth proved a good omen, or so Mariel had said.

"Sorry, Newid," Winne called out, but the cat ignored her.

Pop! Another ripe berry landed just inches from Kathryn's right knee and splattered ruby juice into the dirt, changing it to a rich black color. Kathryn turned and faced her assailant.

"I see you, Winne! Don't think I don't see you hiding there behind Mum's rhubarb."

Winne ducked behind a hollyhock and giggled softly. Eventually, she couldn't hold it in any longer and threw her head back, spilling out a throaty, infectious laugh. Kathryn joined her cousin, and soon the two were laughing uncontrollably.

When she'd finally regained herself, Kathryn clicked her tongue against her teeth. Instantly, a hummingbird appeared.

"Go on, just enough to irritate her," she whispered to the bird. The creature darted to one side then flew behind Winne's blonde curls and hovered there. Its beating wings pounded the air beside Winne's left ear.

She jumped up and swatted at the buzzing. The tiny bird darted easily out of the way.

"Stop it now, both of you," Mariel said and stomped her foot. She clicked her tongue while holding one finger outward, and the hummingbird immediately lit upon it. "No need to be part of their pranks, sweet *colibri*," she said. The tiny creature's Gaelic name, spoken with affection, did not let on to Mariel's growing impatience with her granddaughters. "Go feed and rest yourself there." The hummingbird darted off her finger and landed inches from the sidhe stone. She watched it settle before turning her attention to Winne and Kathryn. "You two are much too old for this. It's no wonder that neither of you have married yet."

"Winne has a suitor," Kathryn insisted.

"Aye, 'tis true, Mum." Winne nodded her head.

"Indeed! Ye'll have a suitor until he discovers the mischief bottled up inside ye, Winne!" Mariel stomped her foot and dropped her hands to her hips.

"Kathryn summoned the hummingbird, Mum – not I," Winne tattled.

"Ye both own a part," Mariel responded. "Come now, we've supper to make ready."

The cousins shot each other a look, and Winne sent one more rogue berry through the air. Quickly, she gathered her skirts and followed Mariel.

"Winne, you are a naughty scamp," Kathryn said and nudged her cousin with an elbow.

"I don't know what you're talkin' about, Kat," Winne responded, darting toward the cottage, leaving Kathryn alone in the green.

The enchanted garden came alive with colors as the sun sent scattering gold and amethyst rays glinting on leaves and pedals. An aroma of mint and licorice blended with the lavender from the front entry path. Kathryn inhaled deeply, taking the bouquet into her lungs. She could smell rain in the air, different from the ocean spray. It was sweeter, and reminded her of freshly washed grass from the heathland. Winne could smell it too, and stopped in the doorway to glance up at the clouds billowing overhead. Her impish smile dropped as her eyes became glued to the darkening sky.

"Oh, Kat, the moon…the *moon*!" She jumped up and pointed. "There's a ring around the moon! Mu-u-um!"

Kathryn's eyes followed Winne's outstretched finger. There she saw a hazy moon surrounded by a dull circle of light. "The sign of trouble ahead," she whispered.

Mariel made her way over to the doorway, her eyes fixed on the skies. Although pale in the sunset, the orb could be seen clearly – an ominous sight. Mariel motioned for Kathryn to join her.

"Ring 'round the moon, trouble 'fore noon," Mariel whispered the rhyme just under her breath, and then pulled her granddaughters close. "We must be watchful. Come."

Holding the young women as if under protective wings, Mariel turned her back to the sky, escorting Winne and Kathryn to the cottage. Kathryn ducked away momentarily to retrieve her basket, forgotten in the row of tubers.

"I don't want to leave it," she said to Mariel. There was a momentary scuffle near the lavender running alongside the footpath. A fox the color of honey made its way across the stones. It followed Kathryn for a moment before disappearing behind a meadow-sweet bush.

"Even the fox is alert to something." Winne glanced at Mariel who nodded in agreement.

Recently, Kathryn had been leaving bits of dried meat for the little creature in hopes that it would leave Mariel's goats and chickens in peace. Interestingly, the fox had shown no interest in the livestock. Instead, it seemed intent on Kathryn – though, of course, the scraps left behind didn't hurt. Most days, the fox would follow Kathryn at a distance. For now, the little creature seemed content to eat the bits of food left out on a rock near the path and keep watch over the cottage from the brush.

"Rather strange behavior in a fox," Mariel had commented once as she observed Kathryn feeding it. "The creature seems rather enamored by you, Kat, as if it were your pet."

"That's silly," Kathryn had responded, but she never failed to leave a morsel for the creature after that.

Today, however, Kathryn had forgotten and the fox simply waited and watched from its hiding place. She reached into the pocket of her cover-apron and threw out a few pieces of bread leftover from an earlier meal. The canine snatched up the offering and darted back into the brush.

"Silly little thing," Kathryn muttered, and shook her head. She picked up her basket and looked skyward a final time before glancing back to the brush. The fox was safely hidden within the undergrowth. Pearly dusk glistened from the cobblestones, illumination given off from the ominous moon. It made Kathryn nervous, and she nearly tripped as she rushed across the stony path back to the cottage.

"Close the door behind you, Kathryn darlin'," Mariel said, glancing over her shoulder.

Inside, in a large black kettle, their supper simmered over a low, burning fire. The fireplace was broad and situated in the middle of a windowless wall. A low table sat in the center of the room with benches positioned on either side. Bread and a wooden ladle were perched there with three pewter cups placed in a circle. Mariel hastened across the room. A row of candles had been meticulously positioned in a straight line along on the top of the mantle. She lit the largest with a kindling stick, then moved across the room and lit a lantern hanging on a small hook just outside the doorway. Those who possessed the *Gift* knew that an enchantment cast by the light of a lantern would offer protection from an omen's warning.

Tonight was a night of omens, and Mariel left nothing to chance. She spread a line of salt across the threshold and each girl was handed a sprig of tightly woven sage. The same kindling stick used to light the candles ignited the tip of each branch. Winne and Kathryn had done this many times before, and quickly separated to opposite ends of the cottage. Each waved her burning sage in circles, moving from corner to corner, nearly dancing as she smudged the cottage. Mariel watched with approval, and soon began to whisper prayers as she moved with them from one end of the small cottage to the other.

This went on until the fire had burned low in the fireplace. With light illuminating from candles and lantern, and the ritual of sage and prayers completed, Mariel motioned both girls to sit at the table. She poured steaming tea into the three waiting cups, then tore chunks of bread and passed them to her granddaughters. As she filled the three wooden bowls from the kettle, the meaty aroma of mutton stew filled the tiny room.

"We should give thanks. Tonight we remain safe," she said, but the nervous smile that crossed her lips suggested otherwise. They ate their warm meal in silence, sharing only the deep love of family.

Newid hopped through a window, slipping inside by means of a crack in the shutters. He made his way to the hearth, stretched, and cozied up to the fire. Night crept over the cottage with a slow rolling mist that crawled from the ocean and along the rocky hillside. Kathryn could still smell rain as she walked toward the nearest window. The shutter sat ajar and she cocked her head to look through it at the moon. The eerie ring of light had grown brighter, and the night had deepened. She felt a slight chill run down her spine. Mariel watched Kathryn as she stood motionless, staring out the window.

"Do not be concerned over things you have prepared for, Kathryn," she said, and placed a gentle hand on her granddaughter's shoulder. She nodded toward the lantern that was still burning, a beacon of safety to those inside. Kathryn turned to put her bowl and spoon in the wood crate for washing in the morning. Oblivious to the concerns of the night, Winne flitted around the interior, humming as she busied herself clearing the remainder of their supper. It was the indifferent joy of her cousin that gave Kathryn an unwelcome twinge of envy. She could find no indifference to the ominous moon, and her eyes traveled skyward once more.

"What is it, Mum? The ring around the moon." Kathryn could not take her eyes from it. "It feels evil."

"We'll soon find out. Methinks its an omen but I canna be certain just yet. For now we're safe."

"But has it a name?"

Mariel did not answer.

"Come, sit with me, Kat." Winne's effervescence beckoned to her. Kathryn could barely resist the invitation and decided to put away thoughts of the omen for the time. The rest of the night was spent seated near the fireplace, listening to Mariel's tales of days long ago when she was a little girl. Mariel always told wonderful stories while she rocked in the old maple chair at the hearth. This was where Kathryn could feel safe and secure, resting her head on her grandmother's knee.

The hour had grown late, too late now for Winne to make her way back down the footpath to her own modest home. Winne's mother would know. Somehow, she would sense that her daughter remained safe with Mariel. Besides, Mariel's concern with the moon omen made it impossible for the young girl to leave now, so Winne settled in for a night at the cottage. The skies were nearly black, and lightning threatened to erupt with an angry storm behind it at any moment. That, alone, was excuse enough for Winne to stay.

"You can use the loft tonight," Mariel said, and prepared the linens used on the straw beds upstairs. It was not unusual for the cousins to spend the night together – it was a time for the telling of secrets. Both Winne and Kathryn nestled under the fluffy hand sewn quilts and soon were blissfully whispering.

Late into the deep night, long after they had finally given in to sleep, Mariel maintained her watchful vigil, seated next to the fireplace. With a wary eye on the burning flames that danced in warning, she watched for signs. Kathryn had been right – tonight held evil within it, and the elderly woman sensed it. She sat at her post until sleep overtook her. For one night, the cottage stayed secure under the protection of charms and prayers while the ominous moon radiated eerily in a lurid sky.

Nineteen

THE NEXT TWO DAYS WERE uneventful. During the evenings, Mariel remained attentive, always keeping a watchful eye to the heavens, particularly keen to changes with the moon's omen. Fortunately, Winne had made her way home uneventfully after that first morning, leaving Kathryn alone with her grandmother to tend to the animals. Typically, these were pleasant tasks that Kathryn looked forward to.

Today was different.

Darting between the goats in the pen, she made her way to the garden and managed to forget the ever-present sign overhead. Although the sun rose, an oblique sky held onto the clouds through which the full moon glared. There was an uneasiness that hung in the air, with a mist that blocked out the sun and stole her attention from the outdoor chores. Kathryn and Mariel stayed close to one another during this time, mostly communicating through their eyes and smiles, or lack of them.

"The skies haven't changed, Mum. I'm certain the moon warns of something…something evil."

"Aye, it does. And ye're astute to notice." Mariel smiled, hoping that would be all. But Kathryn's curiosity hadn't been squelched just yet.

"What is it? Why won't you talk of it?"

Mariel sighed. "Alright then. I'll tell ye." She patted the ground next to where she waited by the Sidhe stone, and waited for Kathryn to sit. "Methinks it's the Midnight Omen. A terrible sign of trouble to come. Most likely, the moon waits to find the soul its omen's meant for."

"But how…?"

"I need be showin' ye this…" Mariel chose not to finish her sentence but, rather, nodded in the direction of the candles on the hearth and mantle. Their flames had long gone out, and the burnt stubs from the previous night had been tossed. New, fat ones had taken their place, and Kathryn noticed their number had increased.

"Aye, Mum," Kathryn replied. She followed her grandmother inside and waited to be taught more of the *Gift*. It was apparent that there was some urgency about the task, given the moon omen and her grandmother's mood recently.

"Come to me."

The elderly sorceress stood next to the mantle with her arms outstretched. It was a welcoming hug, of sorts – something Mariel often did when she wanted to hold her loved ones close.

"There be times when it be necessary ye use the powers God's seen fit to give ye. Mark me word, it must be subtle and well calculated. Those not gifted mustn't witness ye healin' or makin' magic, for they will not understand…as was Rhiannon's fate."

Kathryn alerted to tone of Mariel's voice. As she listened, Mariel moved decisively and leaned into an unlit candle. With a slow, controlled breath, she exhaled and lifted each arm from her side, then pushed both palms away from her body in rhythm with her breathing. Everything was done with a single-minded intensity directed at the candle. The wick ignited in a soft flame.

"Now, do the same."

Kathryn leaned forward and breathed out the breath of life, pushing both palms ahead of her toward a neighboring candle. A weak flicker sputtered on the wick but died out almost instantly.

"Use the wind. Call to it from within your soul." Mariel's eyes were bright. She nodded to continue.

Kathryn closed her eyes and envisioned a blazing flame. She inhaled deeply, drawing from the image, and gently blew toward the candle. Slowly, the flicker grew until it strengthened and ignited into a bright white flame. Kathryn opened her eyes. The flame then settled itself and the wax began to soften as the candle steadfastly burned. She beamed and heard her grandmother sigh in approval. The elderly woman's eyes twinkled, and she nodded again. "Well done. Well done!"

"I saw the flame inside of me. I really did, Mum," Kathryn exclaimed.

"That's why it burns so now," Mariel said and clasped her hands in front of her apron. "Indeed, ye are *Gifted* as those before ye have been."

The night etched on as numerous other incantations were taught to Kathryn. During the late evening hours in the nights that followed, the younger witch drank in Mariel's teachings with a thirsty desire for more. Every lesson was followed by a sense of relief that settled over the worried mind of the experienced old woman. It was clear that Kathryn's skill was improving.

One night, as Kathryn slept, Mariel glanced out through the window and stared at the skies. "Indeed, the *Gift* is a far greater protection against ye and your wicked omen than all the charms and talismans I could produce." She cursed the moon in Gaelic and settled in for another long night.

On the third morning, Kathryn rose to face an empty cottage. Mariel had gone out early to gather small bits of bark from the east side of the majestic birch trees that stood alongside the footpath. Peeling each piece of bark with great care, she placed them one by one in her apron pocket, and then made for the cottage rather hastily. Upon her return, Kathryn welcomed her with a quick kiss to the cheek and silently watched as she set the bark on the table. When she had finished arranging them, she turned to the fireplace. Next, Mariel lifted several long strands of amber twine from a basket near the hearthstone. Carefully wrapping the twine around each of the pieces of bark, she began to chant.

"Gathered from earth and sun and rain

Protection for he who carries this maintained…"

She repeated the chant over and over again, and, as she did so, delicately wrapped each piece in a scrap of white cotton cloth. Mariel then passed each bundle three times into the smoke from a large candle that burned near the center of the table. When she had finished, several bundles lay neatly stacked, ready for the final spell. Kathryn said nothing as the sorceress finished the ritual. She then turned to face her granddaughter. The old woman's expression made Kathryn's heart skip.

"What has happened?" Kathryn swallowed against a dry throat and waited for Mariel's answer.

She did not reply, but instead, shook her head then busied herself with tidying the last of the talismans. One by one, she placed each white bundle carefully into a basket. Kathryn's stare fixed stubbornly on her grandmother until the elderly woman finally relented. Sighing, she turned and locked eyes with the young girl. A sorrowful smile crossed Mariel's lips as she extended a large piece of glass to Kathryn. It was the one they frequently used as a mirror.

"My girl, see your face here," she said.

Kathryn grasped hold of the mirrored glass with trembling hands and lifted it. Her face turned pale as she viewed her own image reflected in the glass. Quickly, Mariel placed one of the smaller white bundles inside the waist of Kathryn's nightclothes and tied it firmly in place. When she had finished, she paused and held her granddaughter's hands tightly. Fighting back tears that threatened her wise grey eyes, she waited as Kathryn stared into the mirror.

Try as she might, Kathryn could not look away from what she saw reflected in the glass, nor did she feel reassurance from the amulet snug against her waist. She only knew that she stared at another omen. Something grave was about to happen and it involved her. Gazing back from the mirror, she beheld the same ominous ring around the moon – only this one had attached itself to her. Her own face and hair had been encircled by the same glowing light as the bloodless moon hovering above.

The omen had chosen Kathryn.

Twenty

"I'm frightened, Mum!"

"I know, child. So am I." Gravity clouded the elderly woman's face as she tried to soothe her grand-daughter. It seemed an impossible task – there was no escape from the icy fear that wrapped its vice-like tendrils around her soul.

Kathryn fled through the arched doorway. Once outside, she stopped and stared with wide eyes at the inky sky. Fog crawled up from the ocean to where Kathryn stood, eagerly lapping at her bare feet. She scanned the moon with its ominous ring, then back again to her own reflection in the mirror, still clutched in her trembling hands. The eerie rings were identical. The sign could not be denied, and was meant only for Kathryn. There was nothing anyone could do. With sadness, Mariel stepped over the threshold to join her.

The lantern behind them burned with a new taper that fiercely spit out a glow meant to cast a steady shield of protection against evil. Mariel questioned its influence. The candlelight was only slightly visible and did not seem to work against the powerful Midnight Omen. Its flame blended with the light from the newly rising sun – and all of that had been hooded by a mist that hovered just inches above the ground.

"Ye have part in this, Kat. The sign be a warning, and ye must be ready." A mourning dove echoed Mariel's sentiment as it sang somewhere nearby and was joined by two or three others. "Come, there is much to be done. I have something for ye."

Together, they entered the cottage where Kathryn took a seat and patiently waited at the table. Mariel gently removed the mirror from Kathryn's clutches and hid it in one of the back rooms. Within moments, she returned with a small wooden box. Its lid was covered in dust, evidence of having lain in hiding for who knew how long. Mariel set the ebony box on the table in front of Kathryn and lifted the lid. Inside, resting peacefully on a bed of human hair, lay a white stone. Etched over its surface were odd little symbols – raised circles and cascading swirls in various sizes. In the center, surrounded by ancient Celtic letters, were crossed orbs that formed delicate scrolls, encasing a seven-pointed star. At the top, a long silvery thread had been fastened.

"The Scarlet Seren," Mariel whispered. She watched Kathryn's eyes fix on the snowy white talisman. "This be for protection, and once worn, must never be removed except when the soul's at peace."

"For protection?"

"Aye."

Kathryn had been uncertain about what it had all meant, but decided to keep her questions to herself. In truth, she didn't want to hear the answers.

"There be three symbols which combine into one to make the Sigil of Defense. These here…" Mariel pointed to the orbs. "Each one provides very powerful protection that is handed down from the Celts – always to be worn next to the heart."

Mariel traced her finger in a clockwise direction from the bottom of the stone, following the pattern of the etchings on the stone's exterior. "The Lathrind. The pattern of protection." She then pointed to each joined scroll. "Triadic Spirals." Finally, her finger touched the center of the star that glowed a dull pink under her fingertip. "The Cipher of Angels."

Kathryn watched her grandmother's graceful finger settle over the center star. A soft pink glow shadowed the center for a brief moment before blanching snowy white as Mariel pulled her finger away. Kathryn peered, dumbstruck, as she watched Mariel cautiously take hold of the liquid silver thread. She lifted the talisman out of the box and solemnly walked behind the young girl. Gently, she hung the stone about Kathryn's neck. The girl felt its resting place cool against the skin above her heart.

"Many of our line have worn this talisman. Our bloodline is most privileged to be in possession of it now. We call this Sigil of Defense, the 'Scarlet Seren'."

Mariel paused, rested her hands on her granddaughter's shoulders, and smiled. "A grave admonition there be with the Seren – it is not to be occupied lightly."

Kathryn looked into her grandmother's eyes and saw fear wash behind them. "Aye, Mum."

"Remember this – never remove the stone or touch it with ill intent. It seeks its own, and peace be its source. Death comes to he who touches the Seren in anger."

Kathryn nodded and blinked away tears.

"Never forget this, child," Mariel added.

"I won't…I'll remember. But why…why is a trinket meant for protection still so dangerous to its owner?" Kathryn's eyes were filled with tears by now.

"It is more than a mere trinket, child. The Scarlet Seren is a very powerful talisman. Only with stillness, love, and pure intent can it be controlled. With peace, it can be taken from its place. With animosity, it will awaken and destroy."

"I…I don't want it." Kathryn reached for the stone. "Take it from me. I have no intention for it," Kathryn protested.

Mariel grasped Kathryn's hands and clicked her tongue against her teeth to quiet the young woman. A childlike fear had crossed Kathryn's face. *A good thing*, Mariel thought. She sighed. "Ye canna remove it in ye're state. Beside, ye be in need of it, sweet Kathryn. The omen seeks ye out, and this be the only power to protect you from whatever comes for ye."

"Comes for me?"

Mariel nodded and lifted a finger to Kathryn's lips. "Should guile or ill will fill the soul who wears this stone, the powers of the Seren turn inward to destroy the source." She paused and added, "Then... death is certain."

Kathryn blinked tears that quickly stained her cheeks. "But I do not wish it…"

"A guileless heart with pure intent will summon power to protect she who wears the Seren – even protection from death."

"I don't want it!" Fear prickled Kathryn insides.

"But I do. And the Seren is the only hope ye have against the Midnight Omen, Kathryn. It is what I want for you … I insist!"

Kathryn sighed. For some reason, Mariel would not relent. "Aye, as ye wish," she whispered, fighting back the lump that had risen in her throat.

The Scarlet Seren's purpose was clear, and Kathryn understood that the heavy white stone hanging from her neck had the power to protect *and* destroy her. But exactly what she needed protection from, she was not certain.

"Keep peace in your heart and find stillness should you ever take this from your neck. Return it only to this box. But do not remove it without purpose. It is to remain with you always." Mariel kissed her cheek. Kathryn swallowed back a sob that pounded from inside. There could be no forgetting the not-so-subtle glow of light that encircled her head. "This is difficult, my Kathryn, I know and…"

"Aye, then. I'll do as ye ask."

Mariel nodded. "One more task remains." She raised her hands toward the heavens and began to chant in the ancient Celtic tongue.

"Diffyniad…Dyfynnu

Cyrchu ar Hogan."

Silver hair flowed behind her as she glided gracefully in a circle around Kathryn. Finally, she stopped with one hand hovering over the Seren. The last few syllables were uttered as Mariel touched the center of the stone. The center star was illuminated in brilliant radiance for one brief moment.

"Selio Deffyniad Rhag Drygau"

When the elderly woman had completed the chant, Kathryn lifted the Seren, still hanging from her neck, and studied the markings on its surface. The stone remained snowy white at her touch. Somehow, there was calm – a strange, new energy transferred to her as she touched it. Mariel knew she had made the right decision, bestowing the powerful amulet to her granddaughter. She smiled with the thought.

"And now for the rest…" Mariel said. It was time to focus on other preparations. She swept both hands down the length of her cotton tunic, and then turned back to the fireplace. As Mariel made her way to the stone hearth, she clapped her hands and exhaled. A billowing flame ignited, disturbing the cottage cat that leapt onto the windowsill. The cat hissed and instantly dropped out of sight and into the dense grass just as its fur changed color to match the shadows.

Kathryn stood up from the table and allowed the Seren to fall back into its resting place against her chest. She took the steaming cup of tea her grandmother had handed to her, plucked a sprig from the bundle of cinnamon hanging from a beam above, and dropped it into her tea. Thoughts of Winne and the way she would season her tea without ever touching the cup brought little comfort, although she wished Winne were with her, given the circumstances. She stared at the tea. It was Winne's magic that would move the stirring stick to circle and bubble froth to the surface. That was Winne's signature spell, and Kathryn could always tell the last place Winne had been by the location of her cup sitting quietly on a ledge or shelf somewhere.

Kathryn smiled and yearned for a new day – one where she could run freely into the garden to cause mischief with Winne – but fate clouded that hope. She picked up the rectangular wood box that housed the Seren and caught sight of something scratched into the top of the blackened lid. A message had been inscribed there. Kathryn peered closely at the writing, unable to decipher it.

"Mum, see here…there's something written on the box."

"Aye, a message it be. Read it aloud, my dear," commanded her grandmother.

"Lo — A'dorned mid peace e're bondage ne'er cease."

As she read, her voice softened to hushed, reverent tones. Mariel smiled and nodded in agreement. Kathryn knew it was the same warning her grandmother had given her earlier, passed down to each destined to wear the Sigil of Defense.

"I understand," she said, and took the smooth box back to the loft where she slept. She pulled out a large, tattered crate and gently placed the little box inside, tucking it next to her most precious things, so as not to lose it.

"We canna control destiny, dear Kathryn…but we can prepare for it."

"Aye, Mum." Kathryn stared silently at the crate and wondered what her destiny would be. The glow of the Midnight Omen trickled from her face, and Kathryn sighed. "It won't be easy."

"Come, help me," Mariel called out, snapping Kathryn from her thoughts. She could her Mariel bustling over the hearth.

"Aye."

Mariel had made quick work of poaching eggs in a kettle over the fire, and by the time Kathryn made her way to the hearth, the food had been plated and ready to eat. As they ate their breakfast together, the two of them began to talk of other things – people they knew and places they longed to see. Mariel recited tales of the sea, and Kathryn listened intently, thinking of her father, who had sailed off on a merchant vessel a little over a year ago. Her spirits lifted a bit, though she could not forget the omen or the Seren that felt heavy over her breastbone.

After an hour or so, the table was cleared and Kathryn had begun the task of washing the plates. Mariel rose and walked over to the same beam where Kathryn had snapped a cinnamon sprig. Dozens of dried leaves and flowers hung upside down in bundles, filling this part of the cottage with an array of fragrance. She pinched off sprays of dried buds and herbs from various bundles and placed them in the fold of her apron. Then, she carefully placed the sprigs in a bundle on the table, and began to arrange stones and candles, as well.

Kathryn knew this meant they would devote the rest of the day to creating medicine charms and lucky amulets – talismans for the future – unless, of course, her grandmother had planned to season meat. But because there had been no slaughter in the village for quite some time, Kathryn felt safe in assuming it was the former and gathered bits of white cloth and string stored on the highest shelf just for this purpose. Mariel set the herbs and dried blossoms in the center of the table.

"Bugleweed for bloody breath," she stated matter-of-factly and set the sprig of dried green leaves in the middle of a white piece of cloth. "Set this to the side as we must add more 'fore it be bound."

Kathryn did as she was told and set the unfinished charm aside. Mariel continued to pinch off bits of each kind of herb, which she spread across the table. These she joined together in odd combinations atop the white cotton cloth. Kathryn kept busy alongside her grandmother, mimicking her as she pinched and sorted the dried plants into piles. When they had completed their task with the herbs, Mariel fetched a large basket. She lifted a small green-black stone from the basket and placed it on top of the Bugleweed.

"Black Star," she announced. "For broken bones and cut limbs."

This was handed to Kathryn, who tied up the contents of the cotton cloth with string, creating a pouch that could be opened and tied up again with ease. Each bundle was tied the same.

"For use against evil vapors," instructed Mariel as she handed Kathryn another pouch.

"To bring love…this will lift the fevers…protection from bad spirits…to heal the heart." Her grandmother paused, and studied Kathryn, who blushed in spite of herself.

"Why do you look at me?" Kathryn said, dropping her eyes.

"Destiny...ye'll be wantin' that one, methinks." She tapped the bundle with a finger.

"Destiny? I'm not certain I like destiny's plan for me!" Kathryn glanced out the window at the moon.

"Humph!" was all that Mariel could muster.

Finally, Mariel labeled each pouch aloud as Kathryn made a mental note about them. When they bundled the last amulet, they set the entire lot upon a stone tray and placed it safely next to the unused cloth. Another day would come for additional charm-making, but for that day, it was enough.

Kathryn stretched her legs and patted Newid, who had returned to the cottage and was now sitting on the edge of a stool, watching them. The cat stayed slate in color, its yellow eyes fixed on their work as if giving final approval.

Eventually, Kathryn made her way across the room. Dusk had fallen, and she glanced at the lantern that still burned outside the open door. The mist was unchanged across the grassy earth, but the moon was no longer visible in the sky. Kathryn remembered her own milky aura, but chose to push the thought out of her head; hopeful it, too, had disappeared with the mist's arrival. She turned her thoughts, instead, to the Seren, still hanging around her neck, and wondered what power it had over the ominous moon.

"I can no longer see a moon, and the lantern still shines brightly. We must be safe by now…" But the words trailed off as she quickly discovered she'd spoken too soon.

Glancing down at the sea, her eyes caught sight of sails on the sunless horizon.

Twenty-One

IVORY SAILS LOLLED FROM SIDE to side as the looming vessel navigated the ocean currents. In the distance, they appeared to be the size of tiny scraps, though set atop a massively tall ship. It was apparent this vessel was making its way toward the cliffs. Kathryn knew the ship would end its journey at nightfall at the narrow dock just below the rocks.

She glanced at the decayed stretch of plank used by local fishing boats and offered silent thanks the torches had remained unlit this night. Perhaps the ship would hit the reef. No vessel was ever outwardly welcomed to shore there, except for the fisherman. She hoped the dark, weathered dock would convey an unwelcomed air, but her instincts told her otherwise.

The sailors aboard those types of tall ships were typically bred to sail rough waters. Mostly, the crewmen would come ashore in search of shadowy ports to work their dark deeds. This ship was no different, and the darkness of an unlit port did not deter them. Perhaps their black intent was better served without light. Kathryn shuddered as the truth of it registered. She watched and waited, mesmerized by the tiny grey sails' movements over the water.

"Kat, come away from the window and help with this mess," Mariel said casually as she brushed the discarded pieces of plant and stone from the large table.

There was no response. Mariel cocked her head and studied her granddaughter. Unusual, it was, for Kathryn to ignore her so. She glanced beyond her and noticed something on the water.

"Kathryn, what do ye see, now?" Mariel stepped to up to the window. She gasped and rushed to the front entry, unhitched the latch, and pulled the door wide open. Mariel stared up at the dank night sky.

"I see it."

Kathryn walked to the threshold and stood close to her grandmother with eyes locked on the sea. "There," she said and pointed.

An uneasy stillness settled over the evening, menacing and dark. Eerie shadows crept across the night's sky and extinguished the stars in their wake. Mariel drew in a breath.

"Malevolence," Mariel said softly. "It ripens as the night sky grows black."

"What? What did you say?" Kathryn glanced at her grandmother.

"Hush!" Mariel stepped over the threshold, and brushed past Kathryn and into the darkness. "Just as I feared."

"Do ye see it? There – a ship moves to shore."
Kathryn pointed to the sea.

"Aye."

They stood together in silence and watched – the
elderly woman's eyes on the skies and Kathryn's on the
sea. Kathryn's heart pounded – there was something
about that ship, the sea, and the sails that called to
her. The sails grew larger and Kathryn drummed her
fingers against a beam. The sound caught Mariel's
attention, and she shifted her attention back to the
sea. A fine mist crept between the sea caps and pier
that made it difficult to see much beyond the shoreline.
Mariel leaned forward and peered beyond the ocean
mist. Suddenly, she moved. Lithe as a young bairn, she
stepped with catlike footfalls over the grass and beyond
the now sleeping garden.

"It answers in summon, methinks," Mariel
said aloud.

"The ship? How can a ship answer…?" Fear flashed
behind Kathryn's eyes as Mariel nodded.

"Aye, perhaps."

She strained to see the ship's mast and scanned its
length for the customary flag. It was still too far away
to make out details, and still too small to see its colors.
Dread gripped her heart at the thought that perhaps
this ship brought ill intent. She squinted against the
darkness but was unable to tell if its ensign meant foe
or friend. Merchant vessels had long abandoned the
use of the worn-out pier below and opted instead for

the port located just north of the cliffs. They were safer waters, where ships could make landfall with fewer rocks and less treacherous currents. Unless the ship was lost, there would be no reason to dock at the mooring below, and this ship was not lost – Mariel could sense it. She strained again to get a better look.

"What do you see, Mum?" Kathryn asked, and panic lifted the pitch of her voice.

"It sails with purpose," Mariel said aloud, but the words were not meant for Kathryn. "There is no standard raised – no flag to be seen at all from this distance – and the ship remains far offshore." Secretly, Mariel hoped it was a good omen but her gut told her otherwise.

Colored ensigns of principled seamen were always raised at sea. Those who sailed under shadows hailed only the darkest of colors atop the mast. These flags were meant as a warning. Those types of ensigns depicted more than just where their homeport lay. There was little to do about it now.

"The ship below hails no flag. I suspect that is intentional." Mariel decided to think no more of it for fear of losing her wits to worry. The vessel would certainly reach shore within a few short hours. She could fret about it then. There were more pressing matters to fuss over, and the omen was the most urgent of them all.

"Why would a ship intentionally find its way to the cliffs? There's no shore and the pier is unstable."

"Soon enough we will know its purpose here," Mariel said, and then added as an afterthought, "Such precious little time!"

"I don't know what you're talking about, Mum. I'm afraid, and…"

Mariel grasped her granddaughter by the shoulders and spun the young woman to face her. There was urgency in the old woman's eyes that brought tears to Kathryn's.

"Listen well, Kat! The skies grow black with a life force I canna yet comprehend, though I know it's dark and filled with evil intent. The ship ye see afar off sails to us, and not by error." Kathryn shuddered and Mariel pulled her close. "This night brings mischief, an' that ship sails in secret under darkness. Take heed and remain alert. We must be prepared. I fear most for your safety."

Kathryn choked as she tried to form into words the terror wedged in her soul. Tear-filled eyes glanced with momentary hope at the flickering firelight of the lantern. The flame offered no reassurance.

Just then, Winne bolted through the door and gathered Kathryn into her arms. "There'll be no harm to you, Kat. Not while I am breathin' and this heartbeat sounds in me body," she said. She tapped an open palm over her chest. Her eyes darted to the sea. "I'll be at your back, I will," she added.

The cousins clung to one another as if that would provide asylum from the dangers of the night. Mariel shook her head with her hands on hips as she studied the two girls.

"Danger lurks in the dark corners of night, Winne. Did ye not think of ye're own safety?" Mariel said, and then added, "An' what of ye're mum? What if she needed ye? Did ye think o' that?"

"Aye, but Kat needed me more."

Kathryn pulled away and studied Winne's face. "Why did you come back, Winne?"

"I felt that…" Her eyes darted to the moon, then back to Kathryn's face. "I sensed you might be in trouble." The smile disappeared from Winne's face as she spoke.

Mariel allowed them only a moment before clearing her throat. "Indeed, we'll both be needin' ye tonight. I fear it won't be long before company arrives."

"What company?" Winne asked, but Mariel refused to answer. Instead, she urged them to start new tasks. A detailed docket of undertakings needed to be completed before the ship made landfall, and little time remained to accomplish it all.

"That is none of ye're concern," Mariel said. She smiled, but the urgency in her voice startled them. "We need eggs and cream, then back inside with the both o' ye." Mariel sent them both to their tasks. Kathryn ran off to gather eggs from the makeshift coop as Mariel prepared goat's cream for churning into butter. Winne wandered to the garden and disappeared in the berry bushes.

Few hours remained before they would soon find themselves hosts to hungry sailors. *Aye, and I pray that be me fate this eve – true sailors given over to lives of honest work at sea.* But Mariel knew better as an ominous sense of foreboding washed over her and truth gripped her heart with icy fingers.

Twenty-Two

IT SEEMED ONLY MOMENTS LATER that Kathryn gathered a dozen or more eggs and placed them into a large woven basket on the doorstep. She paused to bless the sidhe stone before heading to the garden. Her eyes riveted to the angry sea below. Try as she might, she was unable to keep her focus on the soft earth beneath her hands as she plucked beets and carrots from the garden.

The ship had drawn nearer. With each passing moment, she made a mental note of the narrowing gap between the shoreline and the vessel that looked the size of a small coffin by now. It moved swiftly over currents as if the sea was smooth ebony glass shining in the moonlight. This, she could tell, was a large vessel built for rough seas. Indeed, it would not be much longer before it made landfall. Mariel noted its swift movement as well, occasionally standing on tiptoes for a better view over the rocky cliff's edge. Too quickly another hour passed.

Before turning back to the cottage, Mariel gazed at the shoreline a final time and saw the great ship sitting motionless just offshore. Their fate was set. Several men, each shouting orders as they tended the ropes, lowered two smaller dinghies from one side of the majestic vessel. Their voices rose in harsh, animalistic grunts that carried over the cliffs on biting sea spray as the current shifted angrily.

Mariel motioned for the girls to join her. "Quickly now. Their arrival is imminent."

Kathryn left the safety of the sage-lined pathway and moved to her grandmother's side on the edge of the cliffs. Mariel placed strong arms around both girls' shoulders and noticed the ring of light had disappeared from Kathryn's face. This she hoped was a good sign, looking skyward to the moon for confirmation. The mist allowed only a cruel, momentary glimpse of the pale orb. Hope was shattered as Mariel caught sight of the moon still encased in a ghostly ring. She had not been able to make sense of the signs. Foreboding returned, icy and painful, to clutch at her heart. It was too dangerous to give in to her fears, especially as they centered on her beloved Kathryn. She knew she had to shift her thoughts to protect them all, but the only distraction available had sailed in from the sea. Surrendering, she turned her resolve back to face the ship and the sailors' arrival.

Two dinghies pulled up to the dock below, and Kathryn leaned closer into her grandmother as fear of the foreign ship was quickly replaced by an overwhelming curiosity. Mariel pulled her granddaughter closer, but the elderly woman could not prevent the young Kathryn's inquisitiveness as she watched the scene unfolding below them.

Filthy sailors, dressed in tattered trousers, with curved blades tucked into colorful sashes tied about their waists, leapt nimbly from two longboats.

"Seven…I count seven of them." Mariel clutched her hands in front as if prayer could help them now.

"There are more than seven. I sense it," Winne added.

The men held no reserve about their arrival, thrashing about in the water before clambering onto the weary, sea-worn dock. There was a great deal of commotion as each made his way ashore. One by one, they prepared to climb the steep path leading through the cliff rocks where they surely would end their journey on the flat grasses and heather near Mariel's little cottage. The largest of the group heaved a bulky bundle over his shoulder, and with great effort, began the climb up the craggy path just below where the women stood.

After several minutes, Mariel turned away and rushed into the cottage while muttering under her breath. She paused only briefly to chant in Gaelic and wave symbols over the sidhe stone. Kathryn followed closely but was afraid to learn why her grandmother had reacted so. Winne trailed behind, but seemed less distracted by Mariel's antics than by the moon.

"Make ready. These be hard men a-callin'. We have much to do." Mariel ran her hand over the wood table in the center of the room to brush the last remnants of herbs onto the floor. "Quickly now, gather the bedding and bring it here."

The lines of her forehead deepened. With a flick of her hand, she waved off the young girl, much the way Winne would do when distracted. Kathryn rushed to the loft and returned a few moments later, arms heaped with crisp linen. One of the more weathered quilts was placed into Mariel's outstretched arms. She shook it out briskly before laying it flat and stacking each piece of bedding one on top of the other. Kathryn opened her mouth to speak, but thought better of it and glanced instead at Winne, who returned a wide-eyed stare in silence.

"Stop gawking, Winne. We haven't much time now. Water needs be boiled. Fetch it…make haste!" The tone with which Mariel ordered her granddaughters sent Kathryn scampering outside to the shallow stream to collect water. "Not ye, Kat. Winne shall fetch the water. Kathryn is not to leave this cottage…and do not question me mandate at this moment," the elderly woman snapped. It was clear Mariel was out of sorts, and neither girl wished to cross her.

The elderly witch began to break off sprigs from the beam again, and placed each one on top of the cooking surface. Winne promptly returned with the bucket of water, dumped the contents into the waiting cauldron, and hung it over the fire. Mariel had some-how ignited the flames without ever leaving the table.

Indeed, the magic happened in this manner only when urgency demanded it. Side by side they toiled, trapped in an unwanted race with the advancing mariners not far off.

The light shifted and, for a moment, the house became still – all except the fire that flared an insistent warning. Mariel's breath caught and her eyes darted to the door.

"What? What is it?" Winne breathed, barely a whisper.

"Hush. They've arrived."

Irascible, garbled syllables sounded from just outside the cottage door. Mariel bristled at the foul interchange. Each muffled phrase was chased by hoots and howls. Perhaps the girls hadn't heard, she hoped, but Kathryn's flushed cheeks and Winne's telltale grin suggested otherwise. These were no ordinary sailors. Rough men, these were – most likely with ill intent.

"Avast an' let us enter, witch," growled a deep voice. The lantern flickered angrily but remained lit in spite of the intrusion. It was as if the firelight itself had come to life as sentinel – a warning to all that dare approach. Kathryn prayed that the flame would do its job and keep bad spirits at bay, particularly those who now tried to enter the cottage.

"Peace to you. Enter in peace." Mariel's voice sounded surprisingly calm.

The rant escalated on the other side of the door-way, growing in pitch as more voices joined the first.

Someone groaned and the women heard the hinges creak reluctantly. The lantern cavorted in protest against the intruders.

A large, filthy hand gripped the edge of the oak door. The skin was stretched taught between thumb and forefinger to reveal a crude brand – the letter *R*. Chalky scars crisscrossed over the entire hand, obvious remnants of injury inflicted by razor-sharp weapons not so long ago. His fingernails were encrusted with grime and smelled of fish and pomade. A gold hoop dangled from one ear, and from over his left hip, anchored snugly with a leather bandeau, hung a short, curved cutlass.

"Pirates!"

Kathryn gasped and stared wide-eyed as she backed into a dark corner of the room. All thoughts of safety evaporated with the man's entrance. She didn't recognize the voice that had cried out, but quickly realized it was hers and clamped both hands over her mouth, but the effort was in vain. The large, dirty man had already spotted her, glaring at her through slits for eyes. A second, bloke pushed forward, shoved the first aside, and broke the brute's fixed stare on Kathryn. This one was slightly larger and carried old sailcloth bundled over his broad shoulders.

"This be yer ward, sorceress," he said as he flung the item violently onto the table. A sickening, hollow thud echoed, in spite of the linen placed there, as the contents hit sturdy maple planking.

"Aye, he's bad off." Another pirate wormed his way through the door.

A portion of the wrapped sailcloth parted slightly to reveal the broken body of a man. The brute stepped back. Katherine assumed the body heaped atop the table was already dead, but Mariel's alarmed expression suggested otherwise. *The wretched soul's barely alive!*

She stepped forward and, with a swift wave of her hand, threw off the coarse cloth covering the rest of his mangled body. Mariel's expression soured as she studied the heap lying on her table. He was missing a limb, granted, but there was more. She stared hard at the disabled man, which deepened the lines in her face – a sign of seething Celtic anger.

"Foul beasts!" she spat. In that instant, she took command as she went to work. It was evident from the way she moved and the tone of her voice that she held nothing but contempt for them all. In spite of her effort, the injured man did not respond.

"Ye bring him 'ere like this?" She shot a venomous scowl at the large pirate who had shouldered him, and he froze. Mariel was not one to be trifled with when riled. "Ye should be hanged, the lot o' ye."

No one moved as Mariel worked her healing magic, all the while be-damning the pirates under her breath. Her brows knit together and she cursed them again, and still no one dared cross her.

Silent as church mice, the last two pirates made their way through the cottage door as she spat out the last expletives. Mariel's scathing words had hit their mark. A grimy hand flew to the hilt of a razor sharp cutlass, as a deep growl rattled through the pirate's bared black teeth. Mariel's eyes flashed pale steel, her own warning to be certain, but she said nothing more.

One of the others reached a large, calloused hand out to the agitated comrade. "Think again, mate. Ye don' want to act with impulse here, not now."

"Why not?" the first pirate hissed.

"Because yer in the company of a witch."

Twenty-Three

No one else moved – no one except Kathryn, who had inched her way out from the shadows. Her intention, to gain a closer look at the injured man, seemed clear. But something familiar about the size of his hands and the way the curls fell about his face caused her breath to catch in her throat. She crept to where Mariel had been clearing the damp, bloodstained shirt from the man's chest and gazed at the body. Suddenly, reality clouded her thoughts as she recognized the man lying there.

"Papa!" Kathryn fell over him in horror. "Oh, Papa!" she cried out. Her voice mirrored the contempt heard in Mariel's.

Kathryn pulled away from her father and faced the pirates. Fear vanished as Celtic fire took its place. "What sort of foul, loathsome beasts are ye?" Hate washed behind her icy blue eyes. "Certainly not men to foul the lives of innocent people, I say. Scum o' the earth!" She spat at the closest pirate and her aim soiled his already befouled boots.

Blood rushed to her cheeks and matched the color of the stone hanging about her neck. The Seren had transformed from white to a glowing, blood red color. A warm sensation had accompanied it, which she could feel growing in intensity over the skin above her breasts.

"Kat…" Mariel tried to hush her.

"Indeed you're not fit to clean his boots and a curse of the pox shall find all of you for this! *Mae'r sêl ff arnoch*!"

"Kathryn!"

A woman's anger found its way from deep within and surfaced as Kathryn felt lusty eyes shift to her. Carnal greed reflected in the pirates' pupils that danced back and forth between her youthful features and the Seren. The stone grew hotter against her skin, matching her fury.

"Damn you! Damn you all to…"

Out of nowhere, a large hand flew through the air and struck Kathryn on the jaw, knocking her to the ground. For a moment, Kathryn was unable to focus. The act had caught her off guard and Kathryn's mood shifted from one of angry indignation to bewilderment. Tears pooled and threatened to spill over onto her cheeks. Immediately, the stone around her neck faded to a pale rose color, and the heat that accompanied it began to cool. The side of her face stung, and she could feel the telltale welt beginning to rise on her left cheek.

When she glanced up to view her assailant, she caught sight of her grandmother, instead. Mariel stood anchored with hands on hips, positioning herself defiantly between the burly man who had just delivered the blow and Kathryn still sprawled on the floor. She kept her back to Kathryn and issued a warning to the pirate.

"Ye tread where ye best not venture. Not here. Not in a house filled with witchcraft!"

"Aye…the wench cursed us!"

The pirate stumbled backward, though he never took his eyes off Kathryn still sprawled on the floor. A few of the others sidestepped to the doorway. Then to everyone within earshot, Mariel said, "This be my house and ye'll not foul it, or ye account to me. Ye do not wish to meet my wrath. Mark me words on this."

No one dared move.

"No offense meant, ma'am," squeaked a voice from behind.

"Aye! She's likely cursed ye. The girl be my descendant and his daughter. Ye've affronted us both!" Mariel snapped.

The largest pirate stepped backwards into his pack of cutthroats, nodding ever so slightly as Mariel stared at him. She then held out a hand to Kathryn and lifted her from the ground.

"The lass spoke harshly, witch," another piped up, a little more boldly this time.

"She be kin and has the healer's hands, passed down through me own blood," Mariel responded. She spun around to look each man in the eye just to be sure she'd been understood. It seemed clear that she had.

"Her hands have the magic way about 'em, and ye be fortunate she shows mercy to ye now, after ye strike her so. Do not make that mistake again, or ye'll meet her fury along with my own."

Eyes dropped to the floor, and the entire lot looked much like a row of disobedient schoolboys. This was likely due to their superstitious fear of being hexed by witches. The two largest pirates retreated to either side of the room. The rest inched backward with their hands hanging loosely away from cutlass hilts.

Satisfied, Mariel turned back to her injured son. Kathryn's jaw still throbbed from the blow. She stood and took her place next to Mariel. The man she'd called "Papa" had a seasoned face, as grimy and weatherworn as the pirates. Yet there was tenderness lining his eyes, and she saw the same curve of his mouth that graced her own lips. Sorrow pulled at her soul, and she prayed silently that Mariel's *Gift* would be powerful enough to bring him back.

In that instant, Kathryn felt the cold, hard stare of eyes bearing down upon her. She spun on her heels and looked to the source. Several men eyed the white stone she wore. Kathryn looked away and swallowed hard against the contempt she felt toward these cutthroats. There was magic to be done and her father to save.

A soft cadence hummed and the candlelight flickered as Mariel began to chant softly. Outside, the cry of a lone wolf wailed, and the wind joined its howling. Suddenly, the cottage door slammed shut, sending the candle flames into spasms. Mariel raised her eyes to the pirates, conceding her own power over the elements. Her eyes twinkled and the men seemed transfixed. She smiled – a baleful turn of her lips – and then poured liquid into her injured son's mouth. Patiently, she watched as the viscous amber ran down his throat. She then lit a small bundle of dried yellow flowers, blew the smoke in circles overhead, and whispered chants in Gaelic that followed her movements.

Upon completing her ritual, Mariel returned to the fireplace and lit three large candles that she placed on the table, one at the man's head and the other two on either side of his feet. The light shone in a large triangle. Closing her eyes, she raised her hands over-head and chanted again. The candles danced in time with the lilt of her voice then, suddenly, fell still as her hands dropped to give thanks. Finally, she opened her eyes and surveyed the room. Satisfied, she turned to face Kathryn.

"Ready something for them to eat," she said.

"Eat? Mum, are we really to feed…?"

"Do as I say," Mariel said sternly. "You as well," she said to Winne, who'd remained invisible until that moment

Kathryn set about immediately, gathering the boiled vegetables from the kettle, while Winne broke cheese onto wooden plates. The young women tossed an occasional glance at their grandmother, who would not meet the their eyes. It was apparent she had chosen to ignore them, focusing instead on the incantations needed for her son. Kathryn and Winne chose to fill the plates in silence.

Each pirate was handed a helping of hot food. The single loaf of crusty bread was set on a side table then Kathryn backed away. She wiped her hands on her skirts and stared, perplexed, at her grandmother's hospitality. How could she be so generous to these malodorous scallywags, particularly now? She glanced at Winne, who kept her eyes to the floor. She knew Mariel had reasons, and dared not cross her.

"There be no grog here, only tea. It serves well against the cold," Mariel announced, and then turned back to her labors.

She crushed additional herbs scattered strategically along the table edge. Over the man's arms and forehead, she sprinkled the finely ground powder, then rubbed it into his skin as she droned.

"Rhwng Byw a Marw

Anadl Einioes

Cusan Adfer"

A few of the more gullible men stopped gorging themselves to watch the old woman work her magic. Eyes wide and mouths gaping, the pirates stared at the witch. Kathryn ignored their ignorance and passed out wooden cups filled with the anise and mint tea that had been brewing on the hearth. The cutthroats sat upon the floor and never looked up from their plates as they wolfed down their meal. Vegetables were a luxury on most sea voyages and, which to this crew was no exception, apparently. The men devoured the beets and carrots as if they would be their last. Their mannerisms fascinated Kathryn, who suddenly seemed oblivious to the incantations and ministrations taking place in the middle of the room.

The aroma of food aroused the cat. It rose from the warm hearth and arched its back. As if sensing the vulnerabilities of gullible sailors, the creature prowled in front of the pirates and deliberately crossed the path of a half-wit. The man's eyes grew large as he watched the cat make its move. Terrified, he jumped upright, dropping his plate and spilling its contents to the floor. A loud yelp followed, as the silly man crossed himself and spun in circles on one foot before darting through the open doorway, where he spat upon the nearest rock.

"Come here, Newid," Winne whispered. But the cat flicked his tail and ignored Winne, focusing instead upon the ludicrous little man's histrionics. It snatched a piece of discarded meat and padded out the door, changing its color to a deep, midnight black with each step.

The other pirates shuffled away from the cat as it passed, toppling over teacups and scattering plates in the process. A few made a fragmentary sign of the cross. Each appeared unwilling to part with his own plate and quickly turned back to the meal, leaving the stout pirate outside to hop and spit on rocks on behalf of them all. Kathryn chuckled and shook her head, amused by the odd ritual.

"Disposable castoffs from what was left of a solid ship's crew," she whispered under her breath. Winne shot her a look.

"What did ye say, lass?" The pirates lips barely moved. She dropped her eyes and looked away, shaking her head.

"Nothing."

"Best not say anythin' foul 'bout me mates, savvy?"

Kathryn forced her stare away from the men. Their superstitious antics made them comical. At the very least, she vowed to keep a mental note about the pirates' superstitious ways – she'd laugh about it when they were all gone from the cottage and back to sea.

Without warning, a low, tormented groan rose from the table. Kathryn's attention immediately snapped to her father. Muffled sounds percolated from the man's throat as he opened his eyes. Mariel's intense chanting softened at the shift in her son's condition. The creases lining her forehead seemed to relax just a little, too – a good sign, Kathryn supposed. Mariel poured more of the liquid into his mouth and waited for him to swallow.

He might actually live! Kathryn's frayed emotions gave way to some consolation. She rushed to his side and saw that he appeared less distressed than before. It proved to be a soothing balm against the fear that pricked her wits. In that moment, her father's eyes drifted to her face. *He's alive.* The thought became an elixir to her emotions. She began to cry as she watched the corners of his mouth turn upward ever so slightly.

"Papa," she whispered and leaned in closer. He placed a weak hand over his daughter's. Mariel was peacefully silent. Stepping back slightly from the table, she kept vigil over them both. Inwardly, she felt sure she had performed her art well. Winne drifted to her grandmother's side, and tucked herself safely behind the elderly woman's skirts, as a protective arm encircled her.

"Papa, I'm here."

"Kat." His whisper was enough.

The group of men finished eating, and, silently murmuring between themselves, rose one by one from their places on the floor. Kathryn suddenly felt protective of her father. Panic crawled up her spine as she tried to push away the notion that the pirates could take him away from her again. She did not know just how her beloved Papa had come to share company with men such as these, but she was sure it was not of his own accord. He had set sail only fourteen months earlier as a privateer assigned to the Royal Navy. Since that day, he had not corresponded. Returning home as such, carried over the back of the filthy pirate was certainly not something her father had planned in advance.

"Finish and be gone." Mariel's watchful gaze darted back to the men who'd begun to gather at one side of the tiny room.

"We'll be takin' our cargo back wit' us, then." Their voices had become more animated, matching their gestures. As if reading the men's thoughts, she advanced.

"He'll be recovered mind ye, but he'll not be settin' sail with ye this day. His body's too weak to do yer biddin'. Have ye thought on it?" Mariel tapped her foot against the floorboards. "Likely not, else ye'd know it best to avoid bringin' a broken mate to yer captain." Mariel's voice sounded caustic.

It was true. They faced a nasty predicament. Knowing they couldn't bring an injured sailor back to the captain was something she was using to her advantage. It would fall hard on any man who couldn't pull his own weight onboard the ship. No one wanted to be held accountable for returning a millstone crewman.

"Aye," murmured amongst the pirates.

"What'll we tell the capt'n?" The stout pirate piped up.

"Aye. He'll want full account of ole Cully, 'ere."

Looks darted to Mariel as a sly grin crossed her lips.

"Ye best be tellin' yer captain that this sailor passed on an' died even while I made my best magic over him," she said. "Tell him the witch was powerless over death…this time."

The warning hit its mark.

Twenty-Four

"THE WITCH IS RIGHT. WE can't go onboard with deadweight."

All eyes fixed upon the silver-haired witch.

"Aye! It'd be the cats for us, it be."

Uncertainty mounted as the pirates considered their options. The consequences would be grave should the old woman prove right. Their murmurs rose to squabbling as the cutthroats bantered about ideas for a believable story. Eventually, a plan was agreed upon – they'd use Mariel's tall tale: *The man they carried up to the sorceress died under her care.* Surely the fib would suit their captain. The pirates began to craft a convincing alibi.

"She be a right foul witch, at that."

"Aye, the wretch up and met wit' the devil hisself, even with all her cursin' and spell castin'."

The pirates spat, crossed themselves, and hopped in a circle anytime someone referenced the devil.

"The old witch proved she's not a very good healer after all."

"Aye, an' good riddance to the burden we carried on our backs anyway!"

"I carried him, Skyrme an' don't ye be takin' the credit for it!" The pirate wearing the gold hoop hissed as he spoke.

"Let the old woman bury the incapacitated wretch herself. Surely it be her mistake."

"Aye!"

The men agreed to the plan, assured they had manufactured a convincing story. Mariel said nothing as she listened to their scheme. Secretly, she was pleased at how easily the ludicrous group of men could be fooled merely by the power of suggestion. Convincing them to leave her injured son behind in the safety of the cottage had been an easier task than she'd anticipated. She knew, with time, her son would be as well as he would ever be. He had lost the lower part of his left leg – that appeared to be the worst of it. The flesh was scarred and had been wrapped in worn rags that were filthy and had obviously been placed there a long time ago. But that wasn't the nastiest of his injuries – the stump appeared well healed and no longer problematic. No, there were signs of bleeding and contamination in many of the other wounds – at least, the ones she could see. These newer injuries, which were indeed grave, would take more time to heal.

It wasn't long before Kathryn once again felt the heavy weight of the men's eyes lingering on her. Three pirates near the back seemed particularly engrossed, as dark looks passed between them, and they whispered amongst themselves. Their eyes darted in calculated glances that dropped from the white stone hanging from her neck to the top of her corset. Chills crept along her spine.

She moved her hand slowly so as not to be noticed, reached behind her long skirt, and snatched a sprig from the herbs lying on the table. She fingered the pigweed which, when sprinkled over exposed flesh, would cause great welts to appear. There was just enough of the crushed herb to dust at least one of the pirates. To her relief, their scheming continued, long enough for Kathryn to work her mischief. Once in a while, a lusty eye would dart her way and all whispering would stop. These men wanted Kathryn.

Covertly, a step at a time, one then another began to advance. Kathryn's eyes narrowed as she watched the pirates creep toward her. Still hidden behind her back, she clenched her hand into a fist and ground the dried pigweed into fine bits. Soon, the men stood within feet of her. She froze in anticipation, keeping her fist hidden within the folds of her skirting. When the first man was nearly within arm's reach, she raised her fist and took in a slow, deep breath. Bit by bit, almost imperceptibly, she uncurled her fingers to expose the crushed pigweed. Kathryn readied to cast the spell.

The pirate inched closer, and Kathryn could smell his acrid stench as her heart pounded within her chest. Just then, a burly arm reached for her throat. In one forceful discharge, Kathryn blew the contents of her hand. Venomous particles exploded from her palm, hitting the brute's exposed skin. He cried out, desperately clawing at his eyes and cheeks, as he stumbled backwards into his accomplices.

"Bloody wench! She's hexed Slade!" one of the pirates shouted.

"She's a witch! A necromancer same as her kin. Ah, Slade's in a bad way, he be!" Another shouted profanities at her.

Chaos erupted, and the wailing pirate cussed and scratched at his skin where large welts began to rise.

Terrified, Mariel's eyes darted to Kathryn. She knew instantly what the young girl had done. Kathryn locked eyes with her grandmother, who stood behind the center table and shook her head, but it was too late. The spell had been cast, and the pirate caught off guard.

"Th' lass ambushed Slade blind, she did," a pirate growled through yellowed teeth. He leveled a black stare on Mariel. "We all saw it."

There could be no recourse now – Kathryn had placed herself in grave danger. She looked from her grandmother to the pirates and back to Mariel again. *Why do you not react?* Kathryn thought. *Why would anyone question my attempt to fight off these brutes? These are the same conniving group of pirates who captured my father and invaded our home!*

Mariel once again shook her head fiercely, *No!*

Kathryn paused, her brows drew together, confused. She dutifully brushed the remaining contents of her hand into the fireplace, igniting the yellow flame into a sizzling green before it died back to its original burn. Only her grandmother and father saw the change in the fire. Dismay showed in Kathryn's eyes. *Why don't they understand?* Kathryn fought back tears and shifted her gaze to Winne, who cowered in the shadows behind Mariel. Winne simply shrugged her shoulders.

Yelping the cry of a flea-bitten dog, the pirate stumbled out into the deep night air. The rest fell deadly quiet as the cutthroats' leader slowly turned and, with slits for eyes, glared at Kathryn. His voice sounded venomous as he hissed at Mariel.

"Our terms have shifted, Madame. We'll be makin' a trade. Ye keep the damaged goods and we be takin'…" His voice trailed off as his arm slowly rose. The intent became clear as all eyes tracked the muscular arm to one outstretched finger.

The enormous pirate pointed to Kathryn.

Twenty-Five

"No!"

It was the first coherent sound Kathryn's father had made since being brought to the cottage by the pirates. He was propped up on one elbow and reaching toward his daughter.

"No! She will not be goin', not with any o' ye." He fell back onto the table, too weak to protest further. Despair clouded his expression as his head lolled onto the linen used as a pillow.

The father is helpless to save his daughter.

Kathryn had no idea who had given rise to the thought, but she'd heard it loud and clear. She crouched back into the closest corner and froze – a small animal trapped by its predator. Her pupils dilated within her pale blue eyes – a sign of terror. This was no bargain proposed by the ugly pirate. She'd be lucky to get out of their sights on her own. She glanced around the cottage, frantically looking for an escape. Just then, Mariel stepped forward.

"The girl stays here!"

The effect was not the same as before, stopping the pirates in their tracks. No, this time the cutthroats only sneered, and the largest stepped toward Kathryn. She crouched deeper in the shadows and tried to become invisible, but it was to no avail. He slowly shook his head. A calculating grin spread across his cracked lips where rotting teeth peeked through.

"Aye, that little lass with her gifted ways be right useful to a ship of fightin' men," he hissed.

Mariel charged, but the brute swept a thick arm, catching the old woman unawares. He easily tossed her across the room. Mariel stumbled back and caught herself with outstretched hands as she fell toward the wall. Kathryn cried out, but the pirate caught hold of her as well. He laughed at her struggle, and Kathryn gagged as the pirate's rancid breath filled her nostrils.

"Now, lassie. Ye be payin' the price for yer mischief this day," he hissed. "We've got plans for the like o' ye!"

"No!"

Her voice squeaked and eyes pooled with tears, blurring the features of the brute whose face was just inches from her own. She winced as a massive hand took hold of her left arm and grimy nails pressed into her soft flesh. With the skill of a mercenary, he spun Kathryn around and bound one arm behind her back, ready to snap the bone at the slightest resistance. He easily held her secure in a one-handed grip. From beneath a sash tied about his beefy waist, he withdrew a dagger and positioned the razor-sharp edge against her throat. Kathryn felt the sting of steel slicing through her skin ever so slightly with each swallow. She could not speak.

"Ye best keep yer thoughts to yerself, lass. Open yer mouth and I'll sever yer windpipe," he growled in her ear.

Kathryn dared not move. He stepped forward, pushing the captive girl forward. His strength matched his size, and she struggled to walk as he wrenched her toward the middle of the room. All the while, his blade stayed fast against her delicate throat.

"Let's move, men!"

A raspy voice piped up from the opposite side of the cabin where the others waited. "The capt'n's in need of the healin' hand hisself. He's in a bad way, and sure to be rewardin' us with the likes of her."

Heads nodded. Mariel glanced up from her place on the floor and grimaced when she noticed the hole in one pirate's face where an eye had once been. The rest of the cutthroats stared at Kathryn held prisoner by their massive crewmate. The brute hesitated, cocking his head to one side as he considered before finally loosening his grip on the girl. Kathryn wriggled away as he withdrew the blade a bit, allowing her to speak.

"Get your filthy paws off me, scum!" she cried out. The large, grimy hand released her arm and took hold of her wrist instead, dragging her toward to the door.

The twist in the pirates' plan had terrified Mariel, who stared wide-eyed and unsure of the best course of action. Any attempt to thwart the cutthroats' scheming would only make things worse for Kathryn. No, her best option would be to arm her granddaughter for what lay ahead. It was apparent these atrocious villains were now in control and setting the rules. The healer's mind worked swiftly, calculating the potions and amulets waiting on the shelf. She knew she had to get to them. She'd have to give them to Kathryn, along with a talisman that would connect them both while they were separated – and they would part ways, it was certain. Mariel feared it could happen at any moment, should she not act fast enough.

"Murderers and thieves! The lot o' ye!" Kathryn shrieked at her captor. "Let me loose!"

The pirate held firm in spite of her protests. She kicked and scratched at him with her free hand, but all of her thrashing did nothing to stop the brute from lugging her along. In fact, his wicked expression revealed nothing but sheer amusement at the fight she was putting up.

"Aye, she be a right spirited one, she be," he chuckled and hauled her farther across the room.

Laughter peeled from the other pirates. Mariel's face went ashen. The moon's warning had revealed something evil would befall Kathryn. Mariel feared those events were upon them now, and her lips began to move in silent prayer for Kathryn. Mariel could only hope to protect her through magic.

The others kept Winne and Mariel at bay with cutlasses drawn, ready for a swift strike. Kathryn was dragged kicking and biting to the doorway. The pirate leaned his rotten mouth near her ear. Bile rose in her throat as she felt the heat of his foul breath as he whispered.

"We slit the old witch's throat first, then yer father, and ye be watchin', lass. After that, the girly with the golden curls goes next. Think well on me offer and we be lettin' them live. So says I."

Her mind had clouded, and fear blocked any chance to think clearly. It was her instinct to fight back, yet he held her fast. With pleading eyes on her father lying across the room, she begged in silence for rescue. He could only cry out in response, and it was obvious he would not be able to help her. Just then, she caught sight of the garden skewer buried in the basket she had carried in earlier. Her eyes darted from the sharp tool to her grandmother. Mariel caught sight of Kathryn eying the skewer and her focus snapped to attention. Silver eyes bored into the deep blue of Kathryn's.

Not in this way Kathryn…do not think on that blade in the basket there…it is not meant to be done this way. They will kill you for certain!

Kathryn had heard the voice in her head though Mariel's lips remained still. Her eyes held Kathryn's. Apparently, no one else had heard the voice, not even Winne.

Nay, Kathryn…think not on the blade. I be warnin' ye against the thought o' fightin' these loathsome pirates. There's another way.

Again, the voice went unnoticed by anyone else. Mariel's stare was fierce and fixed on Kathryn, who glanced at Winne, wide-eyed with terror. *She's overwhelmed.* Winne must have heard, though, because she instantly snapped her attention to Kathryn and shook her head. "No!"

None of it made sense. Kathryn wanted to ignore them all and lunge for the sharp garden tool, or better yet, one of the raised cutlasses. *At least I'd be able to dispatch one.* Winne's eyes pleaded with Kathryn and she mouthed *No!* again.

Something must be done, at least to distract them or scare the savages off. She could think of no other way to free herself from the brute holding her tightly. There was the blade still held only inches from her throat to contend with.

Not this way, Kat. Mariel again. *We must beg for time. I have a plan.*

In the back of the room, the rest of the crew had grown agitated as anticipation started getting the best of them. No blood had been spilt that day, which was unusual for pirates who ventured ashore.

One by one, the pirates began to make their way toward the door, forming a human wall that blocked any escape. If the girl continued to resist, perhaps a fight would break out and their bloodthirsty need for ransacking could be quenched. All hands stayed ready at the slightest provocation, but Kathryn had become still, no longer resisting her captor. Mariel was fixed as stone – a bad sign.

"So then, we've an accord, aye?" The brute holding Kathryn laughed.

Although their faces showed disappointment, the pirates soon accepted their comrade's plan. Still, there would be no mayhem ashore – a bad omen for any cutthroat. They would have to make up for it later with a rally to swords and spilt blood elsewhere.

"What say ye, witch?"

Mariel stood her ground and her eyes flashed with anger. When she refused to respond, the large pirate curled his lips, and, with a wolfish grin, shifted his gaze to Winne. Kathryn caught his eye and realized her cousin was in trouble – they both were.

"I'll go!" Kathryn shouted. Winne's cheeks glistened as tears spilled over them. Still, she was afraid to speak.

"No!" Mariel cried out. A blade glinted as it moved against her throat. She waited for the slice, but it never came.

"An' so we take our leave." The pirate swept a low bow to the old woman with a mocking touch of his brow with his free hand.

His grip never relaxed as he made the gesture, which forced a slight curtsey from Kathryn as he pulled her downward in one jerk. She grunted but dared not speak, remembering Mariel's warning. With a suitable bargain made, Mariel and Winne were released. And as the large pirate dragged Kathryn out the cottage door, Mariel rushed forward.

"Hold! She be in need of her remedies and cures. She's no good to yer capt'n without her means for curin' him. How could she be?"

The pirate stopped abruptly and glanced back at Mariel. He cocked his head to one side.

"A good point made, indeed, witch."

It was apparent that while the brute was repulsive, he had carefully considered her words. *So much the better!* Mariel thought, and Winne nodded in agreement.

He shoved Kathryn toward the old woman. Large purple bruises marked her wrist where his fingers had been, and she rubbed the spot with her other hand. Another shove sent her sprawling. Kathryn's eyes never left Mariel's. She sensed a plan was about to unfold – one that had been hatched by Mariel. And although she had no idea just what that would entail, Kathryn knew it would include magic.

Twenty-Six

MARIEL'S GLANCED AT THE SHELF filled with conjuring materials. Amulets brimming with thick syrups, dried veined gossamer, and flecked crystals rested there, waiting to be summoned. Their power lay dormant but not forgotten. Kathryn caught Mariel's glance and knew her grandmother had something brewing in her clever mind that involved the *Gift*.

"Come here, Kathryn," Mariel commanded. "You need to collect your supplies. Quickly now, so as not to keep these men waiting."

Kathryn obediently made her way away across the room to the shelf. Swiftly, the two women located the white pouches that had been placed there earlier that morning. On the uppermost shelf lay a large book made of old parchment and bound with dark maple leaves dipped in resin. Mariel reached up, took down the book, and placed it in Kathryn's hands. She then snatched several different bundles, some of which had been created that very morning. Mariel selected the pouches one at a time, ceremoniously handing them to her granddaughter.

Although the words were meant for the girl, Mariel's voice carried loud enough for the pirates to hear.

"These ye shall use for the healing of evil spirits. These be for binding of bones. This," she said and held up a large, red, dried thistle, "ye use to bring evil curses upon those who think to thwart ye."

Each of the pirates began to fidget. The old woman eyed the cutthroats, then turned back to Kathryn.

We must distract these simple fools...I have a plan. Mariel had sent the message, and while it was meant for Kathryn, Winne's eyes popped wide open as she watched from the corner.

Do ye understand?

Kathryn nodded. Winne nodded, too. Mariel scowled at the pirates. A few dark eyes looked elsewhere. Trepidation and mythos easily conquered what little confidence they had, and Mariel knew just how to play on it.

Their superstitious, gullible minds are easily manipulated. Do not forget this, Kat.

Kathryn took note and nodded as she watched the pirates' reaction to Mariel. The old woman opened the cover of the book resting in Kathryn's hands.

"This be powerful magic, lass," she said. "Mark well the need for using it, and do not deviate from the writings thereon."

"Aye," Kathryn replied, her voice barely a whisper.

Mariel turned the pages and gently worked her way to the middle. Unusual writing seemingly danced across each page as symbols faded in and out of view. The book was alive. She paused a moment, then pulled against a worn page. As the parchment ripped, the book screamed – a horrifying shriek that made the pirates cross themselves again.

"What happened?" Kathryn began but a look from Mariel cut her off. Whispering in ancient Gaelic, Mariel ran a finger along the torn edge of the page to soothe it and the screams faded.

Written on both sides of the parchment was faded script. The ink moved constantly with squirming little black symbols that swam over the pages. They appeared agitated. Mariel spoke again in Gaelic and the squirming symbols rested peacefully. Then she folded the sheet and put it into the waist of Kathryn's skirt, brushing her hand over the living folio.

"There. They're at peace now," she said, then touched the satchel she had tied several days ago before handing it to Kathryn.

"Who?" Kathryn's eyes were glued to the book. Mariel smiled in response, and, with one hand, she reached out to touch the stone still lying against Kathryn's chest.

"These keep ye safe from the filthy dogs who will take ye from me now."

Kathryn's eyes darted back to her grandmother's face. She understood – there would be none of Mariel's magic to stop fate.

"Take me?" Inside her chest, her heart skipped and a dull ache filled the cavity that housed her soul. Her eyes welled, but she did not speak.

"Mind what ye have learned and remember the power of the Seren," Mariel said. "Use it wisely, and never remove it until your soul be at peace and your mind be still."

Dread clawed at Kathryn as she blinked away the hot tears that washed over her cheeks.

"Listen in your heart, me girl. I will be with ye. Be still in the silence and ye shall hear me whisper to your spirit again."

"No! Mum, she cannot…" Winne cried out, but was silenced with a searing look from her grandmother and the glint of a blade that was suddenly pointed directly at her.

"I…I…" Kathryn could not find the words. How could this be the plan? It was as if no one had any regard for the desperation she felt. Was there no other way?

"She's stalling, Slade," a pirate said.

"Enough!" the brute barked from the doorway. "We leave now."

"Ye shall hold," Mariel snapped. "There is one last thing she'll need."

She reached for one of the dried plants hanging from the beam above their heads, then took down the sharp chisel used to chop herbs and snipped a lock of Kathryn's hair. This she quickly tucked out of view. Then, she cut a lock of her own silver mane and sliced the length of her palm with the sharp edge of the chisel.

Next, she clenched the hair in her palm and drew the strands from the top of her fist. She looked at the bloody cord and nodded in approval, then reached for Kathryn hand. With precision, Mariel sliced diagonally across the palm of Kathryn's open palm in the same way she had cut her own.

"Ahh," Kathryn cried out and flinched. The blade bit her flesh at the same time a line of blood rose to the surface, but she did not draw back. Mariel pulled out the lock of Kathryn's dark hair and threaded it through Kathryn's fist. When she had finished, she took a long grey leaf hanging directly above their heads and placed it over the length of the gaping wound in Kathryn's hand. She then wrapped it with some of the cotton cloth they had used to bind the herbs and stones into amulets earlier. Once satisfied with the dressing, Mariel bound her own bleeding hand.

"This be dark magic, indeed," one of the pirates said.

"Aye." Shuffling feet and whispered objections followed, but no one interfered.

While Mariel finished securing the dressing, she walked to a candle that still burned on the table where Kathryn's father lay. Cautiously, so as not to catch fire to the charm, she dipped both bloody strands into the hot wax, sealing the blood and hair together in two separate, dangling cords.

Protests followed while the pirates observed the spell. Mariel made her way back to Kathryn and placed the silvery charm into Kathryn's uninjured hand.

"This be from me own body – my blood and hair. A portal to keep us together always." Mariel lovingly curled the youth's fingers around the wax-encased talisman. Finally, she took the charm made of Kathryn's tresses and tucked it into her pocket, along with the steel chisel.

"Again I say, listen, and keep this with ye as ye look to the wisdom of your grandmothers."

"Aye, Mum."

"Stay still…at peace, no matter the cost," Mariel said, and locked eyes with her granddaughter for a moment.

Suddenly, she spun on her heels and faced the pack of cutthroats. Fire rose in her veins and her expression turned lethal. With catlike agility, she raised the needle-sharp chisel and lunged forward with the piercing banshee cry that accompanies attack. The old woman drove the spike deep into Slade's exposed flesh.

He let out a howl and spun in an effort to free himself, but Mariel gripped the spike solidly with both hands. As they grappled, the metal barb sank deeper into the muscle. In desperation, his thick fingers clamped vice-like over Mariel's fragile wrist and snapped the bones in two like dried twigs.

She screamed as her hand fell backward, awkwardly, onto her forearm. Searing pain shot up her arm, and, with a swift swipe of his calloused hand, the pirate clubbed her across the face. The force sent her reeling until she collided with the wall at the opposite side of the room. There was a sickening, dull thud as the back of Mariel's head hit the stone masonry.

Kathryn screamed and Mariel lay unresponsive. Winne rushed to grandmother and knelt over her limp body. Large, bloody hands grasped hold of Kathryn, crushing her arm in their vice-like grip, to restrain her. She fought wildly to free herself, but to no avail. The brutish hiss of the savage sounded low, deep, and threatening as he snarled into the back of Kathryn's neck.

"Ye be wishin' ye be dead jest like the ol' witch, after I be finished with ye."

He pulled the chisel from his fleshy shoulder. Blood oozed from the gaping hole and dripped the length of the spike, running in streams down his brawny arm. Kathryn felt her own skin grow hot and sticky as his fresh blood pooled where his fingers gripped her forearm.

"Never!" she cried out. Tears blinded her as she thrashed to break free from his steely grip. A warm sensation pulsed on her chest. The talisman glowed a pale crimson.

The Scarlet Seren had awakened.

With a flick of his wrist, the brute pitched the chisel across the room and sent it clattering loudly against the floor. Mariel lay crumpled with Winne bent over her. A wiry pirate crouched low with his cutlass raised and ready to land the final blow.

"We should finish this an' take the other, too," he said, and looked at Slade for approval.

"Two for th' price o' one, aye?" Slade leered at Winne.

Just as the pirate raised his blade to strike, Kathryn shrieked.

"Stop! I'll go with ye and ye can do with me as ye please." She glanced at Winne. "Only let the others alone." Kathryn choked out the last words in between sobs.

"An' why would we do that?" the pirate said with his cutlass still poised overhead.

"Because killing a witch brings death," she said. Although she didn't believe the fable herself, she hoped the pirate did. The ruse worked. The pirate dropped the cutlass and stepped away from Mariel and Winne.

Just then, Kathryn felt the Seren grow hotter against her chest. Silently, she reached up and took hold of the stone, then whispered a prayer for protection. One by one, lusty grins crept over their faces, and Kathryn knew her ruse was not enough to scare them away.

"Consider this, ye bloodthirsty mongrels ... I'll willingly go along and spare another curse – one worse that the pox that's already befallen each of you here. Should ye liberate my kin, perhaps the power of the seas will heed my call and bring you favor with the Gods and your capt'n. Kill my family, and you'll be cursed by the Morrigan to do with as that devil-God pleases. The choice be yours."

The pirates said nothing but stared dumbfounded at her. From the center of the room, her father moaned

– a sound that comes from only deep within the heart. Head held high, she marched willingly into the crowd of waiting pirates. They parted slightly to let her through. A subtle fear of the trinkets she carried with her, and the power carried with them, kept grimy, wandering hands away from Kathryn as she passed. Stepping across the protective salt line scattered down the length of the threshold, she heard her father call out once more. One by one, the pirates followed her out through the arched doorway and into the misty night. Kathryn moved ahead of the pack, feeling only contempt for the men she now led down the cobblestone path and away from her home. Her tears lessened and her heartache faded as hate took their place.

She thought she heard the weeds rustling slightly near the footpath. Instinctively, she looked near the rock where she fed the little fox. Glowing in the moonlight were two black eyes nestled in a white muzzle. The fox's head tilted slightly to one side as its ebony eyes watched the procession moving down the path. Kathryn begged silently for her little friend to go back into the brush and remain safe. As if the fox could hear her thoughts, it silently scampered away and went unnoticed by anyone but Kathryn. She felt a sense of relief as she looked back to the path, urged on by the men behind her.

Her cheeks had become wet, but she refused to wipe them dry – her last act of defiance. Nothing mattered anymore, and she felt certain that she would soon join her mother in the afterlife. Fog crept over the ground and licked at her feet, making it difficult to see where she walked. She looked up through the misty night air at the moon, still encircled by its ominous ring of hazy light, glowing its warning for her. Suddenly, the eerily still night was pierced by her grandmother's anguished cries coming from the cottage.

Kathryn paused, and intense heartache pierced her for only a moment before she stepped off the path toward the waiting ship below.

Twenty-Seven

THE PIER LEADING UP TO the ship heaved with the tide. Decay had stripped the wood of its strength with each slap of the tide. More than likely, the entire dock would lie at the bottom of the sea in less than a decade. As Kathryn stepped onto the rotting wood, the ramp pitched with the weight of each step. Her captors traipsed behind her, paying no mind to the bounce of the feeble dock. Their stomps threw her off balance. She stumbled forward and nearly tripped into the small boat waiting for her, but caught herself at the last minute by grasping hold of the nearest pirate for balance.

"Leave off me, wench," he spat. He shook off her grip, moved out of reach, and gingerly hopped into the shallow boat.

Rough hands shoved her toward a bench mid-boat that had been occupied by another pirate. He moved aside and she flailed for balance. The longboat tied loosely to the pier was just large enough to accommodate the men and their captive. It pitched violently under her weight as she sat down and steadied herself.

"Ye best be gittin' yer sea legs on, missy," a gruff voice said, poking fun at her.

"Why she's likely to go tumblin' into the drink an' meet ol' Davy Jones a'fore we git off this here dock," bellowed another.

Hoots and howls followed as the pirates each boarded the waiting longboat. Another rough shove drove splinters into her thighs. She winced and tucked her hands underneath her backside for padding. At her heels lay her scant belongings. She pushed these beneath the bench, using only her feet.

Ahead, a formidable ship rested at anchor. The vessel lingered not far off, leaving little time for an escape. Flickering light from lanterns – a sign of life onboard the ship – seemed to blink wild, radiant eyes upon the smaller boat. The crew darted about the rails, eyes cast down at the water in anticipation of the long-boats' arrival. There was little here that looked familiar. Kathryn closed her eyes and focused on the rhythm of the ocean currents as they matched her pulse.

"Ho!"

Kathryn jumped and the boat rocked.

"Hold tight, missy." The pirate caught hold of her, steadying the boat. "Sit yerself still, else I'll tie ye to the bow like a proper Neptune's wooden angel."

Hoots followed and all at once, two pirates took up the oars.

"Ho!" Sinewy muscles rippled along their thick arms as they began to row. They reminded Kathryn of pack animals – only these were men who worked together against the supremacy of the ocean. Clearly, the sea tempered a man's body the way fire tempered steel. She'd seen it before, and knew these were not men to trifle with. She struggled to stay put as each pull of the oar caused the boat to lurch against the choppy water. Mostly, she fought back the pain in her heart as the men carried her farther away from the cliffs. She knew she would likely never see home again and glanced at the black water just inches away.

Death would be a welcome guest. Should she jump overboard to escape these cutthroats? It seemed less foreboding than facing the massive ship. She glanced at the crew. Black eyes kept watch, carefully trained to read their captive's intentions. Any thoughts of escape were frivolous.

"Heh-heh-heh," snorted a pirate as he pulled against the current. "We got a nice lit'le surprise waitin' for ye, missy."

Kathryn turned her head the other way. The other pirate joined his comrade, laughing a high-pitched squeal that sounded like a pig at slaughter, or so Kathryn thought. Chortles echoed across the surface of the dark water, and both men eyed her with lusty satisfaction.

Slap-pull, slap-pull – everything seemed perfectly timed. Kathryn thought she would be sick. Hopefully, she would get her wits about her before boarding the vessel. She'd had little time to collect herself. Within moments they'd reach the vessel. Who knew what she would face there. It loomed overhead as they approached. Kathryn stared wide-eyed at its terrifying beauty.

"It be a Merchantman – the class, as it were," said one of the pirates. He pulled with an oar and nodded his head.

"Impressive," she whispered. She had been taught the names of many vessels used for privateering ventures by her father. *Merchantman* – a class of ship that's name originated from its intended use – to carry merchandise for trade, usually for the East India Company. This ship had obviously been seized, fitted, and now used for illegal gain – certainly foul play.

She looked straight ahead at the starboard side where a part of the long railing had been removed. An enormous opening yawned, waiting to take her in. Dark, leathery faces peered over the rails and stared at the boat's occupants. The pirates' whispers accompanied their random jabs to a neighboring ribcage as they gawked and pointed grimy fingers at her.

Panic swelled to constrict her chest. She couldn't breathe. It was as if the beastly ship was sucking the life from her. She looked around for an escape, anything to get away, but a heavy hand forced her to stay put.

Several thickly knotted ropes were lowered, along with a narrow wooden plank that was laid between the opened side of the ship and the dory. The large pirate who had held her captive had again taken hold of her with the same vice-like grip. He forced her out of the longboat and onto the narrow plank. She pushed back, gasping for air.

"Wait," she wheezed. "Just one moment…I…I…can't…breathe…"

Unable to walk the few steps up the plank, she grasped hold of the nearest thing to her, which happened to be Slade. He lifted her from her feet and shoved her forward. She stumbled again and nearly toppled into the sea below.

"The cap'n waits for no man," he growled. The beast shoved her again and Kathryn stumbled up the plank and landed one step away from the deck. The surface was remarkably polished for the dreadful barge that it was – a beast that would steal her from her home on the heath.

She strained to take in the hillsides. This would be her last glimpse of the tiny cottage set precariously on top of the cliffs. She barely saw it. Pin dot light blinked from the lantern where it hung at the cottage door. Seconds later, the scene blurred as tears filled her eyes. Just then, hands grabbed hold of her skirts to jerk her back and drag her blindly up the rest of the gangplank. She wiped the tears from her cheeks and turned away, filled with the same heartache as her loved ones left behind on the cliffs.

"Step up, missy. Get yerself through the chains and make haste o' it. The capt'n be waitin' fer ye," said a voice behind her, accompanied by another violent shove.

She grasped hold of the "chains" for support. These were railings that ran the length of the ship, lined with rows of black, grimy faces all staring directly at her. Slade heaved Kathryn onto the polished deck, then stepped aside. With hands on hips, he paused to allow the rest of the crew to admire his human plunder. Kathryn landed on hands and knees, and her belongings landed nearby. She dared not move, but quickly took in her new surroundings. There would be no escape now.

The length of the deck had been completely stripped and cleared of anything previously built on it. Situated mid-ship were two large masts and some actively worked by the few of the crew who remained aft. This had obviously once been a naval "ship of the line," and had commanded respect from those who'd sailed onboard, before it had been re-commissioned for privateering. She shook her head. What a sad state of affairs – the ship had been captured by pirates and sentenced to servitude…and, now, so had she.

Men pounded planking into broken seams – scattered evidence the vessel had recently seen battle. Kathryn guessed this was commonplace, which accounted for the cannons that were mounted facing outward through gun ports located just below the chains. A quick estimation suggested there were about twenty cannons onboard, ten to either side of the deck.

Only those crewmen at the gangplank noticed her. The rest seemed preoccupied with different tasks around the ship. A few took leave, and momentarily glanced her way before they disappeared to take up various positions. Others scurried across the well-scrubbed deck and paid no mind, too busy to gawk at the female just brought onboard. Women were bad luck, anyway – everyone knew it. This was an unwelcoming crew. Their sole purpose was to hunt the innocent at sea. Her new home would be daunting, at best.

"Now, what lil' bit o' booty have ye brought us here, Mister Slade?" crooned a sneering, high-pitched whine from somewhere ahead of her.

"Booty fer the crew?" Cornelius sniggered.

"The capt'n decides," Slade growled.

Another shove sent her further out on the deck, and several disheveled, strangely clad men stood up and made their way toward her, dissecting her with ravenous eyes. She froze like the trapped quarry of ravenous predators. Who knew whether she would live long enough to see the next sunrise, and more to the point, who cared? She was fodder for their amusement until the marauders tired of her.

"She's not bad to look at."

"Aye, better than the last."

A rush of laugher followed, each crewmember poking at her in turn with their grimy fingers and taunting with their catcalls. One of them, a tall, bony sailor that looked frail enough for Kathryn to break in half, reached out and took a handful of her wavy hair. He sniffed it with his black, sticky nostrils. She swatted his face and thought she heard more than just the crack of her palm against his skin. She hoped it was his skull.

"Hah, Fenn. She popped ye one, she did!"

Kathryn stood and stared back into black eyes. These scoundrels were no better than a pack of circling sharks, playing with their food before the frenzy begins. Not long after that, the water always ran crimson from the blood of the victim. She wondered how long they would circle her before her blood stained the scrubbed surface of the deck beneath her feet.

Another shove from someone behind sent her stumbling once again, this time into a massive chest. Stinking arms encircled her, constricting any movement. The foul sailor who embraced her started to bounce and weave. Held tight in his arms, he forced her to dance with him, a drunkard's gambol. Someone started to whistle, and the others clamored for their turn with her, pushing and shoving each other out of the way. She heaved her elbow into the man's gut. The rogue let loose and bellowed a boyish "oomph," then doubled over, staggering backwards. No mercy was shown towards the bloke and laughter pealed out from the circle of pirates.

"Leveled by a mere lassie, eh, Scribbs? Poor matey can't hold his own wit' a female."

The crew bellowed again, then suddenly, a deep, commanding voice boomed from somewhere near the bow.

"Mister Scribbs!"

A slight rise in the deck known as the forecastle was home to the front of the ship and was designated as the crew's sleeping quarters. Standing at the pinnacle was the most magnificent being Kathryn had ever laid eyes on. Dark, wavy hair tied back in a queue danced in the sea breeze. Wisps that had come loose tousled around his forehead. His bronzed face contrasted against the linen shirt that covered the skin of his muscular chest.

"Mister Slade, what 'ave ye done? Have ye no mind to the Articles by law?"

The circling men stepped back to leave Kathryn standing alone as she faced the captain. His jaw was tense, but the expression he wore appeared gentle. Still, he was commanding and carried with him an obvious authority that commanded respect. She couldn't take her eyes off of him.

"Aye, Capt'n, I know the Ar'cles an' be mindful of 'em. This wench is a witch healer, same as the old crone up yonder," Slade replied, and nodded his head in the direction of the cliffs.

Silence followed as the captain eyed her. Kathryn caught her breath. It was as if he looked right through her soul. His eyes narrowed slightly as he took her in. One brow lifted, and Kathryn was certain she saw a fleeting look of compassion cross his face. The captain set his jaw and scanned the crew.

"Bring her to me," he ordered.

"Aye, sir!" the men answered in unison and gripped her by each arm.

Kathryn was hauled up six narrow steps to the landing on the forecastle by a seedy pirate and two others. As she made the ascent, her eyes stayed glued to the captain. He carried a strange familiarity about him. Riveted by the most imposing man she had ever met, she could not look away. The moon with its accompanying ring cast a pale halo behind him, giving the illusion he was more than a man.

"A human God…that's what he is," she whispered.

"Too late for prayin' lass," one of the pirates said, and stared to laugh. The captain paused at a doorway, then turned to wait, statuesque and regal. Kathryn's escorts shoved her toward him then stepped away, leaving her to stand alone to meet the imposing captain of the pirate ship, *Revenge*.

Kathryn lifted her chin and looked into his face. Her breath caught again as she locked eyes with his. Pools of emerald green. His were eyes that she knew somehow. His features were well defined, suggesting Greek descent, and his muscles taut beneath the linen shirt. There was an air of defiance – perhaps even rebellion – about him. It was clear that this man could not be fooled by silly superstitions as the others had been.

He said nothing, but stood there, studying her. The others eyed her as well, waiting for any sign from the captain to indicate approval or rejection of their prize. After a few moments, he spoke, but never took his eyes off the young woman who stood before him.

"Where be the injured sailor ye were set off to shore with, Mister Cornelius?" A Scottish brogue indicated an origin similar to her own.

"He's dead." Kathryn heard the words come from her mouth without realizing she had spoken. "Dead," she repeated a little softer.

"Is he now?" the captain continued, eyeing the girl. "What say ye, Mister Seymour?"

Angus Seymour, a stout little man from some fishing town near southern France, spoke with slurred syllables. He had only one eye – a misdirected cork shot from a rum bottle had popped the other from its socket. Angus maintained he'd been ambushed and stabbed in the eye with the tip of a dirk, although no one believed him and the short dagger used by the Scottish buc-caneer was never found. Still, Angus maintained the story was true, but because he could never lie well, the tale always sounded a bit too tall. It was his inability to fabricate a believable narrative that singled him out as the best person for truthful interrogation, which is likely why the captain sought him out now. The stout little pirate shuffled his feet and kept his head down.

"Did ye not hear me, Angus? Did ye lose an ear for hearin' as well as an eye?" asked the captain, irritation edging his tone.

Speaking falsehoods, otherwise known as telling a bold-faced lie onboard a ship, was cause for a good flogging at the mast, and Angus knew he would not be spared if he tried to pass off anything less than the truth. He also knew he'd be caught. Struggling with the words, Angus repeated the tale that Mariel had proposed, the one they'd all agreed upon in the cottage earlier that day.

"Sir, he be dying when we took him to the witch woman. She danced and cursed him, but he fell back and died."

"He died?" The captain cocked his head and stared at Angus.

"Aye." It was the truth, within reason, spoken convincingly by Angus. The burley pirate standing behind Kathryn nodded his head.

"Aye, sir, that be true, it be. We be needin' a healer ever since the surgeon got run through and passed on. This lass be a keeper o' the craft – the same as the old hag practicing in the cottage. We saw it with our own eyes, sure as God be a witness."

Angus tossed the large pirate a scowl with his one good eye. A pirate wearing a large gold earring stood silent behind them all, shuffling his feet.

"Aye, aye, Cap'n, it be true." The gold ring in the crewman's earlobe glinted in the sun as he muttered.

Kathryn listened to the tale woven by the cutthroats and tapped one toe in agitation, but kept her peace. These men weren't so formidable, stammering in front of their captain. A cynical smile crossed her lips. She whispered ancient Celtic words, and in response, fresh sea air blew across the deck and filled her lungs. She took it gratefully, clearing her thoughts.

The captain noticed the sudden breeze and glanced at the sky, then to Kathryn. "Witch, ye say?"

"Aye, sir," Slade spoke up.

"What, pray tell, happened to ye, Mister Slade? Ye look as if ye've garnered the pox while ye were afoot," the captain said and stepped back.

Slade's eyes narrowed. "The lass, there," Slade said and pointed at Kathryn. "She did it."

"The lass?" There was amusement behind the captain's eyes as they darted from Slade to Kathryn. She cocked her head and smiled at Slade.

"Aye, sir. Slade met with the end of a bad spell, he did." Angus nervously shifted his weight, taking care to keep his only eye averted.

"An' she cursed us all while she was at it!" Cornelius added.

The captain swallowed back a chuckle. "Well, then. That makes our situation interesting, now, doesn't it?" He paused for a moment to size up the young Celtic threat. "It seems ye have a prize, indeed. I'll see her below in me cabin, Mister Cornelius. And you, Mister Slade, attend to your wounds. There's little room for more in the sick bay, as it is." He pointed to the remaining men and ordered, "The rest of ye, to your duties!"

"Aye, aye, sir," the pirates sang out in unison as they scampered away in opposite directions. Cornelius took hold of Kathryn's arm and dragged her back to the stairs and the waiting quarters below.

"Prepare to cast off, Mister Archer!" the captain shouted. Orders were given to the deck hands below, directed by a wiry, grey-haired chap donning a scarlet rag tied snugly over his head.

The quartermaster acknowledged the order. "Aye, aye, Captain!"

He barked another order and crew suddenly grew large in numbers. Each man shot a glance to Kathryn before scattering. The crew was incredibly agile on their feet in spite of the sudden lurch of the ship. Kathryn watched their movements and wished for the same sure-footedness. It would be something she would need to learn soon.

The last lingering stare left behind made her feel vile. She looked to its source and saw dark eyes that belonged to the quartermaster.

Twenty-Eight

His eyes narrowed, and, for the first time, Kathryn felt real fear settle within her bones. She looked away, hoping he would disappear along with the others, but he didn't. Instead, the pirate stood fast and watched her for a while, assessing her, as it were. Kathryn was certain she wouldn't measure up to whatever standards the quartermaster held. Mostly, he'd find fault because she was a woman. She was certain of that.

John Rose Archer had been elected quartermaster, and as such was second-in-command. He was mean and heartless, and none dared cross him. Even the captain maintained a respectful but guarded distance. Archer was a dark man with a dark past. He had defected from the crew of the notorious pirate Edward Teach, nicknamed Blackbeard by those who'd had the misfortune of crossing paths with the notorious pirate. Monikers were doled out based on reputations. Anyone laying eyes on Teach's thick, coal-black beard, which covered nearly the whole of his face, would easily understand how he came to be known as Blackbeard the pirate.

As it turned out, the crew of the *Revenge* had elected to make Archer their taskmaster only eight months earlier. He was chosen mainly due to his fierce understanding of the islands, his skill in battle, and his unusual swarthy manner. He was harsh with the men, but had never been voted out of office. In truth, no one dared elect another to take his place. Since the day he had joined the crew, the men had slept with one eye open.

With the exception of one – a young hooligan, who appeared to be on guard and distant, employed against his will or so it would seem – not a single crewman displayed a lack of experience at sea. The coarseness of the men did not surprise Kathryn in the least.

Still, there was the captain.

He stood apart from the rest, eloquent as he observed the men at their duties. After a moment of watching them, he shouted again to Archer. "We'll put to sea within the hour."

"Aye, sir," Archer responded.

Satisfied, the captain then turned his attention to the young rogue, who sat on a pile of coins and crumpled sailcloth. It was clear he was not one of the crew, not really, and Kathryn wondered if he had also been kidnapped. Likely, he had been dumped atop the sailcloth for lack of knowing what to do with him. His eyes were on her, amusement dancing behind them where it should not have been.

"See this scallywag below decks, and then help me to me quarters, Mister Gow. Make certain his pockets be clean."

"Aye, Capt'n," Gow responded, and began to frisk the rogue, who didn't flinch as he was lifted up and patted down. His focus was locked on Kathryn.

"What're you lookin' at, girly?"

Slade stepped up next to Gow. His pustule-covered face grimaced as he took hold of Kathryn's arm.

"Take your filthy hands off me!" she shouted, kicking and clawing at his blistered face. Slade let her go and crossed his broad hands over his face to guard himself.

"She's mad!" Slade shouted.

"Best do as the captain said, Slade. Go see to yerself. I'll handle the wench," Archer said. It was not a suggestion. Just then, a third mate stepped up to help, and snatched her by the sleeve. He lifted his fist overhead, ready to strike.

"Leave off her, you bloody cutthroat," the hooligan shouted. He broke free of Gow's hold and lunged. Fists flew and the youth took an elbow to the gut that leveled him flat to the deck. He pushed himself up and spat blood through split lips. "Is that the best ye can do, old man?" Another punch left him face down on the deck.

Kathryn bit down hard on the hand that held her wrist. For a moment she was free. The brute bellowed and she darted away.

"Nab her, Cuddy," Sam shouted, nursing the bite mark on his wrist.

Gow had recovered enough to grab her as she ran past. He held her around the waist, his grip nearly doubling her in half.

"Stay put, wench," Gow hissed. She felt his breath, hot against her neck, and gagged. "We're not done wit' ye yet."

"Not till I've paid ye back for this!" Sam snarled, and held up the bite marks for all to see.

"Murderers! Thieves! Leave off me!" she cried out, kicking and clawing against the brute that held her from behind. Struggling against the pirate did little, and his grip only tightened to cut off her air. Tiny stars filled her vision, and suddenly, everything went black.

Just then, the young hooligan scrambled to his feet and snatched an oar lying nearby. He returned to the fray, swinging it wildly. The flattened end found its mark and hit Gow squarely between the shoulder blades. With the wind knocked out of him, Gow released his grip on Kathryn. She stumbled onto her hands and knees where she stayed, gasping for air and coughing violently.

Gow regained his footing, though he could scarcely call for help. But that hardly mattered as newly gathered crewmen stepped into the skirmish, happy to lend their fists to a frisky fight.

"She be a right spirited one, she be," someone called out, followed by hoots and hollers from the others.

"Aye. Th' scurvy pup's the problem!"

Several men moved forward with fist and cutlasses raised, but the swinging oar managed to hold them off. During the scuffle, Kathryn's belongings had spilled over the deck, commingling with the few coins left behind with the sailcloth. It posed a new dilemma for the pirates – booty tainted from the private effects of a witch. The temptation was great, but their superstition was far greater.

"What 'ave we here?" a lanky fellow said, bending over the talismans scattered in front of them. Kathryn tried to cry out, but she was still too winded.

"I wouldn't touch that, mate." The solemn voice was familiar.

"And why not?"

Both pirates looked identical. *A crew with twins in it? Now that's interesting*, Kathryn thought and watched them as they hesitated over her things.

"There's conjury in those effects. I've seen it with me own eyes," the one they called Flint answered. He had been in the cottage and had seen Mariel cast her spells.

Indeed, these are superstitious men, Kathryn thought and watched the twins back away.

"They be phylactery and bad luck to anyone who touches it, says I." Kathryn wasn't sure which of the twins had spoken.

"Make the witch take it all up. The conjury's covered up the gold."

"Aye, the witch be the one…before the booty's been conjured, too!"

Kathryn waited with eyes glued to Flint. He seemed the most knowledgeable about Mariel's casting, so he'd be the one the others would listen to. Best intimidate him, if possible. She lowered her chin and looked up at him, trying to give a more menacing look. It worked.

"Aye, get yer…yer stuff, witch. All of it!" Flint said, waving a hand over the spilled belongings.

"As you wish," Kathryn said, and quickly gathered her belongings, tucking them – along with a few hidden coins – into her bag. *They owe me this – at least a little of it. I may be in need of gold to buy my way off this bloody ship!* When she had finished, she tucked the bag under an arm and rose to face the crew.

Behind them, the hooligan waited, eyes dancing around the ship, no doubt looking for an opportunity to slip away. Kathryn gasped. She recognized his face. He glanced at her for a moment, likely sensing her stare, but had little time to make the connection. The lad had been trapped and the oar confiscated. He suddenly pitched forward, shoved by an unseen hand, and landed just feet from where Kathryn stood.

"Please," she said, and glanced at the twins standing to one side. "We've been brought onboard against our will. This filth there…" She pointed to Sam. "…has been rough with me and nearly broke Seth's ribcage just now."

Horror filled the hooligan's eyes, and he shrugged his shoulders, wincing as he did it.

"Marvelous! Now they know my name!" The lad cast her a dark look. "How do you know it? I've never seen ye before in me life!"

She scowled at him. "Indeed, you have, *Seth*. Your thieving antics go far beyond our village's boarders."

Archer stepped forward and began to circle them both. Slowly, he pulled his cutlass from the sash cinched about his waist. Kathryn ignored him and continued to berate Seth.

"Your pirate *mateys* have been less than gentlemanly, as you can plainly see." She held up a torn piece of her skirt, motioned to the bag under her arm, and then wagged a finger at him. Through clenched teeth, she snapped, "So don't fuss at me over a name, *Seth*!"

"The lad can be trained…forced to be a crewman, perhaps." The quartermaster leveled the tip of his blade at Seth, then suddenly moved it to point directly at Kathryn. "But the wench be naught but trouble, an' best be done away wit'. A bad omen to sail wit' a lass at sea, says I." Archer lifted his cutlass over Kathryn's head. Seth gasped. Just as the quartermaster was about to deliver the blow, the captain's voice boomed.

"Hold, Mister Archer! There'll be no blood shed this day." Archer froze mid-stroke. The captain stepped down the causeway and onto the deck in front of Kathryn and Seth. Reaching one hand out to the lass, he turned his attention to the ruffian. "Seth, is it?" Seth nodded and the captain smiled. "Well, then, Master Seth, help me below to me quarters." The captain threw the men a warning glance, and Kathryn stared wide-eyed in return. There was a strain in his voice he could not disguise.

"Aye, sir," Seth said.

"And for those who cannot follow simple orders to take a woman below – without a round of fisticuffs – I'll deal with ye later."

"But, Capt'n…" Finn began but was cut off with a stern look.

Seth stepped forward, taking hold of the formidable man's arm, and placed it around his shoulders. In unison, the two turned and made their way slowly, one step at a time, down the short staircase to the captain's quarters. Droplets of blood landed silently on the smooth wooden deck behind them – a telltale sign that all was not well with the captain.

"Bring her along, Mister Gow, if ye can control the lass this time," the captain called over his shoulder.

The bosun growled. "Aye, Captain!" he said, and glared at Kathryn.

Gow snatched her arm and, this time, his grip held like a vice. He led her ahead of the others to the captain's quarters. There they waited until the captain approached, still oozing beads of crimson over the burnished wood flooring.

"Thank you, Mister Gow," the captain said, and motioned for them to follow.

Kathryn stepped back. An ornately carved door stood ajar, waiting to swallow the captives into the bowels of the pirate ship. The ship groaned and pitched. Kathryn stumbled forward and, without knowing it, entered the soul of the pirate ship, *Revenge*.

Twenty-Nine

WAVES LAPPED AGAINST THE HULL of the merchant ship, rhythmically coaxing it out to sea. Rolling it back and forth, watery arms rocked the *Revenge* as sea creatures danced beneath her. The motion soothed Kathryn, who soon found her eyelids growing heavy in spite of her fear. Deep night would soon arrive, and the motion of the ship on the water, combined with the dark skies, lulled her to sleep. Minute by minute, she fought the urge to sleep, instead focusing her attention on the décor inside the cabin. She stood near a tapestry settee, facing a miniature harpsichord that had been strategically positioned against one corner. It was dusty and appeared to have been forgotten. Windows checkered the back of the ship and lined the longest wall of these quarters. The flicker of moonlight on water danced through dusty glass panes, matching the pitch and lull of the ship.

Without warning, a door groaned as it closed, and the stately silhouette of the captain shadowed the dimly lit walls. He walked to the farthest end, heavily supported by Seth still under his arm.

"There, lad," the captain said, and they made their way to a modest bed tucked against the far wall. Both seemed unaware of Kathryn, who had made her way into a corner. She said nothing but watched them from a distance as Seth lowered the pirate onto his bed. Seth's arms bulged with muscles far too thick for his age. Kathryn watched as they contracted into tight mounds beneath his sleeves as he braced the captain. And though gentle, the captain winced as he lay back, although he refused to cry out in agony.

"Ye'd make a fine cabin boy, I suppose, though the crew would have ye hung at the yardarm. Perhaps it's me duty to save yer hide, given that ye've shown some care to an injured sailor." A grimace crossed the captain's face and he closed his eyes.

"I'd appreciate it, sir," Seth responded.

"Consider it done, then. Help me off with these boots."

Seth carefully removed each boot and set them neatly next to the bed. Next he placed the captain's cutlass on a side table within reach. When all was laid neatly aside, he slid over to the table where he poured a large goblet of wine, then handed it to the captain.

"We'll be needin' three, Mister Seth."

Seth nodded, and Kathryn caught a sideways glance from the corner of his eyes as he poured two more goblets. When he was finished, he paused with one in each hand.

"Take one for yerself, lad…and the last is for her," the captain said, and looked to the shadows where Kathryn stood.

Seth drained his first, and then set the last on the table, glowering in Kathryn's direction. She scowled, but did not move.

"That will do. Take some o' the platter with ye, too, lad. But leave the bulk of it on the table." The captain pointed to a large platter in the center.

Seth spun around and helped himself to a handful of figs and nuts. He shoved them into the pockets of his britches and greedily popped a sugarcoated date into his mouth.

"Now, be off with ye." The captain waved him off.

Seth bowed low. "Aye, sir. Where exactly do I go?"

"Here." The captain tossed a coin to Seth, who deftly caught it between his thumb and forefinger. "Take this, and when the crew accuses ye of piracy, they'll be right and you'll be me cabin boy."

"I…I…beg pardon?" Seth was incredulous.

"Just take it and tell anyone who crosses ye that I slipped it to ye for service in me quarters as cabin boy."

"But no one will believe me," Seth said.

"Ay, that they won't. They'll think ye killed me cold. Most likely, the men will be taken by curiosity to seek the body here in me quarters…if ye follow."

"I don't," Seth said bluntly.

"Are ye daft, boy?" The captain lifted his head and stared at Seth, who shook his head. "Well then, listen, because it pains me to speak too much. The crew will come searchin' for their dead captain. Instead, they'll find me here, safe and sound in me quarters, asleep with the little lassie there."

Seth eyed Kathryn and nodded. "Aye."

"If there be any question about the matter, they'll take it up with me and, likely as not, I won't be happy about being awakened so rudely. Savvy?"

A grin crossed Seth's lip. He understood and was grateful the captain had come up with a plan that would save his neck...unless the crew got to it first. "Aye, sir," Seth replied, and pocketed the coin.

"Find the bosun – Mister Gow – and have him introduce ye to Jonesy and Dobs. They're doppelgängers – brothers, twins, and extremely nimble with weaponry. You could learn a thing or two from 'em. They'll teach ye the ways of privateering and philandering, unlike the folly that landed ye here this morning."

"What about her?" Seth tossed Kathryn another scowl.

"She's none of your concern, boy. Keepin' the skin intact o' your bones is, however. Now get!"

"Aye, sir," Seth replied and glared at Kathryn as he made to leave. It perturbed him that she'd be drinking grog or wine, and eating sweetmeats from the silver platter, instead of him. He hadn't had a full belly in a while and his stomach grumbled in protest. He walked out and shut the door a bit too abruptly behind him.

Kathryn kept her eyes glued on the captain. His shirt was stained a dark crimson and was torn along one side. Blood oozed from the spot and dripped rhythmically onto the coverlet, staining it as well. He shifted and his head lolled back onto the roll used for a pillow. Kathryn's eyes grew wide as she caught sight of an open gash, exposing one side of his ribcage. The captain lay motionless with one arm slung over his forehead, as if by doing so could dull the pain.

"Excuse me, sir," Kathryn whispered. There was no response. She crept a little closer to where the captain lay. "Capt'n?" Still no response. She slid one hand into her bag of herbs to retrieve a long cluster of leaves and a small vial of rosemary tincture.

"The men know nothin' o' this. Savvy?"

Half expecting him to be dead, she startled and caught her breath. "Aye," she whispered. It would be far worse should she fail to keep his secret, so the promise was easy to make. "Let me tend to your wounds. I can help. I have the medicines ye need." The proposal sounded muddled, but the offer was sincere. Still, he heard genuine concern in her voice.

He turned to face her. Kathryn was instantly drawn into his alarming green eyes and could barely breathe.

"I…I have ways to help," she whispered.

"What are ye called, lass?"

"Kathryn."

The captain's focus on her intensified, and his emerald eyes seemed to grow larger. His expression grew perplexed before he looked away.

"Well then…missy," he said, refusing to speak her name. "Ye'd best be about it and ne'er a word on it. Mind me well on this."

Gently, she pulled back the torn muslin shirt and exposed the gaping wound. Dark, meaty flesh oozed fresh blood from between the clean edges of his sliced skin. There was no stench – no indication of a brewing sepsis. However, given the conditions of the ship, it wouldn't be long before infection set in. From the appearance of the injury, she couldn't be sure how much attention it had received. She scanned the room for any sign of fresh water and found a drinking cask with enough to fill a teacup. It would have to do.

"Water for drinkin' be scarce at sea. We use grog or wine to quench our thirst." He waved a weak hand in the direction of the full goblet still waiting on the table.

"I need to clean the wound," she said, snatching up the water. "And somethin' to sew the flesh?"

The captain sighed and directed her to a dark leather satchel lying on the floor. "Bring me the bottle as well."

A dark green bottle lay on the sideboard next to a pile of maps, parchment, and strange little instruments she assumed were used for navigation. Within moments, she'd retrieved the bottle and satchel and returned to the captain's side. She handed him the half-empty bottle, which he gratefully accepted and bit the cork between his teeth. After a loud *pop*, he spat out the cork and took in long, hard swallows of the amber liquid that Kathryn guessed must be rum.

She knelt beside his bed and laid the leather satchel beside her. Next, she unrolled a long line of what could only be the dead surgeon's medical instruments. Most of the tools were stained dark or rusted. Nearly all were foreign. Kathryn studied each one and had no idea what to do with them. *Would Mariel know what each is used for…at least well enough to make clean work of saving lives?* Kathryn sighed. Rummaging deeper inside one of the leather pockets, she found a long semi-circular needle that looked more like something used to mend sails than skin. She took it up, along with a piece of thick thread lying loose near a small wooden mallet.

He set the bottle on the floor and sighed. "We'll need more."

"May I?" She did not wait for an answer, but lifted the bottle to her nose. The smell of sweet, raw alcohol hit her in the face, and she knew this was stuff that would kill anything it touched, except maybe the insides of a man's gut. Carefully, she dumped some of the rum over both needle and thread.

Mixing water with what was left, she poured it over the gaping edges of his flesh. He winced, but did not move. She paused momentarily to allow him some reprieve from the sting of the alcohol, but he urged her to continue. She repeated the process, and, when satisfied, rose to snatch as many linen napkins as she could find from the great table. The captain did nothing, but watched with interest as she made herself privy to his belongings with no thought to the consequences of plundering a pirate captain's quarters.

Returning to the bed, she knelt alongside him, took the long, curved needle into trembling fingers, and prepared to sew. The captain purposefully turned away, which Kathryn was secretly grateful for – she dared not look into his green eyes while piercing his flesh with a needle.

He nodded for her to begin. She looked deep into the open wound, still oozing with the liquid mixture poured over it. Bone, yellow fat, and sinew peered out through gaping muscle. Kathryn studied it, but could see no evidence of injury to bone or organ. She decided she could close the wound safely. Pinching the tender, moist flesh between her fingers, she stabbed the raw edges with the needle and began to sew with long, even stitches. The cut was clean but would take a while to close properly. Kathryn settled herself into the task.

Once, quite accidently, he moved and the back of his hand brushed her fingers. Her heart leapt. With steady fingers and a quaking heart, she tried to distract herself by humming the tune of an ancient Celtic song Mariel had sung. The tune was old, one she'd heard from the time when she was little. Kathryn's youthful voice rose and fell…and the melody seemed to soothe him.

"There, Captain, we're almost done," she said after a while. The procedure had taken nearly an hour. "You'll be fine but will have to take care until the edges have healed properly."

When she finally finished, she laid the bloody needle aside and reached for her medicines and herbs. She pulled long silver leaves from her pouch and placed them one by one over the newly closed wound. She then poured a tincture made from rosemary and rare Chinese Da Ji blossoms onto several of the napkins, which stained them, a pale jade color. These were gently placed over the top of the silver leaves. Almost immediately, the lines in the captain's face softened – a sign the tincture had effectively dulled his pain. Ever so slightly, his lips parted and he smiled. Indeed, the captain seemed captivated by her.

Kathryn placed the prepared bandage across his chest and let it rest there while she finished rubbing the tincture over his newly sutured skin. For a moment, she allowed her hands to rest upon his bare chest. The muscles beneath his skin rippled at her touch, and her heart leapt again. It was as if electricity had passed from the beating of his heart into her palms. She pulled back, a bit startled by the sensation. None of it went unnoticed by the captain.

"Healing hands," he said. It was a simple explanation that allowed Kathryn to save face. She nodded and felt grateful that he had spared her an explanation. She blushed, and he smiled at her innocence.

In truth, her unsophisticated air was refreshing. A corner of his mouth lifted into a crooked grin. Kathryn's face grew hot as the blood rushed deeper into her cheeks. In an effort to avoid his gaze, she shifted her attention to where she looped the last of the bandage covering the wound. She then dropped her focus to the floor. The warmth of his skin against hers still burned across her palms.

Without warning, he reached out, and, with a gentle touch, lifted her chin and peered into her sea-blue eyes. He said nothing, but studied her features for what seemed like an eternity.

"Sir…I," she stammered, her cheeks flushed again. "I don't even know your name."

He said nothing for a moment but continued to stare, which unsettled her further. Kathryn began to nervously tap a foot against the floorboards, but refused to look away.

He sighed. "Phillips. Captain John Phillips."

She repeated his name softly. They sat together for a moment, suspended, rising and falling with the lift and lull of the ship, eyes locked. Fire crawled along Kathryn's spine and she instinctively pulled away, turning from him. A low chuckle rolled forth from him as she attempted to compose herself. On the center table she saw a goblet that she quickly snatched up, and drained its contents. He chuckled again and amusement danced behind his eyes. Then, he motioned to the table.

"That's yours," he said, and pointed to platter. "Drink a bit more…then eat sommat. I won't have ye wasting away when I'll likely be needin' your assistance again. Ye'd best think on takin' up quarters with me where ye'll be safe this night."

Her mouth opened in protest, but before she could object, his hand rose and stopped her. "Rest yerself there." He pointed to the settee on the other side of the room, then laid his head back on his bedding. The strong drink and tincture had finally taken hold. The pirate captain closed his eyes and slept.

Kathryn faced the platter of fruit, nuts, and biscuits. She was hungry, and the food was inviting. Silently, so as not to disturb anything, she made her way to the table and helped herself to the food spread out there. With the water crate now empty, there was nothing else to quench her thirst except for the spirits, so she drank. Once satisfied, with dusty biscuits and dried fruit, she moved to the settee and allowed herself to sink into the cushions. A dull ache of exhaustion had spread through her muscles. Candlelight burned from the lantern that was suspended from one of many sconces. Not wanting to extinguish it, she watched the flame dance, and soon began to feel the effects of the drink as it warmed her body and numbed her mind.

The sound of wind and waves crashed against the sides of the ship to mix with male voices that sang, vibrant and full, somewhere on the other side of the cabin walls. For the first time since that day's sun had risen above the heather outside her grandmother's cottage, her heart was at peace.

Rocking with each swell of the ocean, she drifted off to sleep without dreaming. Night crept forward and the moon smiled down on the *Revenge*, which bobbed like a cork on sparkling ebony waters. There was no longer a ring around the moon as the stars danced in and out of lacy clouds.

And so it remained through the night as the great ship sailed out to sea and farther away from a young witch's home on the cliffs.

Thirty

EACH CREWMEMBER ONBOARD THE *REVENGE* took a turn as sentinel. Mid-watch was the most difficult for any sailor to stay alert, but a good flogging waited for anyone who ill-fatedly fell asleep during shift. As the 4 a.m. hour rolled around and morning-watch commenced, the winds began to intensify. It was a good sign when accompanying a clear, golden sunrise. The seas would be favorable this day, as indicated by the morning dew that blanketed the surface of the ship and glimmered in the rising sun. Mindful of the hour, Archer rousted the crew. He called to unfurl the sheets, hoist the mainsail, and commanded the men about their duties.

The faint morning light stole through the glass panes lining the rear wall of Captain Phillips' cabin. It slowly crept along the floor to the settee where Kathryn slept. Sunrise settled over the divan, blanketing her in gold. From another part of the ship, a constant pounding on wood planks and the sound of male voices suddenly woke Kathryn with a start. She dared not move, but, instead, tried to familiarize herself with her surroundings.

"Haul up the ratlines, the fore an' maintop bowlin'.

Haul up the ratlines, the bowlin', haul!"

The song rose in pitch as it was sung at a faster pace that matched each shouted, "Haul!" with a strike on the planks or a tug on the ropes.

"Haul up the ratlines, the bosun he's a growlin'.

Haul up the ratlines, me hearties, haul!"

Kathryn blinked a few times, listening to the song sung by the crew as the sails were worked. She scanned the cabin for anything familiar and sluggishly recalled the events of the night before. Her eyes fell upon the bed on the opposite side of the room, and she remembered the man lying on top.

She was not alone. The dressing she had wrapped around the sleeping captain's chest the night before remained intact. Scant amounts of yellowish-pink fluid had soaked through on the sides, which meant she would need to change the dressing sometime before nightfall. But bandages were nowhere to be found in these quarters. Eventually, she would have to venture out of the safe haven of the captain's quarters and search the rest of the ship for some kind of dressing material. She rose from the settee and silently made her way across the room to where the captain lay.

His breath moved in an even tempo as she watched him sleep. With an unsteady hand, she reached out to feel the temperature of his skin. *It's imperative that I touch him…to make certain the fevers haven't taken hold*, she reminded herself. Gently, the back of her hand met his forehead, then travelled to the side of his cheek. There was heat as she touched him, but not from a fever – a flush warmed her skin as her heartbeat quicken. Yet, his flesh felt cool.

Kathryn pulled away. Relieved the night had not brought a bad turn for the pirate, she allowed herself to feel the first real emotions of a woman. Gently, she reached to the top of his head and stroked the dark tresses there, soft to the touch – so unlike the coarse brigand they belonged to. This man was beautiful, meant for more than just ravaging the seas…perhaps meant for her.

Without warning, a hand shot up and seized her by the wrist. Kathryn froze, afraid to move for fear he would think her a thug. She stared wide-eyed at the captain, who appeared to be asleep. He was still, except for his hand gripping her wrist in mid-air. Surely, if she moved, he would snap it in two. Still, his eyelids were closed and his face was relaxed. She whispered the ancient Celtic prayer for peace and waited for it to take effect. Gradually, his grip loosened its hold and his hand fell limply back to the bed.

Shaken, Kathryn backed away, carefully retreating so as not to wake him. She silently moved toward the door. Midway there, her back bumped into something painfully solid. Fearful that the barrel of a pistol lay squarely against her spine, she turned ready to meet a foe. Instead, she faced the knobby corner of the oak table placed in the middle of the room.

"Oh, Kathryn," she whispered, relieved, and eyed the contents of the tray placed squarely in its center. Food from the night before lay spread out, undisturbed and waiting to be consumed. Kathryn snatched one of the apples and moved swiftly through the cedar doorway, leaving the captain to snore soundly in the cabin alone.

"At last," she breathed.

Sunlight greeted her with blinding radiance that caused her to blink against it. She stood at the bottom of a short set of stairs and waited for her eyes to adjusting to the brilliant morning light. The deck of the *Revenge* had already come to life. Men were everywhere, moving in sync as they pulled on the lines to set the sails in time with their robust song. Wind had picked up from the north, filling the canvas and increasing the ship's speed to approximately 18 knots.

"Heave to ye filthy bilge rats. Put yer backs into it, mates!" The quartermaster's voice boomed from across the deck. "Belay the runnings, Mister Moody, an' firm it this time or it be the yardarm for ye."

Kathryn nipped at the apple and watched them at their work. They moved together like a well-oiled machine as they coaxed the ship to greater speeds. It wasn't without a sense of awe that she studied their movements. They may have been called pirates, but they were masters of the sea – a title each had obvious rights to claim. She stepped up to the deck and scanned the horizon, passing Seth, who rushed past without saying a word. He headed to the quarters below where the captain slept, barely noticing her. Apparently, their shared origin in the village above the cliffs was not enough to bind them together as friends. *So be it*, she thought and stepped aside, as he brushed past her and down the causeway.

Surrounding the ship, the water swelled with no sign of land anywhere in sight. Above, the sky bared itself in cloudless blue. She watched the men straining with each pull on the lines. There was a sudden lurch as the sails caught wind, lifting the ship and plunging it forward. Her breath held with the sudden drop that gave the exhilarating sensation of falling.

"That's it, mateys. Now we have the winds on our side," Archer called out to the men.

A few swabs, scrubbing the deck not too far from where she stood, noticed her intrusive stare and decided to take a closer look at the new passenger. Kathryn recognized one of the men – a scallywag who had been part of the small group that had brought her injured father to the cottage and to Mariel. Kathryn edged back as the pirates dropped their holystones and stood, one by one. Slowly, they made their way towards her, eyes on the Seren hanging about her neck.

"Aye, the capt'n be done with the wench and left her to the crew," croaked a greasy, fat man wearing a knitted cap.

"Hah!" burst out from the few, who were now within a yard of where she stood.

Kathryn said nothing, but waited, anchored in place. The pirate she had recognized stepped closer and reached a calloused hand out to her throat. She prepared for the worst, but the gnarled hand paused, taking hold of the Seren instead.

"Aye, an' there be a treasure, as well, a-waitin' for plunderin'," he sneered.

His twist on words did not escape any there, and their laughter pitched louder with the joke. Kathryn understood now. The captain had exercised great wisdom when he'd ordered her to stay the night in his cabin. There, she was indeed safe from the pirates – something that might not be repeated. Sensing the men's intentions, she stiffened and tried to appear confident, unable withdraw as they crowded around her.

"What do you want with me, filthy dogs?" she snapped, and regretted the words the moment they'd left her lips.

"Oh, there's much we'd take from ye, sissy," the pirate hissed. His gnarled hand held firm on the Seren, and Kathryn could feel the color change from ash to amber within his fist.

She remembered the warning written on the lid of the Seren's box, as well as the words of her grandmother: *Lo, adorned mid peace.* She closed her eyes and willed herself into stillness. Forcing her breath to match the rhythmic lift and drop of the ship, she invited peace into her soul. The Seren grew warmer in the dirty pirate's hand, which made the trinket only more enticing to him. He yanked on the stone, and the silver thread separated itself, allowing the Seren to fall easily from Kathryn's neck. Slowly, she opened her eyes, and time stood still as she watched the little group of men cheer on their crewmate.

The thief shuffled his feet in a victory jig as he held the Seren aloft, which was now a brilliant shade of scarlet. He danced in circles, displaying the prize for all to see. The stone deepened into the color of rubies. More men joined the gaiety as they slapped their comrade on the back and passed crude remarks between them. Kathryn did not move but continued watching them in stillness, knowing their moods would soon change.

With his gnarled fingers, the grizzled man placed the Seren around his own thick neck. As he did so, the silver thread magically reattached itself together from behind. Strutting around the circle, he displayed the magnificent stone, which began to pulse while the other pirates cheered. Slowly, the crowd grew larger.

"She's a fine beauty, for certain she be," proclaimed the strutting pirate.

"Th' biggest ruby I've ever seen!"

"That be the property o' the crew and be taken 'fore the mast for biddin'," one of the others called out from the back of the crowd.

Arms flew into the air as several of the pirates scrambled to pluck the Seren from their comrade's throat. He fought back and the Seren responded in kind, changing its hue to fiery red. Steam rose from the stone's surface.

"The Seren has awakened," Kathryn said, but no one heard her.

The pirate clawed at it, whether to protect the stone from the greedy fingers of the other pirates or to lift it from his flesh, she was not certain. But the man's expression had changed to one of terror, and the smell of cooked meat followed him as he moved. He bellowed in distress. Suddenly, the entire party of pirates stopped and gawked at their crewmate. The crimson intensified about his neck. It was clearly magic at work. A few of the onlookers crossed themselves.

"Help me," he bawled.

No one lifted a finger. Each of them merely watched as the pirate fell to his knees. The Seren illuminated, a flaming blood red color, and started to rotate. Spinning in slow motion, the silver thread began to coil. Inch by inch, the strands about his neck tightened until, suddenly, his face turned a deep shade of purple. The solid silver thread had twisted itself into a noose.

The Sigil of Defense was alive and doing its work. Bewitched threads had sealed themselves into one, all the while tightening its grip around the pirate's throat. His flesh reeked as black, charred skin blistered beneath the pulsating stone. He fell onto his back and clutched the Seren but was unable to free himself from it – all the while the silver thread tightened its clutch to cut off his air. The pirate seized in minute spasms while the Scarlet Seren strangled him. Within moments, his large eyes rolled and his legs jerked one final time. A moment later, it was over. Everything stopped as his black tongue fell through a ghastly grin while the bloody whites of his eyes bulged open.

The pirate was dead.

No one moved. Archer had made his way over to see what had happened. The crowd parted to allow the quartermaster a better look. His dark eyes studied the corpse, and then darted to Kathryn. She stepped back, but did not flee – a wise decision in spite of the black gaze that held her.

"What happened?" Archer asked without taking his eyes from her. The response came in muffled "hmmms" and shuffled feet. No one dared answer, which left the burden to Kathryn. How could she respond to the brute? Death would take her with the sharp end of Archer's blade no matter what was said. She swallowed against a dry throat and waited for it.

Just then, Seth mounted the stairs and Archer spotted him.

"Here, boy," he ordered. "Take up that…that thing from ol' Flint's neck. Make haste o' it, boy."

Unaware of the events just taken place, Seth stood, looking over the dead man's body. He bent down to grasp hold of the ruby stone seared into the corpse's chest, but paused to look up at Kathryn. She returned his gaze with a stern warning and shook her head.

"No, Seth, don't."

"And why should he listen to the likes o' ye, witch?" Archer spat.

But Kathryn ignored him and kept her eyes on Seth, instead. "I did not do this. You know it to be true. The scum stole the stone from me and it strangled him for it."

Seth's hand stopped mid-air. "It strangled him? Magically it did this?"

"I don't know what it's capable of," she said and shook her head again. "Seth, please do not touch it!"

He cautiously arose and backed away from the carcass.

"Do it, boy!" Archer shouted, but Seth refused. Archer drew his cutlass.

"Wait!" Kathryn said. "Let me."

As Kathryn moved toward the body, the pirates parted. She studied the Seren for a moment, then began to speak in Gaelic, the way Mariel had done.

Her voice became a whisper and her soul melted back into stillness.

"It's a witch's curse, it be," someone said from behind. No one dared move until she was finished.

"Come forth, Seren," she said at last.

Slowly, peacefully, the silver noose unwound and magically separated into two threads that detached from behind. The brute's throat had nearly been severed. Answering her call, the stone floated upward, landing easily into her hand.

It was as if the Seren knew her. She placed the talisman around her own neck and the two silver threads rejoined. Once again, the Seren lay quietly over her heart. The stone had returned to its original ivory color, becoming cool and comforting to the young sorceress wearing it.

She now understood the power it contained and the protection it provided. Indeed, it was as Mariel had prophesied. The subtle meaning in the warning inscribed on the lid now made sense. She knew she would be safe as long as she harnessed its power wisely and followed the advice of her grandmother.

The circle of pirates withdrew, mouths gaping open with gasps of "Witch" and "Sorceress." A few more made the sign of the cross across their bare chests or foreheads. Kathryn turned to face them – powerful and commanding – much like her grandmother had been in the cottage. She said nothing, only stared at them as, one by one, the pirates backed away and scattered to their individual duties. Archer turned to the last two mates, swabs that shared duties with the dead man.

"Cast the body into the sea, and there be no more talk o' it, savvy?"

He then turned to face Seth, who stood just off from the rest, eyes wide and fixed on Kathryn. Archer swung, striking the cabin boy in the face, brutally knocking him to the ground.

"That be for disobeyin' me orders," he growled. "The next time I tell ye to fetch sommat, mind ye do it!"

Archer stomped back to the sails and the men anxiously attending to them. Seth's face had already begun to puff up, along with his eye. He rubbed the surface as Kathryn moved to him and extended her hand.

"Leave off me! I want none of your cursed ways." He swatted her hand away. "You bring nothing but trouble…just as the legend says," he snapped.

"What legend? The only thing I saw was the quartermaster's cruelty. He's a wretch who doles out punishment where it doesn't belong. You did nothing wrong, Seth. You didn't deserve the back of his hand."

"I disobeyed orders, and I won't be doin' it again. Not for your sake or anyone else's, rest assured on that." Seth eyes darkened as he stared up at her. "You're bad luck, Kathryn."

"I'm not bad luck, Seth." He looked at the Seren. "This was given to me by a great sorceress for protection, so therein lies fate. The dead man had no leave to take it, and that's what killed him. You would be dead, too, if you had followed the quartermaster's orders."

He stood up, but refused to look at her. Just then, the dead man's body was heaved over the side of the ship, followed by a muffled splash.

"And that be his fate for crossin' paths with ye," Seth spat.

"Hate me if ye wish, but do one wise thing today. Take this," she said. From beneath the waist of her skirt, she retrieved the amulet her grandmother had made. Alabaster cloth caught the sunlight and illuminated the trinket momentarily, which caught Seth's attention. Perhaps this was something he could barter with. He took it hesitantly, turning the pouch over sideways, studying its outline. It was obvious that Seth was afraid to untie the strings to peek at the contents inside. Kathryn thought he might give it back out of sheer superstition, but he quickly shoved it out of sight into the pocket of his britches. She smiled in return.

"Wear it always and it will give ye protection from the likes o' him." She nodded her head in the direction of Archer. "This I promise."

"And I'll be sellin' it…this I promise!"

He hastily took his leave and wiped his face with the back of his hand as he disappeared into the shadows of the ship. She sighed.

"It won't be easy makin' allies," she said. No one was around to hear, nobody was listening…except for one. Eyes bored into the back of her skull, drawing her focus to the captain standing below on the stairwell. She returned his gaze, and a tense look of displeasure crossed his face.

Thirty-One

ARTICLES HAD BEEN DRAWN UP for the pirate ship *Revenge* immediately upon John Phillips' election as captain of the ship. These Articles were a list of "rules" each crewmember had sworn to by oath, a promise of loyalty made over an axe, which could only be broken on penalty of death. A promise to uphold these Articles involved laying one's hand over the head of the carpenter's axe and swearing an agreement to follow all rules recorded therein, else suffer punishment at the hand of the bosun, or, worse, John Rose Archer.

The Articles were posted so that none could feign ignorance, and it was to these laws that Captain Phillips now spoke with the crew. Midday had come and the pirates had been called together before the mast.

"Make certain the lass receives an invitation to attend, now will ye, Mister Sparks?" Captain Phillips ordered the ship's gunner. James Sparks was in charge of the cannon and armory – he wasn't a messenger.

"Aye, aye, Capt'n," Sparks said, and then added under his breath, "Why ye would have a woman about a ship such as this is beyond my reckoning…" The captain flashed a look and Sparks quickly made his escape, all the while muttering under his breath as he searched for Kathryn.

Within moments, the entire crew had rushed to the deck and stood at attention, facing mid-ship. Captain Phillips stood before them, surveying his men. There seemed to be little indication of his pain or injury.

He hides his discomfort well, Seth thought as he watched the captain move. Bulky by nature, the Royal Navy's blue coat was heavily decorated with gold overlay and buttons that covered any hint of the bandages beneath. Kathryn had done a fine job of dressing the wound when she'd wrapped it the night before. *Indeed, he does not let on that he is wounded.* Seth cocked his head and smiled.

It was clear by the captain's countenance that he had earned the title of commander. However, the roguish air he carried about him gave clues to his true vocation as a pirate. Still, he had their respect – Seth's included.

"What say ye to this mischief? Have ye forgotten the Articles a'fore ye?" the captain's voice boomed. "None be spared, says I, to the punishment that awaits any man who breaks his oath o'er the axe."

The men shifted uncomfortably, and most stared at their feet.

"It appears Mister Flint has gone the way o' Davy Jones' locker, an' good on it, says I. The dark spot was burned into his flesh this very day," he continued.

"Sir?" a weak voice came from the cluster of men. "The witch cast a hex on 'im. We saw it with our own eyes. The ruby grew angry and burned poor ol' Flint's chest black. That be the black spot he be cursed with."

"Ay…" John Phillips' brogue grew thick. The Welch "ay" preferred over a salty dog's "aye" flavored his tongue. He nodded. "Ay indeed, Mister Cade, that be true. Fate cast its lot on Flint for plundering the stone belongin' to the lass and killed him dead." The captain rebuked them all. "Mind ye well the Articles o' this ship. Fate killed Flint dead for breakin' the third, which speaks on lootin' and plunderin."

He tapped with one finger at a line of writing midway down the top half of a large parchment sheet nailed securely to the helm. John Nutt, the ship's navigation master, had taken it down from its post on the quarterdeck and presented it before the crew at Captain Phillips' request.

Article III for the Pirate Ship Revenge
– If any Man shall steal any Thing
in the Company, or game, to the
value of a piece of Eight, he shall be
Maroon'd or shot.

"Sure enough, the devil took Mister Flint. Cursed, he was. Seems he was spared an appointment as the governor ashore his own private island. Mind that ye not be makin' the same mistake as ol' Flint and find yerself cast into the sea for shark folly."

"Aye, cursed…"

More scuffling of feet followed the captain's last statement, which was accompanied by a few men who made the sign of the cross and swiftly spat on the deck. Only a few dared look directly at Captain Phillips – and no one ventured to look at the young sorceress standing off to one side. Their superstitious minds had quickly gotten the best of them.

"Ye best be mindin' this as well." His voice was full and rose over the roar from the waves that crashed against the ship. He pointed again to the parchment, this time near the bottom.

Article IX for the Pirate Ship Revenge — If at any time you meet with a prudent Woman, that Man that offers to meddle with her, without her Consent, shall suffer Death.

"Surely, it be a warnin' to us all as proved by the hex that fell on one of our own this morn." The comment was muttered by one of Flint's swabs. "I watched the whole cursed thing with me own eyes."

This brought the men to hop in a circle as they crossed themselves and spat again. A few stole glances in Kathryn's direction. Archer shook his head in disgust, and Sparks dropped a hand to the cutlass at his side. Both men were staring at Kathryn, but she could see fear behind their black eyes.

Seth had narrowed the gap to position himself a little closer to the captain. He was obviously intrigued by what was being said. Though considered uneducated by practical means, Seth could read, and was one of only a few that took interest in deciphering the handwriting scribbled over the parchment. Kathryn noticed Seth's hand was carefully placed over his britches pocket where he'd placed her amulet earlier. She smiled.

When the captain had finished his speech, he shot Kathryn a stern look, then called on Mister Fern, the ship's carpenter, and the bosun to finish the meeting. He then ordered Archer to follow him, and the two officers made their way through the assemblage toward the ship's stern. Captain Phillips took a position at the helm, his hands solid on the wheel. As the two men talked, they were soon joined by a third, Master Nutt. All three men wore solemn looks to match their voices, which rose only briefly when pointing to charts and then to the sea. Theirs was a private conversation – everyone knew it. So distance was afforded the three men, and the crew kept their eyes averted as all three talked – all but Kathryn. When the meeting had ended, Captain Phillips signaled, and the cluster of pirates that had gathered on the main deck scattered. Fern and Gow made certain the deck was cleared before parting, each going their separate ways.

Soon, the captain moved aside and left Nutt to stand at the helm. Kathryn sensed a shift in the pirates' mood, particularly at the captain's departure, and she knew her presence had become unwelcome. Those that stood at the mast gave her dark looks.

"I'm leaving in peace," she said and crept portside.

"Ye're not welcome here," a voice called out as she moved to the back of the ship. She ignored it and slipped behind the flagstaff, where the ship's colors were flown. Oddly, the British flag was flying instead of the infamous Black Flag she'd heard was used by pirates. As if he'd heard her thoughts, Seth stepped out from behind a pile of old rope.

"There's a reason for that," he said, and lifted his eyes to the flag.

"I don't understand. Why the British flag?"

He tossed back a piece of frayed rope that had been reworked into oakum – used for caulking the seams of the ship. Little onboard a sea vessel was ever cast off as waste, and Kathryn was impressed to see the same held true for a pirate's ship.

"We fly the British colors in open waters," Seth said, lowering his voice. "Then, when we meet a ship we fancy, we hoist the true colors and plunder. They never fancy we sail under the Black Flag 'til we're on 'em, always thinkin' we're friendly…that is, 'till the Jolly Roger unfurls. It's the element of surprise, and a good plan, methinks."

"You speak as if you're one of them," she said.

"You…me…we *both* are. Anyone who sails onboard this vessel sails under the colors at mast, and you'd best get used to the idea of it, Kathryn. Holding a haughty head in company with pirates is likely to earn you the wrong end of a cutlass."

He leaned against the edge of the rail that ran the length of the ship. Kathryn stayed put, eyes focused on the sea. Below, white caps rolled in erratic crests. The ocean was vast, blue, and alive. Cutting through the white caps like a hot blade through iced tallow, the ship moved with ease. Occasionally, a school of dolphin would surface to play in the ship's wake for a time before they would arch and dive off in another direction, or disappear underwater.

"Seth, what can ye tell me about Captain Phillips?" she asked. She kept her eyes to the sea and her voice deceptively light.

"What do you mean? I can tell you quite a lot…but I won't." Biting one side of his cheek, his face implied he'd been insulted by the question. "I'm loyal enough. He's been more generous than most would have been under the same circumstances."

"What I meant to say is, how'd he come about that gash in his side? It's purely for healin' purposes I'm askin'." She kept her focus on the water and shifted her weight. "You're closer to him than I am," she added. Seth began to relax a bit.

"I heard tell of it – a right nasty battle, I heard." He pointed to an empty sea as his mind replayed an image. "There, on the other side of the reef near the south tip of the channel, three or four ships waited."

"Waited? For whom?"

"Who do you think? The *Revenge*, this very ship." A peeved glanced followed the comment, but he continued anyway. "Sallee Rovers, apparently. A mean lot that pirated up and down the coast of Hispaniola."

"But the Sallees do not frequent those waters."

"Not their usual hidey-hole, to be certain. But this band set out with vengeance against the Spanish. The crew sailed right into 'em, and they waylaid the *Revenge*. It's as simple as that."

"There's nothing simple about an ambush, Seth." She leaned back and shook her head. He grinned and shifted his gaze.

"Sometimes it's simple, particularly if it's a Spaniard you're after."

"But the *Revenge* isn't a Spanish ship. The crew's mostly British or Welsh, methinks. Capt'n Phillips is a Scot by his dialect." Kathryn's eyes went to the water.

Seth shrugged. "Rumor has it he's British. I know nothin' about derelicts." Seth shrugged again for emphasis.

"Dialect. By the Gods, Seth, have ye no formal education? The word means…"

He looked away. "I don't care about a word. I'm educated enough. I know the streets and the sea. Somethin' ye'd best learn quickly out here." He waved a hand at the water. "There are those who'd think nothin' of stealin' the ship and cuttin' your pretty throat at the same time."

Kathryn swallowed and thought of the gash along the captain's side. "It's not right, Seth." She tried to appear nonchalant. In truth, she had been drinking in every word that spilled from Seth's mouth.

"The men fought brave, I heard. Most were struck down to meet Davy Jones." He made the cross sign and spat on the deck. "The capt'n was steadfast, I heard – fightin' half their crew by himself." Seth slashed the air with an invisible cutlass, and the effect was dramatic. Kathryn feigned a gasp and he continued. "Then, after strikin' them all down, the Sallee capt'n drew his cutlass and run Capt'n Phillips through – only, the Black Mark wasn't on him that day. When he saw what that scurvy Sallee's blade had done, Capt'n Phillips rose up and cut off the scurvy scum's head in one blow, and sent the cur down to meet the devil hisself!"

"But the capt'n wasn't really run through. Just the gash?"

"Aye." With a final blow of the invisible cutlass, Seth finished the saga and nodded, proud of the fine tale he'd just told. He looked at Kathryn and splayed a toothy grin. "It's true, every word of it!"

She wasn't sure how much of his story to believe – most had been exaggerated for her benefit, of that she was certain. But at least now she understood why the ship had fallen under recent repairs and how the fresh cut had found its way to John Phillips' ribcage.

"What happened to the other ships afterward?" she asked, coaxing him further.

"They say that from the tip of his cutlass, Capt'n Phillips held up the dead man's head for all to see, especially the crew o' the Sallee Rover pirates. Strike their colors, they did, and fled like bilge rats a-runnin', never to be seen again."

"And that's why they came to the cottage, then, to bring my fa…" She stopped mid-sentence. "…the wounded sailor to the healer, Mariel?"

Seth nodded. "I suppose so. I was chased down and landed here by accident. The pirates nearly shot me dead."

"And the capt'n was already injured then?"

"Aye, although I didn't know it at the time. I was too busy watching out for my own skin at the time. They nearly killed me, those bloody pirates!"

"Well, you're alive, so be glad of it," she said, and smiled at him. "I'm glad too, and so is the capt'n, it seems." Seth looked away, his face a bit pinker than before. The pair stood side by side in silence for a time, staring at the sea. Then, breaking the silence, she added, "It was a good story, Seth."

He grinned, and she patted his arm. They remained, as they were, eyes out to sea – caught up in thoughts of the Sallee Rovers, the pirates, and a captain. It all made sense now. The current changed and the ocean swelled as the two considered for a time the story just shared.

A friendship had begun, and Kathryn was certain that Seth could be someone to confide in. She peered up at the helm and caught sight of Captain Phillips, and a new wave of admiration poured over her. Seth followed her gaze and smiled.

"I think he's a good capt'n."

"I do too."

Duty had called and the crew had returned to their posts with the ship at full sail. All was as it should be – they were back to the normal affairs of pirating.

"Come. I'll show you the ship." Seth motioned and she followed. Apparently, it was safe to make way around the ship with Seth as the guide. They eased in and out of the groups of working men, staying mostly unnoticed at a distance. Kathryn took in every detail of the ship, memorizing every nook and cranny. She also made a mental note of each crewmember that they passed.

Mostly, the men stayed focused on their tasks, ignoring the pair as they slipped past. With some, however, an air of edginess took hold as she walked by. Occasionally, someone would stop what he was doing and squint up at her, his eyes darting between her face and the Seren hanging around her neck. As difficult as it was to appear aloof, she returned their gaze, and forced herself to be calm and distanced.

"No one is allowed in, not even those with pipes – only the powder monkeys." He nodded toward a stock of barrels and the unlit lantern hanging from a post at a distance. "One spark and we all blow sky high." Seth chattered on and pointed to the supply of gunpowder used for weapons. The whole of it was tucked deep in the hull, secure from easy access. But the stash made Kathryn feel uneasy. "And that's why ye don't see many crewmen using tobacco, unless its tucked inside a cheek," he quipped.

They made their way to the larboard bow, where Kathryn stopped to watch three men working together to repair the damaged bulwark. A short, round man in a striped shirt and cap worked laboriously with his right hand – the other was a stump.

"Ho, Billy One-Hand," Seth greeted him, and the stout man looked up. He offered a toothless grin to them both. "How do ye do it so skillfully, mate?"

"I use me good one," Billy said, holding up his only intact extremity. "This I use fer stuffin' the pipes," he added, lifting the stump overhead, then cackled and slapped one knee. Kathryn's face blanched.

"He means the bagpipes," Seth said, and bent nearly in half while laughing almost as loudly as Billy.

"Oh," she said, and a sheepish smile crossed her lips. "I didn't know…"

"Learnt to play it in me homeland. I prop it here," he said, and pointed to his armpit. "Then play wit' me fingers. Works a mighty fine toe-tapper, if ye ask anyone."

"I'm sure I'll be honored with a performance soon, sir," Kathryn said and backed away.

As they made their way to the rear of the ship, Seth stopped short to announce that the tour was ended. "You'll find the rest is of no interest," he said then pointed to the causeway. It was the same short staircase that Kathryn had used earlier. "Ye know the capt'n's quarters. Forward of that ye'll find the galley – that's where the grub is set. The rest is stores, cargo, and sick bay, except for a few of the officers' quarters there – but you'll likely not step inside any of those." He yawned, took his leave, and scampered off to some undone task more invigorating than describing the mechanics of ships and seafaring. Obviously, the lad had a short attention span – something Kathryn would remember.

She sighed and looked around to see that she was once again standing alone on the deck. Left to her own devices, she allowed her scrutiny to wander the length of the ship. Toward the stern, Archer had taken station where the captain had once been. Apparently, it was his turn at the helm. She dodged his scowl and ducked down the companionway. Once below, she quickly found herself in front of the large, carved door leading to the captain's quarters. Unsure whether she was welcome to enter again, she paused, listening for signs of life on the other side.

"Enter," boomed the resonant bass voice.

Startled, Kathryn slipped through and into the cabin where she had slept the night before. Captain Phillips was seated in the center of the room with maps spread over the large table. John Nutt stood behind him. Both men eyed her. It was obvious she was interrupting something.

"I'm sorry...I didn't..." she stammered.

"That will suffice, Master Nutt. Ye're dismissed," said the captain while waving her over.

"Aye, aye, Capt'n." The reply was brisk and the navigational master nodded his head once, never acknowledging Kathryn as he disappeared from the cabin.

"My apologies, Capt'n. I didn't know..." she started, but was soon cut off.

"We need speak of things, lass...things likely disturbing."

Thirty-Two

CAPTAIN PHILLIPS FINGERED THE GOLD fob in his palm. Unusual in design, it snapped open with spider-like legs that shot out in all directions from the base of a brassy orb. Kathryn could see that it wasn't really made for a pocket watch. Rather, some kind of device used to navigate. He looked up from the maps and took her in, allowing his eyes to linger.

"It's a dial, handed down from Capt'n Hawkins, made for him by Humphrey Cole," he announced. The inquisitive look on her face deepened. "But, as ye aren't familiar with the technicalities of sea navigation, ye be needin' none o' this."

"I…I've come for my effects," she stammered, and pointed to her bag of amulets. The satchel lay seemingly undisturbed on the floor next to the settee where she had spent the night. She clasped her trembling hands behind her back and waited.

Captain Phillips' gaze dropped to the pouch. He recognized it as the one she'd brought when captured. In truth, he was thankful the scallywags who had snatched her had permitted it. To anyone else, it held nothing but dried sticks and powders, but to this girl, it was a treasure trove – one that she had used on him to treat to a seething wound. Indeed, he was grateful for it. He nodded and she quickly retrieved the tattered satchel, clutching it to her.

"I meant to thank you for lettin' me stay here this past night," she added.

He nodded again, pushed himself up from the table, and walked to the side of the cot, where he retrieved the black leather roll containing the dead surgeon's instruments. They had been cleaned since the night before and placed back inside. *She's a tidy one, as well*, he thought, pleased. He offered it to her and, when she hesitated, took one of her hands in his and placed the leather roll gently in her palm. His fingertips lingered, savoring the feel of her skin. This woman had never been to sea, and the smooth, delicate feel of her flesh stirred him.

Quite by accident, the leather dropped to the floor. She waited with her hands in his and allowed him to caress them. His eyes fixed on her hers, and she glimpsed gentleness behind the green pools that looked deeply into her soul. A shudder passed through her body, which the captain must have noticed, because the left side of his mouth curled upward. The crooked smile only added to his seductive appeal, and Kathryn felt herself lured into the pirate's intoxicating aura.

"Ahem." Breaking the thrall, he pulled away and returned to the center of the room. His demeanor shifted, and he was once again the brazen Captain Phillips, commander of a ship. "These belong to ye now. My thanks for your expert tendin' o' me wounds." He cocked his head to one side as he lowered the pitch of his voice. "A warnin' to ye, lass. These be hard men, and John Archer is one man ye best not cross."

A foreboding knit of his brows indicated he was not to be second-guessed on the matter. He'd given her the same harsh look earlier, when warning the crew. He made it clear that she was not one of them. Indeed, she would not require additional reminders of her place.

"I understand," she said.

"Ye possess a healer's skill, that I know. How ye made the gem about your neck kill ol' Flint, I have no conjecture, but ye best keep to yourself. Your duty be healin' when summoned. Otherwise stay out of the way o' the men – Archer, in particular."

"I'm not afraid of your crew, Capt'n," she said, unable to hide the defensive tone in her voice.

"That, my dear, is your first mistake."

Was this the topic that he so desperately needed to speak with her about? It seemed pale in comparison to the foul deeds she knew took place onboard pirate ships. Leaving the matter alone, she turned to leave, but not before thanking him again for the gifts – both the surgeon's instruments and the warning. The captain swiftly returned to his place at the table, a signal she had been dismissed. But the young woman did not depart his quarters, not just yet. Summoning courage once more, she addressed him again.

"Capt'n Phillips, you need to have that bandage changed. I can find no linen for the task, but fear the fevers will overpower you without proper attention."

Stained across the linen wrap, a dark crimson had set over the bandage beneath his shirt. He glanced down at the mark for only for a moment, then looked back to Kathryn. She said nothing, but held firm and waited for the argument that would certainly follow. Instead, he nodded, dropping his eyes to the charts on the table. Today would be a day he'd wear the overcoat. Hiding the wound was impossible without changing the dressing. It was obvious by his actions that he wouldn't allow it just yet.

"Mister Gow will give ye scraps from the cast-off sails. Most likely, the fabric will be worn and not useable, if there be any left at all. I will summon you when I need ye're healin' skill and not before. There be no more said on it, savvy?"

This was a stubborn man, and Kathryn understood willfulness well. It was a trait she had been blessed with and knew how to use. Swallowing back the lump that rose in her throat, she forced away the thought of approaching the bosun for torn sailcloth… for the moment. Clutching her pouch tightly to her, she prepared again to leave, when suddenly there came a hard knock on the door.

"Capt'n, I be needin' a word wit' ye."

Fate surely had chosen its victim well. Gow's face appeared at the door. As he entered, he turned a fierce look upon Kathryn. The captain studied his bosun, noting Gow's temperament.

"What is it, Mister Gow?"

"Capt'n, the men have cast their vote on what should be done with the witch." Gow's eyes darted to Kathryn again, then back to Captain Phillips. "It be decided she take the dead surgeon's quarters. The men are fearful she'll be walkin' the decks at night, and none want her castin' the Black Spot on 'em while they sleep. They're fearful she'll curse them the same way she hexed Flint."

"You can't be serious, Mister Gow," the captain said, scowling. "She's but a lass, and can't hurt a fly." He flipped his hand at Kathryn. "She's the one who should be fearful. It's obvious she's harmless, especially onboard this ship."

"Not while wearin' that cursed nugget 'bout her neck," Gow hissed. He crossed himself and shifted his weight from one foot to the other. Captain Phillips shook his head in silence. There'd be no swaying men held in the grips of superstition. With little more than the expected reluctance, the captain nodded approval.

"So be it, Mister Gow. Take her to her new quarters, if that pleases the men."

"Aye, Capt'n." The bosun dipped his head in salute. "Follow me, witch."

Kathryn turned from Captain Phillips and followed Gow from the cabin. Curiosity broke John Phillips' attention from the intricate maps scattered in front of him, and he looked up to watch her walk from the room, through the archway, and out of his presence.

"Make certain the lass finds her way safely. No harm comes to her, particularly not from Archer or the others. Savvy, Mr. Gow?"

"Aye, aye, Capt'n."

Captain Phillips nodded approval and clicked the tip of his tongue against his teeth then shook his head, attempting to shake her image from his thoughts. "Blast!" was all he said to the empty room.

Kathryn had some difficulty keeping up with the bosun's long strides, often lagging behind. She guessed the pirate quickened his pace to keep himself at arms' length. *So jittery*, she thought.

They crossed the main deck to the foredeck. Heads craned to watch as she trotted to keep up. Finally, they reached a small door located deep within the forecastle. It had obviously been forsaken long ago. Kicking against the hinges made for easy access. Gow had made it there first and had done the honors.

"This be yer quarters now, missy. Mind ye, keep to yer business and show proper respect for the dead who once quartered here." He snarled at her before turning away, leaving her standing in front of the open doorway that led to her new lodgings.

She stepped forward and paused just long enough to allow her eyes time to adjust. Dim light filtered in through portholes in the far wall to her left and granted little visibility. Gradually, she was able to make out a small writing table in one corner. On the other side was a cot with a dirty coverlet heaped on top.

"Not much for lodgings, but it'll do, I suppose," she said and walked deeper into the interior. Slowly making her way to the cot, she set her belongings down, dropping the dirty blanket to the ground, which sent an infestation of sea-fleas and rot mites to scurry along the floor. Scattered around the room were diagrams of plants, fish, and body parts. Nothing of value remained, and the only stool in the room had been knocked to its side against the opposite wall. Kathryn guessed the surgeon's belongings had been pilfered and the room immediately ransacked upon his death. Likely, the items left behind had been of no value to the thieving crewmates.

"At least they left the walls intact," she said and began the tedious task of brushing thick layers of silt and brine from the scant furnishings. Fortunately, the portholes were built with hinges that Kathryn forced open. Fresh sea air spilled into the stale, cramped room. Near dusk, a light knock on her door announced Seth's arrival. He'd come with fruit, salt pork, goat cheese, and hard tack heaped onto a small platter. In one hand, he carried a pitcher of grog. Amazingly, he managed both tray and jug with unusually steady hands. Kathryn had no doubt Seth had helped himself to the drink long before entering her cabin.

"This be sent from the cook," he announced, setting it on the edge of the writing table.

"Most generous of him,"

"The men cast votes – and you'll not be eatin' with them. They're afraid you'd poison their food and curse them all, 'the same as ye did ol' Flint'." He raised his voice a bit as he mimicked Cornelius' tone.

"Seth, you don't believe the tales, now, do you?"

"Nope." He set out her meal, and then popped a piece of fruit in his mouth as he turned to face her.

"So it seems." She watched as he stood motionless, except for his jaw, which bounced as he chewed.

"I'll not be temptin' fate, either. You have been decent to me in spite of our seedy meetin' on deck… and did give me this…" He patted his pocket where the amulet rested. "So I volunteered to bring ye sup."

"Surely it had nothin' to do with fillin' your own belly, then?"

"Nope," he said again and popped another piece into his mouth.

"Eat with me, Seth. I promise I won't be poisonin' your food tonight." She smiled and hoped that would soften the sarcasm in her voice.

"Thanks kindly, but I dare not, Miss Kathryn," he said with a bow. "Capt'n Phillips, Archer, and Master Nutt are makin' plans in his quarters, and I'll be attendin' to them." As he spoke, he helped himself to hard tack and cheese.

"You've a keen set of ears to listen in then?"

His response came as a wolfish grin that he wore well, especially when his plans included schemes and eavesdropping. Kathryn intended to get to the bottom of it and pushed him a bit further than she normally would.

"What are they planning, Seth?"

"We're headin' for Tobago Island. The winds are favorable and seas calm, so we make way to careen the ship. It's a good plan, methinks." He snatched another piece of fruit before scampering out the door. She watched him and couldn't help but notice there was a slight spring in his step.

Kathryn had no idea where Tobago was or what it would hold for her, but she liked the sound of it. At the very least, it would be an adventure. Never before had she left the shores of her home in Wales to see other lands. Tobago was an island, from the little bit Seth had told her about it, which was something she longed to see since hearing the stories told by her father.

Fortunately, Seth had thought to include a candle and flint along with the platter of food he'd brought to her. The room had become obscure as the sun dropped below the horizon, so she lit the wick and ate by candlelight. The stillness of the cabin, combined with the gentle swells of the sea, brought her an immediate sense of peace. Kathryn felt strangely at home in that instant. She pushed thoughts of Mariel's cottage aside and basked in the moment, quietly dreaming about what lie ahead of her. Perhaps fate would find her on this island with the strange name. Minutes later, a heavy pounding on the closed door interrupted her tranquility.

"A few o' the men would like a word with ye, witch," the gravelly voice on the other side growled. "Ye best make a move on it. Ye don't wan' to keep 'em waitin'."

Whispers seeped through the cracks of the cabin door, pushing her to her feet. It was time to face them. She decided a bolster couldn't hurt. Eyeing the drink at the table, she took a deep swig of the grog. With trembling hands, she opened the door and was met with a group of swaggering pirates ready to take her.

Thirty-Three

A DOZEN ROUGH HANDS GRABBED hold and dragged Kathryn onto the main deck of the ship. Night had fallen, and, along with it, hundreds of stars caught in its canopy overhead. The moon shone bright and full, which illuminated the gnarled pattern of the cedar deck. Kathryn wondered how such beauty could exist around such wretchedness. Her gaze moved to the cutthroats.

They clustered around a stout pirate who sat upright on a crate. His pudgy hands grasped wildly at his thick throat. *A sign of distress*, she thought, and wondered what the blaggards had done to him. Gasping for air, he sputtered flecks of pink phlegm as he gagged and coughed.

"Make…her…stop!" Billy One-Hand spat the words between spasms. He stared up at Kathryn with a pleading gaze that dripped tears over his puffy cheeks. Terror raced frantically behind his eyes, which were bloodshot and running. For no one else but the one-handed sot, Kathryn would do her best – a decision she made then and there. A rough hand shoved Kathryn to the front of a circle of anxious pirates that had gathered around their struggling mate. The circle had already increased in size. Within minutes, a scuffle ensued from the back of the group as Archer pushed his way forward. He glared at Kathryn.

"Heed me words, witch. I'll slit yer throat this very night 'less ye stop yer curse directly!" Archer barked at her with such menace that it forced Kathryn to quake. She studied Billy, who had turned a dark shade of purple. The others slapped him in the face, to no avail.

"Break free o' the hex, Billy."

The struggling pirate's glassy eyes began to roll back into his head and the man slumped onto the deck.

"I be warnin' ye, foul witch, cease that cursed thing hangin' about yer neck. If this man dies, ye be next." The quartermaster spat and ripped a dirk from his belt, then pointed it at her.

Kathryn put her hand on the Seren. The stone remained a cool, gleaming white. The one-handed pirate wasn't dying because of the Seren. Something else was going on.

"Take your blade from my throat or I can do nothing," she whispered.

"Let 'er go, Archer. Billy's a dead man if she can't do her magic on him," someone said behind her.

Archer dropped the knife. "She's shark-bait if he dies."

Kathryn pushed past the quartermaster and rushed to the fallen man's side. Kneeling down, she could see saliva oozing from his open mouth. A smell of cured pork on his breath and chunks of food inside his cheeks leaked out.

"Lift him," she ordered one of the men standing nearby. The sailor obeyed and quickly grabbed the unconscious Billy, yanking him upright. He supported the pirate's limp body from behind, holding him under the armpits. Kathryn drew the sailor's thick arms around Billy into an awkward-looking hug. She then forced his balled fists over the unconscious pirate's belly.

"When I give the word, squeeze your fists with all your might into his gut, ye hear me?" The order caused several of the onlookers to nod in agreement. Others, including Archer, stood stiffly in place, watching her cast what they thought was another powerful spell. At the ready, the quartermaster's dagger gleamed in the moonlight – a reminder it would surely finish her off should she fail.

"Steady…and…*now!*" She threw herself at Billy, planting her shoulder squarely into the pirate's fists. The force knocked all three to the ground. Food and vomit spewed from Billy's mouth. He landed in a heap next to the circle of men, who stood stock-still, jaws dropped and eyes wide open. The men dared not move, trying to grasp what had happened. A few made the sign of the cross over their chests. Archer stepped to the pile of bodies sprawled out in front of him. With his left hand still holding the dagger, he seized Kathryn by the hair. Pulling her to her feet, he held her from behind with the steel blade to her neck once more.

Suddenly, there was a gasp from the once-lifeless body lying on the deck, and the purple face twitched. Billy's cheeks drained to beet red. He coughed and gasped as a few of his comrades assisted him up to sit. Consciousness had returned. He opened his runny eyes and blinked at the faces surrounding him.

"God Almighty, Billy," a voice rang out from the crowd. "We thought ye'd up an' left us."

"Aye, dead. A goner."

Only guttural noises escaped from Billy's lips, but he nodded his head. Although some believed he was a ghost, most were glad to see him open-eyed and grinning. Someone handed him a bottle, which he slowly tipped back to take short sips of the warm rum. In truth, Billy was unsure himself if he had died. Perhaps rum from a matey at sea was heaven for a pirate. But his solace was short lived, even as a few of the men stepped up to pat him on the back and welcome him "back from the grave."

"Ye best get back to work, the lot o' ye." Archer's hold on Kathryn stayed firm as he barked the order.

With the steel blade against her neck, she waited. Billy still needed to gain his full senses before Archer would set her free, if he did at all. As Archer held restraint, the dark stain of a tattoo stared up at her from his leathery skin. Her heart stopped momentarily and she felt her chest tighten.

"Let me loose, Archer. Billy is himself again, as ye can see," she gasped.

"Not yet, witch." He pulled her against him with a stronger grip and the inked symbols on the salt-weathered arm twitched. Hollowed eye sockets stared at her from a faded cranium, its teeth clenched tight across the arched blade set above three marks: *Q.A.R.* There was a message behind the mark that made her shiver. Something about the strange tattoo felt ominous and deadly.

Billy rose to his feet and the knife fell from her neck. She stumbled as the quartermaster shoved her away. Fortunately, Billy could now speak, though he did so in raspy whispers. She bent down to look at him.

"Are you breathin' all right?"

"Get away from him, witch!" Archer spat.

"I must study his vigor…his breathing." She looked back to Billy. "Are you able to inspire, like so?" She inhaled deeply.

He mimicked the breath, then looked up at her. "I…I believe so. Did ye do it? Did ye break the curse?"

A new rumbling passed between the onlookers, murmurs of curses, spells and hexes gone wrong.

"It was no curse. Ye swallowed your food whole and it lodged there," she said, gently pointing to his throat. Fresh gasps percolated between the men.

"Aye, Billy. We be tellin' ye this a'fore. Ye can't be swallowin' yer sup whole like a swamp gator when ye got no teeth in yer skull," Cuddy scolded.

Billy smiled his toothless grin and nodded in agreement. "Aye."

"At least he's not shark fodder."

A few pirates slapped one another over the back, laughing. Others looked on with blank stares, seemingly overwhelmed that their comrade was not dead. Billy One-Hand was soon escorted back to mid-ship, the spectacle concluded, now that he had come back to life.

Archer faced Kathryn with his dagger still clutched in his hand. He adjusted his grip on the handle, though he lowered it to stay near his thigh. The tattoo glared from his forearm, a warning to anyone who saw it. She met his eyes and studied the hate that stared back at her.

"Mind ye watch yerself 'round me, sorceress," he hissed, pushing past her.

The touch of his skin curdled her insides. She held her stance, glaring fiery Celtic willfulness into his back as he joined his men. Finally, as the quartermaster disappeared from sight, Kathryn relaxed. Her knees suddenly felt weak. With effort, she made her way to the rails of the ship. Without collapsing, she grasped the rails and, leaning over, let herself be sick for the first time since becoming a prisoner of the pirates.

Thirty-Four

OVER THE NEXT SEVERAL WEEKS, the *Revenge* sailed in open waters under favorable conditions. The captain had called for Kathryn to tend to his injury several times throughout the voyage, and was pleased to find the gash had improved without signs of infection.

"Time for these buggers to be plucked from me flesh," he announced one day.

"It's a miracle ye didn't suffer from it," she said as she pulled sutures from the wound. A long pink scar remained, but Kathryn was pleased that the edges appeared well healed and intact. At least her ministrations had brought no harm. Likely, it spared his life – as well as her own. Working like this brought a feeling of accomplishment, and Kathryn sensed she was on her way to becoming a practiced healer, much like her grandmother.

With thoughts of Mariel, a keen ache found her reaching for the talisman made from the strands of Mariel's hair. Its silver had grown darker now from the dried blood and salty air. Occasionally, while asleep in the deep night, she dreamt of a soft voice calling to her, *"Blessed be."* But she would always awaken to an empty room. Magically, the talisman had been clutched in her fist.

This was not the day to feel reminiscent. No, today was another day at sea. "Stay focused, Kathryn." She had heard herself say those words more frequently as the days wore on.

The voyage to Tobago was long and difficult. Throughout the entire journey, the crew stayed busy, tending to the demands of a three-masted ship in open waters. Food became scarce as the weeks turned into months. Drinking water was rationed and mostly used for grog, never for bathing. Kathryn had learned to tolerate the drink made with water, rum, and occasionally lemons, the same as the rest of the crew, but she never lost the ache for clear stream water flavored with lavender or mint.

Once she was asked to join a small group of pirates on the main deck where they passed time singing and dancing and sharing grog made with sugar they had stolen from the cook. She knew they would be flogged for stealing from the galley, but the cook was in on their ploy and had pilfered the sugar himself. This was a rare treat, and Kathryn was a bit surprised she had been included. At one point, Billy One-Hand came forward and took Kathryn to the center of the main deck to dance. He bounced like a giant ball, feet tapping a spastic jig while Kathryn ducked and spun around him. The sailors surrounded them to cheer and whistle as they twisted and bounced to soaring voices.

> *"In days long past, 'afore the mast*
>
> *Me hearties, we will sing.*
>
> *Yo-ho-ho, to sea we go*
>
> *A pirate's life we bring."*

Kathryn joined in, her velvety alto smooth against the pirate's warbling. They sloshed mugs filled to the brim with grog. Above them, standing just beside the shrouds, Captain John Phillips observed. Indeed, she bathes the ship with the soft presence of a woman. A smile crept across his face as he watched her, his foot tapping in time to the music.

On several occasions, they passed tufts of foliage and sand – floating islands in a sea of blue that were still uncharted, untouched, and innocent. These were the islands used for marooning pirates who broke the Code. Kathryn wondered what lay on these small pieces of land, as she would see them rise on the horizon, waiting to be discovered. But fate would never allow her time to explore them as they sailed past, and so, daydreaming about them became her entertainment. Mostly, her days were spent in solace, intrigued by the sea, looking for anything out of the ordinary. Rarely, she would see spray from blue whales migrating in groups, up to ten at a time on occasion. At other times, she would sit with Seth and talk about the captain and fantastic pirate adventures at sea.

"You should tie knots."

The suggestion had come not long after she'd sought out the bosun for bandages. He was an older seaman they called Gentleman Harry.

"I couldn't agree more!"

"Be nimble wit' yer fingers and ye' have it 'fore noontime," he's said and showed her the first of many. "This be the standing end and takes the strain."

"Aye. And this?"

"That be the bitter end, what goes 'round the bitts."

She was quick and seemed to have a knack with tying knots. When feasible, she'd practice on her own. Usually this happened at odd moments, whenever she could steal some unnoticed time against the chains. For hours, her fingers would twist and loop a thin lanyard into different nautical knots until Kathryn could tie them as fast as some of the oldest sailors onboard.

Once, as she was leaning against the starboard gunwale, she caught sight of sails on the horizon. Curious, she watched as the foreign ship made its way closer. A look-out posted in the crow's nest spotted it as well and cried out a warning to the crew below. This sent Sparks down to prepare the artillery and cannon for a possible battle. The captain rushed to the bow with a spyglass against one eye. Archer soon joined up, waiting for instructions. The rest of the men scurried under the orders of the bosun, clearing the decks of anything that could become a projectile or trip a scrambling pirate on the move. Minutes later, the captain lowered the telescope and gave orders to Archer, who responded with a brisk, "Aye, Capt'n." He then turned to face the main deck and repeated the captain's orders to the waiting men.

"Hoist the colors! Prepare to do battle."

Kathryn's heart pounded. Skirmish arrived with the approaching ship, and everyone's focus went steadfastly to the encounter as the ship moved closer and closer.

"Hoist the colors."

The captain's orders were relayed, and the Black Flag of the pirate ship *Revenge* was unfurled. Kathryn watched in horror as the toothless skull, emblazoned with a triton beneath crossed cutlasses, climbed higher up the mainmast. Seth was nowhere to be seen, apparently having found a place with the men. Kathryn felt lost without some duty to perform, which left her to search the deck for some means to be useful. Gentleman Harry approached her as she stood gripping the rails, waiting helplessly. The rest prepared for what was about to happen.

"Ye best get below deck, Miss Kathryn. Yer likely to get shot or hit with cannon shot scatterin' across the deck."

"How can I just sit and wait below deck, not knowin' what awaits topside?" Her voice trembled.

"Ye'll be needed later on for certain, as the only sot wit' a physic's background. It's best ye scamper hence, Miss Kathryn. I know that be the wishes o' the capt'n, too." He smiled and nodded toward the causeway leading to her quarters, then turned from her. Skyrme ran past, carrying an armful of grapeshot. "I'm needed at post," Harry said, and disappeared into the chaos.

"But I…" her voice trailed away and she added, "What am I supposed to do?" No one answered because no one cared. At least, that's what it seemed like at the moment.

Kathryn glanced up to the quarterdeck where Captain Phillips had been talking with Archer, hoping for some confirmation that she'd be useful, somehow. The captain stood at the helm, his neck draped with a bright blue ribbon, each end tied to a flintlock pistol. His cutlass and dirk had been unsheathed and readied.

I have to be of value…to someone, she thought, and began to drum her fingers against her hip. They faced danger, and she was useless without value – without skill.

"But ye have skills, Kat. Ye have the Gift." The voice came from nowhere.

"Aye," she whispered. "But more that that will be needed." She silently swore that should she survive. But her next lesson would include a sword and pistol.

Once again, their course was set. The captain glanced around to make sure Kathryn was out of harm's way. She had slipped below deck just in time, his keen eyes missing her by only seconds. Kathryn hurried to her cabin, making quick work of the charms she had yet to cast. A candle lay in the middle of the table. Next to it, she crushed some dried herbs between her palms, then sprinkled them in the shape of a star and lit the wick. Closing her eyes, she fanned the energy of the protective star all around her body as she chanted.

"As the flame burns bright in clear candlelight,

A bright white of protection surround us.

Rhoddi Am Diffyr Ion…

Rhoddi Am Diffyr Ion."

She repeated the last phrase of the ancient incantation five times and tapped her finger on each point of the star. Then, turning back to her pouch, she pulled out another of Mariel's amulets and sprinkled more of the crushed rosemary and sage into a small white sack. Retrieving a smooth piece of salmon-colored stone, she placed the Bustamite into the sack, as well, and tied it closed. "To ward off danger."

The chant was repeated while waving the talisman above the candle flame to allow the smoke to seal the charm. When the last of the Celtic prayer was said, she blew at the candle. The flame was extinguished and the dust scattered across the table and throughout the little cabin. Hastily, she ran out the doorway and back to the main deck, the newly created amulet in hand.

The men were running between stations now, cannons at the ready. Seth ran past her, his arms filled with supplies for the men soon to be in battle.

"Seth," she cried out. "Seth, here."

He stopped abruptly and scrambled to where she waited. His eyes grew wide with excitement.

"Kathryn, truly ye must get below. The enemy approaches, and they be flying the French colors." Desperation filled his voice, and his expression showed the anticipation of a thrill. However, no fear danced behind his eyes – an odd thing for someone new to sea battle.

"Seth, take this to the captain." He stared at the object. "Please. This will keep him from harm's way," she added as an afterthought.

She placed the amulet in his hand. He looked at it, then at her, somewhat perplexed, but did not refuse it.

"You have the one I gave you before, yes?" His eyes gave the answer. "Wear it, else suffer a deadly fate…I'm certain of it. The captain must have this one. Savvy?"

Holding his hands in hers with the amulet secure in his palm, she waited for an answer. He nodded and peered up at the captain.

"On one condition," he finally replied.

"Anything."

"It's this…that you get below decks and tend to the wounded when they arrive." His words stung, but if those were the terms for accepting her protection, she'd take it.

"Aye, so be it. Now get off with you. Make sure Capt'n Phillips keeps it with him, Seth. And take cover yourself." He said nothing, but darted across the deck to where the captain stood, spyglass to one eye.

Kathryn hid in the causeway and watched as Seth bravely approached the captain. It was clear they exchanged words, though just how heated, Kathryn could not tell. Seth waved a hand in her direction, then handed over the amulet and walked away. The captain hastily scanned the deck, but Kathryn ducked out of sight in time. Peeking through the planks lining the stairwell, she watched him place the token in his breast pocket before turning his attention back on the approaching ship. Seth was nowhere to be seen, and the deck was almost cleared. Cagey men hid themselves behind the rails, while others stayed fixed to their battle stations, ready for the order to attack. Everyone except Kathryn had either a pistol or a cutlass in hand.

"Never again, Kathryn!" she said under her breath. "From this day forward, ye'll be one of them…or at least try to be so."

The enemy ship was now close enough that it was possible to make out their crew. Disorder sent most scurrying about the deck of the French sloop, which was a good sign for the pirates. There were other ships farther off in the distance, but they did not approach, and Kathryn had the dark feeling that this would be a battle her own crew would not survive. In one last desperate act, she gathered the last of the rosemary from her pocket and crushed it in the palms of both hands until it became a fine powder. Cautiously, she inched her way out onto the deck and began to chant. Eyes closed, she raised both hands above her head, then slowly opened her fingers. Kathryn let the wind catch the rosemary and scatter it across the deck of the ship and into the sails. She continued chanting, eyes closed, until she heard the roar of the captain's battle cry.

"Prepare to fire broadside. Send a shot across the bow, Mister Gow. Bolster the scarlet flag. We give no quarters!"

Gow sang out the orders to fire the warning shot from one of the starboard cannons, and an explosion followed.

"No quarters!" The command was repeated as smoke curled from the cannon's muzzle. The men waited, prepared to receive incoming fire. Captain Phillips waited at the helm, his cutlass raised as he waited below the red flag. The signal was clear – no lives would be spared without a full surrender. The two opposing ships were close enough now that the insults hurled between both crews lining the bulwarks were easily heard from across a narrowing, watery gap. At the rear of the French ship, a tall, thin man with a red coat and large plume in an outlandish hat stepped forward. He shouted, along with the rest of them, with a thick French accent.

"Where be ze *capitaine*? I will speak only wiss ze *capitaine!*" he shouted at the pirate ship.

"Strike yer colors, Frenchman. I give no quarters this day," boomed Captain Phillips. "You've a pretty little sloop, and twelve guns to her, indeed. I think she'd rather be under my command, sir."

The Frenchman held his ground. "I will not make a truce until I know who I am speaking with, *Monsieur*."

"I'm John Phillips, captain of the pirate ship, *Revenge*. Mind me words, Frenchman, surrender or suffer death…ye and all yer crew, none bein' spared the cutlass or cannon."

A heavy commotion followed on the deck of the French sloop as the officer with the plumed hat gave orders in French. Several of his men shook their heads, some shouting *"Non!"* Their captain turned, addressing Phillips again.

"We are low on supplies…and have nothing of value, all except ze lives of ze men. I have your word? My men will be spared?"

"Ye have me word. Drop yer swords and yer shot, and strike yer colors. Prepare to be boarded and taken as prisoners."

Kathryn watched the interaction between vessels from her place just behind the companionway. She continued to chant, one hand on the Scarlet Seren, which remained cool to her touch. One by one, the crew of the French vessel raised their swords in the air and then released them. Each blade dropped and reverberated with a steel *clang* as it hit the deck. The French flag was lowered and cables were tossed across the rails to the other ship. Long wooden planks fell to link the ships. Lines were cast and the planks secured, but not before the pirates rushed the sloop and took the prisoners one by one, as each Frenchman surrendered. Soon, the entire ship was filled with foreigners, hands held aloft in surrender. Captain Phillips stood against the rails and watched the smooth capture of his new prize.

"It be the French sloop, *Victoire*," Gow said, stepping up alongside Captain Phillips.

In the distance, the other ships retreated, changing course as soon as the French colors had been struck. It signaled surrender, and immediately, a new course had been chosen for the fleet.

"What of the others, Capt'n?" Archer called from the rails, one hand pointed toward the fleeing vessels.

"Let them go. Take the helm of our new prize, Mister Archer. I've a prisoner to welcome."

Archer jumped onboard the *Victoire* and took hold of the wheel. The French captain was escorted aboard the *Revenge* and brought to face Captain John Phillips.

"Take these prisoners to the brig, Mister Gow. Mister Cuddy, form up a crew and man the prize. Ye stay with the quartermaster."

"Aye, aye, Captain," came the reply from different directions.

As orders were carried out, John Phillips cast his gaze to where Kathryn stood. She stepped forward, allowing her whereabouts to be known. Absently, he raised one hand to the breast pocket that held the amulet she had given him. Ever so slightly, he gave her a nod of thanks. Suddenly, his eyes caught hold of hers. Time stopped, as they communicated what could not be spoken aloud. Coordinated chaos had erupted all around the captain and the sorceress, but in that moment, they did not see it. Each had been captured – spellbound by a timeless longing for one other.

Oblivious to Kathryn and the captain, the pirates congratulated each other on a well-earned plunder. The ship buzzed with talk about the miraculous capture just made. Never before had a ship been seized with such ease – with no shots fired under an immediate surrender! This day would go down in history, and the fame of the *Revenge* would spread throughout the Caribbean. The men would continue to expound on their marvelous story, building the tale a little taller with each repetition. And so it continued, until a new figure stepped into the drama. There was talk of the sorceress, Kathryn.

"She cast a spell on 'em, says I," whispered one pirate to another one evening at dogwatch.

"Aye, me eyes saw her waving 'er hands in the air an' mutterin' curses at 'em just a'fore the colors be struck."

"Aye. I heard it said that Skyrme saw it jes' a'fore the cannon blew. Their captain stood stiff as stone an' be mumblin' non-sense, foamin' at the mouth like a whale spew."

"Ah…" They nodded together and crossed themselves.

Kathryn shook her head upon hearing the rumors, but decided to use their superstitions to her advantage. She was certain protection had been placed over the ship. The amulets and magic charms that she had cast had blessed all who'd sailed. However, nothing by her power had been done to the French captain and his crew. The miraculous surrender was purely due to the commanding presence of John Phillips.

Within days, the French sloop was renamed *Fame's Revenge* and – given the speed at which word surrounding the captured vessel had spread amongst the crew – the name was appropriate. Kathryn felt relieved that Archer had been sent to sail the sloop alongside the *Revenge*, mainly because he was no longer aboard the *Revenge* and could not easily get to her. The change in assignment afforded her some reprieve from his contemptuous glares and threatening expletives.

Both vessels sailed side by side en route to Tobago, and Kathryn took advantage of the days at sea to learn more about life aboard a pirate ship. In spite of the amity accompanying the scallywags, their presence evoked a renewed resolution to one day become equally as skilled as they. That vow had not been taken lightly, and it would not soon be forgotten, either.

One day, feeling unusually bold, she approached the ship's gunner and asked who onboard was the most skilled with the sword. Of course, John Phillips and Archer's names were immediately presented.

"Who, aside from Capt'n Phillips and the quartermaster, would you say? Your opinion's the most sought after, I'm told." The flattery worked like a charm. Sparks puffed out his chest.

"Aye, that be true, missy. I be the one who the men look to, after the capt'n, to be sure. Ye best not cross blades with Wynn, either, lest ye be seekin' an audience with Davy Jones."

The surly pirate elbowed her, then burst laughing at his own joke before turning away. Kathryn could still hear him bellowing from across the ship as he moved aft. It was an easy task to bribe Seth into convincing the lanky Emanuel Wynn to meet with her. Seth made the request one afternoon when the winds had died down and the seas had become unusually calm.

"He said he'd meet ye on deck, mid-ship, abaft high sun on the morrow," Seth announced.

"I owe you, Seth. Thank you," Kathryn responded.

"Aye, and ye'd best be a quick learner, too – ye'll have no one to patch ye back together, except maybe me...or perhaps the quartermaster," he said, laughing.

"Therein lies the motivation, Seth." He turned on his heel and walked away. His answer came with the wave of his hand, a passive farewell, as it were.

On the day they were to meet, Kathryn scurried topside and paced the length of the main deck. It seemed her apprehension had gotten the best of her. She couldn't stand still. Not long after, the noon sun suspended itself in the clear blue sky and a small cluster of swarthy pirates began to assemble mid-deck to watch. The swordsman stepped forward and met Kathryn with a bow. With a quick flick of his hand, he tossed a curved blade in her direction, which landed directly at her feet. On point, the tip pierced the deck and stood the blade upright only inches from her right foot. She jumped, startled at the brazen pirate's move. Laughter erupted from the onlookers as the hilt wobbled back and forth mid-air in front of her. She let fly a string of curses.

"Is that the lesson, then, Mister Wynn? Perhaps I'd do better with a sot man enough to offer a blade with some bloody courtesy," Kathryn snapped. Her determination not to be intimidated by him pushed against her reason – after all, he was the one with experience.

"Calm yerself, lass. I was havin' a bit o' fun, is all."

Taking up the cutlass, she stepped forward and the onlookers crowded in.

"All right, Mister Wynn, I'm ready. Teach me what I need to know…or, at least, enough to save my own hide when one of these scurvy dogs comes at me with the blade." She shifted her weight and executed a perfect balestra on a pivot, counter-clockwise, the tip of her cutlass aimed at each of the pirates gathered. "Bloody, scurvy, low-life pirates!" she said through clenched teeth.

Laughter peeled out again from the crew as they met with her fire. With a firm resolve for self-reliance, Kathryn faced Wynn.

"So be it, lass."

Mister Wynn bowed low and she readied herself for the first blow. The signal was given – he tapped her blade gently and smiled. The lesson had begun. Malice found its way behind his eyes. She was certain the expert swordsman would purposefully let his blade slip at any moment, slicing off one of her limbs or even slitting her throat.

She jabbed at him, then swung the sword from side to side. But the pirate met each challenge with tolerance, countering her advances as he demonstrated a proper skill with the blade. In truth, he was less interested in becoming the mentor of a captive than in spending the next hour or so entertained at the lass' expense. Still, he was impressed by her tenacity and eagerness, despite the ridicules flying at her.

"Again!" she insisted, and the parry repeated itself.

"Surely ye've worn yerself out, lass," Wynn chucked and delivered another blow, which Kathryn managed to fend off.

"Never…Again!"

With sleek, curved blades held high, he taught her to slice fluidly through the air and block the same with fierce counter-moves. The clank and clatter of razor steel reverberated across the open deck, evoking eager interest from pirates on the opposite side of the ship. Dirty, calloused feet set a pattern for her to follow as she adopted the footwork into a dance of defend and attack. More rapidly, their cutlasses crossed, and the rhythm of the swordplay increased.

Once she stumbled and nearly took a lethal blow to the shoulder. It was then she decided her long skirt would do nothing but hamper her footwork, so she tied it up in a giant side-knot. As she moved, her lower legs were exposed, inviting shrill, lusty whistles. But she didn't care. Her feet were unencumbered, and she could freely mark the path she needed to parry with the pirate. Ignoring their catcalls, she clapped her blade against Wynn's to get his attention.

"Again, if you please, Mister Wynn."

He bowed low and she caught him off guard. Hungrily, she swiped and jabbed at the pirate. Her skill increased with each pass and Wynn seemed impressed. His black teeth beamed in a hearty grin, undeniably pleased with how quickly his pupil had learned to handle a sword.

By the time Cook sounded the call to evening sup, nearly five hours had passed. It was sundown before they had finished the lesson. When it was over, Kathryn sat back, exhausted. Cuddy offered her a pitcher, which she accepted and drank from heartily, guzzling grog with the rest of the pirates. A few of the men slapped her back in approval as they left for the galley. She smiled in return, but remained on deck, her place still apart from the men as they supped.

"Impressive, Kathryn," Seth admitted, setting her meal on a barrel. "The men are all talking about it."

"What, Seth? My parry with Wynn?" The smile that rose to her lips betrayed satisfaction. "It was just a lesson."

"Maybe so, but it seems you've become Wynn's prize pupil, a rather quick learner, from what I hear."

Kathryn tossed him a date from the plate, which he caught deftly in one hand. Then, tapping his brow, he disappeared below deck with the others. Stars danced in the night sky, winking applause from above, and she murmured a silent prayer of thanks. Across the deck, one of the Frenchmen who had recently defected from the captured ship pulled out a squeezebox and began to play and whistle. Several others joined in the song that rang out across the ship – a perfect accompaniment as Kathryn ate her meal and sipped grog.

"Fine sword play 'tween you and Mister Wynn, lass." The captain stepped forward and took a seat next to her. She smiled and offered him salt pork from the platter. He shook his head, but took up some of the grog from the pitcher and drank.

"We be in dead waters and there be no bloody wind. The crew's talkin' amongst themselves – not good for morale on the ship." He paused to allow the magnitude of his words to settle in.

She nodded her understanding and put a piece of hardtack back onto the platter. "How bad is it?"

"You know little of the sea. A crew of restless pirates brings naught but discontent."

She kept her eyes lowered. "Is there anything I can do to help?"

The innocence of the question caught him off guard, and he studied her for a moment. "Our supplies are low, the food fouled with rot an' maggots. Cook works hard not to kill us all with the spoilt meat, and with water so scarce…" He inhaled deeply. "I need be puttin' some of the crew out. We'll be goin' before the mast to vote. Ye have no voice in this, mind ye. Still, I thought ye should know."

"Will I be one…put out?"

He shook his head. "I think not. Ye're needed for healing the sick and injured. No one else will do it."

Kathryn nodded. They sat in silence, the sultry evening growing hotter. The captain shifted, peeling his shirt over his head to expose his bare chest. The scar on the side of his ribs was clean and white, the dressing long gone. Kathryn suddenly felt restless, sitting next to him as she eyed his bare flesh. Butterflies danced in the pit of her stomach.

She kept her eyes trained on the water, but occasionally stole glimpses of his perfectly formed body. She couldn't help herself. His skin rippled with muscle and sinew against his spine – the kind of back that only sailors seem to keep – tanned, brawny and lean. A pair of crossed tritons thrust through a skull with the name *Revenge* had been inked in black flowing script just below his left shoulder. Without thinking, she raised a hand and touched the lettering on his upper back. It was warm and strong and smelled of sandalwood. Involuntarily, a shudder spilled down her spine. She yanked her hand back, realizing she had touched him without permission. He smiled sideways at her, took her hand in his, raised it to his lips, and kissed lightly along the tops of her fingers. Her breath caught in her throat, paralyzed at his touch.

"Ye did well today, lass."

She could barely breathe.

As if sensing her uneasiness, he nuzzled his face into the crook of her neck and traced her jaw with his lips. She waited for the kiss that would surely follow, closing her eyes in anticipation. But it never came. Instead, she heard him chuckle softly and opened her eyes to look at him.

"I…you…" she stammered, unable to arrange her thoughts into words.

"No," he said, gazing at her. "This isn't the time."

"But you…"

"Ay, and it will mind ye, but not just yet. Not until…" He smiled and stood. "And so, I bid ye a good eve'n." The pirate then bowed, and moments later, stole away into the dark corners of the ship. Kathryn sat alone in silence, unable to make sense of what had just happened. Reliving the tender way his lips brushed her hand, she felt her heart race and begged it to still. The music played in the background, and she heard it once again as her senses returned. She looked up at the stars, thanking them once again for her place on this ship… with a captain she had suddenly grown very fond of.

"Kathryn," whispered a voice from the dark. It belonged to Seth. "Kathryn, look!"

He pointed to the Scarlet Seren dangling from her neck. Unexpected warmth rushed along her skin where it lay. She glanced down and saw that the stone pulsed feverishly, the color of a human heart.

Thirty-Five

ALIVE, THE SCARLET SEREN BECAME more menacing, especially as the color intensified. Kathryn knew she had no time to lose. She threw her hand over the stone and dashed toward the short stairway that led to her cabin.

Seth watched her run off without saying a word – unsure whether to rescue her from the same fate as Flint or dash off to save his own skin. Besides, he could always feign ignorance when the others found her strangled to death by the cursed thing about her neck. He opted for the second and stole away in the opposite direction, certain he would find some sort of task waiting for him. Dodging a nasty feeling of guilt was always best accomplished by staying occupied – something that would surely help him forget about the deadly stone dangling from Kathryn's throat.

It had quickly become apparent that the Seren would react to anger, distress, or apparently, the disquiet sensation of a new infatuation. Kathryn refused to believe the last prospect was the cause since she had just spent several hours defending herself with the sword. Albeit a lesson, aggression alone would better explain the heat of the Seren against her neck – anything other than passion.

"Be serious, Kathryn." She traced her lips with a finger. Could a tender kiss on the fingertips, be the cause? Surely, a rosy glow in the stone matching the one still coloring her cheeks had its source elsewhere. Far better the swordplay awaken the Seren than her heart. Kathryn made a mental note to be mindful of her emotions while wearing the talisman, else suffer the same fate as the greedy pirate. Still, her soul cried out for the captain.

"I am not in love with a pirate!" She stomped her foot at the same time the words flew from her mouth – not a very convincing argument. Snatching a discarded bottle, and guzzling its contents, she dashed from the causeway and into her quarters. Aggravated, she planted herself on the cot and sat crossed-legged, trying to calm her pounding heart, and along with it, the throbbing Seren. With measured breaths, she sensed the even rise and fall of her chest and willed it to match the same roll of the ship over the water. Within moments, the warm tingle of stillness began to trickle first from her head, then trail down through her arms to her fingertips, until finally dripping into her toes. White light penetrated through the top of her head, cooling her heart and the stone lying just above it.

"Kathryn, me girl." A soft whisper rustled through the room.

She stayed tranquil, breathing with the rhythm of the sea, eyes closed in a semi-conscious state of dreaming.

"Hear me now...Kathryn." The woman's voice sweetened as the white light grew brighter from the crown of her head. It was a voice she'd heard before, from her childhood.

"Mum? Mum, are you here with me?" Kathryn forced herself to stay meditative and at peace. It was the only way she could be with Mariel.

"Aye, me girl. Open your eyes and see for yourself. I have need to speak with you."

Kathryn obeyed and opened her eyes. Standing in front of her, Mariel was surrounded by the same white light she'd felt enter through the top of her body. She smiled gently at her granddaughter. Nearly overcome, Kathryn reached out to the vision, but only brushed longing arms through an empty vast of warmth where the image of her grandmother's body appeared. The ghostly apparition did not respond, but instead, lingered as Mariel's figure floated nearly a foot off the ground.

"My dear girl, ye can only embrace the image in your heart, for skin and bones do not stand before ye now, only an image come to ye through the blood Talisman we share."

The silver charm caked with Mariel's blood lay radiating with the same ghostly glow from the cot next to Kathryn. Here was the connection the talisman provided for them both. This was what Mariel meant, the day Kathryn was taken from the cottage, when she had said, "I will always be with ye." It made sense now, and brought a feeling of relief to Kathryn.

"Aye, Mum. I understand now." Kathryn nodded and noticed the lock of her own dark hair clutched in Mariel's ghostly hand. "What have ye to tell me?"

"This be your destiny, child…the path ye were meant to travel."

"Kidnapped by pirates? Surely, Mum…" Kathryn's protest was cut short.

"It's truth, me girl. There is more for ye on this voyage than as captive onboard the ship. Your heart is to be touched and your hands are to heal. This comes from the Runes."

Mariel used runes to glimpse the future. Hers was a divine sight that Winne possessed as well, although it was not as refined. Without question, Mariel held firmly to each prophecy revealed by the Runes, particularly when loved ones were involved.

"I've done that. And I've healed when fate has brought me to do it." Kathryn spoke with some hesitation. "But my heart is troubled."

The apparition flickered.

"A man will come to you. He is fierce and is never to be affronted. Mind ye well on this. But the heart beating in his chest beats for ye. He needs your protection and the *Gift* ye have been given, though he does not know this himself…not just yet."

Kathryn listened intently but dropped her eyes.

"There is one who seeks to destroy this man and all who dwell with him. He's in grave danger, Kathryn. Morrigan looks for him now, her own love spurned and revenge to be taken. Only by uniting two longing hearts can her design be thwarted. Only then can the man be spared."

"I know no man onboard this ship who doesn't already seek to destroy me...except maybe Seth," Kathryn said.

"There is another."

"Who? No one that dwells onboard this ship would care if I lived or died. In fact, most seek my demise. They all speak of it," Kathryn said. She had embellished a bit, but only in an attempt to drive her point home. Mariel would likely see through the tall tale.

"You speak in shadows, Kathryn. The truth lies open to your heart, if ye will but allow it."

"That may be so, Mum. But why would I choose to spare the life of a pirate?"

"Your paths are the same. His fate is yours. You canna escape your destiny – it lies with him. Morrigan seeks to destroy you both."

The young girl's pulse accelerated. Death followed in Morrigan's wake, and the mere mention of the Celtic deity's name caused Kathryn to tremble.

"Make good use of your time at sea, and use the Sigil of Defense as protection for ye both. Know this, that your ancestry loves ye, which love's powerful magic canna be divided by land or sea…or even death."

The silver head bowed and glistening arms reached out as if to embrace Kathryn, but they could not. Still, Kathryn's heart was encircled by new warmth, and unbridled love filled her entire body. Her cheeks ran with tears as she watched Mariel dwindle from view. The whispered words, "Blessed ye be" faded into breezy silence.

Kathryn curled up into a ball and wept. The silvery talisman stayed clenched in her hand while abundant love filled every fiber of her body. Sadness accompanied the withdrawal of Mariel's energy. As she rehearsed over and over again the words spoken by the apparition, truth filled the empty spaces left behind in her heart, and she knew this voyage was indeed fate. Just how close Morrigan was would remain a secret, but the warning had been given, and Kathryn would one day face the formidable Celtic Deity of War.

Perhaps Mariel was mistaken. Perhaps she had seen, unawares, one of Morrigan's sisters. Roane and Macha, who were nearly as fearsome as their eldest sister, usually travelled together, wreaking havoc wherever they went. Morrigan was the most evil of the three sisters, however, and death almost always followed her.

Kathryn trembled. The thought of the Morrigan in pursuit of those aboard this ship frightened her. Yet, she knew in her heart that the predator hunted only one. Her spine chilled as she allowed herself to see the face of the man whom she knew was Morrigan's intended prey. His strong features and livid green eyes brought such yearning to her soul that she wondered what could have caused such hatred from the Goddess toward the pirate.

"I lie down this night with Spirit…and the Spirit will lie down with me," Kathryn began to chant the ancient Celtic prayer of peace for her soul. "In every place wherein they sleep, in the night that is tonight… and every single night."

The image of his crystal emerald eyes danced through her awareness as she drifted off to sleep with no other thought but him. Finally, deep slumber found her curled up on the cot and granted her some reprieve from the troubling warning. She dreamt of beautiful green pools that echoed the words Mariel had spoken. Once more, the overflowing love that filled her soul visited her again that night.

The rest of the ship lay silent, with the exception of the men assigned to the deep night watch, but their noise was kept to themselves. And so, Kathryn dreamt, peaceful at last.

Thirty-Six

MORNING ARRIVED WITH THE CREW already busying themselves with their duties. Most had risen before dawn. The sun lifted peacefully, breaking the dense fog that blanketed the ocean.

Captain Phillips called the crew together. They were to meet before the mast, with plans to divvy up the spoils plundered from the French sloop. The sails were set and Cook had a meager breakfast ready for them. By the time Kathryn had awakened, the men had already gathered at the main mast, and John Nutt was deep in the business of dividing their loot.

Conducting the affair was a simple task, and Nutt handled it well. Each man would be awarded his share according to his rank on the ship. The captain was first handed two shares of everything taken. The quartermaster and bosun were given one, plus another half share each. After that, Nutt set aside the same for himself. Next, the men each received an equal share of whatever was left. Silver reales, otherwise known as "pieces of eight," and gold doubloons were chunked with axes to balance out the shares. The rest, valuable trinkets and other items such as clothing, weapons, boots, and even a French Bible, were placed before the mast for auctioning.

A long line of men stood patiently waiting to receive their share – a rather orderly process for such an unruly gang of thugs. Captain Phillips was treated the same as the rest of the crew, receiving his share and no more. As Kathryn moved up the companionway, a few of the men parted way to allow her passage. The entire process fascinated her – and impressive display of democracy amongst the crew.

Indeed, it was an orderly way of handling the affairs of pirating business. Of course, to its casualties, democracy didn't exist, particularly when it came to pirates slicing the throats of their victims.

There was no doubt in any crewman's mind that the laws of the ship were to be followed, or else suffer the consequences. Oft repeated was the tale of Captain Phillips shooting a man point blank and throwing the body overboard just for smoking a pipe in the hold – a definite violation of the ship's Articles. "It's a wonder we'd not been blown to smithereens!" or so the story went.

As the men waited to receive their payment in coins, they greedily eyed the trinkets and treasure put up for auction. Kathryn stole onto the deck, keeping herself apart from the crew. She knew she had no part in this, although the dead surgeon would have received his share, as well, had he been alive to collect it. As she was not the surgeon, and not a member of the crew, she would not receive any portion, including the leftovers, which would be cast into the hold or thrown overboard for a decoy. This was not a topic she was willing to broach, and did not want to give the impression that she held expectations to that end. Stepping into the crowd would send the wrong message. So she stayed apart from them, silent but observant.

"I have need to speak with ye, lass." She was startled as the captain approached.

"Yes, Capt'n?" Her voice sounded raspy. She hadn't spoken with anyone since awakening and was somewhat distracted. Intrigued by an unusual sand glass poised precariously on the edge of the loot pile, she struggled to appear more attentive. She cleared her throat. "What was it ye need, Capt'n?"

He followed her gaze to the treasure.

"It's a captivating piece, is it not?" His eyes traced the contours of her face. Without allowing time for her to respond, he turned on one heel and strode to the mast. "Two reales for the sandglass given 'afore the mast. What say ye, men? Be any o' ye dogs disinclined to my bid o' it?"

"Nay, belongs to the Capt'n." Mister Nutt's response was left unchallenged.

Captain Phillips handed two silver coins to Gow, who tossed them into a black box set in between him and Mister Moody for safe keeping. John Nutt handed the hourglass to Captain Phillips, who took the treasure in one hand, turned away from the mast, and moved toward the stern of the ship. He shot Kathryn a look that said, *follow me*, which she did, slipping away unnoticed. None of the other pirates spotted her trailing behind the captain since most of them were too absorbed in the bidding. Their voices shouted one over another, and they waved doubloons and silver in the air for bids.

The door to the captain's quarters sat ajar – an invitation to enter. She stepped over the threshold and met him there. With long strides, the captain walked through the dimly lit room. Kathryn stopped just inside and blinked a few times to focus her eyes. From across the room, John Phillips' strong, angular back faced her. He stood next to a tall case filled with parchment and a solid collection of books. He rifled through the parchment for only a moment before selecting two rolled up lengths.

Kathryn assumed both were navigational charts. She scanned the books' spines for titles, curious as to why a pirate would preserve so many books. Sadly, none of them looked as if they had been touched for ages. They appeared neglected and covered in dust. On one side, the table sat cluttered with course-plotting tools and writing utensils that begged for the captain's attention. He held a sharp carving pin in one hand and the brass hourglass in the other, and appeared to be scratching something on the bottom in the brass. When he finished, he stood upright and faced her.

"Take it," he said, offering the treasure to her. "This be me gift to ye for your care with me wounds." He patted the side of his chest for emphasis. And while the comment sounded rather matter-of-fact, Kathryn detected some tenderness in his voice.

"Capt'n Phillips, I watched you bid on this just now, at the mast." She took the beautiful hourglass in both hands and turned it over, admiring it. Tiny grains of sand trickled in a steady stream from one end to the other. "Thank you, sir," she said, and her cheeks colored. She dropped her eyes to the beautiful brass object in her hands. Three initials were scratched in the bottom, *JPB to K.* She traced her fingers over the freshly etched letters.

"Is the last meant for me?"

"The initials be here on the brass so that no man questions your right to it," he explained. The comment was meant to be kind, but it only reinforced her status on the ship and the simple fact that she had no part to any loot, unless given to her. Whether this was an insult or an act of kindness, Kathryn wasn't certain, but his tone indicated he meant no offense.

She looked into his face and smiled, all the while fighting the urge to wrap her arms around his broad shoulders and thank him the way only a woman could. Instead, she did not move but looked deeply into his breathtaking eyes. She allowed him to see her gratitude. Once again, he took her left hand, lifted it to his lips, and kissed the tips of her fingers, one by one, ever so gently, never taking his eyes off hers as he did so. Kathryn's heart leapt, but she willed it to still. This was not the time to awaken the stone around her neck. He lowered both their hands and turned from her, trying to hide tears that had welled in his eyes.

"I need be gettin' back to me men, lass. There's more business at hand with 'em. Ye can stay here or join us, it matters not, but as I said before, ye have no say in the matters 'afore the mast."

"I understand, Captain," she whispered and drew her finger over the initials again.

"John. My given name is John Phillips Buchannon. Those…" He nodded to the hourglass in her hands. "… be me own initials etched there."

"But you don't use Buchannon?"

"No. When I left me home for the sea, I changed it to John Phillips."

"Why? John Buchannon is a fine name." She cocked her head and waited for him to answer.

"To hide my whereabouts. I'd rather not leave behind a calling card known by those familiar with the Buchannon family."

"Ah, I see. It's a common practice among pirates, then?" she asked.

"Ay, it is." He studied her for a moment. "None but a few know my true name, and ye'd do well to keep it to yourself. But call me John when we be in quarters and none else be present."

Kathryn lowered her eyes as he walked past her. There was the scent of sandalwood and cinder as he walked by, and she felt her heart leap again. Without realizing it, her hands began to work the beautiful hourglass, turning it over and over as she admired the steady trickle into the bottom chamber. Only time would tame the blush that tinted her cheeks. It was essential she not be flushed when joining the others on deck – all of which would certainly raise eyebrows and gossip. She turned to the door and moved to exit the captain's chambers.

"The K is meant for you," he said behind her.

"Thank you," she whispered. She walked out of his quarters, closing the door softly behind her, before taking the causeway two stairs at a time.

The men were still gathered around the mast, bidding on the castoff plunder that had been discarded from the sloop. Sitting amongst the pile were several fine pieces, including a full case of green bottles still sealed with wax over their tops. Archer motioned from the sloop and was straightway assured of his share of the gold, plus a handsome pair of boots and two bottles of rum. This was recorded in a leather-bound book as compensation for staying with the French sloop. Manning the *Fame's Revenge* did not exempt the quartermaster from his share, which was exactly the task Moody had been assigned to oversee.

The French captain and his crew had been kept below deck in the hold for most of the days following their capture, but this day they were brought topside to witness the division of their belongings. Grumbling in French, and cursing all manner of profanities, did nothing to change the pirates' proceedings. The captives watched helplessly as prized possessions were slowly auctioned off. In spite of their threats, the French crew dared not interfere, for they were breathing fresh air and remained alive – something that would certainly change with the least provocation.

Sadly, the French captain had been honest about the lack of valuables or shiny treasure onboard. Only scant amounts of gold and silver were found and doled out as payment for the pirates' fine work securing the sloop. Mostly, the plunder included clothing, books, sugar, cocoa, the confiscated weapons, and of course, rum, all bound for the Martinique. To have intercepted the sloop with even this much cargo was fortunate, given the *Revenge* was down to her last supplies.

"We'll still have to set loose a few." Kathryn overheard Gow whispering to Nutt. "Not enough supplies for this many men."

"Th' capt'n likely will send 'em off in the sloop, methinks."

"Aye, most likely indeed."

Bidding diminished the pile. By midday, only a scant heap remained stacked at the mast. Kathryn could barely resist the urge to join in. Some of the items would come in handy for healing purposes. But, mostly, she wanted bidding privileges for the sheer pleasure of breaking the monotony of life at sea. In addition, a pair of barely worn britches sat unclaimed. They were rather small and would likely fit her, which she thought would be perfect apparel for the next time she battled Wynn in swordplay. Alas, it was not to be, as one of the younger lads placed the high bid and won the coveted trousers.

"Ye men 'afore the mast and prisoners alike," the captain's commanding voice boomed. "We're sendin' off the sloop, *Fame's Revenge*, and be needin' a crew and a captain o're it. What say ye?"

"Aye!" sounded the cry from amongst the men standing 'round the mast.

"Whosoever stands with me and the *Revenge*, step forward."

A scuffle of feet brought a division between the French sailors and pirates, all save four men who stayed behind, apparently preferring the cutthroats' ways to those of the French privateers.

"So be it. Ye're all free then to go back to your ship. The rest o' ye, including the four French sailors, follow Mister Gow."

Stamped with the new title of *pirate*, the four volunteers were ushered to the stern of the ship and given jobs. The remaining men looked to Captain Phillips for orders, ready to jump ship and board their newly re-named *Fame's Revenge*.

"Now be the time for electin' your captain," ordered Phillips.

They all offered names, but none voted the former French captain to return to his command. Lacking respect, the French captain relinquished his title and joined his men. No longer their captain, due mainly to the simple fact that he had surrendered without firing off a single shot in defense, he cast his eyes to the deck and awaited orders. Within moments, the men had elected a new leader for their ship.

"I call for Emmanuel Wynn as captain!" shouted a deep voice from the line of men.

"Monsignor La Bouch," crooned a heavy accent in front.

"William Fly."

"Aye, aye," sang out several voices at once. "We say Fly be Captain."

A few of the crew from the *Revenge* moved forward to join those defecting. The prospect of becoming captain over a sloop had become too tempting to pass up. Captain Phillips scowled.

"So this be yer fate, then?" he growled at his men who had joined the French crew.

Heads nodded with eyes downcast as they stepped in line with the rest. The spurned French captain beamed a sadistic grin as he watched the former pirates line up alongside his own men.

"So be it! Ye have no more place onboard this ship!" Spoken between clenched teeth, the threat in his eyes confirmed the anger in John Phillips' voice. "Captain Fly it is, then. Take command o're your ship, sir, and be off with ye. Pray that we never cross paths, for I will spare no mercy to any traitor!"

William Fly moved in long strides to his ship. The men followed him as they boarded the sloop, the last being the former French captain, wearing a smirk and a red plumed hat.

"There be provisions for one week. Mind ye, don't rot 'afore ye reach the Canaries," Captain Phillips called out as the defectors made ready the sails.

Captain Fly stood at the helm and faced his former crewmates on the *Revenge*. Waiving his hat in the air, he responded to Captain Phillips.

"The devil take yer souls an' we see ye again in hell!"

Scarlet flushed John Phillip's face while anger changed his expression. Welsh pride would not allow him to turn away from the insult. Instead, the pirate captain faced the sloop filled with traitors and cowards. Kathryn's gut wrenched as she watched John Rose Archer hop over the rails and back onboard the *Revenge*. Several of his cohorts followed, accompanied by the French defectors assigned to carry the remaining provisions from the sloop. The vessel was left desolate, since everything had been transferred to the *Revenge*, minus the week's rations left onboard. Jonesy, standing near the rails, shot an angry flintlock at the sloop, but the crew on the small ship laughed as they sailed away from the grand merchant ship.

"I'm not clear whether my anger stems from the hasty defection of those I'd called *mates* or the loss of the vessel itself," Captain Phillips confided to his quartermaster after he'd boarded.

"Cursed traitors, that lot. Best we're rid o' them, says I," muttered Archer under his breath. He took his place at the right-hand of Captain Phillips. "They'll be dead 'fore next full moon and lyin' at the depths o' the sea, grinnin' a skull's simper wit' Davy Jones hisself!"

"Ay," agreed Captain Phillips as he faced the sea and watched the ship slowly disappear. "She's called *Fame's Revenge* for a reason, Mister Archer. The purpose was not lost on any man, yet they quickly turned on their own crew and captain. This, I cannot understand."

"It's the pirate's way, Capt'n. The sloop be naught but a prize to that dog, Fly. He'll surely christen her differently and try his hand at piratin'. But mark me words, the lot will find only the gallows waiting at the end o' their voyage…if they survive." Archer spat on deck.

"Perhaps, Mister Archer…perhaps." Captain Phillips shifted his stance, determined to hold his ground until the sloop was out of sight. None of the traitorous crew would ever see him stand down.

"Get back to work, scurvy dogs! I've no patience for insolence this day," Archer barked. The crew gathered up their winnings from the mast and scrambled to the task of sailing the *Revenge*. Kathryn held back, watching the captain. He remained where he stood until finally, the sloop was nothing more than a white pinprick on the surface of a great blue ocean. Satisfied that they were far enough away, he turned and looked at her once before making his way to the helm with Archer at his side.

She watched him go in silence. Her time with him had already been recorded on a gift inscribed with his initials. Still, she longed to steal just one more moment with the captain of the *Revenge*. But it was not meant to be. Clearly, she would speak with him no more this day.

Thirty-Seven

THE *REVENGE* TURNED SOUTH TOWARD Tobago. The food barrels had been refilled with the supplies taken from the sloop, which kept Cook cheerful. Day after day, the men stayed busy with their jobs, and no one seemed to pay any mind to the young woman onboard the ship. Kathryn still cringed at the sight of the quartermaster, who feigned disinterest out of respect for her…or perhaps fear. Both made a point of keeping their distance from one another at all times. It was a good thing, because Kathryn's boredom met with Archer's temper would amount to no good. Blood would surely be spilt on the day the two became entangled, most likely Kathryn's.

Choppy seas playfully tossed the massive ship as it sailed across the Atlantic currents. Though the skies were clear and mild, the seas seemed agitated, as if something on the horizon waited for just the right quarry to skim its surface. Occasionally, a gentle breeze would waft through the open portal in Kathryn's cabin, which offered a brief reprieve from the stench rising from below where bilge water and spoiled meat rotted.

For several days in a row, the water had been rough, pitching the *Revenge* from whitecap to whitecap like a floating cork. Several of the men became queasy, and a few sickened to the point of incapacitation. Kathryn was summoned, and she worked fervently, coaxing remedies down their gullets made of teas concocted from the freshest water she could find. Of course, unspoiled water could only be purchased with bribes. Thankfully, she'd kept the few coins she had been gifted, and had pilfered a few others – a justified act in her mind, given the conditions onboard. With that, she bargained for fresh water and stole whatever wasn't guarded.

On the third day, the skies darkened. Lightning shattered the silence of the stratosphere overhead, bringing with it enough power to cause the hairs on everyone's arms to stand at attention. Soon afterward, rain poured for nearly forty-eight hours. "A gift from heaven," Kathryn called it. The barrels had been filled once again with fresh rainwater, and bribing others to steal much needed water was no longer required. Still, the process of keeping the crew from the sick bay proved somewhat challenging, until the cook grew ill. Once he could no longer hold his head upright, the task became impossible. Too many had become sick, and the ship lacked hands enough to keep a steady sail.

"We'll founder without adequate seamen," Captain Phillips reported. "Ye'd best conjure up a remedy soon, or I'll be forced to wait out the storm and hope we don't sink or be discovered."

"I'll do my best, Capt'n."

"See to it. This bay stinks of vomit and dysentery. I don't know how ye tolerate it."

"I don't…" she replied. But he had already darted topside and into fresh air. She pulled a rag over her nose and set about concocting another batch of tea.

Fortunately, the seas soon calmed, although it was not uncommon to see several men leaning over the rails at the same time to vomit green bile into the blue water. Schools of little fish danced in and out of the stomach matter, feeding.

"They'll never improve if the only remedy they'll take is grog," Kathryn snapped one arduous afternoon. Gow happened to be standing closest and received the brunt of her frustration. "It's tea that's needed, and lots of it! I'll be usin' the freshest water from the barrels before anyone else does, savvy?"

Gow nodded and immediately reported her demands to the captain, insisting she'd been insolent when making them. Captain Phillips only laughed as Gow mimicked her, stomping his foot the way she did for emphasis.

"If that's what the chirurgeon needs, then that's what she'll get," he replied.

"Chirurgeon? The wench has been designated as the *surgeon*?" Gow responded, incredulous.

"Ay, Mister Gow. Unless, of course, you'd rather change duties and take up station in the sick bay?"

"No sir, Capt'n!"

Gow said nothing after that and immediately marched off to another part of the ship. The captain chuckled again, an image of the spirited young woman stomping her foot at Gow still in his mind.

Time passed and the crew slowly began to improve. Her remedies had worked their magic on the men. Finally, Kathryn was able to venture topside without worries of a full sick bay.

It had been nearly two weeks since the sloop and merchant ship had parted ways, and only days since the recovery of the crew from their seasickness. Seemingly, Kathryn had earned a place of respect among the men, but this new status remained only insofar as she found ways to cure them of their ills. She still was not allowed to sup with them. Her cabin stayed off-limits and private for sleeping, for which she was grateful. Still, she noticed most kept their eyes on the stone around her neck. This, she maintained was the reason for their fair treatment of her – a superstitious fear of the Seren. Whatever the reason, she was left to herself and enjoyed the tedious work of the ship's healer without bother.

During the days the cook had taken ill, another had been selected to fix the grub for meals. This wretched soul knew nothing of the preparations required for food, so meals were scant and foul. Kathryn was grateful to eat alone, as she typically found herself gagging on the mess brought to her by Seth. Once, she offered to take the pirate's place in the galley, but the men revolted.

"Surely an' she be poisonin' us with her witch's brew and hexes," came the response as they voted unanimously against it. "No!"

Her duties were relegated to mucking vomit, stealing supplies for teas, and eating maggot-infested hardtack or salt pork along with the rest of the crew. This followed with the unfortunate task of incessantly administrating curatives to the ill pirates as they sought her help from food poisoning and infestation.

"May I have a word with ye?" Seth spoke rather grimly one evening. He held his lips taught across his teeth as he handed her a platter of inedible victuals and grog. "The curse has found its way to most of the crew, me self included. I fear we all soon wither and die."

Kathryn looked up from her plate at pleading eyes. Seth rarely showed fear of anything, and greeted most challenges as child's play when others would cower. This was not like him.

"Seth, what are ye talkin' about?" she asked, using the gentlest voice she could muster.

In reality, she felt a knot grow in her stomach which she knew wasn't from the food, but rather from the thought of losing her only friend onboard. Seth said nothing, but opened his lips wide in a gruesome sneer, exposing his teeth. The pink gums were puffy, the color of sea coral, with blood on the edges where the teeth grew.

"There be men onboard who bleed from their mouths, same as me. It's a curse, for certain, and we'll all be dead next fortnight. Like as not, they'll blame you for it." The words slipped out before he covered his lips with dirty hands.

"Keep your wits about ye, Seth," she snapped. "This is no curse. At least not one that can't be broken, and I have the means for doin' it…if you're willin'."

Seth sniffed, wiped a wet nose along the sleeve of his shirt, and looked up at her.

"Aye…but ye'd best get on with it and make certain ye don't use that mumbo-jumbo what killed off Flint, on me," he said.

"Take me to the others…and don't tempt me. I've a mind to use mumbo-jumbo on ye all just to keep your superstitious minds from wanderin' so!"

"This way." He marched out of her quarters with Kathryn on his heels, but not before she snatched a handful of tiny, dried white flowers from her bag of herbs. Within moments, they had made their way to the bow of the ship. The seas had turned calm and almost glassy as the evening deepened. Several men sat scattered in small groups, passing a bulbous bottle between them, laughing and sharing stories. As they raised their heads, Kathryn saw the same bloody grin as she had seen from Seth.

"Ask Cook where he keeps the fixin's for makin' grog. I'll need lemons," she said quietly in Seth's ear.

"What do you need lemons for?" he replied. But the look she gave warned him not to argue, and sent him scurrying back the way they'd come. A few of the most inebriated pirates noticed her standing nearby, but none paid any mind to her presence. This was typical, particularly when the crew drank and told tall tales.

She watched them, patiently waiting for Seth's return, and when he finally made it back, she could see that he had filled his pockets with lemons stolen from the galley. He handed them to her and she laid them out on a makeshift table. Pointing to the pirate sitting nearest, she motioned for him to come near. He ignored the request.

"Give me your dirk, Mister Taylor," she ordered in the most authoritative voice she could muster.

"Now why would I give a simpering little mouse me only dagger?" He raised a wobbly head to sneer at her.

"I've no time for drunken idiocy, Mister Taylor. Give it to me willingly or I'll take it myself." She raised one hand to the Seren.

Taylor stared wide-eyed at the Seren for a moment before handing over the small dagger he kept tucked inside his boot. He turned away, forgetting almost instantly that she stood above him.

The fool's placed himself in a rather precarious position, turning his back on me. Luck follows the blaggard today, it seems, as I remain sober in spite of the knife in hand. The thought made Kathryn smile as she forced the blade into the lemon.

"She's cuttin' up fruit for grog, it seems."

"Not quite, Mister Taylor. Although you'll be the first to taste my brew, I promise."

Slivered yellow wedges, the size of a sail-rubber's haft, were then pressed with pieces of the white flowers and leaves.

"Now eat this and don't spit it out 'til the juices be drained," she said, forcing the wedge into Taylor's mouth. Then, she boldly handed a sliced lemon to each pirate there. "That's an order!"

"Aye." The responses were garbled but the edict was followed.

Turning on Taylor, she held up his dagger. "This belongs to you." Juice trickled down her arm, which the drunken pirate followed with his eyes. She allowed the juice to tantalize him a bit. "That, however," she added as she ran her tongue down the length of her forearm, "…will never be yours."

Seth grinned at the power she wielded with the feeble-minded pirates. One by one, dirty hands reached up to take the outstretched lemon wedges and shoved them into bloody mouth. The pirates growled as the juice stung the open sores along their gums, but no one dared spit it out under the commanding stare of the ship's healer.

"Now you, Seth," she said, and placed a fresh-cut wedge packed with dried Chickweed blossoms into his outstretched hand. He dutifully placed the lemon in his mouth and sucked the juice, wincing at the tart sting to his gums while the liquid drained down his throat. One by one, Kathryn did the same with the other pirates that sat against the bow's bulwark. Each complied, their faces showing a look of bewildered submission at orders given by a female. In many ways, they looked much like naughty children facing their scolding mothers.

Only after she was certain each pirate had taken his lemon did she turn on her heel and march away from the drunken group of sailors, dragging Seth along with her until they were out of range. "Who else, Seth? Is Captain Phillips afflicted the same?" she asked, staring him down for any sign of deceit.

"No, ma'am, but Archer and Sparks be showin' a bloody grin. And Skyrme, Wood and Fern be, as well," he responded.

"Blimey," she said and stomped her foot. It didn't please her to hear she would need to make company with the quartermaster. "I suppose I'd best get on with it then. Where are they?"

"I dunno." Seth shrugged.

Sighing, she gave instructions. "Well, find them… please…and bring them to my quarters. I'll wait for ye there." Seth agreed and made his way aft while she returned to her cabin.

Once inside, she set the remaining lemons and Chickweed out on the small table and began to cut off hunks of lemon for her expected guests, keeping one for herself, just in case. In minutes, she heard fists pounding on her door and prepared herself to face the quartermaster and his cronies.

"Enter." She was surprised to see far too many pirates than first anticipated. "There be no room for all of you here. Wait for me at the top of the stairs and I'll bring somethin' to cure it."

The men retreated and she followed. Unexpectedly, she found herself in a throng of anxious pirates.

"Well, I must say you've all found your manners," she said as each man politely waited his turn to be fed a lemon wedge.

Dutifully, each took the painful bite of lemon and sucked the juices from it. Without fail, each of their faces puckered just before taking their leave. Eventually, she faced Archer, who glared at her with his black eyes as blood dripped from the edges of his cracked lips. His appearance reminded her of the stories she's heard of the blood drinkers who walked at night. These were the monsters she'd been frightened of most as a little girl. Her hand trembled slightly, but she stood as tall as her spine permitted, then handed the fruit to the man.

"Eat this, every part, and make mind that ye do not spit out any of it, Mister Archer," she commanded with power in her voice.

He took the fruit in hand and left, saying nothing as he departed. She didn't care whether he heeded her words or not. Falling dead to scurvy would be a fine ending for Archer any day, in her mind. Another calloused hand stretched out in front of her.

"I be needin' one too," Sparks said gruffly.

Kathryn handed him the fruit and gave him the same instructions she'd done for the others, which he obeyed, flinching only slightly as the juice hit its mark.

When the group had cleared, she saw the captain approaching. Creases threaded their way along the skin of his forehead. She'd seen that look before – an expression that indicated displeasure about something. She studied him but could see no sign of scurvy. He approached slowly with hands clasped behind his back.

"Tell me…" His tone sounded flat, and she could not read his temperament as anything but pensive. "Ye have a curative hand with the problem, then, lass?"

"Aye, sir. The men have scurvy from the looks of it, and I've passed out lemons to each of them. That should take care of it, methinks."

"Ay." It was the only response he gave before turning to face the ship's gunner. The lemon-rind grin was still spread across his mouth. "I sense trouble before us, Mister Sparks. Ye best get the weapons fit for a fight, for there's somethin' a brewin' that seeks to take us all…I feel it in me bones."

Sparks nodded – his only reply: "Aye, aye, Capt'n." He grunted and spat out the rind.

Kathryn sensed John Phillips was not a superstitious man, at least not in the way the rest of the crew seemed to be. Yet the gravity of his disposition was evident. As he spoke, she double-checked his mouth and saw no signs of scurvy. She knew this meant something else was the cause for his worry. Suddenly, the image of Mariel flashed in her mind. As Kathryn thought about the warning given by Mariel's apparition not so long ago, her color drained and her heart pounded.

"Is it Morrigan ye fear?"

There was silence as the captain spun around with a black stare, his face ghostly white.

Thirty-Eight

"WHAT DO YE KNOW OF Morrigan?"

Captain Phillips stormed as he began to pace. Kathryn followed him with her eyes as he wore a path in front of the table.

"Is she the one you fear? Tell me truthfully, I beg of you."

"Morrigan?" He stopped pacing and spun to look at her. "I am afraid of no one. And how is it ye know so much of Morrigan?"

"I know little, only that your true love is the sea."

"Now is the time for ye to be truthful, lass. It's factual that my first and only love is the sea. But you've failed to tell all, and secrets are not looked upon favorably aboard this ship!" Kathryn winced but held her tongue. "Do not toy with me, lass!"

"I have need to speak with you about this, sir. I have been warned in a dream." She summoned up whatever courage she possessed.

"Bah, dreams!" He began to pace again.

"Do not discount that with which you are not familiar, sir."

He turned to face her, leaning against the capstan. "Pray tell, then, what is it ye dreamt?"

"I…but the men…"

Kathryn was speechless. The moment had finally arrived when she could finally tell all, and her voice had failed her. When she did not respond, he strode to where she was poised, and stood nose-to-nose with her.

"You're free to speak openly. There is nothin' ye could say that my men can't hear as well," he said. "Speak, woman!"

"Sir, I do not wish to offend you."

"Go on."

It was obvious to the others standing nearby that Captain Phillips' anger was not intentionally directed at anyone in particular, including Kathryn. They all knew the history between Morrigan and the captain, and they also knew better than to bring it up. Kathryn cleared her throat, then recounted the story of the night Mariel appeared.

"The warning was clear, and I noted it well, for my grandmother spoke it herself. Indeed, she was specific. *'Morrigan be lookin' for the man now.'* Those are the words exactly as she said them." Pausing, she considered the effect the warning would have on him. She stayed silent and was a bit surprised by the tears filling her eyes. "The ship is in grave danger, Captain."

The mood grew sullen, locking the crowd of pirates into a transfixed silence with every word she uttered. They occasionally crossed their chests and hopped like a litter of rabbits, but no one dared utter a word. Captain Phillips considered her for a moment before turning to the men. Archer was not among them, so he directed his orders to all.

"Make ready the sails. We need gather speed and hasten to Tobago. Fetch the quartermaster." His pitch rose with urgency.

"Sir, there is more," Kathryn added. One hand reached out instinctively as if to take hold of the captain's sleeve.

"What is it?" His eyes followed her hand, and though he appeared displeased, he did not withdraw.

"The ghost told of a way to thwart the demon's plan."

"Go on."

"It said, *'Only by uniting two longing hearts into one can she be beaten and ye and the man be spared.'* Those were the words, exactly, though I don't fully understand what it means."

"Well you best figure it out, then!"

"But, sir…"

The captain did not answer, but turned his back on her and moved through the crowd of men with long, forceful strides. Kathryn was left alone, facing the last of the crew as each man cast cold stares in her direction before making their way to the sails.

As luck would have it, the wind had died down to nothing at all. Not even a whispered breath blew across the water. Likely, the men blamed her for that as well.

"Well, why not!" She stomped her foot and leaned over the rails to study the water. The current barely moved, and the ship appeared to be bobbing up and down without direction. Archer had been summoned and stood with Captain Phillips, receiving orders that he parroted to the men scattered about the ship. Frustrated with the state of the sea and the news of Morrigan, Captain Phillips' temper raged. No one dared cross him at times like this, and orders were followed without question. The crew worked with backbreaking fervor as they struggled to bring the ship to life.

"She won't find the wind, not against the glass and in the doldrums," Seth stated. Gow's ears perked up.

"How do you know, boy?"

"I just do. I sense it, I suppose. There needs be a shift in the waters before we move again, unless the wind can be summoned." Seth glanced at Kathryn.

"This is Morrigan's doing," Kathryn breathed. She locked eyes with Seth and nodded ever so slightly.

"We need wind. The sails won't respond without it." Seth pulled against a line, drawing the canvas taught, but the sail remained lax.

Kathryn could see that the flush in John Phillips' cheeks had not faded since she'd brought up the topic of Morrigan. Something was amiss with the captain, and whatever it was, she suspected it would now include her. She was grateful her grandmother had appeared to warn her of it, whatever it may be.

"Heave!" shouted Archer at several weathered pirates. They all pulled in unison on large ropes attached to the topsails and jibs. "Put yer back into it, mates, ye yellow-bellied maggots."

The men strained against the sheets, the coarse ropes burning the flesh of their calloused hands. Stubbornly, the sails remained slack with nothing but dead air to fill them. Kathryn watched the struggle as together they put their effort into catching any breeze that might move the ship.

The two officers at the helm appeared tense. Large beads of sweat trickled down the sides of the men's tanned faces. But the crew labored in vain. Captain Phillips maneuvered the wheel, hoping a shift in the rudder might find the draft that would move the *Revenge*. But this proved futile and the canvas remained slack.

Seth's gaze burned against the back of her neck. She tried to ignore his incessant stare as she watched the men attempt, through force, to propel the ship into transit.

I know your thoughts, Seth.

Without the aid of precious wind, they would be doomed to bake in the middle of the Caribbean Sea, a victim of its merciless climate.

Indeed, Morrigan caused this. She created the defenseless state in which we find ourselves. Perhaps it's her way to destroy...

Kathryn's eyes darted to Captain Phillips. She had to do something, and Seth knew it, too. She glanced at him. Do something! She heard his thoughts and he nodded. Memories of a day long ago when the wind had tossed berries through the air at Winne with nothing but magic to launch them urged her to use her *Gift*.

"Troubles fill the sails, I see." Her comment was meant for no one. But Archer's gaze pounded her along with Seth's. Apparently, he had heard her.

"Aye, an' it be naught but thanks to boardin' the devil's daughter, methinks." Archer spat and heaved against a large line leading to the mainsail. "Ye shouldn't have been brought to this ship, fiend!"

"Call for the wind, Mister Archer."

His shock at her audacity stopped him in his tracks, and he let the line go slack in his hands.

"What did you say, witch?"

A crowd began to gather. Her eyes scanned their faces and read the deep hunger for conflict in their eyes. They would just have to wait.

"I said, call forth the wind."

The crew shot glances at one another, and Archer's face flushed. Seth joined them, his eyes wide and hopeful.

"I'll not have any part o' yer sorcery, Madame. 'Tis the devil ye summon, and we have trouble enough onboard with ye. I'll be no part o' it."

Kathryn cocked her head, raised the corners of her lips, and then surveyed the assembly. Lifting her chin, she spoke to the bosun. Her voice sounded airy, too serene.

"Well then, you do it, Mister Gow."

He said nothing and shifted his weight, glancing at the trembling sailor standing alongside him.

"All of you, then. Pray. Pray that the winds come and deliver you from our plight. From Morrigan's curse."

Chests were crossed and the crowd size increased.

"Do what she says, Gow," Captain Phillips ordered. She glanced at him and saw a flash of fear behind his eyes.

"I don't know how. She asks th' impossible," Gow finally responded.

"Impossible? Is that what you think as well, Mister Sparks?"

The gunner stepped forward boldly. "I only know me weapons of war. I know how to fill the skies with fire and the seas with men's blood. But I don't know how to pray for wind."

She scanned their faces and rested her focus on Seth.

"What about you? Do you know how to pray?"

"I know how to receive the answers to prayer. But these doldrums will take more than a prayer to break," Seth challenged.

She cocked her head and smiled, then addressed the assemblage. "Is it more difficult to supplicate God for wind in the sails than cross yourselves silly in hopes He sees your lack of faith?"

"Blasphemy!" Somewhere a cutlass raised itself above the men's heads.

"Hold!" The captain's voice boomed. "No blood spilt on me ship, not even the lass'."

"But we don't know what she's askin' us to do, Capt'n."

"Do it thus." Kathryn pursed her lips and blew gently. A soft, low whistle escaped her mouth, resonating in still air. The crew looked at one another, and a few mimicked in silence.

"What is this?" Archer shouted. "Ye'll be as fools doin' a witch's biddin'. See now, there's no wind, even still."

Kathryn continued to whistle and her eyes smiled as she watched the men try it. She nodded approval.

"Is it harder to act on faith with such a gentle supplication to God than face another day at doldrums? Methinks you'd rather rot at sea, Mister Archer," she said.

She drew in another breath and whistling gently again. The mainsail flickered and her eyes shifted to the top of the mast. Instantly, the sound of supplication was heard from the gathered men as pirate after pirate pursed his lips and began to blow. Whistling filled the air along with shouts of, "Look there!" as the mainsail fluttered again. Archer stepped back and crossed his arms over his chest, then dropped one hand to the hilt of a cutlass set over his left hip.

She wondered if, indeed, the men could possibly push wind into the sails with the faith of a whistle. *Better that they think its wind from a whistle than discover the truth.* She stuffed the thought away and stared at the sky. In actuality, she'd been using her *Gift* to summon wind, as she had done so not long ago in the garden with Winne. She could take no chances now and closed her eyes, putting her mind into stillness, then began to pray. Inhaling deeply, she whispered the ancient words, chanting:

"Codi'r awel. Morio O flaen y gwynt.

Codi'r awel. Morio O flaen y gwynt."

Again and again, she whispered the Celtic spell, summoning the wind to the sails. She raised her arms, inching them towards her head, gathering air in armfuls as she inhaled deeply once more. Then, as she slowly exhaled her breath, she pushed both palms towards the sails above her. This she continued for several minutes with her eyes closed, chanting and breathing air into the sleeping sails.

A few of the pirates nearest to her stopped what they were doing and pointed. The inactivity caught the attention of the quartermaster, who squinted up at Kathryn. Contempt filled his soul, and he made ready to put an end to her witchcraft when a firm grasp stopped him dead in his tracks. Captain Phillips had also been watching Kathryn cast the spell for wind.

"Hold, Mister Archer." He took hold of the quartermaster's arm. "Let's wait and see what the she does before you cast asunder our only hope."

Her graceful movements enchanted him and he wanted her left undisturbed.

"She dances," Seth said under his breath.

"She's bringin' bad luck on us, Capt'n!" Archer responded, the bitterness in his voice noxious. "Her witchcraft cursed the wind right off the waters, and we be sitting like guppies to an eel's tooth. I say we hang her and be done with it!" The words were cold and threatening, ripping the captain's focus away from the girl.

"Ye best be careful o' the threats you're makin', Mister Archer," he cautioned. His tone, dark and foreboding, left no error for misinterpretation. The strong fingers of the highest officer dug into Archer's muscular arm just slightly for emphasis. "Your men brought the girl here for healin' and she's done that, to my knowledge, has she not?" There was no response. "Remember, while she sails onboard the *Revenge*, she's protected by the Articles o' this ship. There's the power o' that cursed stone about her neck to mind, as well. Don't forget that."

"Aye, Capt'n." Archer clenched his teeth as he yanked his arm away. "But I'll not be held responsible."

Captain Phillips let the insubordination go. Caught up in Kathryn's antics, he ignored all else. She chanted and breathed into the sails, lifting the air to the canvas with her hands. More crewmen had gathered to whistle and watch her with curiosity. Fear showed in many of their faces.

At least whistling is something to do – productive or not, it keeps the superstitious mind busy. The thought brought a smile as she exhaled breath into the topsail.

"Codi'r awel. Morio O flaen y gwynt.

Codi'r awel. Morio O flaen y gwynt."

This continued throughout the morning while the crew slowly converged on the deck to watch the enchantress as she worked her magic with the wind.

"This isn't working, Capt'n," Slade finally announced. "We've got to do something."

"Aye." A few of the others nodded in agreement and turned as if to leave.

"Wait!" Seth shouted and pointed overhead. "Look there."

Suddenly, as if in slow motion, each sail billowed outward, filled with gusts that appeared out of nowhere, rolling over the water and through the masts. Kathryn opened her eyes but continued to chant. A resonant crack sounded across the ship as the canvas instantly shuddered, then drew taught. She felt the bow lift high above the water and crash down, assuring all that the sails had taken hold. The ship lunged forward through the currents, but no one aboard dared move. The men ventured to do nothing else but whistle.

She stood back, hands on hips, and took in the full sail and roll of the ship. No longer was the chant required, and deep satisfaction accompanied the power of her magic. Archer's eyes flashed, and anger knitted his brows as he glanced from sail to Kathryn and back again. Both the quartermaster and sorceress shared awareness that this one act had made her powerful in the crew's simple minds. She smiled. The *Gift* had brought wind to the sails and fear into the hearts of the cutthroats she sailed with. In gratitude for the birthright she had been given through the unusual women in her family, and the fact that she had been able to harness it to benefit the ship, she lifted her eyes to the heavens and gave thanks, then faced her captain.

"To yer duties, mates!"

As the bow made its second drop, the men snapped to attention, scurrying to their different stations. They were once again underway toward the Island of Tobago. Only Captain Phillips stayed on the quarterdeck with his eyes locked on Kathryn. She regarded him in return and nodded, then turned on her heels and went below deck to her cabin. He had not dismissed her, but then, she hadn't required it…not this time.

"Sorcery," he said under his breath.

For a while, he stared at the empty space she had vacated and wondered what powers she indeed held. The lass would need to be watched closely. He made a mental note of it before returning his attention to his men. Giving additional orders to Archer, who had assumed a position at the helm, he then made for his own quarters. Shaken somewhat by the bewitchment he had just witnessed, he replayed the prophetic warning given in Kathryn's vision. Mostly, Captain John Phillips was rattled by a name – one he had hoped to forget after so many years.

Taking up a quill, he began to jot notes about the weather and the sudden gusts that filled the sails.

17 July 1721 (11°30N 61°28W) –
Lost to doldrums, had prepared to
ride them out until better conditions.
Concern for morale of crew paramount.
Unprovoked, was blessed with a sudden
blast o' wind from the SE.

He paused.

Morrigan certainly could have her sights on destroying them all. It wouldn't be beyond her to try. Yet Kathryn had breathed life back into the dead sails. The deliberation had interrupted his journaling. Memories of a dark time – one whose only companion was death and decay – scattered his logic. As he tried to make sense of it, his head fell into his hands. Images of pale blue eyes and the magical way she moved as she filled the sails with wind took control of his thoughts. Truly the demon Morrigan could never know what lay deep in his heart. Fear for the young healer's wellbeing scorched his mind and hurt his soul.

He stood from the table and crossed the room. The pirate captain kicked the door to his cabin, closing off the clamor from the ship…and thoughts of her.

Thirty-Nine

LITTLE WAS SAID TO KATHRYN over the next few weeks. Even Seth kept his eyes lowered, and his conversations held to a minimum. In truth, she didn't mind. A new respect had emerged for her and a pervading awe accompanied it. This alone would keep her at a safe distance from most of the men, particularly Archer. There was no sign of the captain whenever she was on deck – apparently, he was too busy with the details of sailing his ship. This bothered Kathryn but there was little she could do about it.

The good captain knew more than he was willing to share. *I'm not the only one who keeps information private.* She stomped a foot. *It's a secret you'd best be kept from, most likely, Kathryn.* She would ask of herself on occasion. *You want nothing to do with Morrigan and her sisters if at all possible, now don't you, Kathryn?* The resounding answer always arrived in a chill that accompanied the mention of the evil deity's name. Somehow, Kathryn was tied to Morrigan, and she wanted to break free of it. Perhaps the answers would be found on Tobago. Perhaps the captain would open up and share his secrets with her. *Likely not*, came the answer.

As they sailed farther south, the air grew dense, heavy, and humid. Kathryn noticed the water's color changing as well – from deep blue to turquoise green. Fish were visible, and dolphin often danced in their wake. The crew seemed to notice it, too. Frequently, sea shanties rang out unfettered as they worked the rigging and scrubbed the decks. Merriment returned to the evenings, which soon became Kathryn's favorite time of day, particularly at sundown. She would stand at the starboard rails and watch the sun drop lower into the pale emerald water, leaving a diamond shimmer sparkling over the tops of the water crests. As she daydreamed, she would often find herself humming along with the songs sung on the other side of the ship. Rising and falling with the lift and lull of the ship, she was completely at peace. These were her happiest times.

One such afternoon, she watched a school of yellowtail flickering through the water alongside the ship when she heard a voice shout out from the crow's nest.

"Land – *ho!*"

The entire crew scrambled topside, eyes to the crow's nest, to see which direction the lookout pointed. He waved his arm toward the southeast. Kathryn followed the watchman's direction, which took her gaze slightly to the left of their course. Peeking through a tuft of white clouds lying low on the water, a mossy-brown island floated – a miniature chip in the turquoise sea.

"Tobago! The island rises there!" someone shouted from the group of men assembled.

"Tobago! Tobago!" was repeated over and over between the men.

Cheers rose – a sure sign they would soon put in to port. Everyone celebrated. Backs were slapped, and a few danced with linked arms and kicking heels. The rest just passed around rum. Forgetting that Kathryn was a sorceress, a few sailors swung her around. A pockmarked brigand by the name of Samuel even kissed Kathryn's cheek. For a time, she joined them, enjoining their gaiety even though the stink from their breath caused her nose to wrinkle.

As they made for land, sea turtles surfaced, giving new life to Cook, who gathered hooks and lines to collect the unsuspecting marine creatures. A delectable soup soon waited. Good food only added to the merriment that continued throughout the night until sunrise. There was much to celebrate – bellies were full and Tobago lie directly ahead. They would make landfall by next eve.

By early evening, on the following day, the anchor was cast and skiffs lowered in preparation for going ashore. The captain had made his way above deck, as well. Mostly, he kept to himself, busy about his duties with no indication of leaving the ship. Occasionally, he'd cast an impassive glance at Kathryn, but always turned his focus back to the ship and the island.

Finally, permission was granted for all to go ashore. It was after the bulk of the crew had left the ship that Kathryn sought out the captain. She found him near the galley.

"I am requesting permission to go ashore as well, Capt'n." They'd been many months at sea, and she desperately longed to set foot on land again. "I mean to join the others in the longboats and…"

"The men wouldn't allow it!"

"Capt'n, please! The men would spare a place for one more passenger. Why do you seek to impede me going shoreward?"

"There are many reasons, lass, and I do not owe ye an explanation."

She blinked away tears. "Capt'n Phillips, I beg of you. Grant me leave to go ashore with the rest of the men."

"There's nothing good comes of Tobago."

The captain turned on his heel and made for the gunroom. She followed.

"You cannot ignore me, Capt'n," she said when she had finally caught up with him. "At least I seek permission first."

"I can do exactly that, Madame!" He stopped dead in his tracks. "Ignoring you is just my objective of late."

"So I've noticed," she snapped.

The response was met with silence, and while he hadn't yet granted permission, he did not deny it, either. His excuses only masked his real motive for keeping her onboard. *It only emphasizes that you're hiding something too.* She stomped her foot at the thought and gathered her skirts to follow him. Long strides took him topside with Kathryn on his heels.

Ahead, the men were boarding the last of the longboats leaving for shore. Unless Kathryn convinced him to grant her leave, she would likely miss the chance to board a longboat.

"Time's running out, Capt'n. If you won't allow me to go with the men, I'll likely swim to shore. Either way, I'll go to land."

"That's insubordination!"

"Indeed, and it won't be my last."

He turned to look at her, astonishment cloaking his expression. "It isn't safe ashore."

"Surely you jest! You warn a witch for safety?" She paused but got no response. "I'll be most cautious, I promise. Besides, I have this as protection." She touched the Seren.

His eyes darted to the stone momentarily before locking with hers. She saw fear behind them. "Why? Why do you seek to leave the ship so quickly?" His voice faltered as he spoke.

"My medicines are depleted, and I hope to gather plants to replace those used while onboard." She stared into eyes that matched the color of the Caribbean Sea.

"No other purpose? Only to seek remedies?"

"Yes, of course." It was true, after all. "Seasickness and scurvy has nearly exhausted all the supplies onboard. Ahead lay many more days at sea, and without supplies for the ills ahead. You'll face a significant decrease in manpower should any malady befall the crew. That will never do on a ship this size."

He considered her words momentarily then reluctantly agreed. "Ay then lass. Under those conditions, ye are free to go." Dismay laced his tone. "Mind me well, if ye do not return to the ship, I'll be comin' after ye meself!"

She sensed he was bluffing, knowing full well he wouldn't waste precious time looking for her on the island. But there was something that bothered him – something she couldn't place. And while she doubted he cared little for what her activities on land might entail, he certainly pressed for her return. She tossed a puzzled look in his direction. The thought never crossed her mind to abandon ship…or her captain. Here was a gentle soul, with a tender heart hidden deep beneath a crusty layer. She couldn't help but smile as she looked at him.

"Capt'n John Phillips, I swear on this day that I will return, unless it be against my will. I will not be kept from you." The oath was made holding her right hand upward, palm facing front – all with a touch of sarcasm.

The captain did not return the smile. Snatching his hand, her fingers wrapped through his and she squeezed gently to affirm her sincerity. He said nothing, but his eyes spoke volumes.

"Oh, thank you, Capt'n! I promise I'll return."

Then, abruptly, she kissed his cheek, turned from him, and quickly set off to join the others. And while he stood in place, a faint hint of relief shifted his expression as he watched her step into the last skiff and row off with his men to the white beaches of Tobago. She would return...she'd promised!

As the boat slid into shore, her heart skipped in time with the currents. A sudden thud, as the bow dug into the sand, indicated they had arrived.

Land!

She lifted her skirt and stepped one foot into the warm water, her toes sinking into the soft embankment beneath. She hopped out of the skiff and skipped through the water toward the dry earth, kicking the water high over her head as she pushed through it. Her crewmates jogged up the sloping bank to a small row of buildings with lanterns just lit – an invitation of rum for sailors.

Kathryn made her way across the beach to where the pirates had scattered. There she noticed a narrow path that cut into the thick ferns and palm trees blanketing the seafront. This would be the best place to start her search for florae and stones needed for spells. She stepped onto the path, hoping the fading sunset would give her enough light to see the foliage growing wild in this foreign place. Carefully placing her feet on the path, she started a course uphill, collecting leaves and blossoms. Most she recognized from Mariel's teachings. These she gently placed in her upheld skirt.

Damn, but I meant to bring a pouch of some sort! She berated herself and plucked another blossom. The trail narrowed drastically, so Kathryn dropped her eyes to stay on course. Ahead lay her destination. Blanketing the summit of a small hill, a vibrant patch of chickweed bloomed.

"Drymaria cordata," she whispered under her breath. "Most excellent for the gut and scurvy." She crested the rocky rise.

Moonlight blended with the last of sunset's amber rays, cascading a creamy light over the deep green and pale blossoms. Scooping her fingers beneath the soft earth, she found the roots, which easily lifted from the soil. As she shook the excess dirt from it, something caught her eye. Tucked deep inside a wall of tamarind trees, she noticed a light flickering ahead. Curiosity soon overtook her interest in the chickweed, and she followed the path. The light grew brighter the closer she got to it, until finally, she saw the source: a single torch projected at an odd angle from the base of a tiny thatched hut. Shadows gathered overhead. Her mouth ran dry, and she found herself unable to swallow. A foreboding dread warned of what might lie in wait in this place. Quickly, she turned, anxious to make her way down the path and back to the beach in the dim nightfall.

"Come! Here, dearie."

The hollow voice cackled from a black hole in the thatch. Kathryn froze, unable to move, and looked back at the hut.

"Here, me dearie. Come here." The voice grated its invitation again as a dark figure appeared in the doorway.

Kathryn did not speak. She dared not move, but held fast, waiting for the figure's next exchange.

"I have somethin' ye be needin', me girlie. Come...come!"

Lanky and dark, the woman was covered in tattoos. Her face was pierced with long picks, and the hair from her head dangled wild and matted. The creature glided out from the hut.

"I know what ye be, girly. There be somethin' I have...somethin' ye be needin' if ye seek protection from the Morrigan witch."

Kathryn trembled and a familiar chill passed down her spine. The Seren came to life and grew warm, a rosy glow in the darkening skies. In that moment, the creature hissed and instantly stopped moving.

"I know what that is – what it be that hangs 'bout your neck. But ye need not fear me, dearie. I am one who knows the Scarlet Seren an' would not give ye harm. Indeed, its powers are great, even in this place."

Kathryn took a step forward, an act of defiance meant for the creature. Cautiously, she moved toward the hut, but suddenly stopped again, her muscles tense at the overwhelming feeling of doom that blanketed the place. She could see the woman's features in the torchlight and recognized the markings on her skin.

Obeah.

Mariel had spoken once of the powers of the Obeah and the black magic they wielded. She'd also warned Kathryn to never tempt fate with Obeah magic, should she have the misfortune to cross paths with one. This was such a time, and Kathryn knew to treat the Obeah witch with caution.

"What is it ye want of me, Obeah?" Kathryn asked, steadying her voice.

"Then ye know what I am. Good! Listen well an' know I speak truth," cackled the dark witch. She squat on the ground near the torch and began to draw symbols in the dirt with one finger. Her eyes glowed and her hair flickered light from the torch. Occasionally, yellowed eyes would dart up to watch Kathryn advance one hesitant step at a time. But the Obeah gave no other indication she cared that Kathryn approached.

Upon reaching the edge of the path, Kathryn stopped. She waited, alert – honed in to the squatting Obeah's presence. Kathryn's body tensed as she leaned in to see what the crone had written. The dark witch scratched more symbols and spoke, snakelike eyes glaring yellow at Kathryn.

"Morrigan seeks the man who sails a great ship. She will destroy him and all who sail with him…" the voice droned, trance-like. "The Sister sails on these waters with another, a fierce pirate covered in hair with smoke that billows from each side of his skull. Beware of his ship, for it will find ye and seek to destroy ye, as well."

Kathryn forced a steady breath, taking in the Obeah's prophecy. On bent knee, she crouched, focused and ready for the evil to come to life that surrounded the place. If left unchecked, it would surely destroy her – there, on the edge of an island path. The witch droned on, her yellow eyes never blinking.

"Morrigan shall take the pirate's head from his shoulders an' hang it aloft while his body swims headless thrice about the great ship. Then all will grow dark. Blood will stain the ground as hell swallows with its gaping jaws." The Obeah's croon turned into shrieking laughter and the torch went dark.

Kathryn sensed her own death only inches away. She leapt off the path just as the air thrummed next to her throat. Bark cracked and pitched from a tree trunk just ahead. Laughter screeched again, this time to one side. The Obeah hunted her. Panic rose in her veins. The path was nowhere to be seen. Darkness had blocked the trail, and the evil of night approached. She stumbled, catching her skirt against a branch that tore a jagged line of fabric and flesh. Kathryn stifled the cry that rose as pain shot down her leg.

"I see you, dearie." The voice was a whisper carried on a hot breeze that passed through Kathryn's hair.

She skirted a large boulder, and another pass thrummed alongside her, followed by the sound of cracking timber. Kathryn reached one hand to her neck and found the skin intact. In that moment, the Obeah's breath caught up with her and Kathryn instantly changed course. But it was too late. Something grasped her by the arm, nearly breaking it, and thrust her in another direction. A cry escaped her lips – instantly silenced as a hand clamped over her mouth. She gasped for air.

"Kathryn," a voice whispered in her ear. "Come, quickly."

She turned to face her captor and looked into unblinking, chestnut eyes that darted to one side.

"Seth!" she gasped and his palm fell from her mouth. "Seth, how…?"

"Hush!" He held one finger to his lips and scanned the underbrush ahead of them. "This way."

He dragged her by the hand through dense vegetation, urging her to stoop beneath its cover. In tandem, the pair moved silently toward the trunk of a thick tamarind tree. A dagger had splayed the bark near the center. Seth's nimble fingers plucked loose the ebony blade that had been wedged into the wood.

"What is that?" Kathryn asked as Seth dropped the dagger into the sash tied about his waist.

"My guess is – the means to your death," he said, and pulled her away from the tree, back into the thicket. "She tried to kill you with it."

Kathryn's hand flew up to her throat, remembering a sudden thrum as the blade passed by just inches from her flesh. Behind them, the Obeah hissed and fell silent. Seth tugged Kathryn's hand to follow, and together they retraced his steps through the dense vegetation. Finally, the path revealed itself in the moonlight. They bolted toward the beach, putting as much distance between them and the Obeah as possible. Yet, as they fled, the screeching laughter followed.

Fear gripped Kathryn, and the Seren grew hot against her skin. She forced herself to sprint, heart pounding, until she could no longer breathe. Seth glanced at her, never letting loose of her hand. Faster and faster, they ran – past thick foliage and low-lying branches, until finally, she could no longer move. Gasping for air, she collapsed on the sand with the leaves she had gathered still tied up in her skirt.

"Kathryn…Kathryn." Seth's voice trailed away.

Her body went limp as mercifully darkness over-powered her fear.

Forty

"KATHRYN...WAKE UP...KATHRYN!"

Seth bent over, slapping her cheeks, trying to wake her. Several other pirates stood in a semi-circle and gawked, afraid to touch her with anything more than the tattered end of a leather boot. A stark and rather unruly pirate, appropriately nicknamed Pock-eye Pete, nudged her limp body in the side with his foot. She appeared to be breathing, which Pock-eye validated each time his boot met with her ribs and she let out a grunt. The Seren had subsided to a pale blush and the silver threads lay loose against the skin of her neck. Thankfully, there appeared no evidence that she'd been strangled. Every sailor who stood over her noticed the stone. But no one seemed willing to lay hands on her, except for Seth, who abruptly shook her. Try as he might, he could not revive her.

"Is she dead?" Cade dared not look directly at her.

"Not yet. Look, she's still breathin'." Just to prove it, Pock-eye jabbed her again with his foot. Seth scowled.

"Rotten sprogs! Keep your filthy boot away from her. Can't ye see she's just lyin' there? Quick kickin' her." Seth waved Pock-eye back.

"Aye, her wits fled from her, it seems," Cade replied.

"Look! The devil's sneakin' in." Pock-eye pointed with a trembling finger. "See how she yawns!"

Gasps followed, and several of the men made a cross with their fingers. Seth was beside himself.

"Certain, and the soul be leaving her body as she gasps," Cade sputtered and stepped back, then crossed himself again. As if beckoned to do so, Kathryn inhaled unexpectedly. Seth quickly covered her mouth with both of his hands. The rest of the pirates just gawked, crossed themselves, and hopped on one foot.

"He's protecting her soul from escaping," a wiry pirate, hopping from one foot to the other, explained to his neighbor.

Her body jerked, unable to breathe. *Someone is trying to suffocate me!* The thought blended with the sound of voices echoing distantly as if in a dream. She reached for whatever was clamped over her mouth, and just as suddenly, opened her eyes. Grubby hands clapped over her mouth again and refused to release her. Sinking her teeth into the meat of a finger, she heard someone cry out and instantly was freed. This sent Seth reeling backwards, crossing himself and hopping on one foot like the rest of the pirates, with one finger bloodstained from a rather nasty bite.

"Get off me!"

The pirates stepped back, wide-eyed, as Seth clutched his bloody finger.

"Blimey! She's possessed!" he said.

"Seth, whatever are you doin'? Are you tryin' to kill me?" She wiped her mouth with the back of her hand. "Nitwits! All of you!"

A few of them still circled and hopped vigorously, crossing themselves and spitting, with their eyes fixed in terror.

"He thought ye're dyin' and the devil be runnin' into where yer soul escaped…there," Pock-eye said, pointing to her open mouth. He bounced on one foot as he spoke.

Kathryn cocked her head and stared at the pirate for a minute. "Are you daft, Pete? Dead? I think not!" She stood and brushed the dirt from her skirts. "Silly superstitious minds have gotten the best of you, aye?"

One by one they stopped their antics, and she shook her head in disgust.

"Are ye sure ye're free of Beelzebub? Th' devil's a wily beast who freely enters through yawns not properly covered," Cade said.

"You're a fool, Cade!" The pirate backed down, apologizing.

"Is that what you were doin', Seth? Trying to keep the devil out?"

Seth nodded, then pointed a finger at the pirates. "They made me do it."

"It's a ridiculous superstition! Covering one's mouth with your hands to keep the devil out. I merely yawned, I did! Really, now!" She brushed the remaining sand from her skirts. A bewildered look passed between her and Seth, and she shook her head at him. He'd been trying to save her, supposedly – something to feel gratitude for. As she adjusted the tangled sash around her waist, she scanned her surroundings to get her bearings. Herbs and leaves lay scattered, stark against the white sand. A faint recollection of gathering plants along the narrow path came with the sight of the tiny, pale blossoms and leaves.

"What happened?" she asked Seth.

"Ye were scamperin' through the brush an' fell flat dead 'ere on the beach," Cade piped in. Seth's eyes travelled to the imprint left on the sand where she'd collapsed. "Pete here, tried wakin' ye, but ye were dead."

Pock-eye Pete kicked his boot at the sand and nodded his head.

"I'm tellin' you, I was not dead! Simpleminded scallywags!" She grew frustrated each time one of the pirates spoke of death or the devil. It was then that she pointed toward the overgrowth, recalling bits and pieces of her journey along the path.

"You, Seth!" She turned on him. "You were there at the last. We ran along that path, chased by the…" Kathryn's voice caught in her throat, her face draining of color as she stared at the path. Suddenly, she remembered – the thatched hut and the Obeah witch who dwelled there.

"Ye were there, too?" Pock-eye asked, eyeing Seth suspiciously.

"Aye, at the final moment when the witch tried to kill Kathryn," Seth stated.

"What did you say?" She spun and stared at him. "What do you mean, kill me, Seth? What did you see?"

"Nothin', in truth. I heard a scream and saw a black figure hurl this at you. Methinks it was a demon," Seth said, pulling out the ebony dagger for all to see. The pirates studied the weapon with hungry eyes, but Kathryn backed away.

"Where did you get that, Seth?" She eyed the strange inscription etched over the blade. He held the dagger out to her to take it, but she refused, pulling back further.

"I pulled it from the tree. It missed you by inches and landed square in the tamarind. Don't you remember?" Seth re-sheathed the dagger.

"The Obeah…" Kathryn whispered, her eyes wide. Swiftly, she spun, facing the pirates.

"Take me to the capt'n! Quick!"

Usually, the men would have been happy to turn over suspicious subjects to their captain, but circumstances had changed and left them uncertain about what to do. Kathryn was a designated traveler onboard the ship, albeit not a member of the crew. Recent events led the pirates to question whether she'd be safe onboard the ship or better left behind.

"Aye…he's in thar, with the rest o' the crew," Pock-eye finally announced and pointed to the row of lanterns hanging not far from where they stood. The others scowled at him, for which he only shrugged. "I'd rather the capt'n deal with her than us," he said, and the majority agreed.

Gathering her skirt, Kathryn sprinted through the soft sand with Seth following close behind. Once Seth and Kathryn had gone, the pirates turned back toward the ship and began to pass a bottle between them. Soon, their swagger implied they'd forgotten the girl altogether. In truth, they were no longer interested, now that she'd come back to life and rum was aplenty.

A row of ramshackle alehouses stood precariously side by side with doors open and waiting to welcome any sailor willing to spend his gold on whatever lay inside. There was no time to waste in finding the captain. A lengthy search inside each of these salty "crawls" would certainly eat up precious minutes. So Kathryn tied her skirt into a side knot and stood in the center of four lanterns. Facing the largest doorway, with hands on swaying hips, and using her best salty dog brogue, she began to sing out.

"John Phillips! Capt'n John Phillips! I be needin' a word with ye now."

Heads covered with curly locks or tri-cornered hats appeared through openings that served as windows. Stamped sporadically in graying plank walls, shutters outlined flickering candlelight that danced behind dusty panes. It seemed as if the shacks stared down at her. Raucous laughter pealed from both men and women alike inside. Kathryn swallowed and prayed the ruse would work.

Deep down, she hoped those within would suppose her to be one of the wenches the captain might pay gold for that evening. A wide, saucy grin played on her lips while her hips swayed as she teased anyone who might be watching. She waited for any sign of Captain Phillips. One by one, heads would pop out of windows to look while Kathryn's eyes scanned the onlookers. She prayed the captain had taken enough rum to dampen his certain rage at her display.

"Looks like a mousy little wench be lookin' for ye, John," cooed a silky voice from inside one of the houses. Kathryn's mouth soured.

A few more tri-corn hats poked through the rough openings in the sea-rotted wood. Dirty, drunken pirates from other crews stumbled out to take a gander at the beauty making such ruckus. A moment later, the tall, commanding form of Captain Phillips pushed through an unsteady trio of sailors. Each held his mug aloft in salute to the wench, who brazenly called for a captain's "business." As John Phillips stepped through the crowd and onto the cobblestones, one of the sailors touched his forehead in a gesture of drunken respect.

"She be a right bonnie lass, she be. A right buxom beauty for ye, Capt'n," he slurred. His comrades nodded their agreement.

Captain Phillips faced Kathryn. She motioned for him and he moved toward her with long strides that matched the look of displeasure clouding his face. Despite his apparent anger, she maintained a swagger, swayed her hips, and feigned the role well. Within moments, he was at Kathryn's side, her arm in a firm grasp as he dragged her to the beach. When they were far enough away from the ogling spectators, he released his grip.

"What the devil's the meaning of this?"

"Capt'n, there's trouble for you and the ship… here…on this island."

He could sense the urgency in her tone. He dragged her farther down the beach, out of earshot from the onlookers, ignoring her as she stumbled to keep up.

"This behavior is completely unacceptable!" he growled.

"This is regarding Morrigan. It regards you!" She jerked her arm free and faced him, hands on hips. He stopped at this and stared at her. A not-so-subtle warning flashed behind his eyes.

"You'd best make this count, lass." His voice quaked, lethal and menacing.

"There's an Obeah on this isle. I saw the marked woman myself, down the pathway there." She pointed as she spoke. "The witch spoke of Morrigan and her plans to find you and your crew." Conveniently, Kathryn left off the reproach the Obeah had given. John Phillips' face tensed, and as he stared at her, his jaw clenched.

"The Obeah hag be nothin' more than a crazy wench. She's been a resident on this godforsaken isle for many years. No one pays her mind, which ye best be doin' if ye wish to keep your throat."

"My throat is not your concern! But if ye must know, she did try to kill me."

"And why wouldn't she? You trespassed onto her land," he responded, but angst strained his voice. "Indeed, you bleed." He waved one hand toward her leg that still oozed blood. She wiped it with the backside of her skirt.

"It's nothing," she said.

"It's always something when an Obeah makes threats, apparently," he scoffed.

"Capt'n," her voice softened. "She spoke of Morrigan and the *Revenge*!"

"Macha speaks nonsense. Her mind's foul and her lips speak naught but gibberish." He had grown impatient with the argument.

"Macha? Capt'n, did you say her name was Macha?"

He nodded.

"Oh Capt'n, you and the crew are in very grave danger!"

The Capt'n said nothing, but studied her face, now wet with tears.

"Go on." His body tensed again as he waited for her to continue.

"Macha is the name of Morrigan's sister!"

John Phillips froze. His face darkened as his eyes latched onto hers and her words took new meaning.

Finally, he spoke, his voice brisk and his face inches from hers.

"How came ye to know of this?"

"The Goddess of War and her sisters are well known to my clan. Mariel warned of their evil when I was but a child." She paused, then added, "She comes for me, too, Capt'n." Tears ran freely down her cheeks as she looked with pleading eyes into the captain's face. His heart stirred with a new desire to protect the young woman in front of him.

"Get to the ship and stay with the men. Ye will be safer there than on this wretched island."

She nodded, then took both of his hands in hers, and held them to her cheek. A brief sense of relief washed over her as she felt the warmth of his skin against her face. She would be safe on the ship with the men – her refuge was with the pirates. Ironic really but I feel safest with them. The thought softened her expression.

He watched her, and his heart softened once again. As she lifted her cheek and released his hands, he brushed a lock of hair from her face, kissed her forehead, and then turned away. Captain Phillips then set about searching the small strand of shoreline for his crew. In truth, he needed to avoid her scrutiny. She couldn't know how she affected him.

Gathered together against a sandbank, the little group of pirates huddled together with mugs held high, warbling sea shanties. Seth had joined them, but had remained sober and somewhat aloof. Tucked to one side, the dagger lay hidden from view. Seth's focus was keen – his eye on Kathryn and Captain Phillips.

Beyond them, the waves lapped the shore, melting into foam, tossing the skiffs and bouncing the oars inside. A few of the men, including Gow, stood guard over the rowboats and told stories. They too, were thrown off balance by the tide, teetering with each slap of the current that fell against their ankles. Captain Phillips approached his men, noting the near empty bottle that dangled from each man's hand.

"Mister Gow," he ordered. "Send a few of the men to take the lass back to her quarters. I'll not have her leave the ship." The captain's steely voice left no room for negotiation. "Prepare the men. We sail within the hour."

Forty-One

JAMESBY CAY ENCOMPASSED A PRISTINE beach set in a cluster of tiny islets known as the Tobago Cays. Its shores lay on the opposite side of the strand of islands, apart from where the ship was currently anchored. Mayreau Isle proved a better location for careening a ship. Vast beaches lining the island sloped steeply upward and were exposed during low tides, which made it less difficult to roll the ship to one side. Besides, the locals' assistance could be bought for only a quarter reale as payment. Difficult as it was, the arduous chore of scraping debris from the ships' hull had to be done. In Gow's mind, there was no point to moving the *Revenge* when she could be laid on her side here.

"Makes no sense," Gow said under his breath. "We'd best get it done here, where we've rum and wenches a-plenty."

"Aye, makes for a much easier task, methinks." Briggs stepped to one side and began to loosen the lines. He exchanged looks with Gow.

Dismayed, Gow motioned for the others to help ready a skiff. The captain waved for Seth to join them.

"Seth, stay with the lass and keep an eye on her," Captain Phillips stated. "I need ye to guard o're the ship until I return." The Captain was solemn. Such responsibility had not yet been given to Seth. The obligation was more than welcome.

"Aye, aye, sir!" He stiffened and puffed out his chest.

Soon, Kathryn was escorted to the readied skiff, accompanied by Seth and Briggs, who took the oars. When they were safely launched, Gow returned to the men, who clutched at the remaining skiffs for support. In no shape to walk, the pirates had found refuge near the small boats that had been lined up in the sand – a sure method to keep from being forgotten when the ship would made sail again. The entire entourage was drunk and wobbly, but not fully incapacitated as they watched the first longboat make its way to the *Revenge*. One by one, they began to scramble into an empty boat. Assured that Seth had the skiff safely en route, Captain Phillips gave further orders, then turned from the sodden crewmen and made his way through the sand to fetch the quartermaster.

Archer had found himself in the clutches of two or three wenches. It wasn't surprising, as Archer's stash of coin made him one of the favorites there. The challenge would be to convince the quartermaster his duty lie elsewhere. Captain Phillips marched toward a set of lanterns. Here, he was met with a spewed melody, accompanied by three pirates nestled on the sand bar.

"Where is me wench, me noggy, noggy wench

She is gone for grog and me booty."

Relieved these were not part of his crew, he moved on.

The shanty carried across the water to the skiff where Kathryn sat. She had seen the pirate who worked the oars before. His name was William, she thought, although she couldn't be certain. They had never spoken, and while she could smell ale on his breath, he rowed in straight, strong pulls. Seth kept his eyes locked on her, a taste of self-importance filling him with pride. She refused to look at him and kept her eyes on the ship that was not far off.

As the longboat pulled broadside to the *Revenge*, the song sung on shore faded. Quickly, Kathryn and Seth were welcomed aboard and she moved directly to her quarters. Seth stayed at her heels, though she tried to dodge him once or twice.

"Stop being so stubborn!" he shouted.

She turned on her heel and glared at him. "You've no right to follow me. I'm not your ward, Seth."

"That's not what the capt'n says." He chuckled and hefted her bag.

Stomping her foot, she eked out a, "Thank you," through clenched teeth then stepped inside her cabin. Once inside, she slammed the door. Safe once again in familiar surroundings, she allowed herself a sigh of relief.

Seth, took up post just outside the door and waited for an invitation to join her. It would never come but he didn't care. Mostly, he wanted to demonstrate his newly assigned authority. His cocky attitude was getting to the point that Kathryn could no longer stand it.

"Seth, I know you're there. You don't need to stand over me like this. I heard the captain's orders, and you've followed them well. But I'm safe onboard now and very secure inside my own cabin." Her words seethed.

"But, I still don't know what you're doin' in there, Kat."

Kathryn glanced at the closed door. His use of her familiar nickname was much too bold. "What I'm doin' is none of your business!"

"Perhaps, but you certainly invited trouble when you went lookin' for that Obeah lady up there on the island." He waited for a response, but got none. "Fate would have your throat slit, but I'm the man sent to protect you from it." This time he crossed his arms and waited.

She shot another warning look at the door and mumbled something foul, which Seth heard but ignored. It was obvious to him that his duty far outweighed any quarrel she might have with it.

"Twice I've saved your skin, and twice you've forgotten to thank me." His brashness spilled out with his words.

"We'll talk of it later, Seth, but not right now. Not until my mind has rested and your pride is deflated."

"You owe me, Kathryn."

She knew he would not leave his post outside her door. "That will be all, Seth!" She buried her face in her hands. Instinctively, her hand gripped the Seren that began to grow warm.

"As you wish, then," he said, followed by footsteps that trailed off to silence. For whatever reason, he'd apparently left her to her own defenses for the moment. But he'd soon return, or else be accountable to the captain for abandoning post. Just to be certain, she cracked the door, glanced outside, and saw nothing but darkness blanketing the ship.

Now that she was alone, she made her way to the cabin porthole and strained for one last glimpse of the island. Only parts of it were visible, but she could still see the drunkards gathered on the beach. Staggering pirates clambered into the skiffs, along with supplies. It would be a long night for Archer as he collected the crew and dragged them into the skiffs. It seemed their belligerence rose with the increase in rum. She did not want to cross paths with the quartermaster, not now, and decided the captain's orders to stay put were best followed.

Night found her unable to sleep. Restless thoughts pawed at her, jumping from the Obeah's prophesy to the chaos above as pirates boarded the ship. Throughout the night, crewmen were loaded onto the deck, stumbling and cursing as they made their way back to the forecastle and the crew's quarters. Supplies that had been purchased from the merchants onshore were carefully loaded and stored below. Song erupted as some of the men, unable to find their way below deck, settled into what was left of their evening. Opting for a spot topside, they sprawled out in their drunken state, warbling to a hornpipe played somewhere on the other side of the ship. For Kathryn, these had become the familiar sounds of pirates. After a time, she finally heard the captain's voice call out orders. She relaxed, much safer now that he was aboard. Finally, Kathryn drifted off to sleep.

The shipboard activity continued throughout the night, and, as the first rays of dawn pierced the morning fog, the *Revenge* put out to sea. By mid-afternoon, they pulled north of a long semicircular reef into a cove on an overgrown, tiny island. There they waited for low tide to beach.

When the time had come, the men disembarked and tied the thick lines to the side of the ship, ready to tip her sideways for careening. Kathryn rose with the sunlight and took a place tying knots and working the rigging. The sparkling white sand of Jamesby Cay mirrored the beach they had left behind. Pale turquoise water lapped its shores, and palm trees scattered in a perfect arc that spread outward from the center. Wild birds sang as they flew overhead and gathered exotic fruit in their beaks, while albatross dove for krill or squid in the clear warm water. There was no sign of any other inhabitants on this island, which made it the perfect location to hide a pirate ship.

For three weeks, the crew repaired and groomed the ship. Kathryn was given free rein to explore the island as she liked. Plants and flowers grew abundantly around the perimeter, and she often spent her mornings collecting the rare ones she required for her medicine pouch. As the stash grew larger, she would tie the leaves and blossoms together in bundles and hang them upside-down from the trees. Usually, the salty breezes would dry them in spite of the humidity – at least, this was her plan. Mostly, the crew ignored her. It was without exception that none of the pirates would venture near the hanging collection, instead creating a large path of sandy footprints that arched away whenever they would pass by.

One afternoon, as she worked at binding together beriberi sprigs with abalone shell, a small ship unexpectedly sailed into the cove. From where she sat, it was obvious this vessel was most certainly uninvited. Onshore, the pirates spied its approach and sprang into action, alerting Captain Phillips and Archer at the same time. Weapons were made ready as the small snow anchored on the opposite end of the beach. From where Kathryn sat, the sun blinded all view of the small vessel's mast. Given the generous shade of the giant palm overhead, she barely made out its position. One of the men shouted something, and a small group of about four or five men rushed down the beach toward it.

"A snow!" a voice called out.

"Small but formidable prize, aye?" another said.

Yelping, with swords held high above their heads, the small band scrambled over the sand and rushed their prey. Catching the crew unawares, the cutthroats mercilessly bushwhacked the unsuspecting ship. There was only slight resistance to the onslaught of pirates, but that soon dissipated with threats of waving cutlasses and hurled curses.

Considering the *Revenge* – with the Jolly Roger flying and cannons at the ready – a threat was something that never crossed the pirates' minds. Indeed, in battle they were formidable, but here the Revenge lay at anchor and the crew disassembled. A snow would likely ignore the pirate ship – or so they thought. This was a fishing boat with no defense against bloodthirsty pirates, and likely only yellowtail or codfish for treasure. There would be nothing of value to the pirates except the fishermen's lives. And so it was that the snow surrendered without so much as a single shot fired.

Upon capture, the fishing boat was ceremoniously presented to Captain Phillips, as rightly it should be. But the men guilty of the deed were reluctant to hand her over just yet.

"We waylaid her, Capt'n, and be settin' sights on takin' her crew," bragged Wood. His arrogance seemed rather bold, but Captain Phillips let it go.

"Ay, Mister Wood, that ye did, and a fine ship she be. She'll be flyin' colors to match the *Revenge* soon enough. It's a fleet we're buildin'."

The captain's eyes never left the snow or the men who still plundered her. Only a handful of fishermen manned the snow, and the problem of what to do with them troubled him. He had plenty of hands, but given his desire for more ships, he'd hoped this prize would fare better than the last one had. He faced the fishermen, and with hands clasped behind his back, began to pace a line in front of them. Finally, he spoke.

"As far as I see it, ye have two choices before ye now. Either join me crew and turn to the grand life of piratin' with these merry mates here onboard the *Revenge*, or remain behind as governor o're this island."

The fishermen shared looks and said nothing. In truth, they'd been given little choice at all – join the pirates or die. Marooning was considered worse than hanging, which was something not lost on the terrified fishermen. The men clustered together, muttering amongst themselves. Finally, a decision was made and the fishermen split up – three would join the pirates, while the other, who would not, sidestepped with his head lowered. His decision to be left behind, to face his fate on the deserted island alone, was unusual but respected.

"It's a death sentence," one of the fishermen said. He moved a bit closer to the pirates.

"I'll take my chances," his companion responded, and lowered his eyes again.

"You'll die, marooned on an island…alone."

"I'm a fisherman. I'll get by until another ship comes in." As if to emphasize the point, he distanced himself from his fellows.

Gow pulled the new recruits to one side and introduced them to Archer. Before long, they stood at the mast and had sworn the oath over the axe with the quartermaster as officiator. Pledging loyalty to the captain, the crew, and the Articles of the ship, the fishermen-turned-pirates took their place alongside a gathering of new comrades – all cutthroats and vagabonds. At nearly the same time, the solitary fisherman who had opted to stay behind was given scant supplies and bid adieu.

"Give 'im a pistol and one shot. He can keep one o' their fishin' nets, but the rest be ours now. One bottle, as well," hollered Sparks. The castaway's fate was sealed.

By this time, Kathryn had joined the gathered crew. Her pouch was heavy, and she was forced to reposition it frequently to keep its contents from slipping out through the top. In truth, she welcomed the chance to rearrange her cargo since the marooned fisherman's state had left her fidgety.

"Surely, ye don't mean to do this!" She couldn't help herself, and shifted the bag once more.

"One shot, only!" Sparks shouted, and tossed her a look that suggested she keep her mouth shut.

It was customary to give a pistol and one shot to a marooned sailor, which would look inviting as starvation soon came calling. This was commonplace on such an island, leaving the man choice to shoot himself or starve.

"Well, I won't stay around and watch you act like murderous little boys!" she snapped, and boarded the first longboat shoving off for the *Revenge*.

"Hah!" bellowed the first three pirates that joined her. The remainder turned their backs, leaving the fisherman clutching his knees, sitting on the bank. Kathryn watched with horror as the *Revenge* was towed back out to sea, leaving him stranded there.

Within minutes, a lanky John Fern stepped up to the captain and cleared his throat. Three other cronies stood behind him, shuffling their feet. All three men kept one hand over the hilt of their cutlasses.

"A word with ye, Capt'n?"

"What is it, Mister Fern?" Captain Phillips said, dropping his eyes to the weapons on the three crewmen's hips.

"We…bein' the men who stole the ship right out from under the fishermen…we be of a mind…" Fern paused and pointed to the others, "Wood, Willie, Taylor, and meself…we think it be our rights to man the snow."

The request from John Fern was nothing short of insubordination. But these men had been rebellious since the day Archer was brought onboard and elected Quartermaster. Jealousy pervaded every thought Fern possessed about John Rose Archer. And because of it,

Fern's antics were well known. A reputation for trouble followed Fern, which only added to his cunning disposition.

The captain endured their complaints while sizing up the men. None of them backed down, but rather, pressed their proposal. Feigning interest in the island that was slowly diminishing, Kathryn stayed against the rails, ears glued to Fern's discussion. Precipitously, a sense of foreboding overcame her. She slid closer to the captain.

"We think we've got as much right to man that snow as the rest o' the crew, Capt'n. In fact, we got more rights, provin' ourselves here and sequesterin' the snow without the help o' the men," Fern continued and nudged the man standing next to him to speak up.

"It be a fine bit of piratin' it be, Capt'n." Taylor was an Englishmen and typically showed better manners – but not this day.

Usually, the crewmen were allowed open discussion at any time with the captain, except at battle when the captain's word was law and never questioned. At this moment, John Phillips' irritation mirrored his nagging dread. Most mates would advise to "go with the gut," a feeling that was usually wisest to heed. In truth, John Phillips' gut had warned him about Fern before, so he decided to act.

"Enough, Mister Fern. The bosun be at the helm now, and the rest of the crew be at their duties, which is where the rest of ye should be. Join the crew, if ye like, but permission to board the snow be given from Gow, not me." His eyes narrowed as he spoke to the men confronting him.

Willie was a rather burly man who was not given to eloquent speech, but today he felt the need to respond. He opened his mouth, but was silenced by Taylor's elbow to the ribs. Aggravated, the four men departed and headed for the starboard rails. They called to the crew of the snow, who sailed close enough to the *Revenge* to allow an exchange of provisions or crew without effort. Ropes were thrown, and Fern, Willie, Taylor, and Wood swung across the narrow span of water to the smaller ship. Captain Phillips kept his eye on the men, suspicious of their behavior. Something about them smacked of mutiny. He didn't trust Fern to begin with, and was left feeling more unsettled after they'd parted ways.

Hands flew in the air and voices rose while Kathryn pretended she did not notice. From her vantage point against the chains, she could see the pirates on the snow growing more agitated. Cutlasses were drawn and Gow was forced from the helm. Captain Phillips rushed forward, afraid of what might happen if the bosun decided to resist.

"Ye bilge rat maggots! Ye'll face the sharp side of the blade 'lest ye turn from yer mutinous ways! Set Mister Gow free at once or face the wrath of yer captain and a hangin' at the yardarm!" John Phillips bellowed. The four pirates ignored him as they quickly took command of the snow.

"Ye be no man's captain aboard this ship, John Phillips," Fern shouted back indignantly as he stepped to the helm. "We'll be relievin' the bosun o' command this day."

Willie seized Gow in a cross hold with the blade of his cutlass against the man's throat. He shoved the bosun to portside, and faced him toward the *Revenge*. Then, with a guttural laugh, shoved Gow over the rails and into the sea.

"Here be yer bosun," the pirate roared as he watched Gow tumble head over heels, hitting the water headfirst. "He be lucky to swim without me cuttin' his throat first an' sendin' him to dine with the sharks."

After a time, Gow surfaced, splashing and flailing his arms about him, screaming for help. It was obvious the man could not swim and would surely drown. Fortunately, Slade had been quick to cast a line for him to grab onto. Thrashing wildly, the soggy pirate found the rope trailing in the water alongside the ship and was hoisted from the sea. When he was safely on deck, the pirates turned their attention to the mutinous men making off with their prize. Gow traipsed along the rails, dripping and sputtering like a wet cat, while several others fired pistol shots at the bandits. Immediately, Fern, Wood, and Taylor scrambled for their own weapons. Ramming a ball down each flintlock, the mutineers returned fired moments later.

Curses and smoke billowed thick between both ships. At the helm, Captain Phillips steered hard to starboard, ramming the portside of the small sloop with great force. A small cannon aboard the fishing vessel had been loosely tied with line to the capstan and obviously neglected. It tore free upon impact and spun across the slippery deck, crushing one of Taylor's legs between its weight and the trysail. He screamed out in agony. Unable to move, the leg was pinned between the mast and the cannon. Wood ran over, trying to free him, but was unable to budge the cannon. Taylor cried out again as his limb began to change color. The other pirates continued the battle, unaware of their mate's predicament, and fired their pistols wildly at the *Revenge*. Overhead, pistol shot hissed, just missing Wood by inches. He abandoned the fight with the cannon and, apologizing briefly to Taylor, ran back to Fern's side with his pistol drawn.

Brute force and skill outnumbered the little band of thieves still trying to make off with their damaged prize. It didn't matter – the rogues attacked the crew of the *Revenge* without compunction. Stamped with defeat, their feeble attempt to steal the sloop was brought to a halt within the hour as the larger ship overpowered them.

When the smoke cleared, Wood was dead, shot straight through the heart. Taylor lay screaming, his leg still wedged between the mast and the neglected cannon. The other two men put up no further fight and surrendered, dropping to their knees with arms outstretched. Their swords and pistols were confiscated and tossed out of reach.

"Hands up!" Archer shouted, and both Willie and Fern raised their arms in surrender. The quartermaster made swift work of clapping the traitors in irons and securing them in the brig. Wood's body was thrown overboard, where dark, spotted sea creatures swam close to the surface with their black dorsal fins glistening in the sunlight. Moments later, the water churned red and traces of Wood were seen no more.

It took several men, pulling in unison, to pry the cannon from off of Taylor's crushed leg. His cry turned guttural as the men lifted the weighty cannon off the mashed extremity that flopped with a sickening thud onto the deck. Four of the crew carried the incapacitated man to the *Revenge* and positioned him flat upon the quarterdeck. Presented to the captain, he writhed like a snake, delirious with agony. Captain Phillips simply stared down at him.

Kathryn had been summoned to the scene by one of the onlookers. Approaching the scene, she sensed this would not end well for her...or for Taylor. The captain barked an order, and Kathryn was forced to stand just inches from Taylor, who twisted and jerked with his left leg contorted in several different directions. She lifted his foot from the crimson pool expanding over the polished wood. It did not require close inspection to see there was no way to save the leg, and everyone knew it without needing to voice it aloud. Indeed, the man would certainly die if something wasn't done quickly.

"There be nothin' to do now unless his leg be taken to spare his wasted life," Kathryn said and kept her eyes glued on the flopping extremity. At this, Taylor passed out.

"Mister Sparks." The captain aimed his comments at the ship's gunner without looking directly at him. "What a distasteful turn of events this has been!"

"Aye, Capt'n." It was all Sparks could muster in response.

"Get the carpenter's saw and a torch. The lass can take it off here, now."

Kathryn gasped. Bile rose into the back of her throat, choking her. She coughed and suppressed the urge to vomit. "Capt'n…I can't cut off this man's leg!" For the first time since arriving onboard, she cowered. "My healin' is not for destroyin' any man's body. There's no magic for this, Capt'n!"

He regarded the unconscious man sourly.

John Phillips had been a carpenter before he had turned pirate. His skill with a saw was unmatched. Perhaps cutting a limb from a body was no different than cutting a limb from a tree. He studied the faces now crowded around the unconscious pirate. No one volunteered, avoiding the captain's penetrating gaze with their eyes all cast downward. It seemed the job fell to him, particularly if he wanted to maintain a healthy respect from his men as their captain. He sighed and snatched the saw from Sparks, who had just returned.

"Hold him down while I do the job," he growled at two of the largest men. He then tossed Kathryn a brisk look as he took up the ground meat that once resembled Taylor's leg.

"Capt'n, don't ye think we ought to give poor Taylor somethin' to ease the pain?" Slade's voice sounded weak. He stepped back, his eyes affixed to the bloody, mashed appendage.

"Hold…please, just for a moment. I have somethin' that will save the wretch some of the agony he's bound for."

"No!"

"It'll help to keep him still." Kathryn clutched at the captain, who was bent over Taylor with the saw poised, ready to cut. He stopped to look at her, but before he could refuse, she darted off. Behind, she heard him growl, "Arrgh."

Grabbing the pouch of medicines from her cabin, and tucking the surgeon's leather satchel under one arm, she ran back to the quarterdeck. One of the sailors had been pouring rum down the half-conscious man's throat while two larger men held him fast across the chest, immobilizing him. Kathryn pulled several dried pods from the bag and crushed them between her palms. She then pushed the entire contents into Taylor's gaping mouth.

"Wash this down," she instructed the brute who held the rum. He hesitated, most likely because he did not entirely trust her. "It's poppy and belladonna…for the pain. Do it!" She shouted the last, causing the pirate to jump and the captain's mouth to curl in amusement. He nodded approval, and rum was poured into the man's mouth, washing down the dusty medication. Taylor sputtered but managed to swallow the bulk of it. He relaxed a little afterward, which the captain took as the signal to begin.

"Hold him still, I tell ye. I don' want him thrashin'."

The captain lifted the rubbery, blood-soaked tissue that had once been a leg. The two pirates holding Taylor pinned him to the ground as Phillips tucked the intact portion of thigh under his arm and turned his back. He then began to saw just above the knee. A high-pitched scream followed the first few swipes of the blade across the raw, tender skin. Soon, the screaming droned into a low, guttural moan that sounded like a wild beast – the cry that's first heard as prey is taken down as fresh kill. Mercifully, Taylor fell limp and silent.

Kathryn flinched and turned her head as bile rose to her mouth. Walking away would prove catastrophic for her, particularly as the captain had showed her mercy by undertaking the task himself. Abandoning him now would sorely aggravate any good will he had left for her. Evidence that this would be his last act of mercy was clear. He obviously expected her to finish the job as the ship's healer.

The other men had withdrawn, wide-eyed and terrified. However, they were soon overcome by curiosity as they gawked at the bloody saw that the captain pushed back and forth. Gristle and bone splintered and cracked, shooting missiles through the air that landed in the widening pool of warm, sticky crimson beneath the captain's boots. One of the large pirates turned his head and vomited, but never released his hold of the unconscious man.

Several grueling minutes passed before a dull thud sounded as the mangled appendage fell to the deck. The limb was severed at the thigh. Blood pulsed from the stump still under the captain's arm as he turned the saw over the torch, heating the blade in the flame. Quickly, he seared the raw end of the stump with the white-hot blade to cauterize the meat, bone, and tissue. Then the captain stood upright, dropping the stump and the saw on the bloodstained deck. His eyes scanned the faces ogling the grisly amputation.

"Clean that mess up," he growled in disgust to no one in particular.

Captain John Phillips then turned from the pirates and strode to his quarters, where he stripped off his muscular body, the clothes that were saturated with a traitor's blood.

Forty-Two

THE WRETCHED MAN LIVED, DUE in part to Kathryn's watchful attentiveness and skill with her herbs and amulets. For the most part, Taylor's foul life was spared because of Captain Phillips' brazen act of hacking off the pirate's leg.

In the days that followed the attempted mutiny, and Taylor's subsequent disfigurement, order prevailed on the *Revenge*. Most of the time, the men went about their duties rather solemnly and without much exchange. Even Archer was a bit more reserved, particularly in the presence of the captain. There was never any doubt that the men respected Captain Phillips, but with this show of valor, the captain was awarded renewed respect, almost to the point of fear. Indeed, it took courage to sever a man's leg to save the miserable, thieving wretch's life. The captain had earned his status all over again.

How to deal with the traitorous Fern and his cohort was a matter that still required attention, however. Willie lay in wait to be sentenced by the crew, who voted unanimously to turn him over to the bosun. It was Gow, after all, who'd been held captive by Willie's own cutlass. This was good news to Gow, who found great pleasure in planning the flogging with the "cat o' nines." Just how many lashes to be given remained undetermined, until he thought to put the issue to vote. The crew voiced their decision, which was that each man would dole the punishment with the leather whip, complete with nails and hooks attached to the ends.

"Thrice apiece!" someone shouted.

"Ye'll kill him too quickly," said another.

"Aye, a lengthier flog fits the crime!"

It was decided that two lashings apiece would suffice. Once the vote had been presented, the prisoner was taken to the main mast and tied upright with his chest pressed to the mast and arms outstretched to either side. Willie's back was exposed to the circle of men waiting to take their turn with the whip against his skin.

"For the crime o' mutiny, with the snow belongin' to this 'ere crew, and general debaucheries, ye be brought before the mast." Gow paced in long, measured steps, tracing an elongated figure eight in front of the men.

"Send 'im to meet the cats!"

The vote was unanimous and cheers erupted forthwith.

Lining the deck topside, the pirates fidgeted anxious to get on with the flogging. Kathryn was ordered to remain nearby, ready to bind up the torn flesh, should Willie survive. Already weary of the gruesome consequences for breaking the Code, she understood the necessity in keeping order on a ship this size… but the cats? Keeping a tight lock on her thoughts, she witnessed for nearly an hour the brutal lashings inflicted upon the pirate's flesh. Each crack of the whip preceded a shrill cry until the wail faded to silence. Kathryn was certain the criminal had surrendered long before the lashings finally ceased. Mercy was found in his unconsciousness – or death.

When they were finished, Willie was untied. His bloody body crumpled to the ground, too weak to stand. She moved to it, cursing the Code under her breath.

"Most likely due to the bleeding," she said. "Lift him carefully and dispatch him below."

A few of the men raised Willie's broken body and carried him below deck to the crew's quarters, which was fast becoming the sick bay. Kathryn followed in silence. Quickly, her compassion for the men fled as she met with the dreaded stench that greeted her there. Yet, in spite of the offensive conditions and foul deeds of her patients, she was tender with her ministering. Steady fingers accompanied a rash of inaudible muttering as she tediously sewed up the wide gashes left in Willie's back. The cat had done fine work, ripping the tissue in chunks from the bone.

"You'll have an impressive tale to accompany the scars that'll likely remain…should you live." She cursed under her breath and when she had finished, Willie was placed in a hammock next to the one-legged Taylor. The crippled pirate still sang out in a delirium on occasion.

"They make for good companions, methinks," Skyrme said as he shifted Willie into the center. "One's looney as a dodo, and th' other's out cold!" He laughed, and quickly moved topside to fresher breezes.

The smell of sepsis blended with stale, salty air and made it difficult for Kathryn to remain below deck for long periods of time. She knew this was how she earned her keep however, and so kept complaints to herself.

Fern's fate was left to the captain, who held contempt for the man, anyway. It was obvious, even more so given the traitor's rebellion. Rumor had it that tension between Fern and Archer began the day John Rose Archer had defected from Edward Teach's command. He was swiftly welcomed onboard the *Revenge*, and joined the crew. Soon afterward, he'd been voted as quartermaster, a position John Fern had deemed for himself. It was common knowledge that Fern hungered for the job, and when Archer was voted to take the office instead, John Fern was openly bitter, causing trouble for Archer whenever he could get away with it. Today was no different. Standing on deck, clapped in irons, Fern showed defiance. He cursed the crew, the ship, and John Paul Archer, then spat on the deck to seal it.

"Ye be charged with committing acts of deliberate and intentional insubordination, cunning, and open piracy to your own end against the crew and captain of the *Revenge*." John Phillips directed his biting comments to the traitor. "What say ye, John Fern?"

Kathryn watched the trial with fascination. Most interesting was the accusation of piracy against a crew of cutthroats. Undeniably, there was great merit placed on respect and order, even onboard a ship of criminals. Justice would be served, for which there would be no appeal process, particularly when breaking the Articles of the ship. Indeed, the punishment would be severe.

Fern spat at Captain Phillips then followed up with a string of curses that caused some of the most seasoned pirates to flinch. John Phillips stood solid and commanding, seething with anger.

"The punishment be a hangin' from the yardarm until ye fall dead," ruled Captain Phillips without emotion.

"Keelhaul 'im, I say." Someone had shouted from the back of the gathered crew.

"Aye, Capt'n! Keelhaul the bilge rat!"

Several others joined in, shouting in unison that the crew should tie Fern with ropes and drag him under the keel of the ship, back and forth, from one side to the other. Kathryn steadied herself. Tending to the injuries Fern would likely incur would no doubt strain her skills. Scraping against the bottom of the vessel, brushing against barnacles and other marine growth, in tow by a rope – underwater, no less – would be nearly impossible to heal, if he survived at all. Of course, her service would only be required if Fern didn't drown first or get eaten by sharks. Still, the severity of the chastisement seemed insufferable. Fern blanched at the proposal but remained belligerent. In the face of his accusers, he cursed God and dared them to "Do your worst." This did not go unnoticed by the captain, who heartily agreed with the chosen penalty.

"Ay, so be it, then. Take this maggot to the ropes and feed him to the sharks," he growled, staring at Fern.

The crew cheered wildly and took hold of Fern, dragging him to the portside rails. There, they fastened one line to his hands and another around his feet. These were fastened to opposite yardarms. Fern was forced to stand on the edge of the chains. With the heel of his boot, Archer kicked him into the water, where he landed with a resounding splash. The word was given, and several men on the opposite side of the ship began to pull on the ropes.

John Fern was dragged underneath the ship.

Kathryn, unable to watch, moved to the bow of the ship. Absence from the incident would not be tolerated, nor would she be excused to her quarters, and a quick glance at the captain confirmed that. Her hands clenched the rails at the front of the ship as she tried to hold back the nausea. Focusing on the sea brought momentary distraction from the events going on mid-ship, but the coarse shouts from the pirates as they dragged their crewmate to his doom beneath was more than she could ignore. Her knuckles turned white as she heard the dull wet thud of Fern's body flopping onto the starboard deck, not knowing whether he lived or lay dead.

"This be a hard life at sea, and these be hard men who live it."

She turned to see Captain Phillips standing next to her. He leaned forward, the white of his shirt billowing against his strong back in the salty air. Gently, he laid his hand over hers, warming her heart, and she lifted her fingers to entwine them in his as she gripped the rail a moment longer.

"I understand. Still, it is difficult for me to watch." she said. A woman's heart beat fiercely in her youthful body.

"Ye need not view it then." He kissed the top of her head and paused, his face resting in her hair momentarily, filling his senses with lilac and rhodanthe. He then turned and strode back to the deck and his crew.

Tears welled in her eyes, and Kathryn's heart betrayed her as it filled with longing for the man just at her side. *It can never be, Kathryn*, she said to herself, wiping the tears from her cheeks. She stayed at the rails, feeling the rhythmical lift and drop of the ship most prominently here, at the bow. This was her favorite part of the ship, and the place she now hoped would ease the ache inside her chest.

Hundreds of brightly colored fish swam in and out of coral as the golden sun lowered itself over the turquoise sea. She squinted against the amber rays and watched as, in slow motion, the sunlight danced in sparkling stars over the waves. In that moment, Kathryn resolved herself to the life she'd been forced to assume, and Mariel's words became prophecy. She knew this was the man who needed her and her supernatural *Gift*. His was the heart that she longed for, the heart that would keep her captive onboard a pirate ship without use of irons, blades or Codes. She belonged here, and wanted to stay with him.

Kathryn leaned over the rail, unable to hold back the tears, and wept.

Fourty-Three

SHARKS WERE PLENTIFUL IN THE waters of the
Caribbean, but the small hammerhead shark circling
the ship brought new excitement to the crew.

"It's a sign!" Cade shouted, pointing to the water.

The arrival of the beast indicated the advent of
other predators below the surface of the water. It mirrored those who hovered over the limp traitor.

"He's still breathin'. Give him time to come 'round,
then send him back under again," a raspy voice called out
as two or three men bent over Fern's body. One of them
put his ear to Fern's chest to see if his heart still beat…or
not. Crimson water seeped from beneath his back, a sure
sign he had met with barnacles beneath the ship. No
wonder the shark had been so tempted. Within minutes,
Fern recovered, spewed water, and began to wail.

"It's from the sting o' the salt water in his wounds,
most likely."

"Aye. Bawlin' like a baby!"

"Off for another swim, mate." Moody shoved Fern
back over the edge of the ship. His companions sang
their approval with rolls of discordant laughter.

For nearly two full hours the keelhauling continued. Each time, after surfacing, Fern was allowed a chance to recover – enough to cry out for mercy – before he was tossed overboard and dragged back under. The shark circled, occasionally skimming past the pirate as he was dragged underwater. After the third pass, Fern didn't recover, though he miraculously continued to breathe. He bled quite heavily from deep gashes – whether from shark bites or ship scavengers, it was unclear. Eventually, the pirates decided he'd had enough and called for Kathryn to come collect her new patient.

Her instructions were crisp and succinct, as she directed a few malingerers to carry Fern's broken body to the sick bay. They did so, and she followed behind, her eyes downcast to match her spirit.

John Phillips watched her go below deck. A selfish satisfaction filled his soul – a reassuring impression that Kathryn belonged on the ship…belonged to him. He tried to dismiss her as mere property, but the heat threading out from his core argued otherwise. Little did it matter now that she was fully enmeshed in the ways of pirates, and enmeshed in his crew. If he could just pacify the sea, he would have everything.

"Alas, the sea shall never be tamed…and likely not my Kathryn," he whispered from the bow. The *Revenge* lurched ahead, leaving the sea creatures and dark deeds of piracy in her wake.

*****

The ship headed northeast toward an island called Barbados, where it was rumored gold, wenches, and rum were aplenty. The snow had dropped low on supplies, and it was decided they would take the smaller vessel back to the Grenadines where they could easily restock it. A young man named William White was voted to command the snow to the closest port. He assembled a skeleton crew, all volunteers who longed to see land again in spite of the risks. The rest, including Archer, Gow and Sparks, asked to stay onboard the *Revenge*. The plan was to reunite again in Barbados, but the crew thought that unlikely, knowing the men on the snow were apt to take their chances at pirating on their own. Still, there were no hard feelings as the snow turned south to the Grenadines, while the *Revenge* continued its northeasterly course toward Barbados.

The wind had been in the sails for days, and all onboard maintained favorable moods. Evenings were once again filled with singing, dancing, and rum, which lifted everyone's spirits, including Kathryn's. On rare occasions, she could be caught off guard and coaxed to join in with the singing and dancing. These were the moments John Phillips craved her company most.

On one such evening, as dusk made its way past the horizon, and as voices and bottles were raised in unison, Kathryn found herself next to Seth. So enthralled was he with tales of the sea, that he hardly noticed her standing there. Briggs waved his arms as Pock-eye reenacted the plot, an excellent display of storytelling, if there ever was one. Behind them, the music grew louder as men grew drunker. Suddenly, a firm hand gripped Kathryn and pulled her to her feet.

"Will ye give me the honors o' this dance?" The captain smiled and bowed.

"Why yes, sir, it'd be my pleasure." Unable to hide the sarcasm in her voice, she returned the smile and added a quick curtsey, before offering her hand.

His palm easily found its way to the small of her back as her hand slipped into his. The tempo changed, and he pulled her to him, their physiques touching as they started to move, spinning in time to the music. As if no other soul existed, the captain moved closer. She felt his breath on her neck, and her heart raced. Tenderness filled the space between them as they moved gracefully, young lovers embracing for the first time. The night stood still as their hearts beat as one, passion expressed through their unspoken intent. Desire burned strong, and both knew it could never be quenched. As the song ended, he held her close to him, and time froze for that instant. She blushed, and the left side of his mouth curled. Then he released her, turning his back and distracting himself from her spell as he clapped for the music well played.

"Thank you, lass," he said as he faced her again, bowed low, then turned and walked away.

Too quickly, it was over. The night's festivities continued but Kathryn could not. She retired early to her quarters and hoped the deep night would release her from all thoughts of John Phillips. She slept little that night, but when she did, she dreamt of his touch, and her skin tingled while her soul warmed. Her life was happy once again.

Early the next morning, an abrupt knock on the door announced Seth with her breakfast. As the sun crept in through the portholes and broke into her solitude, she stretched – grinning at her memories from the night before.

"Enter," Kathryn called out, her voice much too animated to go unnoticed.

Seth ambled through the doorway, and his eyes suspiciously surveyed the room while he chatted on about besting ol' Gentleman Harry as they fenced with cutlasses. Seth was obviously searching for something… or perhaps, someone.

"And I won three doubloons in the process," he announced.

The young woman beamed at him. "That's marvelous, Seth," she said, and grinned as he prattled on. Setting out fruit and biscuits, he moved swiftly around her little room, eyes darting to corners and beneath the scant furnishings. He then stopped to cock his head sideways, squinting at her with uncertainty.

"What in the world are you lookin' for?" Kathryn's eyes danced. In a way, the lad's misgivings amused her.

"Nothing," he replied, and slammed the door behind him.

Kathryn was grateful for her friendship with Seth, but he could prove himself nosy when provoked. Still, a momentary reflection of their frequent talks on deck left her with the reassurance that he was someone to be trusted. It comforted her to see that he'd kept the amulet she had given him so long ago.

When she had finished her breakfast, she patted at her face with fresh water kept hidden in a chipped Chinese jar. She'd discovered it one day stashed behind a stack of discarded rigging. Just whom it belonged to wasn't apparent, but Kathryn reasoned that since she was sailing aboard a pirate ship, plundering discarded wares was appropriate. She snatched it up, claiming it for her own. The water was secretly kept for her personal private use. No one needed to know she kept fresh water in her quarters. When she had bathed her face and rinsed her teeth, she made her way on deck and into the welcome heat of the morning sun.

The men were busy with their tasks, but the captain was not at the helm. Sparks stood with hands on the wheel and his focus on the sea. She shrugged it off, not wanting to spoil the splendor of such a wonderful day. Making her way to her usual place on the portside bow, she noticed Archer was nowhere to be seen. Thus far, the morning fared perfectly!

The rails lent her support as she breathed in deeply of the salty morning air. Below, in the water, schools of fish swam in silver ribbons, zigzagging back and forth against the hull of the ship. Without warning,

Cook thrust his head out one of the portholes below and tossed fish heads and bones into the water where the school of feeding fish thrashed. Seconds later, he disappeared inside the bowels of the ship, only to reappear with more slop for the sea. Kathryn chuckled at the sight.

"You look like a turtle popping in and out of its shell." No one heard Kathryn's comment, which was just fine with her.

Azure water filled the horizon with soothing animation. Currents rolled one after another, skimming the surface in rhythmic succession. She followed the movement of each wave farther and farther away from the ship until something piqued her interest. Not far off in the distance, she caught sight of a single dark cloud rolling out over the water. The sky was a clear blue above her, and the seas were calm, but the cloud that touched the horizon suggested otherwise. She cocked her head and squinted against the sun, keeping one eye on the dirty, billowing cloud, and realized she was looking at smoke. Overhead, three men clamored with the sheets, seemingly unaware of the smolder.

"You, there, what say ye to that?" she shouted to the men. They sat, suspended midair, their only lifeline the beams and shrouds, which they clung to as they worked the ropes.

The pirates gawked and shrugged their shoulders. Obviously, they had no clue what she was shouting about. So Kathryn pointed to the circling grey funnel climbing higher into the blue sky. One by one they spotted the plume of smoke that rose from the surface of the water. Soon, the lookout spotted it, who in turn, alerted Sparks, whose only response was to stare. Craning his neck to discover the source of the flames behind the smoke, Spark's reaction stayed cool, though the others shuffled about the rails for a better look.

"Ye'd best get the capt'n and Archer," Sparks said to Seth, who had been taking the last of cook's breakfast to those still locked in the sick bay. Seth peered out toward the sea and took in the spectacle with mild dismay, then acknowledged the order with a weak, "Aye." Moments later, he disappeared down the companionway, leaving food on the stairway, which Kathryn assumed would be delivered later or eaten by foragers.

Seconds later, Captain Phillips stepped onto the deck, his spyglass in hand and aimed at the billowing grey cloud. A hush fell over the men as they waited with anticipation for orders, all eyes on the captain. Archer joined him, but said nothing, awaiting orders like the others.

"Hard to starboard," he called out, the long telescope still held to his eye. "There be a ship afire. Use caution, Mister Sparks."

"Aye, Capt'n." Sparks cranked the wheel to the right.

"Mister Archer, see the men to arms. We won't be caught in an ambush unawares this day."

"Aye!"

Archer shouted orders and the men scrambled to collect their weapons. Kathryn stayed where she was, unobtrusive but alert, eyes fixed on the burning ship as it moved closer. She could see orange flames lapping at the sea as a great copper flash leapt skyward, engulfing the mast and sails. Smoke and ash wafted across the *Revenge* as the distance between the two ships narrowed, leaving an acrid residue in the back of her throat. No signs of life were visible on the flaming vessel or in the bits and pieces of charred debris that floated past in the water, bouncing off the hull.

Suddenly, a dark chill overpowered her. Something was wrong. She could feel evil on the water here. In a panic, she turned from the rails and ran back to where the captain was standing. He stared at the burning ship and did not acknowledge her presence.

"Captain, there's darkness in this…I feel it." She trembled as she spoke to him. He lowered the telescope and studied at her. A flash of genuine concern washed over his face.

"Go on," he urged.

"I can't be sayin' what it is, exactly, but this is wrong. I *feel* it!" Her expression offered no room for misinterpretation.

She shivered again. The captain eyed her for a long time before he turned to address the quartermaster.

"Mister Archer, warn the men to be at their guard." Looking skyward, he continued. "What see ye there, Mister Dunkin?" His eyes darted up at the crow's nest.

A skinny, weathered pirate perched atop the main mast also stared at the flames through a well-worn spyglass. He paused only seconds before hollering his answer to the captain below.

"A brig set afire with nothin' much left o' her. There be another'n behind in the smoke cover, a rather large cargo ship, it seems…an' it be flyin' the black flag, Captain."

John Phillips stiffened. Wasting no time, he ordered the men on deck to hoist the colors.

Uneasiness crawled along Kathryn's spine as she watched the red flag with skeleton and speared heart hoisted up the main mast. Unable to contain the dread that had suddenly materialized, she clung to the rails to steady herself. Archer shouted orders while the pirates quickly cleared the deck and made ready to fight. Kathryn stayed topside, and no one thought to warn her to take cover this time. Her mind raced with thoughts of the imminent battle and the chilling black feeling of evil that surrounded the burning ship. Aware of the Seren's sudden heat, she realized some type of protection was needed. It was her duty to cast a shield over the *Revenge*, or else the ship would be destroyed and all with her. She darted to the main deck and boldly grasped Archer by the sleeve.

"Listen to me, Archer, if ye want to survive." Her glare dug fiercely into his ugly face. Instinctively, she reached for his brawny arm, clinging to it as tightly as she had the rails. He cast one brief glance at her grip on his arm. Hatred flashed in his eyes, as months of harnessed hostility were unleashed on the girl who dared confront him now. He jerked away and spun around to face her, reaching for his cutlass at the same time. Drawing the steel blade from its scabbard, he thrust the tip at her midriff, stopping just a hairbreadth away from piercing her skin. She gasped.

"Ye've crossed me for the last time, missy," he growled as he raised the steel blade in his hand and slashed the air in front of her. She ducked, fell onto the deck, and rolled to her left, just avoiding the curved razor tip.

Above her head, a high-pitched clatter sounded as one of the crewmen launched a cutlass toward one of her hands. *Could someone actually be helping me? Who would dare offer me a blade against the quartermaster's attack?* The thought startled her more than the weapon itself. Likely, the cutlass was just meant to encourage a fair fight, knowing the girl would lose. It skated along the wood planks, stopping just within reach of her right hand. Instinctively, she grasped the hilt and rolled to her right, just missing the edge of Archer's blade as he swung again, hacking into the wood and sending up fine, pale splinters where she had laid a moment before.

Kathryn leapt to her feet and tucked one side of her skirt into her waistband, then spiraled to face her assailant with the cutlass held forward, en garde, ready for the next attack. The air whistled as Archer carved a fierce blow, aiming at her throat. But Kathryn had been taught well and thrust the hilt upward, fending off Archer's blade with a solid strike from the cutlass in her own hand. A resounding clash reverberated as steel met steel, causing several pirates to gather. Faces watched in abject astonishment as she fiercely met the quartermaster's hacks and slices.

Another clash echoed as Kathryn returned blows, this time as the assailant. The tip of her cutlass tore through the linen sleeve of Archer's blouse, instantly staining it a bright red as the meat on his shoulder gaped open. The edge of the dark tattoo peeked out through the torn shirt. Blood ran in rivulets over the inked letters, obscuring them. Crazed, the quarter-master let out a menacing howl and charged again, thrusting and slashing wildly. She moved back and soon required both hands on the hilt to ward off the strength of each blow as it met her weakening parry. Stabbing with each precise lunge, Archer became possessed, a wild beast aimed at dicing her to pieces. She feigned and blocked, but could not hold back the strength with which he assaulted her.

Aligning her blade to match the next impact, she held the steel overhead as a shield. Steadily, her defense was met with hacking blow after blow, knocking her backwards. Her only protection was the blade. Strength fled her arms and fatigue took its place, as all around her sang with the sound of steel cutting through air. One final blow crumpled her as the razor sharp cutlass was leveled directly at her hands, slamming the hilt that protected her fingers. The force split the blade, shattering it into three pieces. The hilt was dashed from her hands. She fell backwards onto the deck, landing hard on her back, the wind knocked from her on impact. Black eyes bore down upon her as Archer moved slowly, a fiend standing over the helpless sorceress.

"Prepare to meet yer Maker, witch!" Archer hissed through clenched teeth and spittle flew from his cracked lips. He raised his cutlass high overhead.

Kathryn readied for the lethal blow. Without thought, her hand grabbed hold of the Seren. In spite of the fierce heat radiating from it, she took hold of the blazing stone, closed her eyes, and prepared for death. The air hissed, followed by a deafening clash as the sound of two cutlasses collided just above her face.

"Choose this day whom ye cross blades with, Mister Archer!" a deep voice bellowed.

Terrified, she opened her eyes. Towering directly above her was the majestic form of Captain Phillips. He wielded a gleaming, curved sword that had suspended the fall of the cutlass clenched in Archer's hand. Both blades held, crossed just inches from where Kathryn's hand still clutched the Seren.

"Ye best stand down, Mister Archer, else face yer captain. I give no mercy this day."

Archer's stare latched onto Kathryn, and she could feel the heat of his hatred boring through her.

"Archer!" A trembling voice pierced the silence from somewhere among the men. "Stand down, Archer!"

Black eyes flickered as Archer blinked, glanced at the captain, and then back to the crossed cutlasses hovering above Kathryn's chest.

"Archer, think on this, man. This is not the day for dyin'." Another voice called out from the crowd of pirates.

The quartermaster jerked involuntarily, his muscles too tense to relax. After moment, he stepped back, pulled his blade away from the captain's, and lowered his sword, his eyes never leaving the girl.

"A wise move," the captain said, and eased somewhat, though his stance shielded Kathryn. "We're facin' a fight soon enough. There's the Jolly Roger flyin' just off the starboard rails and the men need their quartermaster to lead them."

Archer said nothing, but a slight dip of his head offered a sign of agreement. He stepped back and reluctantly yielded his sword to his side once again.

"The lass spoke before ye drew yer weapon. Methinks it best we hear what she has to say. Don't ye agree?" The captain sheathed his sword as he spoke.

Archer cast a menacing look upon Kathryn as she was helped to her feet by one of the men. "Aye, aye, Capt'n," Archer muttered darkly. He kept his eyes locked on her.

Satisfied that the quartermaster was once again under control, the captain turned to Kathryn. She stared back at him, and in spite of his apparent detachment, she saw the fear peeking out from behind his haunting green eyes.

"Capt'n." She exhaled. "I implored Mister Archer – a request that he order the men to gather every lantern onboard and hang them about the ship. We need to light every candle possible." Kathryn choked out the words as she steadied herself. Her head still reeled from the sword fight, with thoughts of an imminent death still too fresh in her mind. The Seren had not yet cooled either – a warning that danger still threatened.

Archer glared at her, seething with hatred, but passive under the watchful eye of the captain. "Ye mock me, wench," he hissed.

A sense of dread found her again. She faced Archer, the fire in her eyes now as bright as the stone about her neck. "And you left me no choice but to defend myself, *pirate*!" She spat, and blood tinged the place at her feet where it landed. She would not back down – not this time.

He dropped his eyes to the Seren glowing at the base of her throat. Sensibly enough, he chose not to challenge her in the presence of the captain. "Mayhem follows a woman onboard, and ye're no exception, witch! I will not accept your presence, and will never stop hunting you."

"Mister Archer, there's evil on the water, and it's comin' with that ship. We need lanterns, and there's no time to waste."

"Do as she says, Mister Archer."

"Aye, capt'n." With one final glance at the captain, Archer faced the men still gathered on deck. "Davis, Reed, and you, carpenter, gather the lanterns and hang 'em lit about. Make swift o' it or I'll tan yer hide meself!"

He shot a final look at Captain Phillips, then nodded adieu and walked away, glancing behind only once before disappearing into the gathered crew.

Relief nearly overwhelmed Kathryn as Archer departed. At least for now, she could be satisfied that her request had been honored. But the cold realization of what lay ahead on the water pulsed through her veins and assured her that there was still more to be done. In the distance, a thick duskiness rolled across the water, growing denser as it moved.

"What is it?"

"I…I'm not certain, Capt'n, but I need to be prepared. Please excuse me."

Malevolence gripped her senses with cold, icy fingers, making it suddenly difficult to breathe. There was little time before the creeping vapor would pervade the ship. She fled to her cabin in search of the bag of amulets, passing Seth on the companionway. He had just returned from below deck when she stopped him.

"Seth, mind me on this. We're in grave danger, and it falls to you to save us all."

"What?" His eyes grew wide and his voice incredulous. "You're overreacting a bit, don't you think, Kat?" He pointed to the pitch. "It's just fog."

"It is not! Hear me out, Seth…for a just a moment."

Seth shook his head. "No. You *do* this, Kat. You get yourself excited over nothing, then bring trouble along with it. I don't plan to follow you there...not this time."

Kathryn stomped her foot and dropped her hands to her hips. "Stop being so impertinent! The men trust you...not me. The captain trusts you, as well. I cannot do what needs to be done. I've no time to argue. The black ship carries something with it that threatens the *Revenge*. The evidence is there...that stuff you want to call fog. It crawls along the water...alive."

Seth glanced again to the vapor. Fingers clawed at the water's surface as it crept closer. She had captured Seth's attention, as well as his ego. His chest puffed as he nodded for her to continue. "Go on," he said.

"Can you gather salt from the galley without cook knowin' of it?"

"Aye, but what...?"

She cut him off. "There's no time to explain." Her eyes scanned the deck. "Take the salt and pour it along the inside rails. It needs to cover the entire perimeter of the deck, savvy?" He nodded and opened his mouth again to speak, but she cut him off once more. "Be certain to line the helm. Off with you, then! The ship and crew are in jeopardy!"

Seth scrambled toward the ship's galley and disappeared below deck. Kathryn rushed into her cabin and grabbed hold of a bound sage stick, several green leaves, and two orange stones split in two by thin black veins that ran through their centers. As she turned to go, she spotted the cutlass Emmanuel Wynn had taught her to use only weeks before. Wishing she had chosen to keep it with her an hour ago, she made the decision to take it now. Secretly, she knew it would do her no good against seasoned pirates, but the cold steel resting against her hip gave her some confidence. Tying her skirt into a side-knot, she tore a long piece of sailcloth meant for bandages and fastened a makeshift sash around her waist. Then, carefully, she tucked the blade under to secure it snugly to one side, and patted the steel for luck. Dropping several amulets into a pocket, she darted up the stairs and onto the deck. By the time Kathryn had returned, the lanterns had been lit and scattered across the entire ship. Seth was hunched over, trailing a line of salt along the inboard. Upon closer inspection, the ship was completely encircled with sparkling white salt crystals. She smiled.

Fine work, Seth.

The woven sticks of dried sage were lit, then waved in a circle, allowing the smoke from the bundles to rise and blend with the smoke from the burning ship. She fanned the musky grey plume that smoldered in curled, drawn-out threads. As she moved, she smudged the ship and chanted the ancient prayers of protection.

The captain caught sight of her waving the burning sage in her hands and watched in fascination as she made magic across the ship, swaying with the incantation and the smoke.

"The lass casts her spell." He spoke aloud to no one, and looked back to the burning ship. "It seems to be her role in keepin' the ship and crew safe."

He then lifted the eyepiece. Mystical powers were afoot. Darkness at sea had set out to find them, and the light danced onboard to protect the *Revenge*, somehow. In that moment, the larger ghost ship adjusted course, sailing straight toward the *Revenge* as the smaller, burning vessel dropped piece by piece into the depths of the sea. He studied the black ship through the scope. Just visible to the naked eye, a tall, dark figure stood boldly on the bow of the larger brig. Smoke billowed from both ears, circling his dark eyes and long, black beard. On cue, Archer stepped up alongside the captain, his eyes glued to the looming, distant ship and the pirate who stood on her bow.

"It's the *Queen Anne's Revenge* an' the mad Captain Teach, no less." He spoke with low tones directly to Captain Phillips.

The captain faced the quartermaster, who held out his arm and raised the bloodstained sleeve of his shirt, exposing the tattoo on his left forearm. The letters Q.A.R. stood out boldly on Archer's leathery skin.

"It won't sit well with ol' Blackbeard when he sees me standin' on the *Revenge*, Capt'n." Archer's warning was a raspy whisper.

"Then we are doomed," Captain Phillips replied, and turned to face his fate.

Fourty-Four

EDWARD TEACH STOOD ON THE bow of the *Queen Anne's Revenge*, sinister and chilling, as black smoke curled around his face. His countenance brought terror in itself, even without the tales that that were told of Blackbeard. The *Revenge* would certainly be taken as his prize. All the crew could hope for was that quarters would be given. It wasn't likely. And given the state of the doomed, burned ship, the *Revenge's* fate was likely sealed as well. As if to confirm their fears, the dark pirate's guttural laugh echoed across the water.

"Well, by me soul! If it's not the great merchant ship *Revenge* and her cap'n, John Phillips," Captain Teach shouted from the *Queen Anne's Revenge*.

He stood with hands on hips as smoke curled from the lighted matchsticks placed under his hat. It was a signature trick used by Blackbeard to intimidate his victims. It worked. The glowing sticks illuminated his murky eyes, creating a fearsome appearance for which some sailors dubbed him, "The being from hell."

Ahead of the ship, the obscure vapor crawled from the *Q.A.R.* On deck, it hovered, followed by a venomous woman who slinked up to Teach's side. Ebony hair trailed behind her sleek body, which was mottled with tattooed symbols of beasts.

"Capt'n Teach," replied John Phillips, bowing low with his hat in hand. "Always pleasant to see a fellow mariner."

"Yet, yer sailin' in me waters. Not canny, says I."

"I meant no affront to ye, sir."

"Aye, an' that be a good decision, Capt'n Phillips, as I might be inclined to jump aboard ye fair ship and cut ye to ribbons!"

Blackbeard laughed – a feral sound that sent chills along Kathryn's spine. The large ship closed in. Kathryn moved into the shadows, not wanting to be noticed. Her vantage point still allowed her to keep a close watch on the woman standing next to Blackbeard.

As if sensing Kathryn's presence, the woman glided forward and began to pace. Her panther-like movements behind the bearded pirate looked deadly. Black eyes focused on where Kathryn hid. The dark witch lifted her hands and her black lips moved, silently whispering to no one. Without warning, the Seren around Kathryn's neck began to vibrate, and then hum, as its color changed from pale crimson to a sapphire blue that matched her eyes. White, radiant light flashed, followed by a blinding beam cast out from its center, illuminating the ship in a spectral glow.

Kathryn put her hand up to shield the Seren, but the light from the stone created a barrier that even she could not penetrate.

"We're on our way to Barbados, Capt'n Teach. Our ship's barren and in need of supplies," Captain Phillips lied. His eyes darted fleetingly to the source of the blue light, then back to Blackbeard. "There be no need to come aboard, lest ye seek only for company and song."

"Nay, Capt'n Phillips!" shouted Blackbeard. "I seek treasures and rum, the likes o' which methinks be found in yer hull."

Captain Phillips shifted his weight, the signal for Archer to prepare the men to fire. It was apparent that Blackbeard saw through the bluff and intended to ransack the *Revenge* before their conversation finished. Slowly, Blackbeard drew out his cutlass, placing his other hand over a row of pistols hanging from ribbons that were slung over his shoulders. Captain Phillips parroted the pirate by dropping one hand to his own cutlass. As the men sized each other up, chatting about pleasantries that didn't truly exist, the dark woman leaned forward and whispered something into Blackbeard's ear. When she had finished, she pointed at Kathryn, then resumed her pacing. Blackbeard paused, eyeing the *Revenge*.

"Well, Capt'n Phillips." The panther-like paces commenced behind his back, and the crew scrutinized their prey. "It seems yer ship's bewitched. I've been cautioned that cursed be the man who crosses blades with ye."

Captain Phillips remained stone still, watching the bearded pirate and his crew for any sign of attack. Kathryn stepped out of the shadows, and the spectral stone radiating from around her neck intensified. In that same moment, the black woman froze. She opened a dark mouth and spoke, her voice a ghostly moan across the water.

"The witch keeps watch with the Seren, John Phillips. Mind me well, Morrigan shall hear of it. The white witch keeps ye safe this day, but not for always," she cackled.

Kathryn's gut clenched, and she balled both fists as the woman gave her the warning. Instantly, the hum from the Seren amplified.

"Morrigan seeks that which she cannot have, Roane. Tell her this from me and get thee hence, devil woman. Take this filthy pirate with ye." The words from Captain Phillips' mouth flew like daggers to the dark woman.

Blackbeard stepped forward, his cutlass held ready to fight. The crew of both ships positioned themselves and waited for the call to combat. Long sticks ignited on one end were brought to each loaded long-gun by the powder monkeys. Everyone waited for the order to fire.

"Hold!" Roane bellowed. "The Seren protects them all. Can ye not see the ship cast aglow with its spell? Ye shall surely die this day, ye who rise up to fight against the Sigil of Defense."

Blackbeard's crewmen froze, cutlasses held mid-air, their battle cry silenced in their throats. The Obeah witch had spoken, and all onboard knew to listen. Blackbeard lowered his sword, then touched the shiny blade to the brim of his hat in salute.

"It seems great powers be with ye this day, John Phillips. We shall meet again, and when we do, yer blood shall stain the decks o' the *Revenge*." Blackbeard roared and gave the orders to take the *Queen Anne's Revenge* into the wind.

Captain Phillips, likewise, gave orders to move ahead starboard, and though the wind was in their favor, the crew began to whistle, calling the wind to blow even stronger. It proved effective as the wind took the sails and the ship cut through the sea to take the *Revenge* out of the path of the fearsome Captain Blackbeard. When the dark ship had changed course, Captain Phillips walked back to the helm and gave orders to Sparks, who steered the ship northeast. The crew stayed glued to their battle stations, unwilling to leave just yet. Some crossed themselves, while others took up the salt from the deck floor and pinched it over their left shoulders.

Kathryn dared not leave her post. The Seren gradually paled as the dark woman disappeared from view. Mariel had spoken of Roane – who was one of Morrigan's sisters. She was an Obeah witch, the same as her sibling, Macha, whom Kathryn had met on Tobago. Both sisters had foretold of John Phillips' destiny. A warning such as this, particularly given from Morrigan's sisters, had a deeper meaning. There was something the captain was keeping from her. Kathryn needed answers from the willful pirate. His imposing stature at the hull created an almost foreboding air about him. The man knew how to direct pirates, but could he command the Celtic witches? She faced him.

"Capt'n Phillips, I must have a word with you."

Fourty-Five

WITH A WAVE OF HIS hand, the captain motioned for her to take a seat on the settee. It was the same one that she had once slept on. Despite the urgency of the situation, happy memories always came to her on that settee. This time, she merely looked at it and waited for the captain.

Kathryn had been directed to follow him down to his quarters where they could speak in private. Apparently, he had something on his mind, as well.

"Sit, at least be seated for the moment."

"I'd rather stand."

She positioned herself at one end of the large table centered in the room. A silver platter rested off to one side, the fruit left over from breakfast uneaten. Captain Phillips pulled out his dirk and sliced a chunk of an apple that he speared onto the tip of the blade. Arm outstretched, he offered it to her.

"Eat then." The deep voice was commanding.

She took the fruit as he faced her with one foot propped on a stool. "Before ye commence to askin' your questions, I need be knowin' what it was surrounded me ship. Ye hexed this vessel, and in so doin', cursed us all." Indignation colored his voice and Kathryn knew she'd best tread lightly. She stopped eating and leaned against the table. With one hand, she took hold of his arm.

"Oh no, Capt'n. That was no curse, and I had no part in it. That was the Seren." She touched the stone with her free hand. "Mariel gave it to me when the moon's Midnight Omen was brightest, just before your men arrived at the cottage. She told me of its powers, that it would be a Sigil of Defense, protectin' me – just as the black witch on the *Queen Anne's Revenge* described."

The captain stared at the Seren. Arcane symbols caught his eye, and while he appeared to be curious, he remained just as apprehensive about its power, as his men were.

"It seems the thing protected the ship and crew, as well. There is no other accounting for Blackbeard abandoning the *Revenge* as he did, without taking her as his prize," he said.

"The Seren senses danger and protects against it." *Your fears lie with the wrong peril, Capt'n Phillips.* She kept the thought to herself. "The dark woman you called Roane was the greater threat."

"I highly doubt that is the case," he snapped. He settled back into a chair, and Kathryn smiled as he bit into the apple.

"It's a mercurial thing, the Sigil of Defense. The one who wears it must be at peace, or else awaken its power. The object seeks to destroy any source of unrest, even the throat it hangs from, if malicious intent be there. That's why your man Flint was strangled."

He cut off another piece of the apple and took it into his mouth whole. "As you say."

"There be evil with the Obeah witches. I can feel it deep in my bones. That black witch onboard Blackbeard's ship warned ye, but it was not the first." She paused, allowing for his reaction.

"Twaddle!"

"John." She spoke his name gently. "The old woman that lives on Tobago Isle is her sister, and an Obeah, as well."

"I know this. Ye spoke of it before! What has this to do with the curse that that wretched thing 'bout your neck cast over me ship and crew?" Impatience filled his voice as he spoke.

"The Obeah witches know of the Seren's powers and are fearful of it. The stone awoke when her evil crossed the water. The black mist sought to destroy the *Revenge* and everyone onboard. Her wickedness could not penetrate the shield cast by the Seren to protect me…and the ship. It was no curse, sir."

The captain stopped chewing and locked his gaze on her. "I supposed there be thanks to be given ye, then, for sparin' us all. 'Tis true, lass, ye've come to us with yer magic, and we're all the better for it." His voice lowered, though remained intense. She had no response. So he took hold of her hand and continued.

"You're welcome," she said, though she wasn't sure he'd just expressed gratitude or made a statement.

He shook his head and sighed. "Now what do ye need of me?"

Kathryn shifted, her hand warming under his touch. She cleared her throat in an effort to clear her mind and forced her voice to sound older than its years.

"Capt'n, what ties you to the Morrigan?"

Her voice betrayed her as it quivered slightly. Suddenly, the captain pulled away and stood from the table. For a moment, he appeared lost in thought, then turned away and quickly covered the distance across the room in three long strides. As he looked at her, his mind raced back to the day his crew stole her from her innocence. It seemed like such a long time ago. He knew the woman he looked upon now was not that same unpretentious lass. Kathryn was no longer the teen stolen from the heath – she was a woman, and a fierce counterpart to the secrets he kept buried in his past. Perhaps it was best to tell her of Morrigan.

"The Goddess ye speak of was once young and magical, much like yourself, although her intent was dark from the beginning. She had evil in her soul at birth and sought her prey in battle.

"Many years ago, I was taken aboard a country ship bound for Newfoundland. I had been hired as a carpenter by the honorable Captain Hamilton and worked an honest man's life. At least until the day our ship met another that flew the black flag. A great battle ensued. Our captain was lost and I was knocked about the head. As I lay dazed topside, a beautiful woman carrying a shield and sword approached. She wore naught but scant armor and ink over the entire span of her flesh. It was apparent she was not of this world. She glided across the deck to where I lay and bent o're me, destined to slay me, or so I thought. Her eyes were as black as the markings on her skin. And as she stood o'er me, she pierced my soul with her dark eyes." He paused and bitterness crossed his face as he relived the scene he was describing.

"John?" Kathryn urged from across the room.

He blinked, his glazed eyes focusing again as he turned back to look at Kathryn.

"As I said, she stared down on me and spoke words not comprehensible to any civil man. It was then she lifted my mangled body from off the deck, though she ne'er touched me. Her hand rose in the air and my body lifted with it." Anger seethed with each word spoken, and Kathryn remembered her own ability to move air into the sails. She shivered but said nothing.

"The wretched thing then spoke words I knew – 'this one be mine' – cacklin' and wailin' like the devil possessed. Some call it the cry of a banshee." He stopped and eyed Kathryn for a moment. "Her dark face drew near to mine, and she tasted me with a snake-like tongue." He tilted his head as he spoke, and lifted a lock of his wavy hair from his neck.

Kathryn swallowed a gasp as she looked upon a glistening scar that ran the length of his neck from his collarbone to his ear. She had seen it before, but assumed it was from battle. Now she saw the kiss of dark magic. She waited and the captain returned to his story.

"The Goddess of War then turned from me, a merciful act o' God, methinks, and gathered me dead crewmates on deck who lay in their own blood. It was then I crawled to the rails o' the ship and dropped into the depths o' the sea, certain to meet Davy Jones himself. But it was not so, as I was fished from the waters by a man named Anstis and taken aboard the *Good Fortune*, aptly named, given me condition."

"What happened to the devil who…" she paused, not knowing how to comment on the wicked scar over his throat.

"She disappeared, but not before killing every man aboard the vessel and settin' it afire. Curses o're the loss of the carpenter followed me on the water." He pointed to the scar as he spoke. "It was Morrigan."

"But why does she still seek you, Capt'n?" Kathryn's eyes were fastened on the glistening scar along John Phillips' neck.

"Morrigan marked me. And she still seeks me out to take me for her own, as promised. I changed my name to John Phillips and stole a ship, turnin' to pirating to escape her."

Kathryn remembered the initials on the bottom of the hourglass, *JPB*. "Buchannon. Your name was John Phillips Buchannon then."

"Aye."

She clasped her hands and lowered her head as she took in the meaning of his words. John Phillips crossed the room and sat next to the young healer, taking her clasped hands in his.

"Ye be in grave danger aboard this ship, lass. Until now, my fate mattered little."

As he spoke to her, she lifted her gaze to meet his and saw tenderness filling the emerald pools of his eyes, which were wet. She reached up and took his ebony hair between her fingers as he pulled her to him and held her tightly against his muscular chest. They clung to each other desperately, and he buried his face in her hair. She felt his heart racing to match her own and lifted her face to meet his. Eyes met, and the woman in her yearned for the pirate. She strained upward and closed her eyes, waiting for his touch. A gentle brush of his lips against hers quickened the desire pulsating through her body. He pressed his mouth against hers, and Kathryn lost all thought but for him. The taste of sweet apple and cinnamon tingled her senses as she parted her lips. He needed no other invitation as he opened his mouth to deepen the kiss. Releasing her inhibitions, she abandoned herself to the moment and savored him. Suddenly, he pulled back and stared hard at her.

"Open your eyes, lass." The huskiness of his voice gave way to a whisper. "It can never be. You're still innocent, and I am not. And, the black witch chases me. Her sisters will surely spread news that I've been found, and then she will come."

Kathryn shook her head. "John, no…I…" she protested.

He cut her off, placing an index finger over her lips. There was no way he could expose anyone else to Morrigan's wrath, least of all Kathryn. More importantly, the pirate in his soul could not be trusted, and he refused to steal anything further from her, especially her virtue.

"It will surely bring sommat worse than death for ye, lass. This I cannot do." His voice trailed off as he stood, and Kathryn saw a tremor rush his spine. He turned his back on her, a signal their conversation had ended.

A lump rose in her throat. Unable to speak, she whispered, "Aye, Captain." Brushing the creases from her skirt, the witch walked out of his quarters.

Fourty-Six

THE SKY HAD TURNED MURKY with ash from the burning ship. Though it burned her eyes, it did not cause the tears that glistened on her cheeks as Kathryn made her way topside. Using the back of a hand, she wiped her cheeks, though they did not stay dry.

"How could he...?" she said to no one. She turned to face the water. It would not bode well for her, should the men see her tears.

Even with the dusky afternoon air, the crew stayed busy at their tasks as the ship lunged forward on solid wind. Barbados would be the place she would call home, hoping to find the island peaceful and welcoming. She knew she could not stay onboard the *Revenge* with her heart held captive by its captain. The man would never be hers. Over and over again, his words replayed their cruel message within the empty spaces of her heart: *It can never be. This I cannot do...*

She moved across the main deck, toward her cabin. Several men stopped mid-task to stare at her. Amazingly, a few of them touched their brow in a show of respect. Seth spied her and rushed to her side, taking her by the arm. He pulled her portside and dragged her toward the bow. This was her favorite place on the ship, but today was different.

"How did you do it?"

"What are you talking about?" she asked, not wanting to be discovered. She wiped her face again and looked away.

"Tell me, Kathryn, how you did it! Tell me about your magic with Blackbeard and the Obeah." His eyes grew wide and his voice more animated.

Little did it matter now – plans had changed and Seth may as well know about the magic. She joined him at the rail. There, she told him about the powers of the Seren – the same story she had given to the captain – omitting the warnings. She was doubtful that Seth would be frightened by it, but she didn't want to risk putting duress on him or the others. The rumors would fly. Mostly, she didn't want to see him hop and cross himself, not right now. She also kept the secret of Morrigan and John Phillips, respecting the story as private. As she talked, Seth wrung his hands, the thrill of besting Blackbeard almost more than he could stand. When she had finished, he kissed her on the cheek.

"I knew this was more than ole Matthias' fish eyes," he ranted.

"Seth, what are you blathering on about?"

He began to hop from one foot to the other in excitement.

"A few of the men said that if you can conjure, then so could they...with the right trinkets, mind ye." He grinned and ducked as if dodging a punch as he chattered on. "Ole Matthias said he'd seen his mum using fish eyes and bones to scare off the crocs on the river. So he and a few others caught about twenty mackerels, popped out their eyes, and turned 'em into fillets."

Kathryn bit one side of her lower lip, stifling the snicker that threatened to break free. It was rather painful to maintain a straight face while listening intently to Seth's prattle.

"Krill and mackerel? Seth, really!"

"Wait! There's more. After a fine seafood gumbo at lunch...well, he couldn't be wastin' it, mind ye...after lunch, they hung the bones with the fish eyes poked on 'em over the bowsprit for luck." Seth nodded the way he always did when he wanted to make a point, as if this made perfect sense.

Kathryn's hands flew over her mouth. It didn't work. Laughter escaped. He cast a sour look.

"I'm sorry, Seth. Go on, please." She cleared her throat. "Go on."

"He hung the bones for luck."

"Where are these bones, Seth?"

This, she had to see for herself. He escorted her a few feet to the point just above the bowsprit off the bow. Leaning over, he pointed to the long wooden pole sticking out from the front. Hung precariously were several filleted fish spines with little eyeballs stuck to the ribs. Scavenger seagulls perched nearby, pecking the eyeballs from off the good-luck charms at will. Seth waved his hands and called out to scare them off, but they stubbornly returned and perched once again, squawking defiantly.

"Well done, Seth," she said, swallowing hard. "Well done!"

He sat back and cocked his head, studying her. She gulped and held his stare. "It's not the bones, is it?" he finally said.

Kathryn shook her head. "There's more to it, actually. But the intention is what brings power to any charm, even bones," she said, hoping to soften the blow.

"I knew it be more than bones with eyes on 'em. You scared off the black ship, didn't you?"

She nodded. "But it wasn't just me." She touched the Seren.

"Ah, I see." He stared at the stone for a moment, taking it in. "Well then, I need to tell the others. Our ship is magical and you seem to be the source. Huzzah!" There was sarcasm laced through his tone, but she let it go.

"You have your own gift, Seth. You know the currents. That makes for a strong navigator, it really does."

He'd already turned from her and began to walk away. She let her eyes drop back to the feasting birds. "Fine work, Kathryn. You've lost favor with the captain, and now managed to injure the only friend you've got.

Barbados will certainly prove to be your last port," she said to herself.

"They're helpless against Morrigan without ye."

The voice came from the wind. Thoughts of leaving the ship dulled as she considered Seth and the pirates.

"But I can't stay…not with the capt'n and the crew and …"

"You know what you must do. Even with your heart at risk."

This was not a truth she wanted to accept, but rather, a guilt-forced acknowledgment. Truth be told, Kathryn had taken a fancy to the sea, even though she sailed with pirates. Perhaps she'd find another way to stay onboard and guard her heart while protecting the rogue pirates she had become fond of.

"Aye then, Mariel. I'll find a way, I suppose."

Dusk pushed its way through dark clouds, and the water glistened fire-orange from the setting sun. Kathryn grew weary and decided it best to retire. Music played somewhere from a far corner of the ship, and voices soon rose in song. By the time she reached her cabin, heavy feet moved in time to the rhythm. The dancing had begun. She entered her quarters and grabbed hold of the grog still lying on the table from that morning. In just three gulps, she'd drained the pewter mug of its contents, then took hold of her grandmother's talisman and settled onto the cot. Her lips moved silently as she prayed for

Mariel to visit her that night, but sleep overpowered her and the supplication was left unanswered. Deep slumber brought with it dreams of wavy ebony locks and emerald green eyes.

Forty-Seven

NIGHTFALL BLANKETED THE CABIN. THE gentle rocking of the ship transformed even the most vigilant sentry into a sleeping baby, but Kathryn was awakened. Her cabin, though tranquil, was a testament that peace was only a deception. Immediately, her senses shifted to a heightened state of alert.

Something was terribly wrong.

Kathryn opened her eyes, gradually allowing her vision to adjust to the darkness in the room. Corners deepened with shadows, offering nothing to her probing stare. Wood strained against the strong currents beneath the ship and groaned rhythmically as the ship rose, then fell, rocking her, enticing sleep.

The intensity pumping through her veins would not allow it. She opened her eyes wider and blinked. There was no meaning to the shapes and shadows of her quarters, although some she recognized as the furnishings of her room. She glanced to the ceiling and caught her breath. One shadow lingering just above her head was foreign and eerily unfamiliar. Her muscles tensed as she kept her eyes fixed on the shadow. Deep down, she hoped to find it merely the shape of an object she'd forgotten about. Perhaps it was only a discarded piece of linen or tack wound tightly that had slipped into disarray. But her instinct told her otherwise – it was too large for anything of the sort, and the realization that she stared at something her memory could not place shot fear into her, as well.

It moved.

She held her breath as her ears strained to hear if the shadow was disturbing the silence. Shifting her focus to one side, she was able to see the shadow better with her peripheral vision. A dark form took shape. Its eyes were black and obscure and filled with evil. Just below what appeared to be the hollow shadows of a skull, an opaque outline took shape – its surface marked with a tattoo. Electricity shot through Kathryn's limbs as she made out the definite shape of a *Q*, then an *A*, and finally, the *R*.

All of the sudden, something scratched the skin along her neck and pressed downward over her throat. Instinctively, she reached up to grasp it, but was unable to take hold of the rope wrapped around her vocal cords. Reflexes moved her arms and she grabbed for the invisible hands binding the band across her throat – but she couldn't reach them. The cord pressed tighter and cut off precious air, strangling her with each passing moment.

She gasped, desperate to draw a breath. Clutching again at the raw, leathery hands, she felt herself starting to fade. Unable to scream, there was nothing to do but fight back. Held fast by the cord, she curled her fingers and scratched the brute's flesh with her fingernails. The only effect was an unyielding weight on the rope that pressed deeper into her throat. Tears filled her eyes, and she felt them bulge slightly as she looked upwards, hoping to relieve some of the force. Just inches above her face hovered the dark features of the quartermaster.

Nooooo! She mouthed the cry, but her voice could not escape. Pressure filled her head as she began to fade further into blackness.

"Ye be the spawn of Satan hisself," hissed the dark face above her. His yellowed teeth glinted only slightly when he spoke, and spittle fell onto her skin in acrid drops. Archer's sneer widened slightly as he buried the cord deeper. Wheezy laughter echoed, more distant this time.

Kathryn knew death was approaching and would soon make its claim. In one last desperate attempt to pry it from her throat, she grasped at the cord. A ring on her right hand scratched against something solid, warm and familiar. The Seren lay against her throat, just beneath her fingers. Grasping hold of stone, she folded her palm over its surface and curled her fingers.

Repel this deadly enemy…for my sake.

The ancient Celtic words filled her mind, and she repeated the chant, silently mouthing the words.

"Gwirth ladd gelyn glas…er fy mwyn i."

"Gwirth ladd gelyn glas…er fy mwyn i."

Raising the Seren, she thrust upward with her open palm and struck Archer's face squarely at the base of his nose. Brilliant blue light flashed as the butt of her palm made contact and hurled the pirate into the air, slamming him violently against the back wall. His body contorted, then dropped to the floor, grotesque and still.

The rope fell limp from Kathryn's throat, and she sucked air through a crushed windpipe. Rolling to one side, she heaved, pulling in oxygen. The room narrowed to black as she faded once again, still gasping to draw air into her starved lungs. The sorceress soon lulled into unconsciousness, panting. Her body responded and fell limp.

As stillness overtook Kathryn, the Scarlet Seren returned to its place, settling peacefully across the raw outline where the rope had left its mark. Tranquilly returned, and the Sigil of Defense rose and fell in time with the unconscious woman's breath, protecting her. All was still, except for the rise and fall of the great ship that contained her.

*****

When Kathryn awoke, she tasted blood. Her head pounded and her breath wheezed as she inhaled. Protruding slightly from her mouth was something soft, sticky, and raw. She tried to swallow, but pain wracked her throat, so she reached instinctively to her lips. Jutting between her teeth was something foreign. Gently prodding the object with her fingertips, she quickly realized it was her own tongue. Searing pain seized her throat again when she tried to open her mouth.

And then she remembered.

Moving her fingers downward, she found that something warm and sticky had coagulated across her neck. She traced her fingers upward and found the raw edge of open flesh. Stamped across her skin was the impression from the weave of the rope that had almost strangled her.

Archer, she mouthed, but no sound came, and the pain burned the inside of her throat once again. Images of hate-filled eyes that had glared at her as he buried the cord in her neck suddenly brought back the memory of the Seren. Kathryn shuddered. Ignoring the pain, her eyes darted across the room to where she recalled his body had landed after being hurled through the air. The space was empty. Quickly scanning the room, she readied for another attack, but found she was alone. He was gone. Relief consumed her, and she fell backwards against the cot, and drifted back into unconsciousness.

Shadows filled her room once again, unobserved and unchecked. Some remained stationary while others appeared to weave and move about the corners of the tiny cabin. None bothered Kathryn again that night. She lay motionless on the stained, crumpled linen that covered her cot, unaware of the movements in the dark.

Forty-Eight

THE NEXT SEVERAL DAYS PASSED uneventfully. Transient ships were seen rarely, and then, only at a distance. Kathryn surfaced topside only on occasion as she made her way to the galley before returning swiftly to her cabin, steaming mugs clutched in both hands. The crew took no notice of her comings and goings, and generally thought nothing of it when someone did. Only Seth held fast to the task of watching her. When he did, it was with curiosity. The telltale signs that something was amiss with his friend were not lost on him.

Of upmost concern these days to the captain was the issue of crossing Morrigan's path. Only passing thoughts of Kathryn made an appearance, but those would flee just as rapidly as they had emerged – quickly replaced by thoughts of his nemesis. Kathryn often caught sight of him standing alone for hours on end, the spyglass held to one eye. She wanted to tell him about the night Archer had tried to murder her, but knew there was nothing to be done about it anyway, particularly as she had never sworn the oath over the axe. In truth, Kathryn was not part of the crew, not officially, anyway. So she kept to herself, nurturing her injury and wounded confidence with hot teas and herb tinctures until the day her voice returned.

Though raspy and coarse, it was audible, and Kathryn soon found the means to make her declarations aloud. She followed a daily ritual of calling upon the power of her *Gift* in the ancient Celtic tongue. Indeed, she would make this right, but first she had to find Archer.

"I must find him," she breathed to Wynn one morning. "Where…?"

Wynn shook his head and clicked his tongue. "Why go seekin' trouble when there is none, eh?"

She had no answer and it pained her to speak, so she pantomimed something about Sparks and the sails. Wynn didn't seem to understand, or perhaps he didn't buy her story. Whatever the case, he just shook his head and looked down at her through wiry eyebrows.

"Ye'd do well to stay clear o' Archer, missy. He'll bring ye naught but trouble, he will. I can't help ye anyway. I haven't laid eyes on him for two nights or more."

Kathryn knew he was lying, but there was little to be done about it. She watched as Wynn walked away from her, shaking his head and muttering.

The quartermaster was nowhere to be seen when Kathryn eventually made her way topside for more than just a trek to the galley. It was time to get back to the activities of the *Revenge*. Still, she kept a wary eye out for him during the day, and rarely slept at night – always alert to the shadows of her cabin.

Days turned into weeks, and though Kathryn's plan for Archer never lost resolve, she once again found joy on the ship. Mostly, her mind cleared, and she felt as if she could breathe again whenever she stood fast against the rails. Almost always, as she stood there, the wind fanned salt air and sprays of sea foam, refreshing against the mugginess at sea. On one such occasion, she sensed that someone was watching her from across the deck. Turning slightly so as to avoid exposing the mark still raw across her neck, she caught sight of Captain Phillips. His majesty and grace generated a golden aura against the grain of the deck and pale blue sky. At just the sight of him, her breath caught.

He stared at her. She made eye contact, he smiled. Full lips parted slightly to reveal ivory teeth set inside his slightly crooked grin. That familiar rush found its way to her soul, and her spirit leapt. His eyes spoke volumes. He loved her as well, but remained aloof – a captain over a ship he loved more than her, and the sea that he desired more than them both. For now, she could only relish in their unspoken devotion. It would have to be enough.

Touching his brow with one finger, he gave her the only gesture of intimacy she would receive before turning back to face his true love – the sea. Kathryn quietly moved to another part of the ship, allowing solitude to become her only companion once again.

And so it continued day after day, until unexpectedly, the sentry from crow's nest sounded an alarm.

"Sails ho!"

The alert boomed a second time, and she rushed to the rails.

"There…on th' horizon."

She glanced and saw familiar sails. The captured snow that had once sailed alongside the *Revenge* was visible in the distance. It wasn't long before the ships crossed paths in close enough proximity for the crews to call out to one another. Greeting each other the way pirates do, they fired pistols skyward. One shot nearly hit Skyrme – a misfire, or so the shooter claimed. The bullet missed by inches, plunging into a barrel of rum that spilled its contents onto the deck.

"Aye, it's a sure sign of good luck, says I," Skyrme announced. It took nothing more to drive the men forward, laughing while filling their mugs from the barrel.

"Mighty's th' generosity o' yer shot, Hornsby!" The pirate raised his mug in salute and Hornsby returned the gesture. As the evening wore on, the men grew merrier. A spilled keg was always a good excuse to get drunk.

Still, Kathryn could not join them.

Later, when the lanterns were lit and the music played, both ships settled into a calm evening at sea. Stories were soon swapped between pirates. Kathryn took a seat near a group of soggy men, who bragged of great skill in collecting prizes and doing battle. Of course, talk shifted to that fateful night they'd run off Blackbeard. The story had changed once again. Escalating as always, the tales grew taller as each man took a turn telling his version of it. Then something caught her attention.

"It be true, I tell ye. Blackbeard be running sails full, fast as the ship could carry a man o're the seas. Scared he be, I tell ye. Our cutlasses raised with the colors aloft and the captain standing mighty against the devil himself." Tate speech slurred as he rolled back and forth against the bulwark. One of the others grabbed hold of his sleeve and pulled him upright.

"They say Blackbeard was sent down to the depths o' Davy Jones' locker." Davis leaned in closer to whisper to his crewmates sitting nearby. "I heard tell the witch woman sailin' with Blackbeard was cast off, maroon'd by her sister." The pirate crossed himself and spat.

"Aye, true that be. It's said the sister be more fearsome than the first."

The other two spat as well, then urged their mate to continue with the sordid details. Kathryn leaned closer, gooseflesh rising on her skin.

"The War Witch be seekin' the *Revenge* an' found her sister instead standin' side by side with ol' Blackbeard. It's said she was so irate at losin' the *Revenge* and the crew aboard her…" the pirate paused for effect. He glared momentarily at the others, whose eyes widened in anticipation. Davis jumped to his feet, cutting the pirate off.

"It's said, by them what saw it, that the Morrigan took her cutlass and cut off the head o' Blackbeard with one swipe. Then, the she cast the body overboard and down to the depths o' the sea."

"Aye," Tate piped in. "Only the corpse didn't sink, not straightaway." Gasps followed, and Tate's eyes grew wider. "The crew watched the torso swim thrice 'round the ship before droppin' to the depths below."

"'Tis true! The witch grasped hold o' Blackbeard's scalp and speared the whole o' his head on the tip o' the bowsprit. It stayed there as she sailed off to port for all to see." Proud of his accounting, Davis crossed his arms and watched his mates cross themselves in earnest, mouths agape and eyes bulging.

"Nay, you've heard wrong, mate. It's that British fella, Lieutenant Maynard, what sailed with Teach's head to Bath Town."

"Aye, an' that be true as well." Tate grinned. "The lieutenant was given the sword still drippin' with Teach's blood."

"Aye. Gave him the ship as well, with Blackbeard's head still hangin' from the bowsprit. Morrigan gifted it to him herself, then disappeared into th' skies, cursin' the seas against the *Revenge*."

Kathryn jumped. Apparently, these ruffians knew the tales of Morrigan. The pirates sat in awe, and nothing was said between them, after that. A few trembled where they sat. Rum was immediately passed around, and their spirits soon lifted.

Kathryn stood quickly and got below deck, anxious at the thought of Morrigan so close. The unwelcome image of the fearsome Teach's head suspended on the bowsprit of his own ship played again and again in her thoughts. She would have to shift her attention from Archer to Morrigan. Preparations would be made in the morning – a vow she made for herself.

Kathryn slept little that night, running the image over and over again in her nightmares. By sunrise, the crew of the snow made ready to sail, bid their adieus, and cast off once again. Most were sorry to see the others go, likely out of concern for the treasure they might find first, and not due to the parting of friends – although, it appeared that way.

As day moved into night, the skies turned dark and a storm loomed overhead. The crew assigned to night watch had been given strict instruction to lower the sails at the first sign of foul weather.

"Aye, aye, sir," Briggs said. Dunkin took post in the crow's nest.

"And make sure the rigging stays secure. Wake me first, then call for the bosun should the currents lift," Archer added, and turned on his heel. His desire for solid shut-eye would likely never happen.

Kathryn's gaze lifted to the heavens, and she watched as slate clouds crackled with lightning above them. Not more than a few hours would pass before the seas would grow angry and the skies would lash out. She moved to her cabin and settled in.

Another restless night passed, and along with it, a nagging dread that something more than the storm awaited them. To clear her thoughts, she again rehearsed her plans for Archer. It brought some relief as she imagined his end at the point of her cutlass.

Forty-Nine

THROUGHOUT THE NIGHT, THE SHIP tossed and tumbled over rough waters, inciting several of the crew. Each took turns minding the sails in the oblique moonlight. By morning, the sails had been dropped, the quartermaster rousted, and the crew reassembled. Rain poured over the ship to mix with the sea spray that washed over the deck. Kathryn awoke to the turmoil and peered out through the little porthole in her cabin. It wasn't difficult to size up the angry ocean. Cresting in the skyline, the cloud cover spilled slate and crimson, shielding the horizon.

"Red sky at morning, sailors take warning," she recited to herself and rushed to the main deck.

A wind blew fierce and the rain dashed down in drops that stung against bare skin. Men clung to rigging as giant walls of water rose half as tall as the mast, heaving the ship to one side, then the other. Wave after wave broke with deafening thunder, spewing salt water and seaweed onto the deck.

"Ye best get below, missy." Wynn shouted in her direction but his voice was quickly drowned out by the shrieking wind. The captain stood at the helm, fighting to keep the ship upright in the churning water. Rivers poured from the lowered sailcloth as they whipped in the wind and were shredded where they were fastened to the yardarms.

Above her, lightning exploded and stabbed through the black clouds with blinding light. There was a deafening thunderclap immediately afterward, a sign that the heart of the storm lie directly above them. Kathryn's hair stood on end, while electricity danced through the darkness. Just then, another illuminated spear shot down from the black clouds above, hitting the water just starboard of the ship. Steam rose in a great hiss from the ocean and the water lit up. Electricity snaked over its surface.

She held onto the side rail that lined the companionway and watched in horror as the sea raged against the *Revenge*. By now, Sparks had joined the captain at the helm and both men were struggling with the wheel in tandem. Random blasts from the squall threatened to rip the sails to shreds. Then, suddenly, the wind tore through the mainsail, shredding it into pieces that flapped dangerously against the sides of the ship. Several of the men, including the captain, rushed down to secure the torn sail. Heavy tarpaulin lashed out, threatening to dash away anything within reach. At any moment, the damaged sail could catch a sailor unawares and cast him into a watery grave. It had to be secured. A few men approached cautiously, alert to the whipping lines and torn cloth.

Without warning, the winds ceased blowing as if someone had flipped a switch. The seas became eerily calm, and the thrashing sails fluttered to the decks. Life onboard quieted as an ethereal calm stilled the sea.

"What is it, Capt'n?"

The men crouched, fear frozen on their faces. Captain Phillips did not answer. Each man turned to look at the miserable sky.

The masts glowed brightly. Colored light danced from pole to pole in an electrical shower that sent sparks falling in tiny stars to the pirates' feet.

"St. Elmo's fire," Cade whispered.

The captain stood upright and stared directly at the mast's upper point, and at the brilliant colors. One by one, the men followed suit and stood – all eyes glued to the eerie, colored light. Suddenly, a large crack exploded. The mainsail yardarm snapped loose and swung across the deck. Unexpectedly, the heavy beam dipped as it soared through the air and caught the captain squarely in the chest. He was thrown to the deck and landed with a sickening thud on his back.

Captain Phillips did not move.

Kathryn screamed and bolted up the stairs to where he lay, crumpled and still. Sparks ran forward as well, with Seth by his side.

"Capt'n, *Captain*!" Sparks shouted and shook the captain's shoulders. But there was no response.

"Do something!" Seth shouted. "Somebody!"

Kathryn fell over his body and placed her hand gently on his chest. She could feel no heartbeat. It did not appear he was breathing, although she couldn't be sure. Tears filled her eyes as she struggled to clear her mind, wanting only for him to live. She bent closer, her head level with his chest, and watched for any sign of the rise and fall that accompanied life. Her eyes caught a glimpse of faint movement. His breath was weak and warm on her cheek.

"He breathes!" she shouted. Still, she could feel no pulse as she desperately prodded his flaccid limbs. Her face turned skyward, the rain softer now, mixing with her tears, and she prayed. In that instant, clarity struck her and she felt peace swell within her soul. There was no question what must be done.

"Seth, grab some rope, there," she ordered. He immediately ran to the loose rigging hanging from the torn sail. "Bring the grappling hooks and poles, and tie them to the mast. Make haste!" Shouting to no one in particular, she glanced at Archer.

Seth cut the ropes as several of the men fastened the long metal poles together, running them up the length of the mast until it reached nearly to the top where the electrical currents danced. It was risky business, but then, so was pirating, and the men were used to it. Within moments, the line was wound tightly around the poles, and secured to the mast with the bottommost part of the grappling poles just touching the deck.

"Bring him here. Gently now, and lay him at the base next to me."

She waited as the men laid his body next to the large mast, and then knelt down next to the captain. Her eyes met Seth's. It was as if he'd read her thoughts. This moment was part of their destiny – for something they had been brought together to achieve.

"You know what you must do," he whispered.

She nodded and looked back to the captain. "Tie my hand to the pole and fasten it well, mind ye." Her voice faltered and tears stung her eyes as she glanced up at the faces surrounding her. "Do it now!" Memorizing each one, she looked each man in the eyes.

Seth nodded, then backed away. He knew Kathryn's intention was severe, and he feared for his friend. But fate had taken hold and he could do nothing else but to go along with it, even though it pained him to do so.

"Stay back." She gave the order and the pirates obeyed.

"No," Seth whispered, then again loudly. "There's got to be another way. Not like this. You can do this differently…Kat!"

Kathryn blinked away the tears as she gazed up at him, beckoning a gentle farewell.

"There is no other way. You know this, too, Seth." She offered a weak smile then turned to the others. "Do it! Now!"

As the men tied her left hand to the pole, she bent over John Phillips' body and placed her mouth over his open mouth, exhaling her precious breath in the same way she had breathed life into the slack sails. Then, sitting upright, she stretching her free hand over his chest and watched as the electricity danced around the metal hooks atop the mast.

"Cusan Adfer

Anad ein I oes."

Ancient Celtic chanting echoed through the bitter rain, summoning the breath of life back to her beloved captain. And as she spoke, the colored light danced wildly, darting in electric prisms around the metal pole. One by one, the men stepped backwards, widening the circle in anticipation of some fearsome hocus-pocus.

"I don't know what yer doin', witch, but none here want any part of it," Archer spat.

"Leave it alone, Archer," Gow growled, keeping his eyes glued on Captain Phillips and the girl lying next to him.

Kathryn said nothing more.

In an instant, a blinding flash sliced through the black clouds, hurling itself toward the mast. The lightening clung to the metal hooks and spiraled down the poles lashed to the mast. As the electricity touched bottom, it hit Kathryn's wrist and arced electric currents through her body. She stiffened as spasms wracked every muscle with fire and incinerated her from the inside out. Sparks flew as electricity hovered, arching her frame before shooting from each of her fingers resting on Captain Phillip's body. His chest lifted in a perfect arc before falling hard back onto the deck. The bolt released the metal and shot back into the black clouds, leaving its victims lying still as smoke curled skyward.

Kathryn was still from within, her body released from the agonizing pain that held it only moments ago. She could not move, but she could hear voices around her, excitedly calling her name as if through a tunnel. She felt the warmth of familiar arms pull her toward a muscular chest…and heard her name being called again.

"No!" the voice cried out in anguish, "No…no… no! Don't leave me."

She heard chimes sounding from far off and felt the warmth of a blanket covering her body. There was total peace now as her spirit lifted from the top of her head while the strong muscular arms cradled and rocked her limp body.

"No, don' ye be leavin' me, not now…not yet!" The voice continued to call out, agony saturating each word as she floated up along the length of the mast.

"I'll find ye, me love. I'll find ye again, my Kathryn," the words whispered, floating with her – his voice, the captain's voice.

The first time he'd said her name aloud.

Chimes resonated, and as her soul floated higher, she looked down upon the pirate captain who cradled her body in his arms, cried out to her, and called her by name.

He lived.

She had saved him – their hearts had become one as the electrical current took life from her and gave it to him. His bare back rocked over her lifeless body, shielding it from the pounding rain. She saw the skull and triton tattooed into his skin shudder each time he called out her name.

"Kathryn! Kathryn! Kathryn!" The deep brogue became a whisper as a mellower tenor voice replaced it.

PART SIX

Emergence

Fifty

"KATHERINE...KATHERINE, CAN YOU HEAR ME?"

The voice resonated. Sandalwood filled the space she occupied, while beneath her hands the crispness of starched cotton crackled.

"Katherine, open your eyes and take in a deep breath. Use this time to awaken." The shaman's soothing tones urged her back to the present.

She inhaled deeply, and incense filled her senses, heavy against her lungs, making her cough. A bony hand pressed her shoulder, urging her to wake. Wooden flutes played softly in the background, and she noticed the floor beneath was still. No gentle roll of the sea – only the stillness of earth supporting her.

Katherine opened her eyes slowly. Blurred images filled her vision, indistinct objects – pale without the vibrant blue and green of the sea. She blinked to focus.

"What...what happened?" she asked with an unsteady voice.

She blinked again and Dr. Strickland's face came into view just inches from her own. A bright light flashed from the end of a stick that he dashed back and forth between each eye as he peered into them. Finally, the shaman stepped back as she sat upright, shaking her head.

"I can't think straight," she stammered. "Where am I? Where's the ship?"

"You've come back. You've had quite an experience, Ms. McCauley, and need to take it slow." He handed her a glass of water.

She drank the cool water in gulps, not having had fresh water for so long on the ship…she caught herself.

"What did you say?" Her pale eyes darted up to the shaman's face, then trailed over the perimeter of the tiny, candle-lit room. She was still in the shaman's office! *Had it all been a dream? Surely not! She could still taste the saltwater on her lips.*

"Doctor…have I been here, with you, this entire time?" She licked her lips to be certain.

"Yes. Yes, you have." A lump surfaced in her throat. He smiled and continued. "And yet…you were not."

His vagueness confused her further. She cocked her head. "I don't understand. What just happened here?" She licked her lips again.

"You are likely very thirsty. Panting like that… you'll need to hydrate."

"Yes, of course." *Of course what? None of this makes any sense.* "But I don't understand. How…?"

"You have just experienced a past life…by means of regression, of course. It was quite emotional for you, and I almost brought you out once, but you cried out and then calmed almost instantaneously. I have it here, recorded for you." He pointed to a laptop sitting on top of a small table next to a bookcase. "It's audio only, but I will download a copy for you right now while you rest…that is, if you'd like a copy."

"Yes, yes, please." She lifted a palm to her forehead and pressed against her temples. "Can you tell me a little more about what happened? What you heard? I mean, I think I was younger, aboard a ship or something." Her cheeks warmed and she stopped herself, hesitant to reveal more.

"Yes, Ms. McCauley. You spoke often about your experience with the ocean and ships and brigands. I believe you must have been aboard a great vessel centuries ago. Your mind will clear with time, and I would advise you to write down all of your thoughts for the next few weeks." He took the glass from her hand as he spoke. "Would you like more?"

She nodded, and the shaman filled the glass from a water cooler across the room. He handed the water to her, then continued on with the explanation while he moved to the open laptop. There, he touched several of the keys and inserted a blank thumb drive into its side.

"It is my belief that most people have lived many lives, returning, reborn, after a particularly violent and unexpected death – a 'premature death', I guess you would call it. We all bring something from a previous life, and are usually surrounded by those we have shared our lives with, although in different relationships, of course. I suspect you will find patterns that you can identify over the course of the next few weeks – months even. You should take note of these." He glanced at her over the skinny glasses perched on his nose. "Those notes will be evidence or memories of past lives. I can regress you again any time you are ready."

How can this man be so passé about what just happened? Her mind reeled. She was still on the ship… or, at least, she should be. And yet, here she sat in this cramped office with a dispassionate shaman, who called himself a healer. *He knows nothing of healing!*

"Katherine? Do you understand what I'm saying?"

"Yes…I…" she said, but her voice failed her.

Bewilderment forced a smile, and Katherine nodded. Her mind raced with thoughts of what had just happened. *Regress me again?* And yet she yearned to get back to the sea, to the *Revenge*.

Perhaps this is the only way.

So much more awaited discovery, but for now, Katherine needed to get out of the incense-laden office. She wanted time to digest the overwhelming memories that lingered of pirates and azure seas and a captain with emerald green eyes, who held her heart captive in another century.

She had to find a way to go back!

As she stood from the table, Dr. Strickland held out the thumb drive. She glanced at it briefly. This tiny piece of plastic contained evidence of a previous life – one lived as a sorceress healer in an earlier century. A life lived while sailing the Caribbean waters onboard a pirate ship.

"Take it with my blessing. It's yours to review at leisure. A recorded history of your previous life, so to speak." He handed her the thumb drive.

This represents my experience…my past life?

She took the tiny memory chip filled with details of her past life, thanked him, and walked out of the office, knowing someday she would return.

Fifty-One

THE DRIVE HOME FROM DR. Strickland's office wasn't nearly long enough for Katherine to sort through the thoughts that spilled into her head. As she merged south, cruising down Coast Highway, she glanced longingly toward the ocean. It made sense. A piece of her soul belonged at sea. She was a stranger in this century, poised behind the steering wheel of a sports car instead of standing proudly at the bow of a ship at sea. She had felt this way before, but never knew why. Now there were answers – reasons behind her apparent "misfit" status. Yearning for days long ago no longer seemed odd.

She rolled the passenger window down and allowed the sea breezes to waft in. The salty air comforted her. Inhaling deeply, she took in the familiar aromas. These grounded her.

Too soon, the road curved away from the water and into the mainland. Anguish accompanied her as she pulled into St. Cimarron. She'd missed her little Sheba, although it had only been a few hours.

Returning to her home with her dog would be comforting, even though present reality would not. Modern days stenches assaulted her senses as she drove down streets filled with flowers and parked cars.

Wendy's BMW was missing from its usual spot in the garage, which meant that her sister was out with clients. A twinge of disappointment pricked Katherine. She wanted to ask her sister about Winne. Perhaps Wendy knew something she wasn't telling Katherine – something about Celtic life in the cottage. Katherine knew without a doubt that the teen hurling berries in the garden that day was her sister in this life, but she doubted Wendy was aware of it. That conversation would have already taken place over lunch at some quiet beachside bistro, if that were the case.

Sheba slept curled up in a ball on the sofa, which Katherine knew would not be permitted if Wendy were home. As she opened the door, the little dog's head shot up. Instantly, Sheba hopped down and trotted to Katherine while wagging the white fluffy tail curled over her back.

"So you're the little fox I'd been feeding all that time." Katherine spoke gently as she bent down to pat her companion. "I'm so glad you're back with me again." Sheba looked up with her coal black eyes and pawed Katherine's leg as if she understood the significance of her comment. "Come on, then. Let's go home." Katherine snapped on the leash. Next, she wrote a quick note to Wendy, thanking her for keeping Sheba.

We must have lunch soon. I have something I need to tell you. K.

The drive home was uneventful. Katherine tried to process the shaman's remarks, occasionally voicing her thoughts aloud to Sheba, who paid no attention from the passenger seat.

Once home, Katherine paused with her hand lingering on the doorknob. She wasn't clear why she hesitated. Perhaps the grandeur of her home, in comparison to her quarters on the *Revenge*, would be too stark in contrast – just as her life had become.

"I'm not sure I'm ready for this," she said, and glanced down at Sheba, who kept coal-black eyes trained on the door. Inhaling deeply, Katherine readied herself to enter back into the twentieth century. Sheba scratched on the wood, which Katherine understood as the dog's impatient intent: *Let's go already.*

"All right, girl, hang on while I find my key."

The house that was her home had not changed. Things remained as they had been left early that morning. A plate that once held scrambled eggs sat next to a half-empty teacup in the kitchen sink, Sheba's bowl stood empty, and the shutters were still open. It was almost nine, and the sunset had nearly disappeared.

Katherine turned on the corner lamp, set her belongings on the table, and a glimmer of light dancing on brass caught her attention. Her gaze moved to the fireplace, where she saw the hourglass resting on the mantle. Strangely, the sand still drizzled into the lower challis. With reverence, she lifted it from the mantle and tipped it over, examining the initials scratched onto the bottom.

Tears welled as she studied the inscription there. It seemed only a short time ago that she stood in *his* quarters and watched as the captain's hands skillfully made those marks. She blinked back the tears, as she recognized the gift she'd been given for healing his wounds nearly four hundred years ago. Mariel had presented it to her again, only this time, when she'd received the timepiece, it had come with a rumor that it had once belonged to pirates. She knew it was true, and that she had been one of them. Tenderly, she set the ancient timekeeper back on the mantle where it would remain as a symbolic reminder of the century to which it – and she – belonged.

Katherine realized she needed to speak with her grandmother, and without delay. They have the same name. Yet now, it carried new meaning for her. Mariel had been with her in 1721, living in the cottage as her grandmother. She'd been with Katherine in the present century, and her name had remained unchanged!

Very serendipitous, Kathryn mused. *Mariel was given to you at birth – the Welsh name meaning, "ocean born" – hardly a coincidence.* It would be very interesting to hear her grandmother's accounting of her ancestors, and her memories.

"Oh, Mariel, you and I have much to talk about," Katherine said to herself as she turned out the lights and made for her bedroom.

The evening brought a soft breeze, which filled her room with the scents of lavender and freshly cut grass. She closed her eyes and recalled the day she had felt the unrelenting urge to plant those flowers just outside her bedroom window. At the time, she hardly understood the significance. There was meaning, now that she recalled the lavender lining the entry to the cottage on the cliffs. Obviously, her love for its scent was no accident.

She curled up in her bed under the canopy and stayed in the moment. The fragrant lavender soothed her as the evening breathed in and out of her bedroom window. Just then, a mourning dove cooed and she smiled as she drifted off into a deep sleep to dream of ancient ships, the Caribbean, and a captain with emerald green eyes.

Epilogue

Morning arrived too early, and the alarm blared its reminder that she was needed at work. Katherine made quick work of readying herself for another twelve hours in the ER. Sheba had already run through the dog-door to wander outside, so Katherine voiced her goodbyes to an empty room. She then took one last glance at the mantelpiece and the hourglass resting there peacefully – a reminder there was more to her life than what the day would bring.

Arriving early, Katherine walked through the ambulance bay, which was relatively quiet except for a lone red and white rig with a big black number 18 printed on the side. She stepped up to the glass doors and waited as they yawned open, parting the red EMERGENCY in two and allowing her to pass. The security guard wasn't seated at his post, which didn't surprise Katherine, as this was the usual time he went for coffee. Maya was at the nurses' station, scurrying back and forth from her computer to a curtained room across the hall.

"Hey, Kat, how are you feeling?" she called out, not waiting for the answer.

Katherine pressed her glasses back up her nose and smiled, grateful her friend was working the shift with her. She turned the corner and made for the locker room, passing Alex, who didn't break step as she made the short walk to her office.

"Katherine, my girl. How are you feeling?" Alex touched Katherine's shoulder, and instantly blanched. Alex knew something had changed within Katherine, and wanted to press her for details.

"Fine, thanks." Katherine smiled, then quickly disappeared through the locker room door.

"We shall see."

Alex paused only a moment, then walked in the opposite direction and made her way past the empty beds lining the hallway. Several were scattered randomly, most likely having been left over from the night before. April was seated at the computer shared by the nurses. She was the night-shift manager, visibly agitated, and ready to go home.

"It was hell last night. I'm so ready to get out of this place," she announced.

"Is there anything I need to know before you leave?" Alex's mind drifted to Katherine. She laid her belongings on top of the cluttered desk.

"Not really," April said, and glanced at the computer screen. Her blonde curls bounced around her shoulders. "We had one sick call, but I think Mark is coming in early to cover part of it. Oh, and Valley Fire just brought in a 'difficulty breathing' case to Room 15." The report was brief, but April was done, and that would be all Alex would get about the incoming patients. She smiled at April, who stood up and snatched her purse. "See you tonight."

"Have a nice sleep," Alex called after April as she slipped through the door.

The new burst of energy was most likely due to April's enthusiasm to get to her car as quickly as possible. She rounded the corner and almost bumped into Katherine, who had just started down the hallway from the locker room. Her hands were full, and she nearly spilled a full can of soda down April's scrubs.

"Oh…sorry, April. I didn't see you," Katherine stammered. She recovered, offered a half-smile, and made for the nurses' station.

"No worries," April said, and exited through the glass door into the early morning…and freedom.

Alex had poked her head through the door and had witnessed the near-collision. Katherine was definitely out of sorts this morning. Alex kept an eye on her for a moment longer and gasped as a medic stepped out of room 15. "It has begun," she whispered.

Katherine stepped up to the counter as a yellow gurney was pushed down the hallway by two of Valley Fire's medics. The gurney was empty, so Katherine assumed they'd just delivered their patient to one of the rooms. They said their 'hellos' to Katherine as they passed, and moved directly through the glass doors. Moments later, another medic emerged from the room. She hadn't seen him before and noticed that he glanced at her briefly as he walked past.

"New recruit," she said, dismissively. *Well, go easy on him. You're a newbie, too, Katherine.* The medic said nothing, but threw a look over his shoulder at Room 15, where he'd just given report.

Something about his walk caught her attention. She fastened her eyes on him as he made his way down the hallway. His gait seemed familiar, and she watched as he waited at the glass doors. He stood nearly six feet, visibly muscular, with black, wavy hair that fell loosely about his neck. As he lifted his medic bag, the strap pulled down on the blue T-shirt he wore, exposing a little of his left shoulder.

Katherine gasped and covered her mouth with her hands. The tip of a triton and skull tattooed onto his tanned skin peeked out from beneath his shirt. As she gasped, he turned to look at her. He grinned and the left side of his mouth curled up in a crooked smile.

He paused for a moment and stared directly at her. Katherine's heart skipped, and she wanted to cry out. And then, as if a ghost from some other time, his eyes flashed – emerald green.

Bibliography

Johnson, C. C. (2002). *A General History of the Robberies & Murders of the Most Notorious Pirates* (First paperback edition, fourth printing ed.). Guilford, Connecticut: The Lyons Press.

Ossian, R. (n.d.). *Pirate's Cove*. Retrieved August 2009, from Pirate's Cove: www.thepirateking.com

Tresidder, J. (2004). *1001 Symbols, An Illustrated Guide to Imagery and Its Meaning*. San Francisco: Chronicle Books, LLC.

Department of Welsh, U. o. (n.d.). *Welsh-English/ English-Welsh Online Dictionary*. Retrieved July, 2009, from Geiradur ar-lein: www.geiriadur.net

Carleton, B. (1916). *Gypsy Witch Fortune Teller*. Hackensack, New Jersey: Wehman Brothers Publishers.

Carmichael, Alexander (1940) *Carmina Gadelica – Hymns and Incantations*. Edinburg, Scotland: Oliver and Boyd.

Glossary Of Terms

Abaft – Toward the back of the ship.

Anchor Rode – Rope or line attached to a ship's anchor.

Avast – "Pay attention. Stop what you are doing."

Botefaux – A tightly woven stick of hemp or rope used to ignite a fuse or lantern.

Binnacle List – A ship's sick list.

Bosun – Boatswain, officer in charge of sails, lines, and rigging of a ship.

Capstan – A drum-shaped part of the windlass used to wind rope or line connected to cargo or the anchor.

Casabel – A subassembly of a muzzle-loading cannon; the backmost part of the cannon.

Cast off – To let go, break free.

Chirurgeon – Surgeon.

Companionway – The main entrance to a cabin, usually a short stairwell.

Dead Ahead – Directly ahead.

Dead Astern – Directly behind.

Dinghy – A small open boat, usually used for transport from a larger ship to another location.

Ditty Bag – A small bag for stowing personal items.

Fathom – Six feet.

Fo'c'sle – Forecastle. A partial deck above the upper deck at the head of the vessel, typically the living quarters for the crew.

Forward – Toward the bow or front of the ship.

Galley – Kitchen or cooking quarters for a ship.

Gangway – The area along the side of a ship where people board and disembark.

Gunwale – The upper edge of the side of a ship.

Halyard – A rope used for raising or lowering a sail, yard, flag or spar on a sailing ship.

Hawsehole – A nautical term for a small hole in the hull of a ship through which hawsers may be passed. Also known as a cat hole.

Hawser – A thick cable or rope used in towing or mooring a ship.

Heading – The direction ahead of the bow of the ship.

Helm – The wheel.

Helmsman – One who steers the ship.

Hoay – A slang version of "hoy" or "ho" – its purpose is to draw attention to something: "Land ho!"

Hold – The compartment below deck used for carrying cargo.

Hull – The main body of a vessel.

Leeward – The direction away from the wind, opposite of Windward.

Line – Rope used onboard a ship.

Monkeys – Guns and cannons used on a ship.

No Quarter Given – Death to all; no lives spared in a capture.

Quoit – An iron ring used to play an earlier version of the game; horseshoes. A Scottish quoit measures about nine inches and is larger than the British quoit.

Rails – A narrow length of wood forming the top of a ship's bulwarks.

Reale – A silver coin; also known as a "piece of eight."

Ribband – Pieces of wood used in shipbuilding that are temporarily nailed on the frame lengthways in order to keep the body of the ship together.

Rigging – The lines that hold up the masts and move the sails.

Sea Chantey – A maritime work song sung by the crew onboard ships while working.

Secure – To make fast; fasten securely.

Shango – A type of Caribbean voodoo.

Sheets – Lines used to control the position of the sails.

Shrouds – Lines running from the top of the mast and attached to the side of the ship.

Slack – Not fastened, loose.

Starboard – The right side of the boat.

Stow – To put something away; to put it in its proper place.

Taffrail – The rail at the stern of the boat.

Transom – The outer surface raked forward or aft; usually bears the name of the vessel.

Waist – The deck between the quarterdeck and forecastle.

Excerpt

Silver Moon
(book 2)

"Help me up, lad. I mean to go on deck."

Seth's sun-bleached hair bounced as he shot her a look. "No! Kathryn, can' be doin' that. The capt'n wouldn't hear of it and I don't fancy a floggin' at the mast."

"Ridiculous! Captain Phillips would do no such thing. I know for myself that he ordered you to watch o're me and tend to my needs."

"Aye, Ma'am, that's exactly what he said." Seth glanced out the window at the sea, obviously wishing he were anywhere else.

"Well, I'm in need of some fresh air and this cabin reeks for want of sea breezes. Now take me topside before I take it up with the *capt'n* himself!"

Kathryn's Celtic temper flared quickly. The staccato of a pirate's lilt was suddenly exposed in her speech, suggesting she'd spent too much time aboard the *Revenge*. Seth glared at her, which she returned with matched belligerence. The two friends dueled in silence, a stalemate that neither would back away from.

"I won't do it," he stated.

In that moment, she realized their friendship had changed. Now that Kathryn had been summoned to life again, suspicion would surely become her constant companion. She would never be viewed the same, not by Seth nor any of the other cutthroats aboard the ship.

A cool gaze fixed upon Seth as she painstakingly pushed herself up to sit. Unexpectedly, she caught the slight movement as his gaze narrowed into a dark stare. *Is he challenging me?* The effect was not lost on Kathryn.

"Seth, you best mind what you're intendin', mate. I'm not your adversary. Nay, look instead to the black soul who seeks to destroy this ship and all who sail aboard her." She paused, waiting for some kind of reaction from him.

Seth defiantly lifted his chin slightly and continued to glare at her.

Kathryn shook her head. "That devil is Morrigan, lad. She's evil indeed, and seeks to collect the dead on land or sea. Her sign is the raven. She's the one

ye ought to reserve your fierce anger for … not me."
Kathryn's voice had dropped to a whisper – a low, lethal
warning.

"Aye, Miss Kathryn," he breathed, as he faced the
witch. "If that's what the chirurgeon orders, then that's
what this ship's mate will do. But I warn ye, there's
more afoot than what ye think and ye'd best mind
yourself. I'll not be party to your mischief again. You're
on your own, Kathryn."

A piercing shriek broke the silence, as they stared
each other down. The deathly scream cried out again
then suddenly fell silent.

Read the full story in Silver Moon, *book 2 of* The Déjà
vu Chronicles. *Available in major retail book stores
everywhere. Published by Doce Blant Publishing.*